Alexei lowered  **his mouth agai** **slight tremble** **n, tasting the sweetness of her mouth** **the erotic slide of his tongue, sensing her hesitation and teasing her into compliance. He absorbed her faint sigh and went in deep.**

Revenge—did this feel like revenge?

Not in any sense.

As his mouth closed over hers the edge of his tongue sought to breach the tight seam of her lips and won, and her resistance faded as she fought against desire.

'Let me go, Alexei. We shouldn't be doing this.'

'Why? You're enjoying this as much as I am.'

Natalya pulled away from him and Alexei let her go, despite wanting to pull her back into the strength of his arms. The kiss had stirred feelings in him he'd long tried to forget. Feelings only Natalya could ever evoke.

'You think I'm willing to just scratch an itch with you, Alexei? Not going to happen.'

'No?'

'No. And if you think so you misjudge me,' she replied, turning away from him—but not before noticing how his eyes had darkened and become almost black.

'As you misjudge me,' he assured her, far too quietly.

Helen Bianchin was born in New Zealand and travelled to Australia before marrying her Italian-born husband. After three years they moved, returned to New Zealand with their daughter, had two sons, then resettled in Australia.

Encouraged by friends to recount anecdotes of her years as a tobacco share farmer's wife living in an Italian community, Helen began setting words on paper and her first novel was published in 1975.

Currently Helen resides in Queensland, and her three children are now married with children of their own. An animal lover, Helen says her two beautiful Birman cats regard her study as as much theirs as hers, choosing to leap onto her desk every afternoon and sit upright between the computer monitor and keyboard as a reminder that they need to be fed…like, *right now*!

Books by Helen Bianchin

Mills & Boon Modern Romance

Alessandro's Prize
Public Marriage, Private Secrets
The Andreou Marriage Arrangement
Bride, Bought and Paid For
The Italian's Ruthless Marriage Command
Purchased: His Perfect Wife
The Martinez Marriage Revenge
The Greek Tycoon's Virgin Wife
Purchased by the Billionaire

Wedlocked!

The Marriage Possession

Visit the Author Profile page
at millsandboon.co.uk for more titles.

ALEXEI'S PASSIONATE REVENGE

BY
HELEN BIANCHIN

First Published in Great Britain 2017
By Mills & Boon, an imprint of HarperCollins*Publishers*
1 London Bridge Street, London, SE1 9GF

© 2017 Helen Bianchin

ISBN: 978-0-263-93514-1

Our policy is to use papers that are natural, renewable and recyclable
products and made from wood grown in sustainable forests. The logging
and manufacturing processes conform to the legal environmental
regulations of the country of origin.

Printed and bound in Spain
by CPI, Barcelona

ALEXEI'S PASSIONATE REVENGE

For my daughter, Lucia, with all my love.

CHAPTER ONE

'GIVE ME A few minutes, then send her in.'

Alexei ended the call, slid the smartphone into the inside pocket of his jacket and stood in reflective silence as he studied the scene beyond the tinted plate-glass window.

Viewed from a high floor in an inner city office building, it appeared picture-postcard perfect with sparkling blue harbour waters against a backdrop of partially dark shrub-covered rock face showcasing glimpses of expensive real estate.

Sydney. The iconic Opera House, the expansive harbour bridge.

A large cosmopolitan city he'd departed beneath a deliberately fabricated cloud.

A city he'd vowed to return to in vastly different circumstances.

Which he had.

With a plan.

One which covered all the bases, and every possible contingency.

Five years ago he'd stood in this office space, denounced and discredited by Roman Montgomery, the owner of Montgomery Electronics, for daring to conduct a covert affair with Roman's daughter, Natalya.

A young woman who had enjoyed a life of wealth and

privilege since birth. Intelligent, having graduated from university with an MBA degree with honours…savvy, and employed as her father's PA.

A life in which a thirty-year-old American *nobody* of Greek origin could never be a contender. As an added insult, Roman Montgomery had laughed at Alexei's expressed honourable intentions, written out a cheque in lieu of notice and issued an immediate dismissal, adding the rider Natalya had merely been amusing herself with a temporary fling. What followed became an orchestrated farce as Alexei's calls, emails and texts to Natalya were ignored, and within a matter of hours he discovered all her contact numbers had changed to an unlisted category.

Security guards posted in the main lobby of her apartment building ensured Alexei was denied access, and a determined attempt to reach her involving mild force resulted in a Restraining Order issued against him.

Which Alexei disregarded…to his folly.

The appearance of two police officers at his apartment with an arrest warrant provided a sobering experience at best. Invoking his right to legal representation ensured Alexei's incarceration was brief.

The desire to vent at what he perceived to be an injustice had been eased…*slightly*…by a harsh soul-destructive session with a punching bag at a local gym. He could still recall the cautionary shout from a fellow member nearby… *'Hey, man, you aiming to kill that thing?'*…resulting in one final vicious hit before he steadied the bag, tore off his boxing gloves, then turned and strode towards the changing rooms without so much as a word.

'Better a punching bag than Roman Montgomery's jaw,' he muttered beneath his breath as he stood beneath a hot shower to dispense the sweat from his body before switch-

ing the dial to cold in a bid to cool off physically, mentally and emotionally.

Within a matter of days Alexei had boarded a flight to New York, reconnected with his widowed mother, his two brothers in Washington and worked every waking hour, prepared to do anything within the bounds of the law—and a few that hovered on the fringes—in order to establish the foundation of an empire to rival others in the world of electronics.

And he had, exceeding his own expectations, aided by a new invention embraced worldwide that had elevated him to billionaire status.

During the past five years success and wealth had provided Alexei with much. Real estate in several countries, including a Paris apartment, a vineyard nestled on the slopes of northern Italy, an apartment in Washington, a Santorini villa inherited from his paternal grandfather.

Women? He'd bedded his share…a selected few of whom he continued to regard with affection. Yet not one of them had captured and held his heart.

While innate ruthlessness had ensured Alexei gained control of Montgomery Electronics, Roman Montgomery's daughter fitted another category entirely.

Five years of planning, negotiating, dealing, had been with one goal in mind. To make Montgomery Electronics his own via the Australian arm of his global ADE Conglomerate.

No money had been spared in implementing state-of-the-art equipment at the electronics plant situated at one of Sydney's industrial sites, together with complete refurbishment of downtown city offices previously leased to Montgomery Electronics.

The media had featured the coup, speculated on the new owner's identity, and relayed Roman Montgomery's failing health, financial mismanagement and the global recession as the reason for sending Montgomery Electronics to the wall.

CVs and performance reports of existing employees had been examined, decisions made, with employment contracts prepared…currently in the process of being offered by Marc Adamson, Alexei's legal advisor, to selected employees for signature.

Among whom was Roman Montgomery's daughter, Natalya.

An act of vengeance?

Against Natalya's father? *Without doubt.*

Natalya?

The decision was personal.

Make that *very* personal.

CHAPTER TWO

THE MEETING WITH the new company's CEO was a mere formality, Natalya assured herself as she left Marc Adamson's office and made her way along a wide corridor with strategically placed alcoves featuring magnificent floral displays on glass-topped stands. Professional renovations, individual reception areas bearing luxe new carpeting, expensive leather seating, artwork gracing the walls.

A major upgrade from the old-school style her father had favoured.

A faint smile curved her generous mouth. New owner, new vibe.

From a personal perspective, there was a sense of satisfaction in having been offered the position as the new company owner's PA. The plus aspect being a very satisfactory salary package.

It would be interesting to discover how many office staff employed by her father had been retained.

As yet the new owner's identity hadn't been disclosed, with one media-projected rumour referring to an American-based billionaire.

If correct, she mentally sketched him as being over fifty, maybe older, with access to inherited family money. Of average height, possibly bearing a paunch, together with thinning hair or a toupee.

A new broom sweeping clean…or perhaps a figurehead content to delegate and spend time schmoozing at various functions with the city's social elite?

Whatever…first impressions were key, and she tamped down the faint onset of nerves as she approached the CEO's executive area.

'We're not fully operational until Monday. Just knock on the door and walk right in,' Marc Adamson had instructed.

Okay, no problem.

She had a signed contract as proof the position was hers. All she had to do was smile, be professional and relax.

What could possibly go wrong?

Natalya curled fingers into her palm, rapped a firm double knock against the open heavily panelled door and entered a spacious office containing high quality furniture, floor-to-ceiling bookcases along one wall.

A quick glance revealed a wide custom-made desk bearing a laptop, various electronic devices, in front of which there were four single studded leather chairs spread out in a spacious semi-circle.

Within scant seconds it made a statement—wealth, excellent taste and power.

It was then she registered the tall broad-shouldered male frame silhouetted against a wall of reinforced plate-glass, affording an angled glimpse of strong features, a firm jawline, dark groomed hair.

A corporate wolf in his mid to late thirties clothed in black designer jeans, open-necked white shirt and a black soft leather jacket was vastly different from her preconceived image of the new company CEO.

A swift unbidden curl of sensation deep within surprised her, and was immediately discounted as a ridiculous flight of imagination.

Alexei held the advantage, one he used without compunction as he slowly turned to face the young woman who'd once shared a part of his life.

Dark almost black eyes regarded her steadily...waiting for the moment recognition hit.

As it did within a few fleeting seconds, and Alexei took pleasure in witnessing the faint widening of her eyes, the way her mouth parted, the quick swallow as if a sudden lump had risen in her throat as she visibly fought to school her expression into a polite mask.

Alexei? *Here?*

Coherent words momentarily failed her big-time, as she struggled to control the feeling she'd been hit by a forceful, if metaphorical, punch in the solar plexus.

Breathe, she bade herself silently as emotions rose to the surface, a gamut almost defying description, for how often had she attempted to cast aside images from their shared past?

Too many times to count.

Nights, on the edge of sleep, were the worst.

For it was then the memories returned to haunt her...the way his smile affected each and every pulse in her body; the gentle trail of his fingers down her cheek to trace her soft trembling lips. His mouth savouring her own, teasing, tasting, as he drove her wild with wanting *more*. The heat in his dark gleaming eyes a prelude to mind-blowing intimacy.

Five years on there was no warmth apparent in his demeanour, just an inflexibility that sent a chill scudding down her spine.

What did you expect...a romantic reunion?

Seriously?

After five years... Are you insane?

From a time when she'd been able to accurately define his every expression, now she felt as if she'd been flung into a maelstrom of wild conjecture where nothing made any sense as he allowed the ensuing seconds to weigh heavily in the electrified air permeating the room.

Her mind reeled with unvoiced questions. Initially, his motive to buy out the firm formerly owned by her father?

Rapidly followed by...how could Alexei Delandros have accumulated so much wealth in the space of five years?

Groomed designer stubble shadowed his jaw, adding an edgy quality, and there was a hardness apparent which didn't equate with the man she'd once known...and loved.

Natalya kept her eyes fixed on his in a determined effort not to escape his steady gaze. An act of defiance...or a mix of self-preservation and stubborn pride?

Both, she conceded.

Alexei took a degree of dispassionate interest as he examined Natalya's slender curves, narrow waist, slim hips, showcased in a black tailored business suit, with killer heels emphasising toned legs encased in sheer hose.

Subtle use of cosmetics enhanced her delicately boned face, emphasising expressive dark eyes and generously curved mouth.

The length of brunette hair styled into a sleek chignon made his fingers itch to free the pins to allow the thick waves to frame her face.

Professional cool...successfully achieved, Alexei admitted.

Absent was the vibrant, fun-loving girl who'd once embraced the world and all it had to offer. The sweet curve of her mouth parting in a laughing smile...eyes sparkling with teasing humour. The touch of her mouth on his own, magical, incredibly sensual as passion transcended to intimacy.

Alexei lifted one dark eyebrow in a gesture of musing cynicism. 'Nothing to say, Natalya?'

Where would you like me to begin? presented a tempting start.

Instead, she cut straight to the point. 'If this is some kind of sick game,' she offered with controlled calm, 'I refuse to be a part of it.'

He'd expected no less of her, given his deliberate act to conceal the new owner's identity from the media.

He inclined his head in silent mockery, enlightening, 'I prefer…a calculated strategy.'

Any sense of calm was discarded as anger rose to the surface, almost robbing her of speech as she fought the desire to slap his face hard.

'What else from a man such as you?'

Dark eyes speared her own. 'You have no knowledge of the man I've become.'

So very different from the Alexei she'd once known as memories flashed through her mind…hauntingly real for a few heart-stopping seconds as she recalled her body beneath his…supple, avid, in a manner that drove her wild.

For him, only him.

Dear God in heaven…*stop.*

Reflection in any form was a madness she could ill afford.

Almost as if he knew the passage of her thoughts he indicated the nest of chairs framing the front of his desk. 'Take a seat.'

Natalya spared him a dark glare, which had no effect whatsoever. 'I prefer to stand.'

He merely inclined his head…and waited.

An action which ramped her animosity up a notch, and her eyes speared his as she sought a measure of calm. 'The employment contract your henchman presented for my signature bears no mention of your name.'

'*Henchman*, Natalya?' The query held a vague musing

quality. 'Marc Adamson is ADE's legal consultant.' He eased his lengthy frame against the edge of his desk as he spelled it out. *'Alexei Delandros Electronics.'*

'Very cleverly disguised in the contract I signed,' she accused as she reached into her satchel, removed the folded document, ripped it in half, then tossed the pages onto his desk, quietly pleased when a few of the torn pieces fluttered onto the carpet.

She wanted to hurt him, as she had been hurt by his abrupt disappearance from her life. Days when she could barely function. Nights where sleep eluded her until the early dawn hours.

Weeks, dammit, spent examining every possible reason he could have left without a word.

An inexplicable action which compounded when she woke one morning feeling queasy and had to make a mad dash into the en suite bathroom. Something she ate became less likely when a second early morning bathroom dash occurred the following day, and the next. A positive pregnancy test had tipped her into a state of shock…they'd always used protection, so *how?*…until she recalled a night when need had obliterated common sense.

A rapid calculation of pertinent dates had merely confirmed a distinct possibility, followed by a host of scattered emotions that briefly pitched her between delight and despair, and the inevitable…*this can't be happening*. Except a further three pregnancy tests over several days had eliminated any vestige of doubt.

Vivid images swirled unbidden through her mind of times shared, long nights together, the joy of love and quietly spoken plans for their future…then nothing, no word as to why Alexei had seemed to disappear like smoke in the wind.

The energy she expended attempting to track him down

without success. Details of staff employed by Montgomery Electronics revealed Alexei's file had been deleted—but she had no idea who by or why.

It appeared he'd intentionally slipped off the radar…but for what possible reason?

She'd lain awake for nights searching for an answer… *any* answer. Only to come up with a few scenarios, none of which seemed to fit the man she thought she'd known so well.

Was she that desperate to locate the father of her unborn child, when he'd presumably taken steps to disappear? And what if she *did* manage to make contact? Would he be someone with whom she'd want to do battle over shared custody?

Seeking medical confirmation was a given, providing the reality of early pregnancy, closely followed by her determination to carry the child to full term. The only person in whom she'd confide was her mother…except she needed the right words, the chosen moment.

Only to have the decision taken out of her hands when she'd suffered a miscarriage just six weeks into the pregnancy.

A tiny foetus not meant to develop and take life's first breath.

There was little solace in medical opinion a second pregnancy would need to be carefully monitored with ongoing blood tests during the initial three months of pregnancy. Facts which didn't begin to equate with Natalya's emotional distress, until Ivana took action by booking flights and accommodation for a ten-day vacation on Queensland's Hamilton Island.

On reflection, they'd shared a lovely apartment with views over tropical waters, restaurants, time to relax and enjoy what the resort had to offer, indulging in facials, body massage, treatments at the Island's Resort Spa.

Sunshine, soft warm breezes, an idyllic beach. A healing period which strengthened their mother-daughter bond.

'Love you, darling,' Ivana had offered quietly as they exchanged hugs while the cab driver transferred Natalya's travel bag from the vehicle's boot. 'Are you sure you don't want me to come in with you?'

'I'm fine. Really,' Natalya assured her, aware once she settled into her apartment and resumed work as her father's PA life would assume its normal pattern...or as close to a facsimile of it.

And it had, over time.

All of which now flashed painfully through Natalya's mind, and served to heighten her anger as she rose to her feet, choosing to icily indicate the destroyed paperwork lying on the carpeted floor of Alexei's office.

'Not even a million-dollar salary would convince me to work for you.'

There was nothing she could gain from his expression, or his demeanour, then one eyebrow lifted to form a slight arch as he queried silkily,

'Are you done?'

Courage...she owned it in spades, Alexei acknowledged. Together with a flash of temper, which showed for a brief instant before she visibly gathered it in.

'Yes.' Succinct, and final.

Natalya turned to leave, and he waited until she reached the door before relaying with drawled intent, 'I strongly suggest you change your mind.'

He watched her shoulders stiffen, their slight lift as she took a calming breath before she swung back to face him.

With determined effort she took in his sculptured facial features accented by scrupulously groomed designer stubble...impossibly sexy, highlighting a raw edgy quality she found disturbing.

Dark eyes…not warm as she remembered, but cool, analytical. The faint groove bracketing each cheek seemed a little deeper, and the mouth which had caressed her own, devoured and taken, was now set in firm lines.

His shoulders…had they been so broad? His hair, so silky she'd exulted in ruffling it into disorder. Matching the dark promise in his eyes, a soft throaty chuckle an instant before he claimed her mouth, her heart…her soul.

Then.

Not now…and it rankled more than she would ever admit to how much the admission had the power to hurt.

She was over him. *Way* over.

Alexei Delandros belonged in a previous chapter of her life. One she had absolutely no intention of revisiting. Only a degree of stubborn pride ensured she remained facing him…when every cell in her body urged she should simply turn and leave. *So why didn't she?*

Because it was the easy way out. And she didn't do easy.

Like she'd even consider working for the man who had ruthlessly set out to destroy her father's business empire?

Natalya lifted her chin and threw him a fulminating glare. 'As far as I'm concerned, you can take your employment contract and shove it.'

She was either a very good actress, Alexei conceded, or she genuinely had no inkling of the verbal bombshell he was about to deliver.

'You might consider leaving your options open.'

Her eyes never left his own. Dignity and sarcasm didn't mesh, but she really didn't care. 'Please don't hesitate to enlighten me as to why?'

Family values had been her strong point. One he'd admired…until he'd dug deep into her father's business and private affairs and uncovered a number of discrepancies revealing the antithesis of the man Roman Montgomery managed to portray.

Had Natalya been aware of her father's transgressions? Possibly not, given Roman's penchant for subterfuge.

There was no point in sugar-coating the facts, nor did he feel inclined to soften his words.

'My accounting team have uncovered an elaborate scheme involving several bogus offshore accounts created by your father for the illegal transfer of Montgomery company funds.'

Alexei watched her eyes sharpen with disbelief. 'There's no way my father would commit fraud.'

It was a gut reaction and, on the surface, genuine, he perceived. Although she'd managed to fool him in the past.

'You're so sure of that?'

'I'd stake my life on it,' Natalya voiced emphatically, ignoring the folder Alexei extended towards her.

'I suggest you examine the paperwork.'

'And if I choose not to?'

He studied her features as she ran a pale lacquered nail over the folder's seam, noted the soft pink colouring of her cheeks, the defensive spark in the depths of her eyes, and for a brief moment he almost felt sorry for her.

Almost.

'The report details dates, account numbers, the series of complicated layers deliberately created to prevent detection.'

Natalya cast him a withering look, only to witness it had no effect whatsoever, and she tossed the report, unread, onto his desk.

'You can't be serious.'

The silence became an almost palpable entity as she refused to shift her gaze. Difficult, when a host of conflicting thoughts swirled through her mind.

If…and in her opinion it was a vastly improbable if…
the report held a grain of accuracy, the question had to be
what Alexei intended to do with it.

At best the details would reveal any fraud had occurred
without her father's knowledge.

At worst…she wasn't prepared to give that thought any
credibility.

'Read the report.'

Only a fool would fail to recognise the steely intent beneath his silky drawl, and she shot him a baleful glare as
she picked up the proffered folder and flipped aside the
covering page.

The first thing she noted was the name of the firm
who'd compiled the data…and recognised it as one of the
foremost sources well known worldwide for its excellent
reputation.

Why did she have the instinctive feeling the goal posts
had suddenly undergone a subtle shift, when it was she
who'd determined to maintain control during this brief…
very brief encounter?

A small ball of tension manifested itself in the region of
her mid-section, and she took a calming breath before she
began skimming the range of figures, dates, only to slow
down as growing alarm escalated with each turn of the
page. Detailed entries tracking each amount as it passed
through an elaborate tracery of accounts.

A trail initiated by direct instructions from Roman
Montgomery.

Amounting to millions of dollars.

Natalya felt as if she needed to sit down, and she froze
for a few heart-stopping seconds as reality hit home.

If the report was brought to the notice of relevant authorities, her father would face restitution, penalties incurred for tax evasion, and probable jail time.

It was beyond belief.

She lifted her head and looked at Alexei with undisguised incredulity for a few unguarded seconds, before reassembling her features into a taut mask as realisation hit.

'There's more.'

Natalya's eyes flashed dark fire as they fixed on his own. 'How can there be *more*?'

Alexei reached behind him, collected a second folder from his desk and handed it to her.

Her reluctance to examine the contents was apparent, and he watched in silence as her shoulders stiffened before she turned her attention to the written details, the photographs, and caught the moment irrefutable proof led to the only possible conclusion.

Roman Montgomery led a double life and had been doing so for many years.

There was an apartment in Paris, occupied by a mistress. A London apartment in fashionable Notting Hill housed a second mistress. Each of whom were maintained by Roman, whose visits coincided over the years with so-called business trips to both cities.

Deeds to both properties were buried beneath a list of subsidiary companies, ultimately tracing back to one man…her father.

Disbelief, together with emotions she was loath to name, coalesced into anger she fought hard to control.

The burning question had to be *why* had Alexei Delandros hired accredited investigators to delve deep into Roman Montgomery's business affairs and his personal life?

Why expend so much time, effort and money?

To do *what*?

Blackmail?

Her father? *Her?*

On the surface, such conjecture appeared unconscionable.

It took considerable effort to remain relatively calm, when her overwhelming desire was to toss both folders onto Alexei's desk and walk out, take the elevator down to basement car park level and exit with a squeal of tyre rubber.

Not the best idea…but incredibly satisfying. Provided she maintained control and didn't crash the car. Or worse, suffer an injury or three.

Her eyes darkened as they fused with his own.

'What do you intend to do with this information?'

Alexei regarded her thoughtfully, noted the tension evident in the way she stood, the straight back, squared shoulders, her eyes fixed intently on his own.

'That depends on you.'

The only visible indication apparent was a slight narrowing of her eyes, followed seconds later by an increased pulse-beat at the base of her throat.

A vivid reminder of past occasions when he'd touched his lips to that pulse, savoured it, before kissing it gently with his mouth. Her soft husky groan followed by a faint gasp as he used his teeth to tease and nibble a little.

Almost as if his body remembered, he felt its damning response, and silently cursed as he shifted position, using the moment to transfer a slim document and pen from his desk and extend it towards her.

Natalya's eyes flashed with fine fury as she recognised it as a duplicate of the contract she'd just destroyed.

'I have no intention of attaching my signature to a document representing *any* company involving your name.'

'That's your final decision?'

'Yes.'

'You might care to consider the fallout if I disclose the information I have on your father to the relevant authorities and the media.'

He'd do that?

The answer was clearly apparent in the chilling darkness in his gaze, and her mind reeled at the impact the exposure would have on her parents, their lives, *her mother* once Roman's infidelity became known.

Anger burned her throat. 'You *bastard*.'

'Language,' Alexei chided mildly.

For a brief moment she wanted to cause him physical harm, unaware how well he was able to read her.

Silence filled the room...ominous, intrusive, threatening.

'Decision time, Natalya.'

The silky warning apparent in his voice acted as a reality check, and earned him a baleful glare.

'I need to consider my options.'

'There are two.' His gaze seared her own. 'You sign, or you don't.' He waited a beat, then added with irrefutable inflexibility, 'It's a simple no-brainer.'

Her father's indiscretions made public. Worse, much worse...her mother's humiliation and heartbreak.

The mere thought of the snide whispers, the disdain as the social elite tore her mother's marriage, her very life to shreds...

A silent curse rose and died in her throat. She couldn't do that to a caring, loving woman who in no way deserved such denigration.

Natalya subjected Alexei to a killing look which should have felled him on the spot, and gritted her teeth in sheer frustration when he displayed no reaction whatsoever.

'Give me the damn paperwork.'

Seconds later she tore it from his extended hand and began reading the various clauses. Carefully checking no word or phrase had been changed from the contract she'd initially signed.

Every detail was clearly defined, stating as his PA she'd be on call twenty-four-seven when necessary, and available to accompany him on business trips within Australia and overseas. The contract would be valid for one year... renewable by mutual agreement.

While a term of one year had seemed perfectly reasonable, *now* it stretched way too long. 'I insist renegotiating the one-year term down to three months.'

'No.'

His unequivocal refusal ramped up her anger to boiling point. 'Revenge or blackmail?' she demanded tightly. 'Which?'

'Neither.'

He expected her to believe that? 'And the moon is a ball of blue cheese,' she offered with deliberate disparagement.

If he displayed so much as a glimmer of humour, she would hit him and be damned to the consequences. Only a forward flash of reality provided her saving grace, and she forced herself to mentally calm down, breathe, and stick to the basics.

'What guarantee do I have you won't go public?'

Alexei spared her a steely look. 'My word.'

'Not good enough,' Natalya dismissed with a retaliatory edge, and glimpsed his eyes harden at her temerity.

'The original certified documentation is held in a bank's locked security box.'

She didn't hesitate in issuing a cool demand. 'Copies?'

'Returned to the bank's security holding after you've signed a new employment contract.'

'I'll require a certified bank receipt in confirmation.'

He leant back against the desk, seemingly relaxed, but only a fool would ignore the restrained power apparent, or doubt his intent to use it. 'Done.'

Her eyes silently warred with his own, her mouth tight

as she fought for a semblance of control as Alexei handed her a pen.

A mesh of angry pride caused her to hesitate for a few seconds before taking it from him.

'Just for the record… I hate you.'

'An emotion which should make for an interesting relationship.' His voice was a smooth drawl which did little to improve her anger level.

'Business-related *only*.' The emphasis was fiercely stressed with finality as she attached her signature to a copy of the contract, watched as he countersigned, then she stood to her feet, walked out of his office, and took the lift down to the basement car park.

Alexei was intent on playing hardball, expecting her to meekly comply?

Comply, yes.

There really wasn't an option.

But meekly?

Not a chance…

CHAPTER THREE

NATALYA ENTERED HER HOME, greeted Ollie, her beautiful Birman cat, caught him close for a customary cuddle, gave a light laugh at his plaintive miaow as she made her way into the kitchen.

'Okay, I get it. Dinner time.' She toed off her stilettos, dropped her bag onto the marble-topped servery, then moved to the walk-in pantry.

'Chicken or fish?'

Unable to answer, Ollie merely butted his head against her chin and began to purr.

'Chicken,' Natalya decided as she extracted the appropriate tin, removed the seal, spooned the contents into the cat dish and placed it on Ollie's food mat. 'There you go.'

Her apartment was one of two situated in a large two-level converted family home in an exclusive bayside suburb overlooking a sweeping promenade bordered by a stand of tall Norfolk pine trees along the seafront.

Inherited from her maternal grandmother three years ago, the home rested high on a sloping hill with sweeping views over the bay and neighbouring suburbs.

Renovated into two beautifully decorated apartments, one of which she leased to a responsible tenant, the property represented a valuable investment, providing Natalya with a place where there were no memories of her shared time with Alexei to haunt her.

Except now he was back.

Food held no interest whatsoever, and she reached for the remote, activated the TV, checked local and international newscast, and scrolled through the host of programmes until she found something that might provide a distraction.

A night in was a conscious choice. Not that she was a social butterfly, although there were a few very good friends whose company she enjoyed…live theatre, movies, social events for worthy charity causes; lingering over a shared coffee, and there was a sports complex she frequently visited with an indoor swimming pool, and several large rooms hosting a variety of exercise equipment. None of which held immediate appeal.

She wanted out of her clothes, a leisurely shower, then she'd slip into something comfortable and carefully examine her copy of the employment contract in the unlikely event she'd discover a possible loophole.

An hour later she tossed the contract aside, aware there appeared no evident room to manoeuvre within the skilfully crafted legalese.

Food was a requisite, and having nibbled without appetite she settled into a comfortable chair and channel-surfed the TV for a while, noticed a much-viewed programme, only to discover it was a repeat episode she'd already seen.

What next? Phone a friend? Skype? Flip through the pages of a current magazine?

Indecision wasn't one of her usual traits, so she decided to retire to bed with a good book. Ollie merely tilted his head in silent askance at this change in his mistress's usual evening routine, and leapt onto the bed when it became apparent Natalya intended to settle in comfort.

Half an hour in, the written word failed to capture her complete attention, given her mind seemed intent on re-living events of the day.

No matter how hard she tried to focus on the story, Alexei's image kept intruding, until she simply gave up, closed the bed lamp, and attempted to sleep...with no success whatsoever.

Emotional reflection eventually tipped her back into a place which transported her back six years to a time when she first met Alexei...at an end-of-year social gathering for employees of her father's affiliate firm responsible for the manufacture of electronic components.

Tall, dark-haired and ruggedly attractive, he'd stood apart from the rest of the men present. For a heart-stopping moment she'd become acutely aware of every breath she took, unable to look away as he turned slightly as if drawn by her attention.

Dark gleaming eyes met her own, lingered, before returning to the young woman who clung to his side. Understandable, Natalya conceded, given he possessed the wow factor in spades.

She could, if she was so inclined, cross to his side and effect an introduction. Hadn't she slowly circled the room achieving the social etiquette required of the boss's daughter separately, and at her mother's side, as the evening progressed?

Except she'd been forestalled by one of her father's foremen, intent on introducing his son, and when she moved on the object of her attention was nowhere in sight.

Shame, she mused, aware she'd probably never see him again.

Yet she did, days later, when she entered a suburban supermarket to purchase a few groceries needed to replenish her fridge and pantry. And there he was, in the same aisle. Their eyes met, and they both exchanged a smile at the coincidence, whereupon Alexei introduced himself, and Natalya did likewise. Coffee, the universal suggestion, worked, and led to conversation and the exchange of phone numbers.

What followed rose to the surface, intact and in glorious Technicolor…a relationship so special, caring, so attuned to each other there had been no need for words. Just the touch of his hand, the warmth of his smile, dear heaven, his mouth as it possessed her own. The hard strength of his body, aroused emotions taking them both to a place where they existed in a sensual world of their own. Erotic, exquisite, mind-blowing.

A time when she'd felt so happy…so *alive*, in mind, body, and soul. Sure in her heart they were destined to share a life together.

Only to wake one morning to find herself alone in her flat, no explanatory note, only a brief text message on her cell phone later in the day indicating little, and not followed up at all.

'*The number you are dialling has been disconnected*', a disembodied robot had intoned, sending her reeling with alarm. Worse, the crushing news he no longer worked at her father's electronics plant.

Five years, with no satisfactory explanation.

For all she knew he'd disappeared off the face of the Earth, followed by months of her agonising *why*. Ultimately, the realisation he didn't want to be found.

Now he was back. Not the man she'd once known and imagined she'd loved, but a hard, resolute stranger bent on revenge—no holds barred. Bent on destroying her father, using her as a tool.

Blackmail…no other word suited as well.

She wanted to hit out…verbally, physically.

Silently didn't begin to cut it.

Getting physical, however, did.

First up, her apartment, which she cleaned to within a whisker of perfection.

A long session at the local squash centre expended excess energy, and there was a certain satisfaction in continuously slamming a ball against the wall, especially as she mentally imposed Alexei's body centre front and deliberately aimed to hit target every time.

Revenge of sorts for his physical image which had entered uninvited in dream form throughout the night, providing vivid memories she assured herself she'd long forgotten.

And knew she lied.

'Why so aggressive?'

Oh, hell.

Natalya closed her eyes, then opened them again as she turned towards her squash partner and endeavoured to catch her breath.

'There has to be a reason.'

Aaron offered her a penetrating look. 'Spill.'

One of the pitfalls of a good friendship being they knew each other too well.

Initially they'd met at a social gathering hosted by her father. A partner in a prominent law firm and the eldest son of a wealthy family, Aaron was sophisticated, charming and considered to be a very good catch in the matrimonial stakes. Only a chosen few knew he maintained a relationship with a long-term same-sex partner.

'Nothing I can't handle,' Natalya assured him as they emerged from the court.

Aaron read her better than most, a good friend who'd provided unstinting support when she'd needed it most.

Such as now, when his teasing anecdotes would do

much to help lighten the dark mood threatening to destroy her composure.

'Share dinner with me this evening.' The invitation was tempting, yet she hesitated as she collected a towel from the neatly folded stack adjacent the locker rooms.

'I'll make a reservation and collect you at seven.' His smile held a tinge of humour. 'Enlighten me or not, your choice.'

She didn't, because she couldn't bear to drag into the open how deeply Alexei's presence affected her. Or revive memories too breathtakingly real to share.

Instead they kept the conversation light, touching on the ordinary, and simply enjoyed fine food, a little wine, and the relaxed benefit of good friendship.

It was a pleasant evening, and Natalya thanked him as he deposited her outside the entrance to her home.

Surprisingly she slept well and woke early, pulled on a Lycra body suit, added a singlet top, affixed earbuds to channel music and took her customary morning run...at a more gruelling pace than was her norm.

Following a shower, she dressed, munched on an apple as she collected keys, shouldered her bag and drove to the nearest mall to stock up on essentials.

As she drove to her parents' home later that day to share Sunday lunch she couldn't help but silently question what was *real*, as opposed to what had been a superbly acted sham on her father's part, given he'd managed to fool her so well. There were no incidents she could recall to indicate her parents' marriage had been anything other than a devoted union. There had been the odd private meeting while in London when her presence as his PA was not required. Likewise Paris.

The knowledge refreshed memories of her father taking time out for a relaxing massage. Personal shopping time. The supposed private business meetings he attended alone.

How naive had she been?

Worse, did her mother suspect?

Doubtful, given Roman had provided the perfect cover by employing Natalya as his PA, ensuring his daughter accompanied him to interstate and overseas business meetings.

A string of silent castigations didn't come close to easing the anger she felt at her father's deceit. There was a part of her that wanted to confront him, rail her fists against his chest and demand to know how he could have put his marriage, dammit, his life, in jeopardy by such selfish careless actions.

Play nice, Natalya cautioned as she eased her car into the driveway leading to her parents' modern home set in beautifully tended grounds.

Smile, chat, and pretend nothing has changed.

Except it had, and the conscious effort to maintain a façade affected her appetite.

It was during dessert the question arose regarding her future plans.

'Darling,' Ivana broached with interest. 'Are you going to take a break before applying for another position?'

Oh, my. Evade the issue, or aim for the partial truth? It had to be the latter...

'No break, unfortunately,' she managed with a credible smile.

'Really?' Disappointment was apparent in her mother's voice. 'I was hoping we might share some girl time. Lunch, shop. Book a massage, facial, mani-pedi.'

'Who will you be working for?' Roman queried, direct and to the point, as ever.

There was no easy way to break the news, other than

to make the truth as simple as possible...then wait for the inevitable fallout.

Natalya met her father's narrowed gaze with outward calm. 'The ADE Conglomerate.'

His eyes hardened, so did the tone of his voice. 'You intend to work for the firm who bought me out?'

Natalya chose not to remind him that technically the bank had foreclosed.

'Is that a problem?'

Roman's features darkened. 'You're aware of the CEO's identity?'

'My interview was conducted by a legal representative.' Initially it had been, and not precisely an untruth.

The media presses would run overnight for newspapers delivered at dawn. In a matter of hours the news would become public knowledge.

'Alexei Delandros *is* ADE Conglomerate.'

'Delandros?' Roman's face grew dark with a mixture of anger and disbelief. *'Alexei* Delandros? What the hell are you *thinking*?'

Of my mother... Except the words never left her lips. Instead she lifted her chin a little and met his anger with determined spirit.

'He made an offer I couldn't refuse.' The truth...just not all of it.

Dark, almost black eyes hardened, and she saw his mouth thin to an ominous line as he made a visible attempt to rein in his wrath. 'How could you even *consider* working for Delandros?'

Because there's no alternative.

'In what position?' The demand was palpable.

With no easy way to break the news...except tell it as it was. 'PA.'

Roman regarded her with disbelief for several long seconds, then he slammed a fist onto the table, sending crockery rattling in protest. 'I'm calling my lawyer.'

'Who'll only confirm the contract was signed without duress and therefore legally valid.'

A telling silence reigned as Roman processed the inevitable. 'I hope you know what you're doing,' he warned heavily.

Her eyes didn't waver from his own for several seconds, then she discarded her dessert fork and pushed the plate aside. The thought of taking another bite of food made her feel slightly ill.

For as long as she could remember, she'd prided herself on being part of a close loving family worthy of her implicit trust.

Now she was forced to recognise the father she had adored was not the man she'd believed him to be, and the pain of betrayal was almost a physical ache.

The desire to leave was uppermost...now, before she uttered words that, once said, couldn't be retracted.

Another hour, that was all, then she could escape.

Consequently Natalya accepted coffee, lingered over it, and accepted Ivana's invitation to admire her treasured garden.

Together they moved outdoors, leaving Roman to add a generous snifter of brandy to his coffee, and smoke a cigar, presumably in the hope the alcohol and nicotine hit would soothe his temper.

Scrupulously tended and picture perfect no matter the season, the beautifully sculptured shrubbery and numerous borders were Ivana's pride and joy. While a part-time gardener took care of the heavy work, Ivana was very hands-on with the choice of plants and succulents designed to provide a glorious balance of symmetry and colour.

'Darling, I'm very concerned for you,' Ivana said quietly as they wandered through the grounds. 'Having to sell Montgomery Electronics was a blow to your father's pride and self-esteem,' Ivana added. 'It doesn't sit easily on his conscience he needs to rely on the money and investments I inherited from my late mother's estate.'

Natalya's grandmother had expressed a dislike of Roman Montgomery from the onset, and had been fiercely against the marriage, ensuring each and every one of her assets on Ivana's demise would pass directly to Natalya.

Natalya had adored her *babushka*, the regular visits with her mother, the joy and the laughter, tales relayed of an early childhood in another land, the treasures representative of a different country and culture...the division between wealth and poverty.

Ivana caught Natalya's hand and brought it to her lips. 'Will you find it difficult working with Alexei?'

The answer could only be an unspoken yes. 'I'm no longer the lovesick young girl of five years ago, *Mama*,' Natalya reminded her.

'Perhaps not. But...'

'I've moved on.'

You have? Like the initial encounter with Alexei Delandros was totally impartial and devoid of any emotion?

'I hope so,' Ivana opined evenly. 'For your sake.'

It was easy to offer a smile and brush lips to her mother's cheek. 'I'm fine.'

Little white lies and pretence. Not something she favoured, but forgivable in the circumstances...surely?

She lingered a while as they leisurely wandered through the structured pebbled paths, pausing to admire numerous plants, commenting on the subtle scent of roses, while listening to gardening tips Ivana chose to share.

There was a sense of relief when they reached the silver BMW parked in the pebbled forecourt.

'Come inside, darling, and have a refreshing drink.'

'Another time, *Mama*, if you don't mind.'

'You're leaving so soon?'

'New job,' she managed lightly. 'I need to check my wardrobe, laptop, and grab an early night.' She leant forward and hugged her mother close. 'Love you. Thanks for lunch.' A quick movement released the BMW's locking mechanism. 'I'll phone during the week.' She slid behind the wheel, fired the ignition, and blew a customary kiss as she eased the car forward.

Not the most convivial lunch, Natalya perceived wryly as she traversed the main road en route to her own home.

Tomorrow was likely to be a whole lot worse.

Working in close proximity to Alexei Delandros featured way down at the end of her choose-to-do list. So how did she prepare to meet her nemesis?

Perfectly groomed, elegantly attired, immaculate make-up, heels to die for…and presenting solicitous professionalism together with a degree of unruffled cool.

Something she achieved following two attempts to acquire the desired effect with her make-up.

Laptop, iPad, leather satchel, smartphone, car fob… *check*.

Minutes later Natalya joined early Monday morning traffic into the city, fought the long delays at numerous controlled intersections before entering the underground parking area assigned to the building housing ADE Conglomerate.

Easier said than done to tamp down the onset of nerves as she rode the lift to a high floor.

She'd been her father's PA for several years, she knew what the position entailed. There might be a few adjustments, but how difficult could it be?

CHAPTER FOUR

NATALYA ENTERED THE ADE reception and was met by a personable young woman who moved forward to offer a polite greeting.

'Natalya?' A hand was extended, which Natalya accepted.

'Marcie,' the blonde enlightened by introduction. The smile was genuine, which helped ease any preconceived tension. 'I'll take you through to your office suite.'

A comfortably large room, Natalya perceived, executive fittings, new state-of-the-art electronic equipment.

'Louise is your assistant, whose office is to your right, separated by a shared lounge,' Marcie offered with a smile. 'I'll introduce you, when we're finished with the tour.'

So far, so good.

'Alexei is at the industrial plant today. His office is to your left, accessed via his assistant's office, and their shared lounge.'

A reprieve, Natalya accorded, aware the day just became a little better.

Space, lots of it with room to move. Comfort, synchronised professional privacy…and far different from her father's former set-up.

Introductions completed, Marcie indicated Natalya's office. 'I'll provide a brief overview of Alexei's schedule for the current week, and answer any questions you might care to raise before I leave to take a mid-evening flight back to the States.'

Efficient, capable and very clear re the CEO's schedule. One which Natalya reluctantly admitted appeared daunting.

Did the man sleep?

Not a wise thought, given it led to imagining if anyone shared his bed, and, if so, whom?

So what do you care?

You hate him, remember?

Focus, she admonished.

'I've printed out notes you may find helpful.' The attractive blonde bestowed a conciliatory smile. 'I'm confident you'll be fine.'

Natalya was sure she would be even if it killed her. For no way would she permit Alexei Delandros to have any reason to find fault with her performance.

As to her emotional heart…it was guarded in self-imposed lockdown. Deliberately sought, to regain a sense of purpose. Sure, she'd indulged in a social life, even flirted a little…if you counted a pleasant smile, intelligent conversation, light laughter.

Did anyone see beneath the façade? Detect her broken heart had been figuratively stitched together, never to be torn apart again? Healed, resolute, as she fought for contentment…and thought she'd achieved it, until a few days ago when Alexei Delandros reappeared on the scene and any pretence of contentment went out of the window.

Worse…unless she was wildly wrong, he'd deliberately taken advantage of her father's misdeeds to place her between a rock and a hard place.

Damn him.

He sought to play hardball?

Then so would she.

'Are you okay with that?'

Marcie's intrusion wrenched Natalya back into the here and now.

Schedule, overview. 'Got it.' At least she thought she had, and, failing that, there was Plan B... Marcie's printed notes.

Besides, she knew the electronics business well. Her father's list of contacts was on speed dial, and saved in her computer's email address file.

How difficult or different could it be?

Different, Natalya discovered soon after she entered the offices of Alexei Delandros Electronics the following morning.

Absent was the relaxed, almost laid-back atmosphere generated during her father's regime. Instead there was a fast-paced vibe as she passed through Reception. The receptionist's usual warm friendly smile was absent, replaced by a slightly harried look, and Natalya arched an eyebrow in silent query, only to receive an expressive eye-roll in return.

Alexei Delandros was in the building, and obviously bent on ensuring everyone followed a high-powered work ethic.

Which indicated she should merely offer a smile in return and walk on through to her office...instead she paused to indulge in a brief post-weekend chat.

Staff camaraderie had always been an important factor during Roman Montgomery's reign...

At that moment her smartphone buzzed and she retrieved and answered it, only to hear Alexei's secretary's voice.

'Natalya. Mr Delandros expects you in his office.'

Now…was an unspoken directive holding a slightly ominous tone.

'Two minutes,' she advised patiently, and fluttered her fingers at the receptionist before heading down the corridor.

A brief stop off in her office to deposit her bag and laptop, then she collected her iPad, breathed in deep and tapped on Alexei's door.

She could do this…and fervently wishing otherwise wasn't going to change a thing.

So ignore the man, smile, be so efficiently professional he'll have no cause for complaint.

Easy in theory…difficult in practice when all it took was a glance at Alexei's arresting features for her heartbeat to quicken. Worse, the sudden spear of sensation arrowing deep within her belly.

What was with that?

Her body out of sync with her brain. Granted, her polite smile didn't waver as she met his impenetrable expression.

The dark superbly tailored three-piece business suit, crisp dark blue shirt and perfectly knotted silk tie did little to tame the predator image.

If that was Alexei's aim…he'd unequivocally nailed it.

Cool, professional, remember? 'Good morning.'

One eyebrow lifted slightly. 'Your lateness is an oversight?'

Natalya checked her watch. Three minutes past eight. 'My usual start time is nine,' she managed civilly.

'I gather you failed to check your smartphone for messages…or your laptop?'

She had. Last night. Not this morning.

'Twenty-four-seven contact,' Alexei reminded her.

'Ultimatum,' she corrected without missing a beat, ignoring the silken warning apparent in his dark gaze.

He rested back a little in his chair and regarded her with a steady appraisal. If she was bent on a confrontational path…he was a few steps ahead of her.

'Written into your employment contract and specifically drawn to your attention during Friday's interview.'

Tough. While she had every intention of being the quintessential PA, and polite in the presence of others, any pretence when they were alone went out of the window.

She was something else, Alexei conceded as he took in her groomed appearance, the smooth chignon, skilfully applied make-up, red lipstick which matched the jacket she wore over a pencil-slim black skirt.

He experienced an urge to ruffle her composure, to dig beneath the professional façade. Then what? Rattle her cage?

His body stirred with sensual adrenalin, unwanted and inconceivable, but *there*. A *need* to pull her close and ravish her mouth…to remind her of what they'd once shared.

To what end? Play it forward to rumpled bed sheets and hot sex? Simply to satisfy an urge?

Evidence he unsettled her could be detected in the fast-beating pulse at the base of her throat, the edge of tension whenever he entered her personal space.

He had never aimed for the grab-and-conquer method with a woman. Mutual attraction and mutual need were his requisite for sex.

Natalya? Why this instinctive feeling there was a missing link? One only she could provide?

Patience. And time…the latter of which he had plenty.

Alexei indicated the structured curve of studded leather armchairs. 'Take a seat. I'll outline the day's schedule.'

Extensive, Natalya breathed as she noted appointments, calls to be made, two afternoon meetings to arrange…and lunch with a business associate.

'Book a table for one o'clock,' Alexei instructed, naming a restaurant with inner harbour views and known for its excellent cuisine. 'Contact Paul, my driver, and arrange to have my car waiting outside the main entrance at twelve forty-five.' His eyes didn't waver from her own. 'Naturally, you'll accompany me.'

Hadn't she attended many business lunches with her father? So why would this be any different? Professionalism ruled as she held his gaze. 'It would be helpful if you could reveal who'll be joining us.'

'Elle Johanssen and her PA.'

Natalya maintained a polite expression. Eleanor, or Elle as she insisted on being called, held a reputation for winning, by whatever means it took. Those among the business sector who'd parried with her and lost were known to refer to the woman as Hell-Jo…an unflattering but self-explanatory term.

Elle Johanssen, the noted ball-buster, locking heads with Alexei Delandros?

A woman associate with whom Roman Montgomery had refused to do business following one scalding episode that had left him red-faced and publicly humiliated.

Lunch should be *interesting*, to say the least.

She could do this, Natalya assured herself silently a few hours later as she rode the elevator with Alexei to the ground floor.

So why did she feel conscious of every breath she took, together with an incredibly heightened awareness that threatened to destroy her hard-won composure.

He radiated male sexuality, too much for any woman to ignore. Especially her, having known how it felt to be possessed by him. Sensual heaven…and then some.

Even now, when she had every reason to hate him, he still held the power to affect her emotions.

Five years…during which time she'd attempted to convince herself she was over him…disappeared like mist beneath rays of the sun.

Not good. Not good at all.

So much for self-survival skills.

And this was only day two in her contracted employ.

So…suck it up.

Which she did. Although there was a moment when Alexei indicated they share the rear seat of the chauffeur-driven limousine.

A deliberate ploy to unsettle her?

Who could tell?

She could analyse it to hell and back, and still not arrive at a definitive answer…so why even try?

The key being to adhere to the rules…a faultless PA during business hours, amenable and highly professional, even if it killed her, for no way would she allow him to glimpse so much as a chink in her emotional armour.

Consequently Natalya entered the restaurant at Alexei's side, where the maître d' offered a deferential greeting and led the way to their table.

Not the bar, which had been her father's preferred starting point. Or, she perceived in retrospect, where Roman plied his guests with alcohol before adjourning to a table where he ordered fine wine with no regard to cost. By which time, business, as such, became a secondary consideration.

Elle Johanssen made her entrance a fashionable five minutes late, offered a faux smile, apologised briefly as she slid into the seat politely held for her to grace it, and took control by ordering wine.

A female shark baring her teeth, Natalya mused, all too aware of the woman's reputation for shrewd deals tailored to her advantage.

In a contest of strong wills, Elle most often won out, her gritty formidability legend. So, too, was her intolerance for fools.

Natalya sat still, aware, alert…and prepared to watch the play between two business titans, each of whom were determined to win.

A little wine, which did nothing to soften Elle's forceful tactics…and the wheeling and dealing began.

It was quite something to watch, as Alexei simply listened while Elle outlined her terms, declared them non-negotiable…only to stiffen defensively as Alexei discounted all but one of them, before stating *his* terms.

Stalemate.

'You're new in town,' Elle dismissed haughtily, only for Alexei to qualify,

'But not new to business dealings.'

'My terms cannot be bettered.'

Alexei merely lifted an eyebrow. 'I disagree.'

'Really? By whom? A firm who'll use a superior to broker the deal, then pass the client on to a less experienced staff member?'

'No.'

Natalya saw Elle's eyes narrow in speculation. The ADE Conglomerate was huge. To have Alexei as a client would be a very large feather in the woman's cap.

It would be interesting to tell which card Elle would play.

'Then there is nothing more to say.'

Alexei's shoulders lifted in a negligible shrug. 'So it would seem.'

The word-play game had just moved up a notch.

A waiter delivered their entrees, which were eaten in supposedly companionable silence.

Was this the final act in negotiations, and, if not, who would concede?

Natalya's money was on Elle, given it was Alexei who held the power.

Conversation during the main course centred on world economics, a subject in which both Alexei and Elle were well-versed.

Dessert was declined, and Alexei chose not to linger over coffee, stating the meeting concluded.

That was it?

Unbelievable.

Alexei indicated Natalya take care of the bill with ADE's corporate card…which she did, following him from the restaurant to witness Alexei's limousine sliding to a smooth halt at the kerb.

It was then Elle moved a few steps to his side.

'Have your lawyer email me a copy of your terms.'

Alexei didn't miss a beat. 'There's no point.'

'I'm prepared to consider a few adjustments.'

Really? Natalya mused as she heeded the faint pressure of Alexei's hand at the back of her waist as Paul appeared and opened the limousine's rear door.

Alexei refrained from making any comment as he followed Natalya into the rear seat and gave Paul instructions to leave.

'Checkmate?' Natalya offered with a tinge of cynicism, and incurred his measured glance.

Wednesday morning there was a courier delivery from Elle Johanssen containing an amended list of Alexei's terms. All of which, with the exception of three relatively minor clauses, Natalya noted, had been accepted.

'Return to sender,' Alexei instructed within minutes of perusing the document. 'With an attached letter rejecting the amendments, reaffirming ADE no longer require her services.'

Natalya keyed the relevant words into her iPad, glanced up and caught his slightly raised eyebrow.

'The three clauses are quite minor.'

Alexei's gaze was impossible to discern. 'I was unaware I requested your opinion.'

Was it her imagination, or did the room temperature suddenly drop a few degrees?

'You were present when Elle Johanssen requested a list of my terms,' he reminded. 'My parting statement to her was clear, was it not?'

'Perfectly. But she's...'

'Playing me.' His eyes seared her own. 'Something I refuse to allow anyone to do...under *any* circumstance,' he added in silky dismissal.

Okay, duly noted. Natalya collected the paperwork. 'I'll ensure this is returned today.'

'Via courier.'

Natalya inclined her head. 'Of course.'

'No further input you'd like to add?'

She didn't miss a beat. 'Nothing you'd want to hear.' Not the best exit line...yet there was a small degree of satisfaction in having had the last word.

And in doing so, she failed to see Alexei's lips quirk with mild amusement.

Natalya Montgomery was the antithesis of the carefree young woman he'd once known. Now she rarely smiled in his presence, which shouldn't concern him, yet it did, for he could too easily recall the way her voice would subside into a husky purr as he pleasured her. The sweet slide of her mouth when she caressed his body, teasing, tasting with such delicacy it drove him mad...until he took control, and it was she who gasped as he used his mouth to trace a tortuous path to the apex between her thighs, edging them gently apart to savour the acutely sensitive clitoris, using his tongue to drive her wild with need as she begged for his possession. And cried out as he moved over her and surged in deep as they both became swept up in the throes of a passion so intense there was only them... devoid of sense of time or place. So completely lost in an acutely sensual climax.

Alexei had contemplated for ever, his ring on her finger, a home, children...the complete package.

Only for everything to suddenly and inexplicably change.

Alexei leant back in his office chair and idly took in the cityscape, brilliantly clear on a mild summer morning. Beyond the many varied buildings the sky and sea appeared to meld as one.

The past couldn't be changed. There was only the present, and the future. Together with a plan...one he was determined to win.

CHAPTER FIVE

IT WASN'T SURPRISING the media channelled social and business reports around Alexei's every move...or so it appeared.

He was the new man in town. Successful mogul, ruggedly attractive with a dark earthy quality that had the social set flooding him with invitations.

Very few of which he chose to accept, preferring two prominent events, the proceeds of which aided worthy children's charities.

Both events drew national media attention, and resulted in photographic evidence of his presence with a different glamorous socialite clinging to his side. Each almost visibly simpering at having gained his notice.

Instructions for flowers...specifically roses...to be despatched to each socialite with the following message...

My personal appreciation for an enjoyable evening.

Really?
How personal was personal?
As if Natalya cared.
Although he did, in her eyes, redeem himself slightly by gifting a sizable donation to each nominated charity.
Laudable, Natalya conceded, or calculated...and men-

tally derided the latter as prejudicial, in spite of the fact he ranked *numero uno* on her list of least favourite people.

On the other hand she had to admit he worked long hours, for it soon became apparent he was the first to arrive each morning and the last to leave. No one could achieve what he managed on a nine-to-five schedule. A factor which had obviously enabled him to reach his current level of success.

His prominence in the business sector seemed to grow with each passing day, as did the respect of his peers.

Everything her father could…and should have had if he'd paid more attention to business instead of frittering company funds with magnanimous abandon.

Three weeks in, Natalya had managed to assume an admirable professionalism—no matter what Alexei threw at her.

And he did. Frequently, without warning.

If he was bent on testing her, she managed to rise to the occasion, and derived a certain satisfaction in holding her own…*professionally.*

Personally? Not so much.

As hard as she tried, she couldn't fault him. And she wanted to, badly.

Staff admired his business nous…especially the men. While the female staff sprang to sparkling attention every time Alexei appeared within sight.

Something Natalya chose to ignore, without much success. A fact which irked her unbearably.

She was over him. Had been for years.

So why did he enter her dreams and force a vivid reminder of what they'd once shared?

It was crazy.

This Alexei bore little resemblance to the man to whom she'd gifted her body…dammit, her soul.

Then he'd surrounded her with his warmth, his affection. *Love*, she amended, prepared to stake her life on it.

A time when she'd thought to hold the world in her arms, when nothing and no one could take it away.

Yet he had. And she hadn't been able to pick up the shattered pieces of her life.

The many nights she'd lain awake in tears searching helplessly for a reason *why*. Hoping, praying for a phone call, text, email…*any* form of contact that would provide an explanation.

Yet none had appeared, and slowly she'd managed to rebuild her life. Vowing she'd never let another man get close enough to melt her frozen heart.

There were friends, the trusted, tried and true kind, of whom Aaron was one. Ivana, her mother, another she'd trust with her life. Leisl, her BFF, who had married and now lived with her husband in Austria, with whom she kept in regular contact via social media, Anja, registered nurse and cosmetician to a leading Sydney dermatologist.

Acquaintances, of whom there were many, but not one of with whom she would lay bare her innermost thoughts.

The insistent ring of her smartphone dismissed any further reflection as she checked caller ID, picked up and briskly intoned, 'Natalya.'

'I'll require your presence this evening.'

Alexei issuing a statement, not a request. And there was no reason whatsoever for the faint shivery sensation feathering down her spine at the sound of his voice.

'I may have made other arrangements.' *May* ensured it wasn't exactly a fabrication. She even managed to sound suitably regretful.

'Cancel them.'

Just like that? 'If you'd given me more notice,' she began, only to have him cut her words short.

'Have you neglected to recall the terms of your salary package?'

Really? As if she could forget. 'Is it too much to expect a degree of courtesy?' Sweet she could do, albeit with a touch of saccharine.

For an instant she braced herself for his comment, only to feel slightly disappointed when he didn't rise to the bait.

'My car will be waiting outside your home at seven.'

Her chin tilted a little, a response ready...only to have him intercede before she managed so much as a word.

'Business, Natalya,' he relayed with an edge of mockery, and named a restaurant. 'Arrange a table for six between seven-thirty and eight.' Business...*naturally*. What else would it be? 'Of course.'

Selecting what to wear wouldn't be a problem, given her wardrobe included clothes suitable for every occasion.

Nevertheless she changed her mind a few times before settling for elegant evening trousers and camisole in deep jade, and teamed the outfit with black killer heels.

Understated make-up, emphasis on the eyes, a light gloss covering her lips, her hair loose framing her face, and she was done.

Her iPad was a given, satchel, smartphone, keys, a fine cashmere black wrap folded over one arm, and she was good to go with five minutes to spare.

Limousine and driver were waiting out front when Natalya checked, and she smiled as Paul crossed to open the rear passenger door.

'Thanks.'

She moved close, saw Alexei already seated, and bade a polite good evening as she slid in beside him.

The night was warm, the air-conditioning within the car set at a comfortable level, and she forced herself to relax as the limousine purred through suburban streets towards the city.

There was a moment caught up at a controlled traffic intersection when Natalya caught a glimpse of Alexei's profile outlined in sharp relief.

An attempt to be analytical failed miserably as she skimmed those strong features. The firm jaw, broad cheekbones, eyes as dark as slate, his mouth…

Don't go there.

Except it was impossible to still the sudden flare of emotion in vivid recall of the way his mouth had wrought havoc on every intimate inch of her body. In the name of heaven…get a grip!

She did, in spite of the effort it cost her, and she offered him a cool glance.

'Do you have anything to add relevant to this evening's meeting?'

All she had was a business dinner for six, time and venue. 'No.'

Great. There was nothing like being unprepared…

'No comeback?'

She shot him a steady glance. 'No.'

For a brief second she thought she sensed a fleeting smile, then it was gone.

The car eased into a sweeping curve and slid to a halt immediately adjacent the entry foyer of one of Sydney's upmarket boutique hotels.

Alexei's associates were already seated as she entered the Bar Lounge at Alexei's side.

Four men of varying ages…three of whom she knew by reputation. And Jason Tremayne, son of one of the city's wealthy scions, who'd come on to her in the past… charming in company, the reverse in private, as she'd discovered to her cost.

The tension racked up another notch.

'Natalya.' Jason's voice was almost as fake as his smile. 'How *fortunate* you were able to score the position of ADE CEO's PA.' He waited a beat. 'But of course, you're old friends.'

The subtle emphasis didn't escape her, yet she managed a cool smile as she took a seat and ordered sparkling mineral water from an attentive waiter.

The evening's focus was business, and she assumed the expected role for which she was employed. A pleasant meal, during which her conversational input would be minimal. A few hours, then she'd return home.

Simple.

Except she hadn't factored in Jason's slightly raised eyebrow, the faint curl of his lip on occasion in a subtle reminder of a reckless mistake in judgment. Hers to have accepted his invitation almost four years ago at a time when she was most vulnerable.

Sydney's social elite were intensely active, organising and attending numerous charitable events for various reputable causes. A scene her parents had once been a part of for as long as Natalya could remember. Roman had considered Jason's late father as a business and social equal. There had even been talk at the time that a marriage between Natalya and Jason would prove a valuable business advantage. Something Natalya had refused to contemplate.

Until one evening, a few too many flutes of fine champagne, a starry night, and a determined need to move on with her life…the result had been a close encounter of the not wanted kind, ending with Jason's harsh words, a few hurtful bruises, and her desperate escape.

Something Jason had never let her forget, nor Roman's fall from grace in the business sector.

Alexei's reappearance in Sydney and his coup in acquiring Montgomery Electronics raised conjecture… So what if Alexei was flavour of the month and the rumour mill shifted up a gear?

Beating herself up about it wasn't going to change a thing.

'Indulging in a little mind-wandering, Natalya?'

Without pause she spared Jason a measured look and recounted a concise review of her condensed notes. 'I believe that covers it?'

She offered the three men a brief smile as the waiter appeared to request a preference for tea or coffee.

It was impossible to ignore Alexei's presence, or the effect it had on her emotions. A contradiction in terms given she had every reason to hate him…and she did. Unequivocally.

So why this simmering awareness? For no matter how strong her denial, her body possessed too many vivid memories to be easily dismissed.

Alexei Delandros was in her face…encroaching her space during working hours, and invading her dreams at night.

She was over him. At least she'd thought she was…until a few weeks ago when she entered the new CEO's office and discovered she'd walked into a living nightmare manipulated by a man she'd once loved so deeply, nothing, no one could possibly come between them.

So much for blind faith.

It was a relief when Alexei called time on the evening, and issued instructions to summon his driver.

'I'll take a cab,' she managed quietly.

'Not an option.'

Why, when the meeting was done and she was on her own time?

With the practicalities taken care of, Alexei's guests exchanged courteous pleasantries and made their way from the restaurant.

Natalya gathered her satchel. 'An emailed copy of my notations will be available on your laptop prior to the start of tomorrow's business day.' Professional efficiency delivered with firm politeness could hardly be ignored...surely?

Alexei pocketed his smartphone as he moved from the table and indicated the main exit. 'My limousine has just pulled into the kerb.'

'I've ordered a cab.'

He turned slightly and shot her a measured look. 'Cancel it.'

'No.'

If he brought up the twenty-four-seven thing again, she'd be strongly tempted to verbally lash out at him. It had been a long day, fraught with delays and interruptions beyond her control...throw in Jason Tremayne, and her composure was beginning to shred. More than anything she wanted the familiarity of her home and a blissful night's sleep.

'Do you particularly want to cause a scene?' His voice was a dangerously soft drawl, and she silently challenged him for several seconds, unwilling to capitulate.

The sight of a cab swooping to a halt directly behind the limousine proved perfect timing.

'There's my ride,' she indicated with polite civility, only to see Alexei cross to the cab, pay the driver, then return to the waiting limousine and indicate the open rear passenger door.

If a look could kill, he should have collapsed onto the pavement. As that didn't happen, she had to content herself with a flame-fuelled stare...one which, much to her mounting anger, he met with glittering dark eyes and held for what seemed a ridiculous length of time.

'Get in the car.' His voice was quiet. Yet only a fool would ignore the steel beneath the deceptive calm.

She tilted her head a little, for even in killer heels her height didn't come close to his own. 'You neglected to add please.'

Are you *crazy*? The answer had to be a definite yes.

He held the balance of power, and thwarting him to any degree was the height of folly.

For years, *hell*, most of her life, she'd complied, content to fit in. Happiness equated to family, good friends, satisfying job, and a pleasant lifestyle. Not that she didn't possess views, nor was she afraid to voice them when the occasion warranted it.

Easygoing, fun, joyful…until five years ago when everything had fallen apart.

Since then she'd toughened up…on the inside. Outwardly there appeared little change in her demeanour. As far as anyone knew, she'd survived and regained her former easygoing persona.

Only she knew it to be a protective shell. There were nights when vivid dreams haunted her sleep, occasionally so painful and stark she'd awake with tears dampening each cheek, emotionally and mentally exhausted by painful images.

'Natalya.'

Okay, enough with the hissy fit. One of them had to give in, and it was clear it wasn't going to be Alexei. Conceivably, how long could they remain standing here, Paul and the limousine waiting, in a deliberate face-off?

She gave Alexei a look that should have seared his soul.

'Go to hell.' The words were quietly spoken, but there was little doubt of the heartfelt meaning as she moved past him and slid into the rear seat, reached for the seatbelt, fastened it, and steadfastly ignored Alexei's presence as he joined her.

Silence is golden?

Really? It felt like a thick fog encompassed the car's interior as it moved quietly through the city streets.

She wanted to lash out at him in verbal rage…so much so it became a palpable entity.

'Nothing further you'd like to add?'

Natalya spared him a hard brief glance. The temptation to tell him precisely what she thought of his macho tactics was almost irresistible. 'Not at the present time.'

For a millisecond she imagined the gleam of humour in his dark eyes, and her own narrowed at the thought he might be amused.

She was tempted to take him up on it. Although the joke would be on her if it could have simply been a trick of reflected light in the car's dim interior.

Focussing her attention on the passing traffic, the bright neon billboards, worked for a few scant minutes, until unbidden memories rose to the surface.

Remembering too well vivid images of his mouth on her own. The way his tongue sought, teased in wicked exploration, and possessed until she became totally lost in the magic of his touch…and the response it evoked as she matched the sensual fervour to a point when foreplay ceased to be enough…

The images came to a sudden screeching halt as her mind went into involuntary shutdown.

She was so not going there.

Couldn't, if she was to retain a shred of sanity.

At least she managed to exert strict control during her waking hours…

Now he was there, five days out of every seven, invading her space, a constant reminder of what they'd once shared.

A deliberate manoeuvre in his plan for revenge.

Against her father...without question.

Her? How many times had she lain awake in the dark of night emotionally agonising for a possible answer?

Too many times to count.

Alexei had done his homework too well, ensuring Natalya's one way out would involve irreparably breaking her mother's heart, and she hated him for it.

Worse, the all-consuming emotional war was gradually tearing her apart.

Had that also been part of his plan?

It said much for her resolve that she managed to regain a semblance of apparent calm until Paul turned off the main thoroughfare and eased to a halt outside her home.

Natalya unclipped her seatbelt, offered a polite goodnight, and made her exit, assuming a normal pace as she walked the path to the front door, inserted the key, entered the foyer, then closed the door behind her.

Inside the car, the driver spared his employer a questioning glance via the rear mirror. 'Seaforth, Alexei?'

He inclined his head, and issued a brief affirmative. Home was a beautiful mansion high on a promontory with enviable views. Professionally decorated and furnished, with staff to cater to his slightest whim.

Hard work, long hours, a penchant for electronic design...add the three Ds, determination, dedication and desire...had seen him succeed beyond his wildest dreams.

Some of his contemporaries had described him as *driven*. Only *he* knew the true reason why he'd deliberately chosen to bring Roman Montgomery to his knees, and make Natalya pay.

There was a personal need to push the boundaries... which surprised him. So, too, did Natalya's concerted intention to become the quintessential PA.

Absent was her smile, replaced by an efficiency he couldn't fault.

Had she changed so much from the beautiful young woman in mind and spirit with whom he'd once fallen in love?

Haunting memories teased his sleep on occasion, and left him wondering if there was a missing link he'd failed to discover.

Yet he'd employed one of the best investigative teams to uncover fact, down to the most minuscule detail.

For a brief second he considered calling one of the few young women he'd dated socially, each one of whom had pressed a note with their smartphone number into his hand, issuing a sultry smile and breathing an inviting call me, any time.

Sex for the sake of it?

He'd taken his share. Indulged in short-term relationships that weren't destined to go anywhere.

Alexei checked his wristwatch, noted the time, aware the workforce on the other side of the world had begun, and there was data he needed to check, calls to make.

'Yes,' he conceded.

CHAPTER SIX

ALEXEI'S PREDICTION OF a full day fell short of the reality, as scheduled meetings ran late; an important presentation was held up due to an unforeseen delay, and there were occasions when the air in the conference room of an affiliate firm could have been cut with a knife.

The pace was relentless. A restless seemingly sleepless night meant Natalya needed to maintain focus, and as the afternoon wore on it took concentrated effort to keep up.

'Did you get that?'

Natalya met Alexei's studied gaze without so much as a blink. 'Of course.'

She did her work, executing each assignment with dedicated professionalism. No one was aware she downed painkillers for a persistent headache, or that her body became limp with relief when Alexei called an end to the afternoon meetings, issuing a curt demand to a contemporary associate to supply the relevant information within three hours or the deal was off.

Then he closed his laptop, gathered his briefcase, spared three associates a brief nod, and strode from the room with Natalya at his side.

Alexei's limousine was stationary in a temporary parking bay as they exited the building, and she slid into the rear seat, leaned back against the cushioned rest and appreciated the silence during the relatively brief ride while Alexei checked messages on his smartphone.

All too soon the limousine slid to a halt in the forecourt of their office block, where within minutes they reached the bank of elevators to take the first available one to their designated floor.

'Have Louise send in coffee, and arrange for food to be delivered here at six,' Alexei instructed, shooting her a glance as they approached his office. 'If you've made arrangements for tonight…cancel them. We'll be working late.'

'Tonight isn't convenient for me.' It was a retaliatory answer, despite being politely couched. More than anything she wanted to finish what was left of the working day, drive home, soak in a hot bath, then crawl into bed.

'Make it convenient.' Without a further word he moved to his desk and opened his laptop.

She was *so* tempted to utter a comeback, and almost did. Instead she turned away, effected an expressive eye-roll, stepped into her office and summoned Louise, who raised an eyebrow and offered, 'You look ready to slay dragons.'

For a few seconds she contemplated her weapon of choice…not that it changed anything, but the image of winning provided momentary satisfaction.

'The CEO requests coffee asap.'

'Hot, black, strong. Got it. Anything else?'

'Dinner for two, to be delivered here at six p.m.'

Louise glanced up, pen poised over her iPad. 'Sourced from where? Preferences?'

Natalya named a nearby restaurant, specified orders, and waited until Louise retreated before allowing herself a faint smile.

Choosing Alexei's least favourite food would afford a slight victory of sorts…and if challenged, she had the perfect answer.

Meanwhile she compiled notes on an extensive report, and transferred it to Alexei's laptop.

Dedication was key, and it said much for her stoicism that she achieved an enviable workload. What was more, she managed cool...albeit polite cool.

By five-thirty most of the office staff had departed for the day, and promptly at six an alert came through announcing their dinner delivery.

Natalya checked the foyer camera onscreen, cleared the delivery, then went to Reception. Minutes later she collected two containers of food, paid the delivery guy, returned to her office and alerted Alexei.

'Take it through to the staff room. We'll eat there.'

Not if she could help it. 'I'll take a half-hour break at my desk.' Plus strong coffee and more painkillers.

Alexei spared her a brief glance as she deposited his food within reach, inclined his head in acknowledgment, and returned his attention to the screen.

Witnessing his reaction when he checked his meal would have been a plus. Although the visual aspect was less important than the deed itself.

The evening ran longer than anticipated, the pace full on...so much so, she began to suspect deliberate payback. Yet she refused to bend, achieving everything he threw at her until enough was enough.

With care she closed her laptop, stood to her feet and extracted her bag.

'You have a problem?' His voice was pure silk. 'We're not finished.'

Her gaze met his, fearless, unequivocal. 'I am.'

The air appeared to chill a little, and she stiffened her shoulders against the icy finger feathering down her spine.

'Angling for dismissal?' Alexei posed quietly as she stepped towards the door.

'Be my guest.' A foolhardy response, but right at that precise moment she didn't care.

'We both know that isn't going to happen.'

Natalya swung round to face him, and for an infinitesimal instant the atmosphere became electric. Her eyes met his in open defiance, silently daring him to react.

His eyes hardened, and a muscle bunched at the edge of his jaw. 'Think before you indulge in a war of words.'

'Really? *Why?*'

He waited a beat. 'Give it up, Natalya.'

'And if I don't?'

He didn't answer. There was no need.

She could plead exhaustion, a throbbing headache... she should probably apologise.

Instead she did neither, supremely conscious with every passing second of being alone with him in an empty suite of offices...no phones ringing, smartphones chirping or the buzz of background noise.

Were there others working in the building, putting in the hours? Who would know?

'Fifteen minutes should wrap it up for the night.'

Refuse or comply? The reality being comply...which she did, with a measure of reluctance. 'Fifteen. Not a minute more.'

Natalya caught his studied appraisal, met it briefly, checked her watch, then she returned to her office.

Precisely fifteen minutes later she shut down her laptop, pushed it into her satchel, gathered her bag, closed her office, stepped along the corridor...and found Alexei waiting in Reception.

'Thank you.'

It was an unexpected courtesy, and she found herself examining his tone for any hint of an edge, discovered none apparent, and merely inclined her head as she pro-

ceeded through the entry foyer to summon the elevator...
which, despite a silent prayer, failed to appear within seconds, and left her little option but to share as Alexei appeared at her side.

Fate chose that precise second for the lift doors to open.
Of course...what else?

Alexei stepped into the electronic cubicle and indicated
the instrument panel. 'Which basement level?'

'Three.'

The small confines merely emphasised their isolation,
and she hated his close proximity, the subtle aftershave
which, unbidden and unwanted, succeeded in heightening her senses.

Nothing more than a temporary madness, she dismissed, more relieved than she was prepared to admit
when the elevator slid to a halt.

The level was well lit and almost empty, given most of
the building's staff had vacated hours ago.

With a brief goodnight, Natalya moved quickly towards
her BMW, aware he remained at her side, and she pressed
the remote button to deactivate the car's locking system,
heard the resultant chirp and leant forward to open the
door at the same time as Alexei did.

The touch of his hand on her own sent heat searing
through her veins, and she quickly snatched her hand free,
shaken by her reaction.

Worse, the unwanted flare of emotion deep within.

Get real. You have every reason to hate him, remember?
And she did, *really* she did.

So why was she temporarily locked into immobility?

Without a word she slid in behind the wheel, inclined
her head in silent thanks as he closed her door, and she ig-
nited the engine, eased the car out of the parking bay and
resisted the desire to speed.

'Idiot,' she muttered beneath her breath, unsure whether the castigation was against Alexei or herself.

Both, she decided as she reached street level and joined the stream of traffic.

Ollie offered a plaintive miaow as Natalya unlocked the front door, and she scooped up his furry body, ran a gentle finger down his throat, sensed rather than heard his responsive purr, latched the door, then entered the kitchen, checked his dry food feeder and water bowl.

Stilettos off, briefcase deposited in her home office, then she headed through her bedroom to the adjoining en suite bathroom.

A leisurely shower, pyjamas, channel-surfing the TV, then hitting the bed were all on her agenda.

It had been a long day…not so much in hours, per se, but the pace. Achieving in one day what would have taken a minimum of several days during her father's regime, interrupted by over-long lunches, time out for one innocuous reason or another.

With hindsight it had been she who'd attempted to adopt a more businesslike attitude in preceding months leading towards the forced sale of Montgomery Electronics.

Takeover, she mentally corrected. Engineered by Alexei via an agent.

Payback. Undoubtedly justifiable revenge on Alexei's part…from his perspective.

How many nights had she lain awake wondering how their lives might have been if she'd been able to reach him when she first discovered her pregnancy?

Five years had passed, time during which she'd carried on with her life, and managed just fine, she added silently…until Alexei reappeared on the scene.

Disturbing her peace of mind, her emotions.

In a deliberate ploy to unsettle her? Subtly remind her of what they'd once shared? The passion...the love.

A time when she could read him so well. The teasing gleam in his eyes, the curve of his mouth when he smiled. The barely disguised passion...a reminder of what they'd shared, and would again. *Soon.*

The light touch of his fingers as he trailed them down her cheek to cup her jaw, the slight pressure as his eyes darkened with passion...the light brush of his lips as they teased her own. The moment *teasing* became more...so much more there was no sense of time or place. Only pleasure of the senses, escalating until clothes became an unwanted restriction to be discarded at will...slowly, tortuously. Or almost torn with urgent hands until they each stood naked, exulting in the magic freedom of skin against skin and the mutual delight of touch to explore, tantalise and exult in mutual passion.

Natalya closed her eyes in a bid to dispense the memory, only to fail miserably.

Alexei's image was there, embedded in her mind, surfacing from a past for which there could be no return. Even now...especially now, there was a part of her that ached for what they had shared.

A past where she could read him so well, aware of the simplicity of curling her hand into his, the subtle trail of his fingers as they brushed her cheek.

Dear heaven, the quiet promise of how their day would end, the love they'd shared—so deep and all-consuming neither had any doubt it was the for ever kind.

Only for Alexei to suddenly disappear...and her world turned upside down, when hope died, together with the fact she needed to get on with her life.

During the past four years Natalya had studied advancement potential in existing technology—projecting how it could and would aid production. Increasing her knowledge in the field of electronics, creating ideas for media attention, publicity via donations to worthy charities…in each of which Roman showed little interest.

Her suggestion she join the directorial board had been dismissed out of hand. Reason being Roman was inured in the theory he had everything under control, and when he chose to retire, the lead role would justifiably be filled by a man.

Women, while delightful creatures, inevitably became tied up in relationships and/or marriage and children. Ergo, their attention became divided.

Natalya's rebuttal in naming women with high profiles worldwide who successfully managed both with admirable acclaim had been airily dismissed, followed by a reassuring pat on her shoulder and the words…together we make a good team. Why change?

Because if you don't, the firm will become vulnerable.

Words she had uttered at the time, to no effect whatsoever.

Never going to happen, Roman had assured her.

How wrong her father had been, Natalya reflected as weariness won and sleep provided a blissful escape.

Reflection served no purpose, Natalya decided as she guided the BMW through heavy traffic clogging main arterial roads leading from the city at another day's end.

A day fraught with action, demands which tested her ability to keep up with Alexei's instructions…so much so, tense didn't begin to cover it.

The man was a machine, geared into top form and take no prisoners mode. So chillingly calm, it sent figurative ice tricking down her spine…together with a degree of sympathy for whoever was his target.

If Alexei's motive had been an exercise in trialling the limits of her professional endurance…he'd positively nailed it.

There was the need for distraction, preferably something physical, where she could don boxing gloves and rid some excess anger against a punching ball…replacing the ball with a figurative image of him. There was a gym bag packed with clean gear in the boot of her car in readiness for a spontaneous workout should the mood take her…as it did now.

A flyer for a new women's only gym in a relatively new complex not far from her home had recently popped into her mailbox, and on the spur of the moment she decided to give it a trial.

Attractive signage, she acknowledged as she parked the car and retrieved her gym bag. Uncluttered reception area, boutique style with strategically placed mirrors, an attractive receptionist who took details, offered a friendly spiel, and alerted an attendant to escort Natalya on a explanatory tour of the premises.

Great state-of-the-art equipment, where a few participants played…the only word Natalya could think of, wearing the latest design in imported gym wear, full make-up, hair artfully tied back, at a pace aimed deliberately to avoid a sweat.

Seriously?

Her own dark grey sweat pants and matching sports top would stand out like a sore thumb.

Then she spotted a woman with a camera, and realised an infomercial was in progress.

'They're nearly done,' the attendant relayed quietly as she indicated a passage. 'The change rooms are accessed to the left. Each cubicle has an individual lock, a cabinet for your personal effects and an adjoining shower.' She handed over a key, offered a friendly smile. 'Enjoy your time here. Any questions, just ask.'

Feminine and functional…a pleasant combination, Natalya approved and she donned gym wear, executed a set of warm-up exercises before hitting the gym itself, initially setting a moderate pace before gradually increasing to near professional speed, maintaining it, then easing off. Taking time to hydrate, before moving on to a rowing machine.

Physical exercise, endorphins helped ease stress and tension…a clinical fact, Natalya acknowledged with gratitude as she took a leisurely shower more than an hour later, emerging refreshed, equilibrium somewhat restored by provided liquid lotions, clean casual clothes.

Natalya offered the receptionist a brief smile as she handed in the locker key.

'That was some workout,' the attractive blonde relayed with a degree of admiration. 'I hope you'll decide to take advantage of our membership.'

Maybe. The venue had high-end equipment, the facilities were fine, and it was close to home. There was no reason why she couldn't split her exercise regime between her regular gym and this one.

She was almost out of the door when her smartphone beeped with an incoming text, and she checked the screen, recognised the sender's number, and muttered something unprintable as she reached her car, aimed the remote, heard the resultant chirp, then slid in behind the wheel to check the message.

Current Passport USA Visa departure next week, destination NY. A.

Okay, she got it. Business, with scheduling details to follow.

CHAPTER SEVEN

THE REMAINDER OF the week progressed without a hitch as Natalya dealt with work, meetings, together with Alexei's seemingly incessant instructions. If, as she suspected, he sought to see her fall in a heap as he ramped up the pressure, she took satisfaction in being one step ahead of him by coping admirably…and then some.

The weekend loomed, with nothing planned other than her usual routine, and maybe a call to her close friend, Anja, suggesting they take in a movie currently gaining rave reviews.

Pleasant, low-key, enjoyable.

So why this sudden feeling of restlessness? As if there should be *more* to her life than a predictable pattern with little, if any variation.

She was happy with the status quo…wasn't she?

Because it's safe, a silent voice taunted.

A conscious choice, she determined. One with which she'd been perfectly content…until now.

The cause, she reluctantly admitted, was Alexei.

There. In her face. Invading her mind…her sleep, as a reminder of what they'd once shared together.

Like she wanted to be caught up in an emotional maelstrom? Alternately dismissing the secret yearning deep in her heart, and the need to rail against him for causing it.

The electric fire of his touch when their hands met on the door clasp of her car in the bowels of the basement car park, when for one wild unprincipled moment she hadn't been able to *think*, let alone move.

Had he felt it, too?

For heaven's sake, take a reality check.

Alexei's sole motivation was revenge. Hadn't he gone to exceptional lengths to ensure he'd covered every possible angle?

So why waste time trying to search for that elusive something that didn't quite gel?

Worse, why was it *she* who was paying the price for her father's indiscretions and financial misdeeds?

Enough already.

Except her weekend plans were felled in one swift stroke with a text message received at ten fifty-three Saturday morning from Alexei demanding she contact him asap.

A soft imprecation escaped from her lips, followed by, 'Who the hell does he think he is?'

Natalya thrust the phone back into her bag and zipped the compartment.

He could wait.

She was hot, sweaty, in need of a shower and change of clothes following a vigorous hour of squash. There was a sense of satisfaction in taking her time, and she emerged into the reception area to find Aaron waiting for her.

'Problem?'

'Is it that obvious?'

'Uh-huh. You have *the look*.'

Natalya rolled her eyes.

'Alexei,' he concluded. 'What does he want?'

'I have no idea.'

'And you're not exactly in a hurry to find out.'

She sent him a faint smile. 'No.'

'Careful, sweetheart. Don't bite off more than you can chew.'

His concern was touching, and her expression softened. 'I'm no longer the vulnerable young girl of five years ago.'

'Nor is he the same man.'

Isn't that the truth.

A faint shiver slid down her spine, only to be instantly dispelled as they exited the building and crossed to the adjoining car park.

'Thanks for the game,' Natalya voiced as they reached her BMW.

'But not the advice.'

'That, too.'

Aaron placed a hand on her shoulder. 'Travel carefully.'

She deactivated the car's locking system, and sent him a sunny smile as she slid in behind the wheel. 'Always.'

Asap equated to urgency. Yet she waited an hour before making the call. Justifying the delay as a need to stop by the food mart for grocery supplies, unpacking and depositing same into her fridge and pantry.

'Your smartphone was on charge; you failed to check for messages,' Alexei pre-empted with undisguised dryness as he picked up on the second buzz. 'Or was the delay merely sheer bloody-mindedness?'

'Good morning to you, too,' she offered with incredible politeness.

Strike one for Natalya.

'Afternoon.'

She made a play of checking her watch. 'By precisely three minutes,' she agreed. 'The nature of your call being?'

Was it possible for silence to be explosive? And why did the thought please her?

'A meeting set up in Melbourne late this afternoon. My

car will collect you at three-thirty. You'll need an overnight bag.'

'Need I remind you it's the weekend? You expect me to drop everything at a moment's notice?'

'Yes.'

'And if I decline?'

'I suggest you reconsider.' His cool, slightly acerbic response hit a hot button, and she tamped down her temper.

Of course. He held all the cards in this diabolical game, with not one in her favour.

Once, just once she'd kill to be able to upset the balance of power between them.

Not going to happen anytime soon...

'Could we make it three forty-five?' Fifteen minutes was a small concession, albeit a deliberate one.

'No.'

Well, there you go. Nice try, even if it failed. With that, she slipped into smooth professional mode. 'Any specific instructions?'

Alexei outlined them with succinct brevity and ended the call.

Hotel. Restaurant. Six for seven. Suitable attire.

Natalya extended the tip of her tongue in an unladylike gesture, then she swept into her bedroom to pack.

CHAPTER EIGHT

HIGH-END MELBOURNE HOTEL, stunning river and inner-city views, *check*.

Top floor restaurant, good table, time and number of guests, *check*.

Luxury two-bedroom suite, each with en suite bathroom, and separated by lounge, *reluctant check*. A familiar business arrangement when travelling as Roman's PA.

However Alexei was not her father.

'I'd prefer a separate suite on the same floor.'

Alexei's eyebrow rose. 'On what grounds?'

She had a few, only one of which she was prepared to voice. 'Privacy.'

The faint lift at the edge of his mouth was so fleeting, she wondered if she'd merely imagined it.

'Afraid, Natalya?'

'Of you?' Her gaze met his with cool equanimity. 'Not in this lifetime.'

'In that case, I don't perceive there to be a problem.' He checked his watch. 'Order coffee in ten. Bring your iPad.' With that he collected his bag and disappeared into the bedroom on his right.

She ordered room service, took the second bedroom, freshened up, unpacked, and re-emerged into the lounge to find him seated at a desk checking data on his laptop.

He'd removed his suit jacket and tie, released the top few buttons of his shirt, and bore a raw masculinity that tugged at her nerve-ends, heated her blood and made her aware of every breath she took.

Not fair. Any of it.

Coffee arrived, and she filled both cups, placed one within Alexei's reach, opened her iPad and went to work keying in minor and a few major alterations to contractual clauses, highlighting the changes, then sent the amended contract to Alexei's laptop and checked the evening's schedule.

Four guests…three men well known in the electronics field and a PA.

There was time to shower, change into black silk evening trousers, attend to her make-up, style her hair, then slip on a stunning red jacket with matching silk lapels. A simple gold chain at her neck, small gold ear studs, a solid gold bracelet and her watch completed jewellery. Killer black Louboutins, and she was ready to go.

At six-fifty, evening purse tucked beneath her arm, satchel in hand, she emerged into the lounge to join Alexei.

Sensation arrowed deep within her as he turned to face her, and she had no control over the heat warming her body, or the way her pulse thudded to a quickened beat.

There was nothing classical about his features. Cheekbones a little too wide, the jawbone strong and emphasised by dark close-clipped designer stubble. Broad forehead, and eyes so dark they were almost black…equally expressive and warm, or cold as Russian ice. A generous beautifully moulded mouth, groomed hair a little longer than the current conventional style, a lithe toned body, an inherent air of power, success.

Unequivocally the *wow* factor.

So what?

She'd come into contact with equally attractive men. Yet none affected her the way Alexei had...*and still did*.

An admission she refused to give the slightest consideration.

Moving right along. They had a business dinner to attend, undoubtedly a late evening ahead, and any delays could lead to a further meeting the next day.

Superb food, splendid views of a stunning nightscape. Tall brightly lit city buildings, neon billboards...and skilled high-powered business as Alexei outlined his terms for a proposed deal involving one of ADE's subsidiary companies.

Interesting and slightly amusing to intercept the occasional glance aimed at Alexei by the super efficient blonde PA, a hint of sultry in her smile, the slow sweep of perfect mascara-enhanced lashes. Little doubt an attempt to signal discreet interest.

Like she *cared* if Alexei returned it? Natalya determined, and focussed on the job at hand.

The conglomerate represented by the three men wanted concessions written into the existing contract, which Alexei refused to consider.

Negotiations moved up a notch, Natalya acknowledged as she declined a second glass of wine in favour of sparkling mineral water.

Power became an effective sword, one which Alexei chose to wield with ruthless purpose, resulting in the spokesman for the group making a calculated attempt over coffee to regain some balance in the power play.

Without success, as Alexei brought the evening to a close by rising to his feet, inclined his head in dismissal, and silently signalled Natalya.

'Gentlemen.'

Obsequiousness was out, but Natalya detected a hint of silent back-pedalling as the head partner attempted to counter. 'We'll confer and contact you tomorrow.'

Alexei didn't hesitate. 'I have another meeting in the morning at nine.'

The implication was clear. Play ball on Alexei's terms, or not at all, Natalya reflected as they rode the elevator in silence, exited at their designated floor, and headed towards their suite.

A faint element of tension curled around her nerve-ends as he used the entry card to disengage the door and indicate she precede him into the lounge.

Professional, remember?

'Goodnight.'

It was easy to turn towards her chosen bedroom, and she was almost there, her hand extended towards the door handle when the sound of his voice caused her to pause.

'I want the evening's report accessible on my laptop by seven in the morning.'

It was all she could do not to grit her teeth. Instead, she turned towards him, inclined her head and added with sweet emphasis, 'An indication of tomorrow's agenda would help facilitate a workable schedule.' A fractional pause accelerated by a steady unwavering look lent intended emphasis. 'Seven-thirty?'

She could have sworn she glimpsed a flicker of amusement in those dark eyes, then it was gone.

'We'll confer over breakfast. Order room service for two at seven-fifteen.'

A minor concession… Whether she compiled the report tonight, or rose early to complete it was neither here nor there.

Without a further word she turned and walked towards the adjoining bedroom.

'Sleep well.' His faint drawl held a tinge of amusement.

Natalya didn't miss a beat as she spared him a glance over one shoulder as she entered her room. 'I always do.'

With that, she closed the door behind her, turned the lock, and silently pumped a fist in the air.

There was something eminently satisfying in having the last word.

A victory short-lived, Natalya conceded as business ruled their early morning breakfast.

A relaxed CEO, she perceived, with the top two buttons of his shirt undone, sleeves turned back, suit jacket spread over the back of his chair.

A casual look she silently assured she was perfectly comfortable with…and knew she lied.

Five years had added a few slight changes if one looked closely enough. Fine lines fanned out from the far corners of his eyes. Close-clipped designer stubble added a ruthless quality to his facial features…and she squashed the stray thought whether it would feel soft or slightly bristly on a woman's soft skin.

Are you insane?

Just…curious, she hastened silently, and filled her cup with coffee. It said much for her level of control that her hand remained perfectly steady. So what if she took the coffee black, strong and unsweetened for the maximum caffeine hit?

Cool, professional, as they ran an updated check on the day's schedule. Tight, Natalya perceived, with little wiggle room for any unforeseen delay.

Vastly different from the leisurely meals she'd shared with her father during his regime when the first business meeting of the day began with an extensive lunch and rarely concluded until late afternoon. Dinner inevitably morphed into a social event with a well-imbibed Roman generously picking up the tab.

Chalk and cheese, she perceived as she drained the last of her coffee, slid the iPad into her satchel, and waited dutifully as Alexei buttoned his shirt, fixed his tie before shrugging into his jacket.

Attired in a black pencil-slim skirt and fitted jade-coloured jacket, killer heels, she felt ready to deal with whatever the day would bring as she preceded Alexei from their suite.

It didn't help that the elevator doors opened to reveal an almost full occupant capacity entailing up close and personal contact with her nemesis. Nor did it aid an increased pulse-beat as unwanted awareness unfurled deep within.

Natalya stood rigidly still, consciously ensuring her breathing remained even, measured, and didn't pound to a rapid beat as it threatened to do.

In a few short seconds the elevator would reach ground level, release its passengers…and she'd be able to breathe normally again.

Did he have any idea how his presence affected her?

Or how hard she fought against it?

There were many reasons to hate him, and she did… vehemently. So why did the light musky drift of Alexei's cologne tease and heighten her senses?

His height and muscled frame proved a powerful force impossible to ignore. So, too, the sexual chemistry he managed to exude with little or no effort at all.

Five years ago she'd relished every stolen moment with him, no matter how brief. His touch, warmth of his smile, the knowledge of more, much more, as soon as they were alone. Did he remember, as she did? Wake in the night wanting, needing what they'd once shared?

Obviously not.

So who's the fool haunted by images of a past best forgotten?

You have a life...or at least she did have until Alexei reappeared on the scene.

Her relief was palpable as the elevator slid to a smooth halt, and she accompanied Alexei across the marble-tiled lobby to the black limousine and driver parked adjacent the hotel entrance.

Any hope she had of occupying the rear seat alone was dashed when Alexei slid in beside her, and she silently cursed his close proximity as the limousine cruised through city streets towards their destination.

'No last-minute instructions?' Natalya managed quietly, and incurred his measured glance.

'None.'

Okay. Time out from idle conversation. Which suited her just fine.

Instead she reflected on the meeting's key points, and the background research she had managed to glean on the major player in opposition.

An open mind, adhere with polite formalities, record all details from both parties...and become the quintessential PA.

In other words, be prepared for anything.

The limousine pulled into a semi-circular driveway and drew to a halt adjacent an impressive entrance lobby.

Showtime, Natalya accorded as they were met and led towards a bank of elevators, one of which transported them to a high floor where they were escorted to a designated boardroom.

There was a brief moment when Alexei's hand inadvertently brushed her arm, and she hated the way her pulse immediately quickened to a crazy beat.

In the name of heaven…*focus*.

The fact she did owed more to the experience of long practice, and she took her seat at the conference table, extracted the necessary iPad, and mini-recorder.

Playing tough in the business arena was an art form Alexei had mastered with unfailing ease as he calmly stripped negotiations to a base level of take it or leave it. Something which didn't augur well, and resulted in harsh criticism of ADE CEO's tactics.

Cut-throat didn't come close. Although Natalya had to concede the methodology worked. A break for lunch involved food eaten in one of the hotel's private rooms… and a review of key points from the morning's meeting.

High-powered, with Alexei's unyielding stance, and his superb negotiation skills.

Natalya could only quietly admire his ability to figuratively pin his business competitor to the wall…while her personal jury remained out regarding the inherent ruthlessness he managed to employ.

The pace increased during the afternoon, with Alexei adamant his terms were final, which led to a hastily arranged meeting the following morning.

'Reschedule our flight to mid-afternoon tomorrow,' Alexei instructed as their limousine took the route to their hotel.

Natalya sent him a killing look as they entered their hotel suite. 'In this technological age legal documents can be digitally signed and emailed.'

'True.' He removed his suit jacket, loosened his tie and tossed both onto a nearby chair as he sent her a piercing look. 'You're questioning my decision?'

'Merely expressing an opinion.'

'Which you feel entitled to do?'

Why did she suddenly feel as if she'd ventured onto

shaky ground? 'It wasn't specifically mentioned in my employment contract.'

Was that a faint gleam of humour in his dark gaze?

'Consult the menu and order a meal to be delivered to our suite at seven.' Alexei waited a beat. 'I'll have the sea-food pilaf.' He reached forward and collected his jacket and tie, then turned towards his room. 'I'll change and go down to the gym for an hour.'

All this *togetherness* didn't augur well, especially from her perspective. She could manage days, business lunches and dinners. It was the overnight thing that bothered her. *Especially* the sharing of a suite, despite it being a sensible business arrangement.

Hadn't she accompanied Roman to interstate meetings? Shared similar suites in several different hotels?

So why, now, did she feel wary? Defensive, on edge?

Yet she did, and it angered her that she should.

Worse, a full-blown suspicion Alexei took pleasure in figuratively ruffling her feathers.

Civil during business discussions in the presence of others, yet when alone with him she detected a watchful element, almost as if he was deliberately intent on...*what*?

There had been a time when she could read him well. Yet the passing of time had wrought changes. Few of which she could condone. For even now, her heart ached for the loss of the love they'd once shared. The pain of him leaving her so suddenly without a word and no further contact, despite all her efforts, still existed...like a wound that had never completely healed.

So go do something constructive, an inner voice urged. *Check out the hotel boutiques. Or better yet, go swim laps in the hotel pool and work off some pent-up angst.*

The pool won out, and she quickly rang Room Service, placed an order, then retrieved a one-piece from her bag, changed, caught up a towelling robe, popped the suite swipe card into one of two capacious pockets, and took the elevator.

Most of the guests were readying themselves for drinks at the bar or in the lounge, and Natalya felt a sense of relief on discovering she had the pool to herself.

The water was enticing, crystal clear and sparkling. Without hesitation, she shrugged off the robe and dived in.

It felt so good as she rose to the water's surface and began stroking laps, one after the other, steady at first before picking up speed. After a while she lost count, content simply to power up and down the pool's length, varying strokes as the whim took her, until she simply rolled over and lazily backstroked to the pool's edge.

How long had she been in the water? Half an hour?

A quick glance at the wall clock revealed longer, and she hastily emerged, dried off, then pulled on the towelling robe. Ten minutes should be sufficient to return to the suite, shower and dress before room service delivered their evening meal.

Alexei was already seated in one of the lounge chairs as she entered the room, and she met his gaze, rolled her eyes, lifted a hand in a silent gesture and hurried towards her bedroom.

Oh, hell, emerged as a silent condemnation as she caught a glance at her mirrored reflection. Bright lights enhanced her damp hair...rats' tails was an apt description...bare face...great!

So what? He's seen you in less...a lot less. But that was years ago when things between them had been different.

Way different.

Suck it up, girl. Take the fastest shower ever, dress and wind wet hair into a knot on top of your head, add lip gloss and go.

Food, perhaps a shared wine, followed by coffee and a recap of the day's business at hand. An hour, maybe two. Then she could escape to her room, duty successfully executed for the evening.

Three hours, slightly more to be exact, Natalya perceived, as she checked her laptop, read and discussed pertinent points, gave her opinion when asked, and provided a requested overview from her perspective.

'Honesty? Or circumspection?'

Alexei leaned back in his chair. 'Both.'

'They want the deal on their terms.'

She was good, he conceded, aware just how well she'd covered for her father during the past few years. Without her, Roman's business would have crashed and burned way before it had become vulnerable to a takeover.

Family loyalty…or desperation? Maybe both.

'Not going to happen.' A statement, no wiggle room.

Of course not. Alexei held the power, and was unafraid to use it.

'You've decided on a predetermined figure,' Natalya ventured. 'I imagine they will offer ten percent lower, then prepare for you to negotiate.'

'Astute.'

She inclined her head. 'Thank you.'

'Did your father request your opinion on any of his business dealings?'

Now there was a question. 'Occasionally.' In a befuddled alcohol-infused state, only to resort to something totally different in the light of day.

'Yet he rarely implemented them.'

The truth hurt, in more ways than one. At peak, Montgomery Electronics could have sold at almost double what ADE had paid for it. 'No.'

'Did you resent that?'

This was becoming upfront and personal. She was a daughter, not the son Roman envisaged Ivana would dutifully bear him.

'Is there a point to this?'

His eyes took on a watchful quality. 'It fills in a few blanks.'

She drained the coffee in her cup, closed her iPad and stood to her feet. 'I think we're done for the evening.'

Alexei silently commended her efficiency, enjoyed the challenge she presented…and wondered what it would take to crack the shell she'd erected to protect herself.

From him? Or men in general?

It shouldn't bother him.

Yet it did.

She offered a polite goodnight and crossed the room to her bedroom suite.

'Sleep well.' His faintly mocking voice curled around her nerve-ends as she reached for the door handle.

What she wouldn't give to best him at something…anything, just for the satisfaction of doing so.

A feeling which continued as she undressed and made ready for bed, rearranged pillows and settled comfortably with a current paperback.

Two chapters, then she'd close the bed lamp and sleep.

Except an escape into blissful oblivion didn't appear to be happening anytime soon, as Alexei's compelling image filled her mind and refused to disappear, no matter how hard she fought to dispel it. Nor her ability to evade dreams of their shared past. The intimacies…erotic, all-encompassing, as she became alive beneath his touch in a mutual gift of passion in all its guises. Lost, so completely lost she had no recollection of anything other than Alexei.

Magical. Transcending to a place where heart, body and soul became one…until the dream began to fade into a reality where she slowly woke to discover her body damp with sensual heat. Bereft, wanting...with silent tears slowly drifting down her cheeks.

Her breath hitched for a second before she caught hold of the now, and the need to shower, dress and face the day ahead. As well as the man who managed to slip through her subconscious and invade her heart.

Their shared morning breakfast was interrupted by the ring tone of Alexei's smartphone, and Natalya lifted her head to witness his eyes darken.

Trouble?

Undoubtedly, as Alexei's voice hardened during a conversation with, she assumed, a spokesman representing the group with whom they'd shared dinner the previous evening.

It didn't sound promising, as Alexei firmly refused to consider any further negotiation.

He ended the call, calmly drained the rest of his coffee and refilled his cup. 'They've requested a two-hour extension. A delay with their bank.'

'In a bid to gain more time.' She made it a statement, not a question.

And you have no intention of playing into it, Natalya conceded. Nor would I, in your position. 'So we wait.'

We...a slip of the tongue, and a throwback to the days when she prompted her father, whenever he required it... more frequently than it should have been.

'They have my number, flight departure time,' Alexei stated. 'The ball is in their court.' He checked his watch. 'I'm catching up with a friend for an hour or two. During which time I need you to complete a few shopping items on my behalf.'

Natalya's eyes widened. 'Shopping?'

'Is that a problem?' There was a hint of wry amusement in his voice, and she met his gaze, held it.

'I gather you intend to supply a list?'

'Note it will be business combined with family while we're in New York,' he enlightened, as she retrieved her iPad.'

Natalya attempted to ignore the slight blip in her heart-beat, and stilled the temptation to tell him to choose his own gifts.

Yet if she displayed the slightest hesitation…

'I guess I can add it to my job description.' Just don't make a habit of it, she added silently. Helping the boss choose family gifts came under personal…and personal wasn't ever going to be in the picture.

'Your mother?'

'Books.'

'That's really not helpful,' Natalya offered. 'Fiction? Fact? Romance…modern, historical, suspense, crime? Shall I elaborate further?'

'Romantic suspense.'

This could go on for a while. 'Favourite authors? Or don't you know?' She named a few, which presumably didn't strike a chord.

'Scarves,' he added. 'To add to my mother and sister-in-law's existing collection.'

'Any particular designer?'

He named a few, then handed over a credit card.

Safe choices, Natalya mused, and two hours later she had acquired numerous gifts beautifully wrapped and placed in a clutch of glossy carrier bags.

Ignoring the occasional brief…very brief moment, she recalled other occasions of shared shopping excursions. A time when Alexei would place an arm across her shoulders and catch her body close to his own. The dark emotion evident in his eyes, and the silent promise of how the day would end.

The memories shouldn't affect her...except they did, and she mentally struggled to put them back into a figurative box, and throw away the key.

She re-entered the hotel foyer to find Alexei standing to one side, newspaper in hand as he appeared seemingly engaged in reading an article.

Alexei's smartphone beeped as she drew close, and he moved aside to take the call, kept it brief while Natalya checked her watch, noted they had an hour and a half to pack, check out, and reach the airport to make their flight.

'The deal has been accepted,' Alexei relayed as he returned to her side.

Of course, she acknowledged silently. Had there been any doubt?

CHAPTER NINE

A FEW HOURS later they disembarked at Sydney's major airport, collected their bags, and were met by Paul in the passenger lounge.

'Welcome back,' Paul greeted with a smile. 'A successful trip?'

Natalya inclined her head as Alexei answered in the affirmative as Paul took hold of their bags, and began leading the way towards the exit.

Confirmation documents digitally signed in ADE Conglomerate's favour had been recorded. Another deal settled, Natalya acknowledged as Paul eased Alexei's limousine away from the terminal.

No matter how many domestic and international flights Natalya had made over the years, the return to Sydney inevitably invited the pleasure of familiarity, the buzz of city traffic, famous landmarks.

Mission accomplished, she acceded...admitting it was good to be back. Within half an hour of her own home, free of an insidious awareness pervading her senses with every passing day.

A temporary madness, she dismissed, due to being in Alexei's presence a minimum of eight hours five days a week...more, if you counted business dinners, travel.

She didn't feel comfortable with it. Didn't condone he

had managed to manoeuvre her between a rock and a hard place by robbing her of choice…aware there was only *one* choice she could make.

It made her want to rail her fists against him…except she didn't *do* tantrums. Couldn't remember throwing any, even as a child. Not that there had ever been a reason for her to do so.

A faint smile curved the edges of her lips. Except one incidence as a child in first grade when a boy…she couldn't even recall his name…grabbed hold of her single hair braid and pulled it so hard her eyes had watered. The taunt of 'cry-baby' had made her so mad she didn't hesitate to kick him…inadvertently where it hurt him most. An act which earned both children a demerit point, a lecture, and a phone call to each of their parents.

A forgotten incident…until now.

The limousine eased to a halt outside her home, and she emerged from the door Alexei held open while Paul removed her bag.

It was a simple expedient to offer Paul a polite word in thanks, reach for her bag, only to have Alexei collect it and accompany her to the front door, wait as she extracted her keys.

'I can take it from here.'

For a brief moment she imagined she glimpsed a tinge of amusement in his dark eyes. The temptation to execute an expressive eye-roll was uppermost. She selected the appropriate key, unlocked the front door, reached for her bag…missed by a mere second or two as Alexei placed it in the hallway before exiting without so much as a backwards glance.

An unladylike swear word slipped quietly from her lips, followed by another as she transferred her bag into her bedroom, tossed her satchel, then dug out her smartphone and rang Ben.

'Okay if I call over and collect Ollie?'

'Sure. He's antsy. I think he heard the car and your key in the door.'

'On my way.'

And there was Ben waiting for her with Ollie in his arms. 'Good trip?'

The fluffy cream seal-pointed cat squirmed with delight at the sight of his mistress, purred as Ben transferred him to Natalya, and she smiled as Ollie smooched his head into the curve of her neck, lightly nipped her earlobe in mild protest at her absence and followed it with another smooch.

'You missed me, huh?' Natalya acknowledged, and received a soft plaintive meow in return.

'Thanks, Ben. I appreciate you taking care of him.'

'No problem. Any time.'

He was a great neighbour, and looked out for her like the brother she didn't have. 'We'll catch up. Soon,' she added, meaning it.

'No rush. Whenever.'

She smiled, aware his life was even more hectic than her own. 'We're good.' And they were, for the pet minding thing was reciprocal… Ben owned an adorable sad-faced pug named Alfie, whom she looked after on occasion. 'Talk soon.'

'Look forward to it,' Ben bade as she crossed to her adjoining apartment.

Time spent with Ollie, smooches, head-butts…the feline equivalent of an adoring, *Welcome home. I missed you*, and food…always a clincher.

After which she changed into comfortable sweats, unpacked her bag, set up her laptop, checked the agreement, itemised the salient points and sent the data to Alexei. Resisting adding an expressive emoji…only to send it separately minutes later.

Time for a light meal, shower, then hit the bed with Ollie curled up beside her, maybe view a television programme.

Surprisingly she slept well, woke early, checked her email…no response from Alexei…then fed Ollie, collected the morning newspaper, made breakfast, then she poured a second cup of coffee and began skimming the daily headlines.

Normally she might have missed the article, except the bold print caught her eye. So, too, did the capitalised name—ADE CONGLOMERATE SCORES MEGA DEAL—together with a photograph of ADE's CEO, followed by brief details.

An approved press release from ADE? Doubtful, given she would have known about it. Unauthorised, damage control would ensue via a statement from Alexei in the late afternoon news.

Exactly as Natalya predicted, followed by a phone call from her father voicing a conspiracy rant, insisting she must have had advance knowledge the deal was about to go public. Concluding with a spiel alluding to the victory should have been his.

Any attempt to defuse the situation proved unsuccessful, and Natalya simply concluded the call, aware a reality check would prove a wasted effort.

Their return resulted in invitations to social events supporting various prominent charities arrived, requesting Alexei Delandros' presence and partner.

Back in the day of Roman's excesses and largess, almost all such invitations were accepted, including Natalya's attendance with her parents from the age of eighteen when she'd adapted to sharing the glitz and glamour as the social elite worked the ballroom.

Natalya checked each of the invitations, listed a few she

warranted would benefit from Alexei's presence and probable donation, and placed them on his desk.

'I'll organise for an acceptance when you've made your choice.'

Would he decide to appear solo...and if not, whom would he choose as his partner?

Like she cared?

Yet deep down she did, and for a brief few seconds she considered attending with her parents...just *because*.

Only to have the decision taken out of her hands when Alexei summoned her into his office prior to an event.

Natalya took a seat, opened her iPad with her fingers poised to tap in an update, schedule or reschedule a meeting...and glanced up when he failed to begin.

It was the end of the day, and he'd removed his jacket, loosened his tie, aiding a casual look that succeeded in ruffling her composure.

'Ensure you're available for Thursday evening's charity event,' Alexei began.

She schooled her expression and met his steady gaze. 'I'm sure you have a few young women on speed dial who would jump at the chance of an invitation.'

'None of whom possess your observation skills and diplomacy.'

'Assuming their total focus would be on charming *you*?' Natalya queried sweetly, sure she caught a faint smile at the edge of his mouth.

'Consider your presence a necessity as my PA.'

Be seated at his side throughout a lengthy dinner? Play nice, when privately she wanted to hit him? An inconceivable action in public view. Something more subtle...an elbow in his ribs, perhaps? *Accidentally*, of course.

'Business-oriented,' she clarified in droll tones. 'I'll ensure the mini-recording device will fit in my evening purse.'

'You've attended several events in the past. I doubt to-morrow evening's event will be any different.'

A number of the people present were repeat guests at several of the city's charity events throughout each year. Wealthy, influential, dedicated in donating funds to worthy causes, active on the social scene…and most familiar with Roman Montgomery's fall from grace in the finance sector.

The fact Roman's daughter would be seated next to, and to all intents and purposes partnered by, Alexei Delandros would be viewed with interest and a degree of speculation.

Poise and sophistication were an acquired façade, and qualities in which Natalya excelled…on the surface. Education in one of Sydney's highly respected private schools and world travel had ensured she could handle almost any situation without falling in a heap.

This evening's charity event would be no different. So why the edgy onset of nerves as she put the finishing touches to her make-up prior to Alexei's timed arrival at her home?

Her expressed insistence she meet him at the hotel venue had been dismissed out of hand, and for twenty-four hours she'd considered defying his edict with a last-minute text…only to abandon the tempting plan.

Instead she visited one of her favoured boutiques and purchased a new gown in champagne silk with an over-lay of matching lace.

Dressed to kill, she observed as she added a diamond pendant on a slim gold chain, attached a single diamond tennis bracelet to her left wrist, adding discreet diamond ear studs…each of which had been gifts over time from her late grandmother.

Natalya ran her fingers over her hair, plumping the loose

waved tendrils touching each collarbone, and reached for her evening purse.

Good to go, with a few minutes to spare.

Alexei's limousine slid to a halt at the prearranged time, and she drew in a deep breath as the doorbell rang.

Nervous tension, Natalya excused, and sought to steady the increased pulse-beat at the base of her throat as she opened the door.

He had presence, an elusive quality that set him apart from most other men. Difficult to define in mere words, but there nonetheless.

Dark eyes that could sear the soul; a mouth which held the promise of sensual sin…and delivered.

Stop, a silent voice echoed inside her brain. Remembering how it had been between them served no purpose.

As an escort he ticked all the boxes. Appearing even more devastating in impeccable evening wear, he could easily have passed as a male model in a photo shoot for Armani. The epitome of the man he'd become…assured, comfortable in his own skin. The acquisition of the fine things in life, its influence and power. An added quality he bore with ease.

The limousine purred silently through the city streets, entering the inner city perimeter until they reached the hotel where the evening's event was being held.

Assembled media, photographers were positioned ready to capture the arrival of well-known guests, and flashbulbs popped as the cream of Sydney's society descended from a moving procession of limousines…women offering practised smiles, should their photograph be one of a chosen few to make the following day's social pages.

Alexei's light touch at the back of Natalya's waist was a courtesy, although only she was aware of the flare of sensual electricity coursing through her body.

Her role was strictly business-oriented. Definitely not personal. She should have organised a pin discreetly emblazoned with PA to clarify her presence.

Natalya offered a slight smile as she accompanied Alexei into the large atrium where guests were gathering for pre-dinner drinks prior to a bank of doors being opened to allow access into the formal dining room.

Waiters circled the atrium offering flutes of champagne as guests mingled with fellow associates and friends, increasing the noise factor as the numbers swelled to capacity.

Natalya offered a smile in silent acknowledgment as she recognised friends among the crowd, aware they'd be able to connect throughout the evening, and when a few scions of industry approached Alexei she achieved each introduction with practised ease.

It became increasingly obvious Alexei garnered attention. His takeover of Roman Montgomery's firm had become a lingering buzz among those in the financial sector, fired by successful deals Alexei had achieved worldwide.

There was media interest in his background, together with any information investigative journalists could dig up about his personal life.

Until now Alexei had declined to give interviews, sanctioning only information his media personnel were instructed to release. Fine in theory, but the gutter press possessed few scruples, and a grain of truth embellished with innuendo could increase sales of varying tabloids tenfold.

'Natalya.' The sound of Ivana's voice captured her attention, and she greeted her parents with affection, formally introduced Alexei to her mother, who offered him a gracious smile and shook his hand.

'You've already met my father,' Natalya indicated, sensing the tension beneath the obsequious smile as Roman extended his hand.

'Indeed,' Roman expressed. 'So pleased you've taken Natalya on board. She's an excellent PA.'

Proficient at covering your back...words which remained silent.

'Ivana, darling. We're seated together.' Aaron's mother, Elvira, Natalya perceived, aware both women were long time friends. 'Roman. Natalya.' Her gaze shifted towards Alexei. 'Alexei Delandros, of course. You photograph well. I'm delighted to meet you.' She turned towards Natalya. 'Aaron is parking the car. Al has been shanghaied by a client. I'm sure he'll manage to escape soon.'

Interesting didn't begin to describe the seating arrangement. Aaron, the gay son whose parents were in ignorance of their son's sexual proclivities; Alexei and Roman... which member of the committee thought to put the fox and the rabbit together? Each table seated twelve. Who were the remaining five?

'Ah, they're opening the doors,' Elvira declared. 'Shall we go in?'

Moving within a crowd involved some inadvertent contact with other patrons, and she stiffened as Alexei placed an arm along the back of her waist...and kept it there until they reached their table, choosing to position her chair as she graciously took a seat. The gesture polite, impersonal...so why did his touch affect her body as much as it did?

A temporary madness, and one which she'd avoid by maintaining a reasonable distance between them. Which worked until a complement of five guests soon joined them. None other than Lara and Richard Tremayne, their two daughters Abby and Olivia, with son Jason bringing up the rear.

Like she needed *awkward*?

Nothing she couldn't handle…and she did, with grace and politeness, expressing amusement at the right intervals, while easing her way through three courses of beautifully presented delectable food.

'Champagne, Natalya?' Alexei queried, and she spared him a polite smile.

'Thank you.'

Definitely a departure from her usual preference of sparkling mineral water, and she caught Aaron's faintly raised eyebrow in silent askance.

On the surface all twelve patrons at their table appeared to be sharing a pleasant evening. Perhaps they were, and she was the only one present who sensed an edge of tension.

It was a relief when the wait-staff began clearing tables in preparation for serving coffee. An action which usually pre-empted a series of announcements, speeches offering thanks for generous donations, the evening's success, followed by music and the voiced encouragement for guests to enjoy the dance floor.

Roman stood to his feet and crossed to Natalya's side and extended his hand. 'Shall we?'

At least her father employed a little circumspection in leading her part-way through the waltz before he lowered his head a little and quietly demanded,

'What in hell are you thinking?'

She didn't pretend to misunderstand. 'I'm Alexei's PA, and seated with him in a professional capacity.'

'Darling girl, he's merely using you to highlight his success over my business failure.'

Natalya looked at him, glimpsed the anger, the frustration evident, and sought to alleviate it. 'Why would he do that, when the media have already printed the coup in various newspapers?'

Roman snorted in derision. 'Didn't you learn anything five years ago? The man upped and left you without a word.'

'That's not relevant to the current discussion.' Her voice was firm as she refused to placate him. 'Shall we rejoin the others?'

Coffee, hot, black, with no sugar helped, Natalya admitted, and she offered a smile as Roman swept her mother onto the dance floor, which left Natalya, Alexei and Jason Tremayne the only occupants at the table.

Not the best scenario, she perceived, wondering if she could escape to the powder room. However luck wasn't on her side as Jason rose to his feet and approached her.

'Our turn, I think.'

'Mine actually,' Alexei intervened smoothly as he rose to his feet and placed a hand on her shoulder. 'If you'll excuse us?'

She could refuse him, plead the need for a coffee refill, and attempt to relax. Instead she inclined her head towards Jason, offered a faint smile, and accompanied Alexei onto the dance floor.

'That wasn't necessary,' Natalya said quietly as she matched his steps with familiar ease.

'No?'

What could she say? If in doubt, don't, and in this instance silence was the better option.

The music slowed, and Alexei pulled her in as they adjusted their steps to a softer beat. The top of her head barely reached his shoulder, and he fought the urge to wrap an arm around her slender body, brush his lips to her temple…as he had done in the past. Enjoy the light floral perfume she wore, aware of his body pulsing with need, and the promise of how the night would end.

He'd been so sure of their relationship, of *her*, envisaging they'd grow old together, having raised a family, and enjoy grandchildren. Until Roman Montgomery had employed strong-arm tactics to ensure Alexei's swift departure from Sydney *and* the country.

Five years on, Alexei had changed, so too had his life.

The human psyche had intrigued him to such a point whereby he'd studied psychological behavioural patterns, mannerisms, characteristics that would provide insight to figurative red flags during his business dealings.

Qualities that had led to his success.

Had it hardened him? Undoubtedly.

His late father would have been proud.

'We should return to the table,' Natalya indicated as the music sped up to a modern beat. 'Considering the duty dance is done.'

'Duty?' Alexei queried as he released her. 'Is that what it was?'

'Of course,' she dismissed. 'What else would it have been?'

Indeed. If he hadn't noted the fast-beating pulse at the base of her throat, felt the throb of it beneath the palm of her wrist, he might have believed her.

The evening eventually drew to a close, with the final speech, the lucky door ticket prize, with guests lingering in the adjoining atrium as they waited for taxis, private limousines, while others continued on to a nightclub.

There were hugs, air kisses, voiced promises to do lunch or coffee…the usual pattern following the end of an evening's social event.

'The limousine will be here within a few minutes,' Alexei indicated.

'I can easily take a cab.'

'But you won't.'

Her lips parted with the intention of arguing with him,

only for her to decide against it. Besides, taxis at this time of night were in short supply.

'Compliance, Natalya?'

She spared him a glance. 'Only because it makes sense.'

And if you *dare* smile…

He didn't, or else she missed it as Paul eased the limousine to a halt at the kerb. The late evening flow of traffic was intense as patrons vacated cinemas, cafés and restaurants until they cleared the inner city and crossed the harbour bridge.

'I trust you both enjoyed a pleasant evening?' Paul queried, and it was Alexei who responded,

'Successful.'

The context had to relate to the capacity crowd, donations raised, and Natalya added, 'Very much so.'

There was a sense of relief when the limousine drew to a halt in her driveway, her set of keys in hand as she released the door clasp and stepped out in one fluid movement, pausing to offer, 'Thanks for the ride, the evening.' She held up her set of keys. 'I'm fine. My porch light is on a timer.' She closed the rear door, then turned towards the gated path, unaware Alexei had joined her.

'I'm quite capable of walking unaccompanied to my front door.'

'I was unaware I implied otherwise.' His voice was a musing drawl, and she was conscious of the sharp tug of awareness, the unbidden heat flooding her body…and silently damned her own vulnerability, choosing to glance at the lit window on the far left of the house.

'You share the house with someone?'

Not an unusual question, given its spacious size.

'It's a large family home divided in half to incorporate two separate units. I occupy one. Ben leases the other.'

Alexei's eyes narrowed. He had no recollection of her

mentioning anyone by that name. And he would have. A sharp memory was one of his talents. 'Since when?'

'Two and a half years ago.' She deactivated security, then inserted her key into the lock and heard Ollie's pathetic wail. 'My cat,' she enlightened as she opened the door, whereupon Ollie leapt into her arms and began purring as he affectionately butted his head against her chin.

Feline love, gifted unconditionally. If only human emotions were as uncomplicated...

Except they weren't, and Natalya offered Alexei a polite goodnight, entered the spacious hallway, then with a brief smile she closed and locked the door. Less than a minute later the veranda light faded, and she released her breath.

'Bed, hmm,' she murmured against Ollie's furry head. But sleep came without success, as she tossed and turned for what seemed an hour or more, only to check the illuminated hands on her watch to witness only thirty minutes had gone by.

Ollie protested and resettled his furry self at the base of the bed as Natalya punched her pillow, counted to ten, and sought a more comfortable position.

But there were too many images filling her mind of the times when she and Alexei were so attuned to each other there had been no need for words. Magical, engaging, special...so much so, she would have wagered her life nothing, no one, could tear them apart.

Yet someone or something had.

CHAPTER TEN

NATALYA MUST HAVE SLEPT, for when she woke Friday morning the sun was filtering through the bedroom shutters, and a quick glance at the bedside clock revealed she had plenty of time to shower, dress, linger over breakfast, flip pages through the daily newspaper and feed the cat, ready to face whatever the day might bring.

But something in the press changed her light mood to one of outrage as she caught a newsprint photo on the social page featuring Alexei handing her into his limousine. Taken on angle the photographer had managed to imply an intimacy that didn't exist.

Worse, the caption—MOGUL AND FORMER LOVER TOGETHER AGAIN?—was endorsed by a brief paragraph beneath the photo.

Without hesitation she tore out the page, folded it and thrust it into her satchel.

Seconds later the phone rang, and she bit back an unladylike curse as she saw the ID.

'Hi, Dad.'

That was as far as she got, before her father launched into a diatribe, which in essence demanded to know what was going on between her and Alexei.

Soothing him down took several minutes, until she cut his words short with the excuse she had to leave for work.

She was barely a kilometre from her apartment in heavy morning traffic when her cell phone beeped with an incoming text.

WTH? Aaron.

Her staunch and loyal friend who'd supported her through the worst of times had clearly seen the same photograph too.

Worse, she garnered a few speculative glances as she rode an elevator to the high floor occupied by ADE Electronics.

All it took was one vigilant employee to start the gossip mill…and who better the focus than Natalya Montgomery, daughter of the fallen Roman Montgomery *and* former lover of the new head honcho, Alexei Delandros?

Dammit. This had to be stopped *now*.

She ignored her own office and in one swift action she retrieved the newsprint page and marched directly into Alexei's office…which probably wasn't the best idea, but she was so angry she didn't care.

If he was surprised, he failed to show it, and she hated that he'd leaned back in his chair seemingly intent on regarding her with detached interest as she crossed to his desk.

Natalya drew in a deep breath, then released it slowly. 'Let's get one thing straight,' she stated firmly. 'I'll act the polite efficient PA in all matters business. Anything alluding to *personal* is off the table.'

He waited a beat. 'Clarify *personal*?'

'Placing me in an invidious position.'

'Apropos of?'

Natalya extracted the page she'd torn from the daily newspaper and placed it on his desk. *'This.'*

She watched as he skimmed the offending caption…and waited for his reaction. Except there was none.

'I have no control over the media's agenda.'

Had the light touch of his hand at her waist been deliberate? Or was she simply being super-sensitive?

It irked he had the power to tie her emotions in knots… She hated that she actively looked for and subsequently judged his every word and action, silently seething if she imagined they crossed the line…*her* self-imposed line.

Her eyes darkened measurably. 'I want a retraction printed in tomorrow's edition.'

Alexei leant further back in his chair and regarded her thoughtfully. 'Don't you think that will only exacerbate the situation?'

Natalya drew a deep breath, then released it as her eyes darkened with anger. 'There is no *situation*.'

He lifted one eyebrow. 'Perhaps you'd care to inform the media of that?'

She pursed her lips, then opened her mouth to deliver a volley of words best left unsaid. Instead she directed him a glare which had no visible effect whatsoever, much to her annoyance, leaving her little option except to turn on her heel and sweep out from his office.

Her silent frustration with the media's intrusion continued throughout the morning, while she fought to qualify they were only doing their job. Not that it helped much. Nor did she feel comfortable with a part of her private life being played out in the public domain.

Natalya ordered lunch in, despatched a text to Ivana, and cursed beneath her breath when Reception notified several calls representing the media had not been redirected to Alexei Delandros' PA.

Like she *needed* this?

Late afternoon a text arrived on her smartphone.

Flight Monday a.m. Sydney/NY. Details laptop. Confirm. Alexei.

Two weeks? Natalya silently queried when she checked her laptop and read Alexei's schedule.

The expected meetings, a few business lunches, three business dinners. Family.

Alexei's family. So, not all business.

Which meant she'd have free time to check out a few upmarket boutiques, enjoy a leisurely coffee in any one of numerous cafés. Me time.

She sent off a text in confirmation, then she turned her chair towards the plate-glass window, momentarily took in the harbour view, and smiled.

Suddenly the day appeared a little brighter.

The weekend involved a close inspection of her wardrobe, a list of items to pack, the need to check with Ben if he could look after Ollie, a phone call to Ivana, who listened, wisely chose to relay a simple, 'Take care, darling,' instead of a litany of words attributed to caution of the personal kind. So not Ivana's style.

When the persistent beep of the alarm woke her the next morning, Natalya had an urge to push the off button, roll over and grab another hour's sleep, only to groan… *not going to happen*.

There was a need to be ready on time. Alexei's text stating she be ready for pick-up at seven-thirty a.m. ensured she was waiting on the front veranda with her luggage, overnight bag and satchel.

Sure enough the limousine slid to the kerb with Paul at the wheel. Within minutes the driver transferred her luggage while she joined Alexei in the rear passenger seat.

'Good morning.' Pleasant, she could do pleasant…which he responded to in like manner.

There was no need to run through their immediate agenda. They could do that once they were in the air.

Not a passenger jet, Natalya discovered, but a private one. Expensive, luxurious and essentially an office in the air with cabin staff who provided coffee, offered a light meal be served once they reached cruising speed.

A review of their agenda required a few adjustments, and their first appointment in New York required only a minor amendment.

'There's a sleeping compartment with a comfortable bed adjoining the en suite bathroom,' Alexei relayed as he retrieved a set of earphones. 'I suggest you get a few hours' rest.'

'What about you?' The query was out before she'd given it any thought.

'I'll take the second shift.' He paused, and his eyes met her own. 'Unless you suggest we share?'

'Not going to happen.' Her response was instant, and his mouth curved a little.

'Relax, Natalya.'

She hadn't been able to completely relax since the first day he'd reappeared in her life.

The bedroom compartment was more spacious than she expected, containing a bed with fresh linens, a small wardrobe, appointed mod-cons, and a comfortable chair.

It took a few minutes to discard her outer clothes, re-move make-up and don a wrap, then she turned back the bedcovers, settled comfortably, and much to her surprise she slept for more than four hours and woke feeling re-freshed. Suitably clothed, she applied moisturiser, added a touch of colour to her lips, then she returned to the cabin, accepted fruit and coffee while Alexei sought the sleep-ing compartment.

Which became more restless than restful as the light

floral perfume Natalya used lingered to taunt him with memories of shared passion, and what he'd believed to be unconditional love.

Elicited fact appeared to prove him wrong.

Yet deep in his gut there was a kernel of doubt based on the occasional unguarded moment during the past few weeks...when he was able to catch a glimpse of the young woman he'd known so well. A momentary warmth in her smile. A faint wistfulness, only for it to quickly disappear.

The slight change in her breathing when he'd held her in his arms on the dance floor. The tension evident in her stance when he escorted her to the front door of her home. There was a degree of vulnerability evident he found intriguing...a quality she endeavoured to disguise. And almost succeeded.

A stopover in Los Angeles for the jet to refuel, Customs, before boarding for the final leg of their flight to New York...where a uniformed chauffeur was waiting for them in the Arrivals lounge.

A service Alexei had obviously used on prior occasions, Natalya observed, given the ease of friendship between both men, and with smooth economy of movement their luggage was cleared from the carousel, carried through the terminal and deposited in the boot of a sleek black limousine which had slid smoothly to the kerb.

A driver *and* a bodyguard?

Elevated status...or a necessity?

New York contained a variety of differing vibes...from extreme wealth and luxury to the opposite end of the spectrum. Alive with a mix of cultures, from traditional to the exotic. A city which moved to a certain beat, glamour, pizzazz, to the bleakness of the Projects. A familiar vibe she recalled from previous business trips she had shared as her father's PA.

Music was key to the difference in attire and speech, and Natalya breathed it in as the limousine traversed the distance between airport to the high-end hotel in the vicinity of Central Park.

Classy, Natalya determined as they rode the elevator to a high floor, with stunning views over the city that never slept.

For the following few days they attended meetings, while maintaining a painstakingly professional façade.

Each day became mission accomplished. The nights, not so much.

Arranging business dinners didn't faze her, nor had attending them when the CEO had been her father. Alexei was someone else entirely.

Five years had wrought changes in Alexei she'd thought she'd known so well. Eyes dark, gleaming, sensual, conveying with just a look how the night would end.

The antithesis of the man he'd become...hardwired, ruthless—*driven*.

Except she was no longer the biddable young girl with stars in her eyes, imagining love would overcome everything.

How wrong had she been? she reflected as she dressed for the evening ahead. Formal, Alexei had forewarned, and she selected a red gown with a high neck artfully draped to cover each breast, leaving her shoulders and arms bare, nipped in at the waist to fall in a swirl of soft material at her feet. Subtle make-up, emphasis on the eyes, bold red lip gloss, her hair styled in large soft waves which fell past her shoulders and curved forward to partly frame her face, a touch of jewellery, she gathered up a wrap in matching red, slid her feet into red stilettos, took a deep breath, and emerged into the adjoining lounge to find Alexei conducting a conversation on his smartphone in a language she failed to comprehend.

Black evening suit, white shirt and black bow tie did much to emphasise his European features, impossibly dark eyes and wide mobile mouth. A mouth that could wreak mindless havoc…as she knew too well.

His cologne held a subtle blend of musk and something she failed to define…a soft sensual whisper that teased, taunted and made her think of the forbidden.

Each breath she took in his presence became measured, *controlled*, as every muscle in her body slowly tightened. In the close confines of the limousine she felt as brittle as the most delicate piece of Venetian glass.

One touch, and she'd shatter.

CHAPTER ELEVEN

THE EVENING AHEAD was a formal occasion. *Very* formal, Natalya noted, given the venue, the sumptuous grand dining room, the quality linen covering the many tables, exquisite crystal, cutlery and tableware.

Security was evident, invitations carefully checked, and guests personally escorted to their tables.

A gala event of note.

'Why me?' she had queried quietly, and incurred his studied look.

'Why not you?'

'This is social, not business.'

'The lines between the two are blurred, are they not?'

Anything else she might have added remained unsaid as a stunning blonde, who appeared out of nowhere behind him, snuggled close against his back, wound her arms around his neck.

'Guess who?'

Natalya caught a glimpse of diamond rings, a diamond necklace, sensed a drift of exotic perfume, heard the sultry in the young woman's voice, and felt her stomach plummet.

A friend? Lover? Mistress?

'Stassi,' Alexei acknowledged with a tinge of amusement as she released her hands and stepped to face him. 'Your signature perfume is unmistakable.'

There was a light tinkle of laughter followed by a staged *moue*…belied by the sparkle in Stassi's eyes as she stood on tiptoe to brush a light kiss to his cheek before turning towards Natalya. 'And you are?'

'Natalya,' Alexei drawled. 'Let me introduce you to my irrepressible cousin, Stassi.'

'Family,' Stassi declared. 'So Alexei is off limits, unfortunately. Although he does duty as a partner on occasion.' She glanced from Natalya to Alexei. 'And you are Alexei's…?'

'Friend,' Alexei declared.

'Uh-huh. Euphemism for…?'

'Friend,' he drawled, undeterred by his cousin's inquisitiveness.

'PA,' Natalya corrected.

Stassi smiled. 'Business *and* pleasure. Interesting combination.' She offered Alexei a teasing grin. 'You do realise your mother is planning a family dinner in your honour? She'll be delighted to welcome Natalya.'

Family? No, not happening. 'I don't think my presence would be appropriate.'

'Alexei will do his persuasive best,' Stassi stated with a light laugh. 'He's very good at it.' A slow smile curved her lips. 'I really must return to the parents. They have plotted to introduce me to a gorgeous man who, according to my darling mama, displays excellent potential as future husband material. Should be a fun evening.' She kissed her fingers and playfully touched them to Alexei's cheek. 'Take care.'

She turned towards Natalya. 'I'll look forward to catching up with you again.' With a mischievous smile she began threading her way through the numerous guests.

'Your cousin is delightful,' Natalya ventured politely, and caught his musing expression.

'Yes, she is. She's also intelligent, with a degree in criminal law. Loves life, has no intention of marrying, now or in the near future. Much to her mother's despair.'

'She obviously hasn't met the right man.'

'Is marriage so important?'

Sticky question, and not one Natalya was prepared to answer. Five years ago she would have said marriage represented a lifetime commitment, enduring love, growing a family…including qualities such as trust, faith and respect. Sharing the good and the not-so-good times together, without blame or regret.

'No comment, Natalya?'

She managed a credible smile. 'Much depends on one's life plan, don't you think?'

'And yours is?'

'Personal.'

For a moment she glimpsed a slight change in his expression, then it was gone, and she was left to ponder if her imagination was playing tricks.

'Perhaps we should take our seats,' Alexei indicated smoothly, inclining his head to a staff member waiting to escort them to their reserved table.

Society's glitterati at its finest, Natalya noted, as she sipped an excellent French wine. Similar to, but different from, she perceived, other charity functions she'd attended in the past. For there was ample evidence of extreme wealth apparent in the women's designer gowns, and their jewellery alone could have funded housing and food for a poor nation.

Cosmetic enhancement appeared to be *de rigueur* for the mature women, varying hairstyles combed and teased to within a whisper of perfection.

Nor, she suspected, was it confined to the women.

It was akin to viewing a movie on screen, where the

majority of guests were actors playing a part, prepared by stylists, make-up artists, such was the achieved element of perfection.

The ballroom was enormous, and soon seated to capacity. Soft background music became almost lost to the chatter of voices as stylishly clothed wait staff ensured champagne and fine wines were replenished with reputed flair.

'Darling Alexei,' a female guest seated opposite at their table inclined with exquisite poise. 'I heard you'd touched down in this part of town.' All that was required to complete the woman's image was a long cigarette holder, for she had the pose down pat of the lead actress who played the original role of Auntie Mame in an old movie. 'So delighted you could grace us with your presence. But then, you have a vested interest in the nominated charity.' Her smile held graceful interest as it settled on Natalya. 'You've brought along an interesting new friend. Natalie, I believe?'

'Natalya.' It was easy to smile as she offered the correction.

'Of Russian origin?'

'It was my great-grandmother's name.'

'How interesting.'

Her great-grandmother's history *was* interesting…the story of a family who escaped a life of poverty to settle on a distant relative's farm in northern Europe. As a young girl of eighteen, she'd entered into an arranged marriage and bore four children…the youngest of which being Natalya's grandmother, who'd fled to America as a teenager, found work and lodging in a Californian vineyard, borrowed a sewing machine and made children's clothes long hours into the night. Embroidery was her specialty, and at first her exquisitely embroidered gowns sold by word of mouth, until she was encouraged to sell direct to a childrenswear shop in a nearby town. In storybook style, her grandmother had married the vintner's son, bore two children, a girl and a boy. Sadly her husband and young son were killed in an accident together with her husband's parents. Stricken with grief, Natalya's grandmother attempted to run the vineyard, only to sell it within two years, and start a new life with her daughter Ivana in Australia, settling in Sydney, where she set up shop, employed minimum staff, and gradually expanded over time to export her childrenswear overseas.

Natalya's cherished Babushka...so morally and emotionally strong. A woman who had worked every day of her life and for whom family was everything, and who left behind so many memories of love, wisdom and laughter.

'More champagne?'

The sound of Alexei's voice intruded, and the ballroom with its numerous guests returned in sharp focus as Natalya offered a polite smile together with a quietly voiced refusal.

Background music faded, and there was the introductory speech of welcome, followed by the purpose of the charity in question, funds raised, together with a plea for guests to be generous with their donations.

In terms of success, the event topped the scale, given the plaudits offered throughout the evening. Guests appeared at their sparkling best, the food superb and the champagne flowed.

Polite small-talk appeared to be the order of the evening...the best party a few of the society doyennes had attended, who were present, snippets of gossip, and descriptions of apparel...designer of course, and who wore it best.

Different country, another major city...familiar scenario, merely on a larger scale.

Natalya briefly compared the evening with some she had attended with her father; the increasing tension as his alcohol intake rose, and her attempt to minimise the fallout. The relief when the evening came to a close and they could leave.

Now there was tension of a different kind, arising from her emotional reaction to Alexei's presence. Sexual sensuality…a heightened awareness that threatened her sanity. The question being…what was she going to do about it?

'We'll be dining at my mother's home this evening.' Alexei's seemingly normal statement following breakfast the next morning caused Natalya's breath to momentarily catch in her throat.

We?

Her fingers momentarily paused from keying words into her laptop.

Surely she'd misheard?

'I'm sure you'll enjoy spending time with her,' she offered with genuine sincerety as she set her fingers tapping on the keys.

There was a need to transcribe recorded notes from the previous day's meeting, prior to lunch and a mid-afternoon consult…when casual attire would be exchanged for suit, heels to present a more professional image.

Vastly different from his current casual attire of black fitted jeans and black tee shirt which emphasised the breadth of his shoulders, powerful flex of toned forearm musculature…the taut stomach, narrow waist and six-pack abs. The fact he worked out was evident in every move he made.

It made her want to explore. To track every muscle, the hard flex and tone with her hands. Purr with pleasure at the thought of dragging the tee shirt from his body, to tease and caress his bare skin…with the familiar touch of a lover.

Exult in his response, the faint catch in his breath when she unbuckled the belt at his waist, slid the studded button free, then slowly freed the zip of his jeans in a slow sensuous play that could only have one end…almost crying out as he mimicked each movement she made, slowly, with exquisite care. The almost reverent touch as he cupped each breast, lowered his head to taste one nipple, and drove her wild as he used his mouth to draw it deep and suckle, before slowly withdrawing to shift focus to its twin.

The way she trailed a hand over his stomach to trace the extended length of him, feel, rather than sense his indrawn breath, the shift in his body as he lifted his head and claimed her mouth in erotic possession…until extended foreplay wasn't enough. Nor the whispered words inciting the sensual promise of sexual pleasure.

Stop right there, a silent voice echoed in Natalya's mind. Mentally reliving an erotic memory of what they'd once shared served no purpose.

Almost as if Alexei knew, his dark eyes lifted and held her own for what seemed to be a long minute, when it could only have been a few seconds.

She couldn't move, nor did she have the power to utter a word.

A lost moment in time, brief…but it took an age before she managed to gather herself together and gain a sense of focus on the prosaic…laptop, transcribing notes.

Yet her mind lingered… Five years on there was a maturity evident, an innate knowledge of the man he had become. A certain ruthlessness apparent that almost alluded to an element of danger should anyone be sufficiently foolish to attempt to thwart him…on any level.

He possessed charm, respect, loyalty, and employed

each characteristic facet with ease. Yet he possessed the ability to freeze an opponent with a mere glance; the power to walk away from a prospective deal without so much as a second's hesitation.

Was that how he treated his women?

Don't go there.

'The invitation includes you.'

Natalya's fingers inadvertently touched a wrong key, and a silent epithet echoed inside her head as she turned towards him.

Professional, she could manage. Sharing dinner with Alexei's mother was in a different category entirely.

'Will I be required to take notes this evening?' The query held polite civility, and one as his PA she was entitled to ask.

Alexei's expression remained unchanged. 'Possibly, given my two brothers and I form part of a European-based business partnership. Although primarily the evening will be a family gathering.'

Her stomach executed a slow roll of discomfort. She didn't do family...specifically not an ex-lover's family.

A slightly hysterical laugh rose and died in her throat. Like she'd had more than one lover?

A couple of close encounters that hadn't ended well, when there had been the expectation of more than she was prepared to indulge.

'Given the evening is family-oriented, and any business matters are unlikely to be discussed on a level requiring my presence,' she inclined, 'I'll—'

'Pass?' Alexei lifted one eyebrow. 'My mother is expecting you. My sister-in-law will be delighted to have you there to tone down what she refers to as excessive male testosterone.' A faint smile curved the edges of his mouth. 'Despite qualifying affection for her two brothers-in-law.'

'I don't think it's appropriate.'

'What are you afraid of, Natalya?' His eyes held a glimmer of dark humour. 'We might be issued an invitation to stay overnight?'

In the same bedroom? How much of her former relationship with Alexei was his family aware of?

Almost as if he knew the passage of her thoughts, he offered quietly, 'Any fears you might have are completely groundless.'

Were they? So why this feeling of heightened awareness? She didn't want or need a reminder of what they'd once shared. She'd dealt with the past, moved on, created a pleasant life for herself.

Who do you think you're fooling?

'I agree,' she managed firmly. 'For each of us.'

Alexei moved in close before she had time to draw breath and laid his mouth over her own in what began as an explorative kiss that soon changed and became something else.

She wanted to protest, and lifted both hands to create a distance between them, only to have them falter as the years melted away as she was transported back to a place and time where everything was right between them.

She had no recollection of the passage of time...only the assault on her senses as he brought her emotions alive in a manner that tripped her heart into rapid beat.

Heaven, and then some, as she began to respond, uncaring at that moment where it might lead...and if it did, would she gain the emotional strength to step away?

Then he released her, and the room came into focus... together with reality.

There was a need to breathe in a conscious effort to still each throbbing pulse in her body...acutely sensitive to the once familiar touch personally geared to send her totally undone. As it had in the past.

'An experiment, Alexei?' She even managed to inject a shred of disdain into her voice, caught the dark glitter in his gaze before it was masked, and she valiantly ignored the sudden lump that rose in her throat.

There was only the heavy thud of her heartbeat as she sought to bring wildly swirling emotions under control. The words I hate you remained unsaid...*just*.

Or was it herself she hated? For momentarily succumbing to the special magic they'd once shared. And its vivid reminder.

'An answer.'

Which didn't sit well with her at all. 'You think?'

With forced calm she crossed to the mirror, extracted her lipstick, repaired the damage, then she caught up her satchel, included her laptop, recording device, added sundry necessities...and moved towards the front door of their hotel apartment, all too aware of his close proximity as they rode the elevator down to lobby level. Prepared, in essence, to become the quintessential PA as business meetings were due to unfold for the day ahead.

CHAPTER TWELVE

CALISTA DELANDROS RESIDED in an elite part of Georgetown.

A slender elegantly attired woman who welcomed her son with a warm hug, before extending a hand in greeting to the young woman who stood at his side.

'Natalya. Welcome to my home.' Her smile was genuine. 'The family are waiting in the lounge. Let's join them, shall we?'

Beautifully appointed, fine handcrafted furniture, framed family pictures on the walls. Warm, welcoming, Natalya perceived as Calista indicated a large comfortably furnished lounge where two men stood... Alexei's brothers, without doubt, given the likeness in height, stature, and facial features. A young woman displaying the slight emerging bump of early pregnancy held the small hand of a young girl.

'Cristos,' Alexei greeted and clasped his brother in a brief hug before indicating, 'Cristos's wife, Xena, and their daughter, Gigi. My younger brother, Dimitri.' He turned to include Natalya. 'Natalya. My PA.'

Natalya smiled...a smile was good. Polite, professional.

It was Xena's daughter who captured Natalya's attention. Petite, dark curls framing beautiful features, offering a smile to melt hearts.

'Gigi is a lovely name,' Natalya said gently.

She was rewarded with a polite, 'Thank you.'

For a few fleeting seconds it proved difficult to ignore the faint wistful ache in the region of her heart.

It was relatively easy to converse, to fit in, as the evening progressed. A skill she'd mastered since mid-teen years, together with an interest in current world affairs and a degree of genuine charm.

She accepted a small measure of wine, which she sipped as she observed family dynamics, their affection, and genuine interest in the current play in each of their lives.

Cristos headed the New York arm of the family business, while Dimitri travelled to interstate branches, and maintained an active social life...very social, Natalya surmised from the slightly wicked gleam in his eyes.

A family originating in Greece, as had Calista's late husband. Evident in some of the classical pottery on display in a few of the glass cabinets.

A faint lilt, not exactly an accent, in Calista's speech on occasion.

Xena, who was charming, and delighted the babe she carried was a boy.

The food was superb, and Natalya felt at ease...comfortable, she amended silently. Gigi began to tire, willingly retiring to bed for an overnight stay at her grandmother's home.

They were a pleasant family, Natalya perceived, extending polite interest in Natalya's role as Alexei's PA, her familiarity with the field of electronics...although not why, how or where she'd gained that knowledge.

It was after eleven when the evening drew to a close.

'You seem surprised,' Alexei drawled as the car cleared the drive and headed towards the inner city.

Perhaps because she'd expected...what? Cool reserve?

Why, when Alexei hadn't imagined it necessary to mention her existence in his life?

'In what way?' She could do cool, and tempered it with a touch of deliberate sweetness. 'Because you chose not to out me as my father's daughter?'

He shot her a quick glance before returning his attention to the traffic. 'Would you have preferred me to do so?'

'Perhaps I should thank you.'

'Give it up, Natalya.'

The atmosphere had taken a subtle change. A personal element that didn't sit well, for too many reasons she was reluctant to explore.

Consequently it was a relief when Alexei drew the car to a halt outside the hotel entrance, where a uniformed attendant hailed a waiting employee to drive the car down into the underground parking area.

A few words, a generous tip, and a leisurely pace through the foyer to the bank of lifts…one of which swiftly transported them to their designated floor.

One day led to another, as Alexei, Cristos and Dimitri conducted high-powered meetings, each with their individual PAs in attendance, as they brokered deals, added valuable real estate to their company portfolio at a pace which left Natalya in awe of their combined expertise and staying power.

Ruthless power, she added silently, at the end of a particularly fraught day…one that was far from over. Debrief, dinner, highlight pertinent points from recordings, send same to Alexei's laptop. Shower, bed, sleep…

Except sleep proved elusive, and she lay staring sightlessly at the darkened ceiling for what seemed an age before emerging from the bed to pull on a wrap and quietly emerge into the lounge, where she crossed to the wide floor-to-ceiling glass sliding doors, parted the drapes a little and looked out over the brightly lit city, lingered on the kaleidoscope of neon signage on numerous city sky-scrapers.

'It's a bit late to be admiring the view.'

Alexei's quiet drawl caused her breath to hitch as he moved to stand at her side.

'It beats counting sheep.' The words were out of her mouth before she gave them thought.

'Something is bothering you?'

You, she wanted to throw at him. *There, in my face...all day, every day. A constant I don't need or want.*

Because...she didn't want to explore the *why* of it.

Okay, she totally got the business part. What she hadn't bargained for was the constant twenty-four-seven away from home bit. Far away from where she could retreat at day's end to her own home. Dammit, her own sanctuary.

'Go to bed. We have another full day tomorrow.'

'Perhaps you should take your own advice.'

Admit he couldn't sleep? Her image haunted him, firing the need to pull her into his arms, claim her mouth with his own...and let whatever would happen, happen.

So why hesitate?

With any other woman he'd play the seduction game, accept the unspoken invitation and enjoy the sexual activity...heart untouched.

Natalya...their shared history was gaining too much intrusion on his original intention to gain revenge. So why now question what he'd believed to be fact?

Something didn't add up...but *what*?

He felt compelled to do the unexpected, and lifted a hand to trail light fingers down her cheek. And felt her tense.

'Don't.'

His mouth curved a little at the slight huskiness apparent in her voice. 'No?'

If she acted on sexual need, she'd tear the clothes from his body...and to hell with the consequences.

How many nights had she lain awake restless with the aching need of wanting him? *Only him.* Fighting an overwhelming urge to stem the tears that filled her eyes, angry with herself for lapsing into an emotional watershed as she wretchedly fought for control.

Alexei watched as she turned and escaped into her bedroom suite, heard the faint snap of the door clasp...and remained where he was for several long minutes, unaware of the night skyline, the many lit buildings, flashing multi-coloured neon, the traffic.

Instead he became caught up by her reaction...the faint quiver of her lips, the warmth of her cheek beneath his touch.

All too aware of his own body's damning response.

For the past five years he'd worked eighteen-to-twenty-hour days, fuelled by the need to succeed beyond measure in the name of revenge, ruthlessly crafting each move, each strategy in a personal vendetta where there could be only one survivor...*him.*

He'd won. Big time.

Satisfaction should be his...and it was.

So why this feeling a subtle shift had come into play?

The weekend provided a welcome change from the hectic week's business schedule. It was a beautiful day, and Natalya decided to revisit a few of the many glamorous stores and fashion boutiques New York city had to offer.

She was entitled to take some down time, to savour a coffee, a delicious pastry, browse a little...simply explore where the mood might take her. Sit a while, and watch the people walk by. Enjoy the cosmopolitan atmosphere.

Not to mention relax away from Alexei's powerful presence.

Something which earned a studied look from Alexei on learning her intention.

'Ensure you have your smartphone for contact, should it be necessary.'

It was simple to voice the few necessary words. 'Of course. Although I might remind you it's my day off.'

'But not the evening. The Delandros corporation sponsor an annual invitation-only dinner to commemorate my late father's love of his birthplace and Greek heritage. My mother insists you join us.'

Now there was the thing…an invitation from Calista Delandros made it difficult to refuse. 'I don't think it's…'

'Appropriate?' Alexei prompted.

'No.'

His smile held a tinge of amusement. 'Your reason being?'

'It's a significant occasion for family and friends. My position as your PA doesn't fit either category.'

'Consider it a personal request.'

'Personal is not on the agenda.'

A musing smile curved his mouth. 'The lines are becoming a little blurred.'

'Not,' Natalya confirmed, 'from my perspective.'

He wanted to change her mind, and would…soon.

Subtle persuasion was an art form, one he'd mastered at a young age. Only to realise seduction didn't equate to love, and while some women were content to play a part, he had tired of that game.

He wanted *more*.

'My mother will be disappointed if you refuse.' Manoeuvre and conquer was a skill in itself…one he owned unequivocally, and didn't hesitate to use to his advantage.

Natalya recognised it, wanted to call him on it, only to concede defeat. 'I accept, given the invitation came from your mother.'

The faint gleam of amusement momentarily apparent indicated he was one step ahead of her. 'I'll book a limousine for seven o'clock.'

'I'll ensure I'm on time.'

There was a sense of freedom as she rode the elevator to foyer level, declined the need for a limousine or taxi, and began to walk, choosing one of her favourite department stores in which to browse a while.

Coffee and a sinfully loaded pastry in a small café, followed by a gift for Ivana, a colourful top for Anja, a cute little doggy bow tie for Ben's pug Alfie.

It had proven to be a relaxing, enjoyable afternoon, and she entered the hotel suite ahead of time to discover it empty, a note in plain sight, which she quickly read before heading into her own suite.

A male could shower, dress and be ready in less time than a woman…

Nevertheless, Natalya was ahead of Alexei by five minutes, poised, attired in a tailored black skirt, matching camisole and a red silk box jacket. Stylish, flawless make-up, matching red lipstick, and diamond studs her only jewellery.

He did evening wear with superb masculine style. Designer stubble added an edgy touch that set him apart, adding to an overall masculinity impossible to ignore.

'A drink before we leave?'

Natalya shook her head, and he checked his watch, caught up door swipe cards, then ushered her out of their suite.

The evening lay ahead…different from the usual social occasion, together with the pleasure of Calista and her family's company.

A limousine took them to a private venue in the city's outskirts where cars lined the streets, and the subdued beat of Greek music resonated in the evening air, softening as the four limousines carrying members of the Delandros family drew to a halt adjacent the main entrance of a large single-storey building.

'Smile,' Alexei bade quietly as the driver opened each door and ushered them to join Calista, followed by Cristos and Xena, then Dimitri.

The guests were greeted personally by each family member, which took a while, given a numbered ticket, until everyone was accounted for, seated…and the evening began.

An evening which was a mix of formality, anecdotes relayed in turn by Alexei, Cristos and Dimitri of a much-loved father. Reminiscences of times past, interspersed with the serving of food. Specialties of the region where Calista's husband was born. And laughter.

Truly a celebration of a life well-lived. Of honour, hard work, and the joy of family.

Later there was music, gentle, like the air drifting over the seas lapping the islands that made up Greece, the fishermen who dragged the nets, and the men, like Calista's husband, who had built many fine houses and villas on his beloved Santorini.

'Nothing like you expected?' Calista queried with a slow sweet smile as Natalya shook her head. 'We share this each year, and the money raised is gifted to those less fortunate. Soon there will be dancing, the music will become a little loud as the men move to the strains of the bouzouki. Each invitation carries a number for the prize of a ten-day cruise around the Greek Islands, including a three-day stay at a villa on Santorini.'

It was a beautiful sentiment, and Natalya said as much.

'My husband worked hard to provide our sons with a good education, to appreciate the good things in life, and to always remember where they came from.'

'Their success is a testament to you both,' Natalya offered with quiet sincerity.

'Thank you.'

The music proved enticing, and couples moved onto the dance floor, initially led by Alexei and his mother, followed by Cristos and Xena.

'Our turn,' Dimitri indicated, glimpsed her faint hesitation, and smiled. 'I don't bite.'

'Good to know.'

A younger version of Alexei, tall, well-built, easy-going with a sharp legal mind. Evidenced during the most recent meeting the three brothers had held with one of their competitors.

'Will you object if I pull you in a bit closer?'

She got it…or at least she thought she did. 'You're attempting to attract someone's attention?'

'Uh-huh.'

Natalya offered him a teasing smile. 'I doubt you'd fail attracting any young woman you chose to pursue. So you want me to appear as a decoy date,' Natalya teased. 'May I ask *who* has captured your attention? The gorgeous blonde eating you with her eyes? No? Hmm… The auburn-haired angel on the next table to our left, looking to kill you first chance she gets?' Given there was more than one titian-haired sophisticate in the room, Natalya added, 'The one wearing a stunning bronze-coloured gown, with a strand of diamonds showcasing a dazzling pendant showcasing her elegant décolletage?'

'You're more than just a pretty face,' Dimitri inclined with a faintly rueful smile, and she offered a light laugh.

'I'm trained to observe.'

His eyes assumed a musing gleam. 'Something you obviously do well.'

'Are you going to tell me who she is?'

'Curiosity, or genuine interest?'

'Interest,' Natalya answered quietly.

'A corporate lawyer in her father's firm.'

She smiled a little. 'Does she have a name?'

'If I told,' he enlightened as the edges of his mouth quirked a little, 'I would have to kill you.'

She wanted to laugh. 'Got it,' Natalya offered solemnly. 'So… Alexei?'

That came out of left field…and unexpected. Dimitri's eyebrow lifted a little. 'What's with the vibe between the two of you?'

'Your misinterpretation.'

His smile widened a little. 'I beg to differ.'

The music increased in beat, as almost everyone joined in with the laughter, and those couples dancing on the floor took a few missteps…which didn't appear to matter at all.

Voices rose, and Natalya gave a startled sound as Alexei appeared at her side and led her onto the dance floor before she had the opportunity to protest.

I don't know the steps, remained unsaid.

'It doesn't matter. I'll guide you.'

He did, and she soon mastered the rhythm, laughed a little when she almost missed a step, which Alexei faultlessly covered.

For the moment she simply let go, lost in the moment, the music, ambience…and the man who led her.

Until the moment the music slowed…and Alexei drew

her close for timeless minutes, when it took all of her inner strength not to lean in against him, rest her cheek close to his heart, and just let the evening, the music, take her wherever it might lead.

Except there was an awareness of time and place, the haunting music, the slight pathos that seeped into her body, making her wish for more.

Did Alexei feel it too?

Who would know?

The sound of strings stirring from the bouzouki teased the air, and the chatter of conversation ceased as the pace lingered, dwelled, then began to quicken in tone and pitch. Stirring memories for most, of times past, and present for those who returned to revisit again and again in order to relive the magic merging of old and new, the history, the future.

Special, Natalya perceived, and felt the touch deep in her heart.

Coffee, thick, aromatic and strong, was served, after which the duplicate numbers handed out at the point of entry were presented in a circular glass tumbler, spun, and Calista, by tradition, extracted a ticket and read out the winning number.

There was a shout of victory, applause from the guests, the music lingered as the evening wound down, guests began making preparations to leave, with the sound of pleasurable laughter, affectionate farewells, car doors opening and closing, engines starting up as the streets slowly emptied.

It had been a memorable evening, and she said as much as she thanked Calista for the invitation, bade Xena, Cristos and Dimitri goodnight, before sliding into the limousine Alexei had summoned to return them to the hotel.

'You enjoyed the evening?'

Her mouth curved into a generous smile. 'It was great. The venue, the music. Uplifting to witness everyone coming together for a specific purpose. Reliving memories of times past, sharing lifelong friendships. Tradition,' she offered quietly.

Alexei shifted slightly to take in her vivacious features alight with pleasure, and held back the desire to pull her close, take her mouth with his own, and absorb her response.

There was a heaviness in his groin...needing, wanting what she could give him, as he would gift her. Sex, as a means to define love?

It didn't work that way. Love was a gift from the heart, inviolate, unconditional. A force of Nature shared by two people whose lives were inexplicably bound together for all time.

Hadn't he searched for its likeness in the intervening years? Only to despair a woman's interest was more attuned to his bank balance than his heart, his soul.

It hadn't been enough to put a ring on any woman's finger. Call him cynical, but he wanted *more* than a facsimile.

The limousine slowed and drew to a halt in the curved apex adjoining the hotel's main entrance. It was late, but the inner city remained alive with guests returning from drinks after the theatre, parties.

A city which never slept, Natalya acknowledged, as she rode the elevator to their designated floor.

The vibrant hype of the evening began to dissipate as she preceded Alexei into their suite, and she toed off her stilettos, discarded her jacket, and bade him goodnight.

He let her go.

And silently cursed...for lost opportunities.

Need...for a woman. Not just any woman...he could have any one of many who would give whatever he wanted.

A wild eroticism among tangled sheets, each aware it was merely satiation of the senses, nothing more.

To his credit, he was selective...upfront, no false hope, mutual pleasure for as long as it lasted.

Sexual satisfaction for a price.

None of which applied to Natalya. For what they'd once shared rested deep within. A memory he'd failed to expunge...no matter what method he chose to apply.

She was *there*, as much a part of him as every breath he took...every beat of his heart.

Steely control...he possessed it in spades. In the boardroom.

Only a door separated him from Natalya's bedroom. He could breach it, seduce, and maybe succeed in gaining her compliance.

So why didn't he?

Damned if he knew.

Yet he did.

Aware losing wasn't an option.

CHAPTER THIRTEEN

THE FOLLOWING FEW days were business-oriented, with meetings between Alexei, Cristos and Dimitri as they explored strategies for a major takeover of a company on the brink of financial collapse.

Natalya's recordings were lengthy, the content involved as each man added input, opinions regarding the need for further investigation, relevant sources…calling a coffee break for a short debriefing session.

A relief from the intensity of the past few hours, Natalya accorded as she placed an order for coffee.

'Amalgamated will play ball,' Dimitri projected as they regrouped. 'They don't have any option.'

'Unless United undercut you,' Natalya offered, immediately aware of three pairs of male eyes refocussing their attention.

'An interesting observation,' Cristos declared. 'Your basis being?'

'They tend to sideline, then jump in just as a competitive deal is due to be struck.'

Alexei's eyes narrowed as he leaned back in his chair. 'They're not one of the major players.'

Dimitri leant forward. 'You have experience of their tactics?'

She inclined her head. 'They know how to play the game.'

'So do we,' Cristos answered, shooting Alexei a glance. 'A back-up plan alternative, and play our hand close to our chest?'

Good thinking, aware just how well United had tied her father's negotiations in knots two years ago, and left Roman red-faced, bluffing, and totally out of his league.

'Well, there you go,' Dimitri accorded softly. 'PA is a misnomer.'

'I imagine Natalya's observation skills saved Roman Montgomery's lack of attention in the field of negotiations.'

If her father had listened, she added silently. Unfortunately he rarely did.

Natalya indicated the carafe. 'More coffee?'

Each man declined, and she bore Alexei's scrutiny with equilibrium, caught the faintly speculative gleam, and gathered the carafe, cups onto the tray and moved it to the sideboard.

The meeting continued, the pace broken from time to time as Dimitri sought to lighten proposed strategy with a little levity.

Which he did very well, causing Natalya to smile at his efforts, laugh a little at one of his witty takes on one of New York's scions of industry, known for his slight pomposity.

It was light fun, momentary, although at one point she had to stifle her laughter...which earned Dimitri a searing glance from Alexei.

The afternoon wound up, with paperwork dispensed into briefcases, with Dimitri heading out as Alexei accompanied Cristos from the apartment.

'Natalya is a highly valued PA.'

Alexei directed his brother a non-committal glance. 'I agree.'

'She is also Roman Montgomery's daughter,' Cristos

commented. 'And the young woman you were involved with during your Sydney sojourn.'

'Apropos of…?' Alexei queried. 'Besides being none of your business.'

'You chose not to elaborate why you returned to New York following your sojourn in Australia.'

'Missing home, family, was a logical reason.'

'More than that, unless I'm mistaken.' He waited a beat, then added, 'Dimitri flirted with her. You didn't like it.'

'Natalya is my PA.'

'Dimitri likes to play. We both know it's harmless. Yet you considered Dimitri's attention inappropriate.'

'Out of place during a business meeting.'

'Dimitri was bent on getting a reaction.' Cristos sent Alexei a musing look. 'That he succeeded proved…interesting.'

Alexei's dark glare was accompanied by a terse, 'Back off.'

Cristos lifted both hands in a gesture of silent compliance, offered a commiserative smile that required no words, then turned and headed towards the bank of elevators.

Natalya focussed on what she did best…encapsulating key points during the day's board meeting. Ensuring lunch reservations were in place, and displaying smooth efficiency as she dealt with unforeseen interruptions, while remaining cool, calm and collected.

Everything her position entailed and required.

By day's end, all she wanted to do was change, shower, slip into comfortable clothes…and chill.

Good luck with that, a tiny voice taunted, as a call came through stating the power brokers affiliated with the financially ruined company were ready to deal.

Chilling was out as she accompanied Alexei to the bank

of elevators, one of which would deposit them to the floor housing several boardrooms where a take no prisoners negotiation took place, which the Delandros brothers won. A deal reluctantly struck, legalities approved, paperwork signed.

A coup to add to the Delandros portfolio.

Any form of celebration would be delayed until the legal formalities were complete.

Natalya glanced at the wall clock, made an attempt to shake off the weariness creeping through her body as she followed the men from the boardroom.

She was tired, it was late, she required time to de-stress, and importantly gain a few hours' sleep before rising soon after dawn to begin dealing with the follow-on from the evening's meeting. Right at that moment she silently acceded she earned every cent of her generous salary.

'Congratulations,' she offered as Alexei closed the door after they entered their suite, watching as he shrugged off his jacket and loosened his tie.

He spared her an intent glance, noted the shadows beneath her eyes, the tense edges of her mouth, the faint droop of her shoulders…and felt a degree of empathy for the long day, the even longer night.

Without a word he tossed his jacket onto a nearby chair, followed it with his tie, then he crossed to stand within touching distance, laid a hand on each shoulder, and began massaging the tight muscles, easing out the kinks, the tightness.

Natalya didn't move, couldn't…it felt so good, as he worked his magic easing the pain, and gradually the stress began to ebb…to be replaced by something…*more*, as he removed the clips from her hair and trailed light fingers over her scalp, soothing, taking her to a place where it would be so easy to succumb.

The touch of his lips to her forehead, lingering at her temple, the gentle whisper-like touch as he reached the edge of her mouth, savoured a little, then brushed the soft seam with a wicked promise of seduction.

A slow savouring persuasion, which left Natalya spellbound, uncaring where it might lead…only to baulk as reality began to descend.

She'd been down this road before, become pregnant and suffered a miscarriage. Hadn't the obstetrician advised in future certain steps should be taken prior to falling pregnant in order to avoid another miscarriage?

Birth control…she wasn't on any. Her mind spiralled… what if Alexei wasn't prepared? And even more alarming…what if she fell pregnant?

She closed her eyes, then slowly opened them again as a voice in her head silently screamed no.

'I don't do casual sex,' she managed carefully.

'I want you in my life,' Alexci said quietly.

She took care to meet his eyes, unsure what to say…or whether to say anything at all.

He lifted a finger and traced a gentle path over her lips. 'Is it too much to ask we share what we once had?'

She was willing to swear her heart took a downward flip. Lover? Mistress?

She closed her eyes, then slowly opened them again.

'I don't do the mistress thing,' she said carefully.

At that precise moment she hated herself for letting her guard down. Tempted, just once, to have him take her mouth with his own, to feel sensually alive. To accept whatever he offered, and to hell with the consequences.

She almost succumbed, knowing how easy it would be to lose herself…and that made her angry beyond measure.

Without thinking, she wrenched herself out of his arms, grabbed her jacket, the suite's swipe card and walked out of the door, uncaring of anything other than the need to get away from him, the hotel suite…to be *anywhere* but here.

Instead of summoning a lift, she chose the stairwell to the next floor down, made it to an elevator about to close, and took it down to street level.

The air was crisp, and she pulled the edges of her coat together as she exited the foyer.

The area was well lit, traffic moved quickly, and right at this moment she was too angry to consider the wisdom of walking alone late at night in a city not her own.

One block, crossing on to the second, becoming increasingly aware she should turn back.

Fool, she silently berated. What would this achieve?

Nothing. Other than reveal her lack of common sense.

One more block, then she'd turn and retrace her steps.

By which time her anger would have lessened, together with the dawning reality of place, time and the foolishness of walking alone on a New York street, prey to… whatever, whoever.

Enough.

Quickly followed by the realisation she'd left so quickly, she didn't have a bag, money…just the hotel swipe key.

Angry tears filled her eyes, and she brushed them away, turned…and witnessed Alexei closing the distance between them.

'You were *following* me?'

'A few metres behind you.'

'That's…' Words temporarily failed her as he moved in close and silenced her with a savage kiss, before easing into something else, gentling as his hands moved from her shoulders and slid down to cup her bottom, lifting her against his hard arousal, holding her there, his mouth softening to tease a little, then tangle her tongue with his own, sensuous, arousing, until she became lost to his persuasive touch, unaware her hands had crept unbidden to clutch his face, holding him close.

The sharp blast of a car horn, followed by a male cat-call and a laughing voice demanding, *'Get a room!'* acted like a bucket of icy water, and Natalya released her hands and wrenched her mouth from his.

Her eyes changed from slumberous to startled fury as she began to struggle free...only to fail miserably.

'We're going to talk.' His eyes became dark ominous pools. 'Back at the hotel.'

Without warning he turned to face the opposite direction, holding her hand, pulling her along with him as he began walking, not even so much as flinching as she curled her fists and hammered his shoulder-blades...anywhere she could reach with as much force as she could muster.

Alexei just kept walking.

She bore his silence for several long minutes, then she launched a punch into his ribcage...with no physical reaction whatsoever.

'Alexei, slow down,' she demanded. Causing a public scene had never been on her agenda...waiting a beat before adding, 'Please.'

'Will you behave?' His anger was quiet...too quiet. She drew in a deep breath, aware in a moment of clarity just how ridiculous it was to attempt to best him.

Temporary capitulation was the only option as she released her breath and briefly inclined her head. Relieved as he finally slowed down and released her hand.

There was wisdom in silence, and she refrained from uttering a further word until they reached their hotel. Together they crossed the marble-tiled foyer to the bank of elevators, all too aware the air between them could be cut with a knife.

Tall, dark, and silent, Alexei resembled a dangerous

force as electronic doors opened, and two other couples followed them in.

Natalya deliberately looked straight ahead, ignoring him until the elevator reached their floor, choosing to walk ahead of him along the carpeted passageway to their suite, swiped the room card and she took three steps into the lounge before swinging round to face him.

'I want *out*.' Anger was a palpable entity she barely managed to control. She indicated the desk. 'My formal resignation will be there in the morning.' It provided a measure of satisfaction to turn her back and walk towards her suite.

Right at that moment she didn't give a *damn*.

She was *done*. With *him*, the situation she'd been manipulated into…all of it.

'I didn't figure you for a coward.'

Alexei's voice reached her as she was about to open the door to her suite, and she turned to spare him a scorching glare.

'Why? Because you kissed me?'

'You were with me every step of the way,' he offered quietly.

'I'm no longer the girl you once knew,' she retaliated.

'No?'

'You saw to that.'

His eyes darkened, sharpened. 'Enlighten me…how?'

'There's no point to this conversation.'

His entire stance stilled. 'I think there's every point.'

Natalya suddenly felt as if she was standing on the edge of a precipice, poised between the need to lash out in anger…or live to regret not imparting fact…as she knew it?

She tensed, every muscle in her body tightening as she recalled in minute detail the devastating discovery he'd disappeared out of her life.

'You left without a word. I called you. Many times. I

made enquiries… *"The line has been disconnected."* I checked your apartment, hospitals, any and everyone I could think of who might have a clue to your whereabouts.' She tamped down the helplessness, and resorted to anger. 'I sent you texts. Emails. Desperately pleading for an answer. An explanation.'

She clenched each hand into a fist, felt her nails dig in each palm…and didn't even feel the painful sensation. '*Anyone* who could tell me whether you were alive or dead.'

The pain of him leaving her…even after five years, was still there…raw, aching, like a wound that had never truly healed.

Anger rose to the surface. 'Do you know what it's like to wake each day…and hope *today* a call, text or email could ease the heartache? God willing in the best way possible? Only to fade into despair? Until eventually there's a need to accept whatever path you thought your life would take no longer existed?'

'Yes.'

She couldn't stop until she said it all. 'Worse, the agony of not knowing what went wrong? Why texts and emails remained unanswered?' She took a deep breath. 'To consider the worst scenario in each of many guises?'

He moved towards her and closed his hands over her shoulders. 'Back up a little,' he demanded quietly.

Her eyes blazed in anger. *'Why?'*

The ensuing silence became electric, and she closed her eyes in an effort to shut him out…only to have them widen as he took hold of her chin and tilted it.

She opened her mouth to berate him, except no word emerged as he pressed it closed.

'I didn't receive any texts or letters.'

She tore his hand away. 'You expect me to believe that?'

He stilled, his features hardening as a muscle clenched

at the edge of his jaw. 'I left messages on your answering machine. Texts.' His eyes darkened. 'Are you saying they never reached you?'

The colour fled from her cheeks as uncertainty left her temporarily speechless. 'No,' she managed as her mind reeled. 'Nothing,' she said in a shocked whisper.

First and foremost, how it could have happened, followed seconds later by why?

She was reluctant to explore who, for it appeared highly unlikely anyone had access to her laptop, smartphone, snail mail.

Except…memory resurfaced in minute detail…her move to another apartment building, misplacing her smartphone, her father's decision to replace all their phones, both business and personal, with a different provider and new numbers. As well as a new email address for a reason that appeared valid at the time.

When?

Years ago. Her mind momentarily retraced the events back then, examined each sequence in detail, unaware of Alexei's narrowed scrutiny as he witnessed every fleeting emotion on her expressive features…and caught the moment she realised she had stepped into an unbelievable nightmare. Surely…it couldn't coincide…except it did.

Her father.

'How could he do such a thing?' Natalya's voice was an agonising whisper.

'Roman wanted you to marry up. I didn't come close to being a prospective candidate.'

'Tell me.' Her voice was calm…too calm. 'I need to hear what my father did. All of it.'

She deserved the truth…which he whittled down to essential detail. Leaving out his emotional turmoil, anger. Worse, the desperate need to discover *why*.

'Roman demanded I end my relationship with you, and presented me with a substantial cheque in a pay off. I tore it up.'

For the love of heaven. That her father would dare to go to such lengths to destroy their relationship was unconscionable. Unforgivable.

The disbelief, the silent anger.

The loss of *five years* of their lives.

Dear heaven, her miscarriage.

Natalya felt a cold hand clutch her stomach.

Sickened, almost literally, she briefly closed her eyes in an effort to retain a sense of calm. Opening them again, her eyes pierced his own, held steady, controlled...when inside she felt like screaming.

'He fired you, didn't he.' A statement, not a question. 'And threatened to make it impossible for you to get a position with any electronics firm in the country.' Her eyes locked with his own as she sought confirmation.

He didn't confirm or deny it...but then he didn't have to. The truth was there. Ugly, untenable, damning.

Did she realise how well he could read her? See the silent rage simmering beneath the surface?

She closed her eyes as Alexei reached for her and drew her close. There was magic in his touch, the way his lips sought the sensitive curve of her neck, savoured there, then he gently traced a path up to settle in the sweet hollow beneath her earlobe.

Evocative eroticism stirred something deep inside and spread through her body in sweet sorcery, dispensing with inhibitions and making her want so much more.

A faint groan emerged from her throat as he lifted and carried her into the bedroom.

He felt the warmth of her silent tears seep through his shirt, and brushed a kiss to the top of her head.

With care he slid her down his body to stand on her feet, and his gaze held her own as he carefully removed each item of clothing from her body.

She felt the warmth of his fingers as they trailed up her ribcage and unclipped her bra. Free, her breasts burgeoned in anticipation as he cupped each mound, and she bit back a gasp as his fingers sought the delicate peaks, traced them until they hardened beneath his touch.

Sensation arrowed deep inside, and she couldn't utter a word in protest as he lowered his head to one breast and took its peak into his mouth to lave it with his tongue.

Liquid fire coursed through her veins, heating her body to a point of madness.

Almost as if he knew, he lowered her evening trousers, traced a path up the inside of each thigh and sought the throbbing clitoris…brushing his fingers against the sensitive folds as she arched against him, unaware of the whispering plea emerging from her throat.

She was beyond sanity, filled with an aching need for his possession.

His clothes became an unwanted intrusion and were quickly discarded as they sought to touch, explore, as she became lost in the delight of tracing warm flesh, tight musculature, the sheer strength of his arousal.

She didn't want to wait. Wasn't aware of her soft cries as he inserted a finger into the damp warmth between her thighs and skilfully brought her to orgasm, absorbing her guttural cry as she shattered.

It wasn't enough. She needed more, so much more, and he knew, teasing a little, taking time to lay his mouth against her own in a slow kiss that became sensual foreplay as she met and matched everything he gifted…then she gasped as he used a hand to pull aside the bed covers and lower her down onto the sheeted mattress.

She kissed him, teasing as he had teased her, and explored his body with light kisses, circling the tight masculine nipples, using her teeth to nip, the slide of her lips to soothe, before trailing to his navel, delicately laved it, before she turned her attention to the thick jutting arousal pulsing beneath her touch as she stroked its length with her tongue, reacquainting herself with its shape and throbbing size…heard his husky groan, and delighted in his throaty *you're killing me* an instant before firm hands took hold of her hips and eased her onto her back, holding her hands fast above her head as he trailed a path down the quivering flesh of her stomach. Lower, and she cried out as he suckled the damp flesh, nipped the sensitive folds with care, then used his tongue to send her mindless.

Her entire body felt as if it were on fire, and she gasped as he shifted over her and drove in deep, held still as she absorbed him, then he gently rocked, lengthening his thrusts until she reached the edge and came, as he did in unison, and there was only the euphoric ecstasy of two lovers in perfect accord…mind, body, heart and soul as they gave everything there was to gift…before easing down to the sweet exhaustion of sexual fulfilment.

'Amazing,' Natalya whispered, and felt his lips drift gently over her skin, soothing her rapid pulse-beats, before exploring her lips, caressing with such tenderness she fought to hold back tears.

Lost, so completely *lost* in him, there was no sense of time or place. Only the need to cling to the pulsing thrum deep inside her body, and exult in sexual nirvana.

The musky scent of sensual heat combined with the dawning knowledge they'd just shared unprotected sex…

Dear heaven, what had she done?

They, she corrected silently. There were two of them

in this bed, two who had seduced, shared, and exulted in their mutual passion.

Alexei caught each fleeting expression as the reality widened her eyes, the brief few startled seconds as her eyelids shuttered closed, only to open again as instinct kicked in together with a sense of *déjà vu*. Unfounded, according to rapid silent calculation.

She pushed at him, endeavouring to escape without success as he caged her in, his eyes dark as the blackest slate as he took in her expression.

Without a word Alexei rolled off the bed, scooped Natalya into his arms and walked into the en suite bathroom, turned on the shower and carried her beneath the pulsing water, collected the liquid soap, and began smoothing the lightly scented fragrance over her body in a slow sensuous slide that drove her wild...wanting, *needing* to respond in kind. His mouth curved into a sensual smile. 'Patience. You'll have your turn.'

She did. Eventually. Only it took a while. And later, towelled dry, he took her to bed, drew her close in against him.

She couldn't find the words—not the right ones. The extent of Roman's intervention devastated her, and merely confirmed the extent her father was prepared to go to in order to rule not only his company, but his family.

'There's something you should know,' Natalya said quietly. At the time she'd borne the heartache in the light of day, and let the tears fall during the dark of night when she was alone. Until there were no more tears to shed, and she gathered the resolve to get on with her life.

'I discovered I was pregnant.' She faltered in an effort to find the right words, and her mouth trembled as his hands shaped her face. His eyes were dark, silently questioning, and she couldn't look away.

'Why didn't you tell me?'

Her features paled, her eyes dark with an edge of pain, and he swore softly beneath his breath.

'I drove to your apartment after work.'

A lump rose in her throat, momentarily preventing speech, and she swallowed compulsively in an effect to allow her voice to emerge. 'You weren't there.' The words tumbled out. 'I rang your phone. No answer.'

Alexei stilled, his eyes almost black. 'When did you ring?' His voice was hard, urgent. 'What time?'

'Is time so important?'

'Yes.' He bunched his hands into fists. 'Dammit.' Yet he already knew. 'Think…please,' he added in a strained voice.

'After six…maybe six-thirty.'

He closed his eyes briefly in silent anguish at the hand of Fate. Ten…fifteen minutes after the police had taken him from his apartment, arrested by the hand of her father. His phone confiscated.

Theos.' The soft imprecation left his lips with the realisation she'd had to cope without his knowledge, or the benefit of his support.

Silent anger consumed him, together with the imminent need to take Roman Montgomery apart with his bare hands.

Her words hurt like a stab to the heart as memory surfaced in vivid Technicolor detail.

The anger…helpless rage at Roman Montgomery's manipulative machinations.

Natalya felt his lips rest against her forehead, then trail gently down her cheek to rest at the edge of her mouth, soothing the trembling seam as he held her close.

Roman, Natalya determined fiercely, was about to be called to account. She'd call and invite him to share lunch with her, then calmly…surely she could *do* calm several hours from now?

'He's going to pay.'

'Natalya,' Alexei cautioned, and she shook her head.

'You don't understand.'

But he did. All too well. The silent rage that had almost destroyed him, the desire to succeed beyond measure.

Not the least of it, to throw that success in Roman's face. As he had with deliberate intent, using his business nous to prove he could. Then plotted his revenge against the man who'd wielded God-like power…using Natalya as a weapon.

Ill-founded, as he discovered…and beat down the rage simmering beneath the surface.

How could a father do that to his own daughter?

As easily as Roman succeeded in deceiving his own wife. A self-absorbed narcissist who put his own needs first and foremost…without exception.

Alexei wanted to slam a fist against something…for a few brief seconds he almost did. Just for the hell of it.

Almost as if she knew, she lifted a hand to his cheek.

'Natalya…'

Her eyes seared his own, steady, obdurate. 'There's nothing you can say to stop me confronting my father.'

He waited a beat, then offered quietly, 'Think it through,' he advised gently, and watched her eyes narrow.

'He doesn't deserve consideration.'

CHAPTER FOURTEEN

THERE WAS A need for planned strategy. An assemblage of irrefutable facts. Cool, sans anger. Absence of a public scene.

In Roman's true sense of style, he'd vetoed a small restaurant in favour of one of his favoured upmarket haunts noted for its fine cuisine.

Natalya entered the boutique restaurant several minutes past the appointed time, for, in truth, she wanted her father to be seated and waiting.

It helped that he was there, charming the wait staff in his typical style. The smile, a flirting tease in his eyes… just enough not to offend, but holding a silent invitation, should it be accepted.

Natalya touched a hand to Roman's shoulder to catch his attention, and he turned at once, offering a warm greeting as he caught her hand and lifted it to his lips.

'Darling girl.' Ever the showman, he gave the waitress a knowing smile. 'Better late than never.'

Did he ever stop? And to think she'd always put his teasing down to his consummate charm.

'Have the sommelier choose the finest champagne and have it brought to the table,' he instructed the waitress in a grandiose manner, 'A celebration.'

He might think otherwise by the time their meal concluded.

'Problem with traffic?' Roman enquired as Natalya slid into the chair opposite.

'Parking,' Natalya enlightened, and when the champagne was presented, checked, approved and opened she instructed, 'Just a small amount. I have to work this afternoon.'

She waited, sipped superb champagne and exchanged small-talk as she selected an entree, refused a main, and settled for a lemon sorbet to follow.

The waitress served coffee, and Natalya added milk, sat back and mentally directed...*now*.

She kept it brief, citing irrefutable fact with admirable restraint...and took some satisfaction as her father stiffened, blustered a little, then paled as she relayed knowledge of each pertinent detail...the coincidence of her lost smartphone and its replacement with a different provider and new number.

Coinciding with Alexei's disappearance from her life.

'Don't,' she cautioned as he attempted to speak, 'attempt to justify your actions. Your manipulative meddling was unforgivable.'

'I wanted the best for you.'

She battled with anger, and fought to contain it.

'Without thought for my right to choose?'

'Delandros had nothing. He could never have supported you in the style you deserved.'

Leave now, a silent voice urged...before you say something regrettable.

Natalya rose to her feet, caught up her bag and walked to the cashier's desk, produced a credit card, paid the bill, then she emerged onto the sidewalk, covered the three blocks to where she'd parked her car.

Alexei was at the industrial plant, the rest of the afternoon was hers, and there was a need to occupy her mind and minimise any inclination to dwell on her father's actions.

She aimed the car remote, then slid in behind the wheel, had a flash of inspiration and delved into her bag for her smartphone. Minutes later she engaged the engine, eased out of the parking bay and headed towards fashionable Double Bay.

A relaxing facial, some one-on-one time with Anja… what could be better?

'Thanks for fitting me in,' Natalya greeted with affection as she took her place in one of the beauty rooms.

Bliss, absolute bliss to simply close her eyes and let every muscle in her body slowly relax as Anja worked her magic.

'Are you going to update me? Over the past few days a number of regular clients have quizzed me if the rumours are true about you and Alexei.'

'Which you refrained from providing.' It was a statement of fact.

'You know better.'

Yes, she did. They'd shared much over the years, and maintained a mutual trust.

Yet she hesitated…the sex with Alexei was great. Okay, *fantastic*. The question being what their future might hold. Or if they had a future.

There were words left unsaid, and while she ached for the whole package…did Alexei want the same? Or would it be her fate to remain his PA with benefits?

'Hello?' Anja prompted. 'Natalya to Planet Earth?'

'There are issues,' Natalya admitted, and glimpsed Anja's faintly wry smile.

'Resolve them. Anything less is a cop-out.'

'What would you suggest?' Natalya queried, *sotto voce*. 'Grab Alexei by the scruff of his neck, pin him to the floor, and demand his intentions?'

'That would be my modus operandi.'

Natalya bit back a light laugh. 'I'll remind you of that when the love bug strikes.'

'Not going to happen anytime soon.'

'Famous last words.'

'Keep your eyes closed,' Anja ordered. 'I'm not done yet.' Firm hands created their own magic, and Natalya uttered a pleasurable sigh. 'Something you're not telling me?'

'Nothing to tell.'

Not yet, Natalya perceived. She could wait, and would, aware there was a time and a place, and now wasn't it.

Natalya's phone chirped with an incoming text as she entered her home.

Dinner tonight. I'll collect you at six. Alexei.

She checked her watch, saw there was ample time in which to change, and then took a leisurely shower, towelled dry, stepped into her bedroom, and riffled through the contents of her wardrobe. Formal or semi-formal?

The latter appeared a safe choice, and she selected a stylishly cut dress in emerald-green.

Ear studs, a simple necklace, black heels, a black clutch with essentials, then she caught up a black wrap and she was good to go within minutes before the appointed time. On cue the security gate buzzer sounded and she crossed to the video link, identified Alexei and released the locking mechanism.

He was waiting for her as she opened the front door, attired in casual trousers, open-necked shirt and casual jacket. Tall, ruggedly attractive... Her stomach flipped as heat flooded her body as she walked into his outstretched arms, lifted her face for his kiss and breathed him in, relishing the moment as his arms pulled her close.

Nice. She could have stayed longer…resisting the urge to invite him in, suggest they forgo dinner, and eat later. Much later.

Except he trailed his mouth to the sweet curve of her neck, savoured briefly, then took hold of her hands linked behind his neck and brought one to his lips.

'Food,' Alexei opined with a wicked smile, and led her to the sleek Aston Martin waiting kerbside.

Natalya wondered which restaurant Alexei had chosen as he eased the luxury car into traffic. A boutique place in one of the suburbs, or city venue.

Not a restaurant, she discovered as the car headed towards one of the elite northern suburbs where residences commanded multimillion-dollar prices, and were guarded by high-tech security.

Alexei turned into a tree-lined street and slowed the car before a wide set of high black elaborately scrolled gates, beyond which stood a graceful two-level residence at the apex of a semi-circular driveway.

Were they dining as guests at a private home?

His home, appeared the correct answer, as he used a remote to open the gates and eased the car towards the front entrance.

Immaculate lawns bearing some decorative sculpted shrubbery, and there were borders bearing a beautiful array of flowers lining the driveway.

The front door opened as he disengaged the engine, and a middle-aged woman stood waiting to welcome them.

'My housekeeper, Lisette,' Alexei informed her quietly as he curved an arm across Natalya's shoulders and drew her forward, effecting introductions.

Together they entered a large circular foyer with a marble-tiled floor, showcasing a sweeping double staircase leading to an upper level.

Lisette greeted Natalya with a pleasant smile before turning towards Alexei. 'I expect you would enjoy a drink in the lounge. Dinner will be served at seven in the private dining room.'

'Thanks, Lisette.'

He turned towards one of four heavily panelled doors leading off from the lobby and led her into a spacious lounge, closed the door behind them, then pulled her close.

What began as a gentle kiss soon became an evocative tasting as he explored her mouth, and she met and matched him, luxuriating in his touch as she lifted her arms to link each hand at his nape.

Natalya's entire body came alive, as the kiss moved up a few levels, where the urge to dispense with his clothes… and have him remove her own, became almost impossible to ignore.

She wanted to slide the palms of her hands over his naked skin. Explore the tight muscles sculpting his body, admire the strength apparent, and savour every inch with her mouth as she drove him wild.

Then welcome him into her body as they became lost in each other…lust, avid, earthy and beyond mere words.

Love, as it had been in what seemed to be another lifetime when they had implicit trust in each other.

Alexei gently shifted his hands to cup her face. He traced her cheek with his thumb, his eyes dark as he examined her features.

'I'll get you a drink.'

Did she look as if she needed one? Probably. 'Preferably non-alcoholic.' It was a while since lunch, and she recalled she'd eaten very little. 'I'll have some wine with dinner.'

Alexei moved to the drinks cabinet, retrieved two crystal wine glasses, filled one with mineral water, the other with white wine, then he retraced his steps and placed a glass in her hand.

She avoided the prosaic, and went for the most relevant.

'I had lunch with my father today.'

His eyes sharpened. 'He upset you?'

'In hindsight...not so much.' Surprising, given how much pain Roman's actions had caused her. 'I said what I wanted to say, paid the bill, and walked out of the restaurant.'

She possessed an inner strength. Yet he sensed the hurt, her loss of trust for her father's almost criminal meddling. Worse, perhaps, for having been totally unaware of her father's other life.

Roman had created the perfect cover in choosing Natalya as his PA.

Which bore the question of Ivana's wealth and social standing...somehow it didn't add up with the woman he'd come to know. Her values, her unconditional love for her daughter.

Perhaps a woman was entitled to her reasons, none of which were his to attempt to explore.

Of one thing he was certain. Natalya's total loyalty to her mother.

'You have a beautiful home,' Natalya complimented as they entered a tastefully furnished dining room.

'Which I will show you after dinner,' Alexei said as he led her to the table and withdrew her chair.

The housekeeper had excelled herself, providing a sea-food entree, followed by perfectly grilled salmon steaks accompanied by a delicious salad, with fresh fruit compote for dessert.

Later they took coffee on the terrace, relaxed following a pleasant meal. The view over the harbour to the city with its buildings lit and rising high against a darkened sky presented a superb panorama. Coloured neon signage promoting varying products, the moving headlights of passing traffic…mere pinpricks observed from this distance.

Peaceful, tranquil. A place that could be a home, filled with love, perhaps children…

A vision of which the stuff of dreams was made. Not always the reality.

So where did they go from here?

The word love hadn't been mentioned.

Alexei unwound his length from the chair, leant forward to take hold of her hands and gently pulled her to her feet and into his arms.

His touch, the brief flare of unguarded emotion in his eyes…dear heaven, his kiss…sensuality at its peak as his tongue curled around her own, tasted, teased, gentling a little at the sound of her despairing groan as he went in deep, persuasive, pervading as he gifted his heart…his soul.

It was more, so much more than she believed possible, and seemingly an age before he lifted his head, his eyes dark as he glimpsed her flushed cheeks, the soft mouth slightly swollen from his touch, and caught the faint quiver as she visibly sought control.

He lifted a hand to smooth the pad of his thumb over the fullness of her lower lip. 'Stay with me tonight.'

Her eyes lit with a tinge of humour. 'Presumably this isn't a work-related request?'

'Not even close.'

'I'll give it some thought,' she said, delighting in teasing him.

Without a word he led her inside, secured the terrace doors, set the security alarm, moved towards the beautifully curved staircase leading to an upper floor and the master bedroom.

He took it slow and easy, removing each item of her

clothing, as she unbuttoned his shirt and slipped it from his body. Loving the muscular chest, the tight abs, the strength apparent in his broad shoulders.

'Don't stop.'

Natalya reached for the belt at his waist. 'Just savouring the moment.'

'Uh-huh. You want some help there?'

She traced the bulging length of his arousal pressing against the zip, and offered him a witching smile. 'Got it covered.'

'Uncovered is better.'

'No foreplay?'

'As much as you can take.'

'That sounds interesting.'

Interesting didn't equate to what they shared as he slowly removed each item of her clothing, pausing to press his lips to each pulse, his hands intent on shaping every curve until she trembled, on fire, wanting, *needing* him inside her...so much, she was unaware of the faint sounds slipping unbidden from her throat, the way her hands moved on him...and her satisfaction as he took her mouth with his own in a kiss that sent her over the edge.

'You want to hear there has been no one who mattered since you?' Alexei queried quietly.

In one easy movement he leant forward and stripped the covers from the large bed, then he laid her down on the cool sheets and moved over her body.

Now...or she'd have to beg.

And then she did, as he trailed his lips down her stomach to the moist heat below, using his mouth, his tongue, to drive her wild.

Then he positioned himself and drove in hard, exulting in the feel of her, the way her inner muscles contracted around his length when he began to move, slowly at first, building sensation to an exhilarating peak, held them both there as an intense orgasm took them high, consuming mind, body and soul.

So excruciatingly sensual she had no memory of crying out in ecstasy…nor was she aware of his own groan of release as they lay joined together, too caught up in the deliciously slow ebb of exquisite pleasure.

Natalya didn't want to move…wasn't sure she could, until the wonderful lethargy consuming her body settled a little.

It felt good, so incredibly *right* to snuggle her cheek into the curve of his neck, to bury her lips into the hollow and savour his musky heat, feel the strong beat of his heart as he tethered her close.

Later, so much later, Alexei gathered her up into his arms and headed to the en suite bathroom, set the shower into action, and held her beneath the pulsing warm water as he smoothed liquid soap over every inch of her body with such evocative slowness it was nothing less than seduction.

With a witching smile Natalya took the container of liquid soap from his hand, moved to stand behind him, cupped a handful of soap and administered slow sweeping strokes across his shoulders, down his back, covering the taut slopes of his buttocks, then turned him round to face her.

She could do evocative slowness as well as he did, and his eyes became dark, faintly hooded, as she teased a little, plucking lightly at his nipples, felt them tighten beneath her touch, then she moved to his shoulders, his arms before trailing down his ribcage to settle a hand on each hip.

'If you stop there,' he declared with a throaty drawl, 'you will suffer.'

'I'm afraid,' she mocked quietly, and offered him a mischievous grin as he caught hold of her shoulders. 'Very afraid.'

'Witch,' Alexei accorded with dangerous softness as he lowered his head and took her mouth in a passionate kiss that robbed her of breath.

At the same time his hands slid down her back, cupped her bottom and lifted her high against him, caressed the softness of one breast, then sought her burgeoning nipple, tasted, teased, before drawing it into his mouth.

Intense sensation spread through her body, coalescing at the most sensitive part of her femininity, and she gasped as he trailed a hand over her stomach, palming the indentation as his mouth moved to render a similar salutation to her other breast, where he took her almost to the edge as he teased, tasted and lightly caught the nipple with the edge of his teeth.

Heat rose deep within, and she gasped as his hand trailed low...way too low as he sought the sensitive folds protecting her clitoris.

Her mouth parted with a soft gasp as he stroked the delicate bud until she almost reached begging point.

He slid a finger into the moist passage, heard her unbidden groan and felt the restless movement of her legs, aware she needed more...*more* than this slow delicate, exploratory, teasingly intimate foreplay.

Natalya curled her fingers around his thick arousal, squeezed a little, and sensed Alexei's quick intake of breath.

In one easy movement he carried her into the bedroom, tossed back the covers, then he sought her mouth with his own, staking a claim that seared every erogenous pulse in her body as he brought her to tumultuous orgasm, stilled a little, then he began to move, slowly at first, then with deeper intensity, driving them both towards a mutual orgasm that left her temporarily bereft of the ability to breathe. Sensual overload...and then some.

There were no words, just a whisper of a heartfelt sigh escaping from her lips.

She didn't want to move…didn't think she could as Alexei held her close for what seemed an age, until sleep overcame them both.

Only to wake in the early morning hours to the touch of his mouth against her own as he made love to her with such exquisite gentleness she wanted to weep. Lazy pre-dawn sex, infinitely sensual, Natalya managed as Alexei curved her close to his muscular frame. Exquisite and a beautiful beginning to a new day.

'Sleep,' he murmured as he pulled up the bedcovers.

The next morning, showered, dressed, they shared a wholesome breakfast together on the terrace, took a refill of coffee, after which Alexei drove her home, settled his mouth on her own, then headed into the city.

There was time to feed Ollie, exchange her clothes for office wear, a slimline skirt, silk blouse, jacket, make-up, check her satchel and head into the city.

A day where *work* took priority, which was a blessing, for it allowed Natalya little or no time to think…or in her case, over-think.

Alexei slipped easily into professional mode, moving it up a notch as he liaised with Marc Adamson, chaired an intense meeting, took a business lunch which ran over time and by day's end she required every ounce of energy in order to match Alexei's pace…while he appeared as if he'd enjoyed a good night's sleep instead of a mere few hours.

In truth, she was in a state of ambivalence. Unsure of what their future held.

One day led to another, each following a familiar pattern as Natalya dealt with everything Alexei threw at her.

While the nights were something else…spent at his mansion, her apartment. Emotive, passionate.

Until one evening when Alexei offered the words she longed to hear.

'Marry me.'

Not I love you…can't live without you.

'I want you in my life.'

Want, not need. 'In your bed,' she managed evenly, and saw his eyes narrow slightly as she slid out of his bed and began pulling on her clothes in the moonlight streaming in from the night sky.

'That, too.'

It took all her resolve to utter the one word she'd hoped never to have to say to him. 'No.'

His expression remained unchanged. 'Marriage is not important to you?'

Yes. Just not merely another merger added to your life portfolio.

'I'm content with my life the way it is.'

'What if I want more?'

Five years ago she'd believed their love was inviolate, a permanent entity that would entwine their lives for a lifetime.

'Qualify "more".'

Your heart, gifted unconditionally. Words she couldn't, wouldn't voice.

She needed her own space, her own bed. Without a word she gathered up her bag, her keys, bade him a polite goodnight…and left. Waiting until she used the remote to close the gates guarding Alexei's residence.

Fool, she silently chided as she traversed the streets towards her home.

CHAPTER FIFTEEN

NOT THE DESIRED result Alexei had envisaged.

Five years of hard business negotiations had resulted in paring details down to the bare essentials...cut-throat minimalist facts.

Successful in the business arena.

A complete failure when it came to proposing marriage.

He wanted to hit something, and almost did...except doing so wouldn't achieve the desired result.

There was a flashback to the night he'd intended to ask Natalya to share his life.

The champagne on ice. Flowers...her favourite roses, tastefully assembled in clear cellophane with a note expressing his love. The for ever, until death do us part in poetic prose. The ring, the delicate diamond, the best he could afford at the time, put on hold and paid off in increments from his fortnightly wage. Her favourite food.

The evening she didn't arrive.

Her smartphone cut off.

Alexei's arrest.

History.

Which had no part in the *present*...or the future.

He picked up the phone, punched in numbers, made a few calls, cancelled two appointments, and set the next day in motion.

A day in which Alexei spent time with Marc Adamson caught up in meetings with Marc's PA in attendance. Not entirely unusual, Natalya perceived...nor was the late afternoon text requesting her presence at a restaurant on the other side of the city.

Despite the location not being one she perceived Alexei would normally choose. Who was she to judge? Presumably privacy was key, with no intrusion from the media.

Parking wasn't difficult, and she slid in behind Alexei's Aston Martin...a surprise, given his preference for the limousine with Paul at the wheel.

Whatever...it hardly mattered. She was here in her capacity as Alexei's PA, with no time to delay if punctuality was key.

She walked through the door, and paused, initially puzzled at the lack of patrons. There was only one occupant... Alexei, who rose to his feet as she crossed to his side.

'Has there been a delay?' She glanced up as a waiter appeared out of nowhere and pulled out a chair for her. 'I take it your guests are late?'

'No guests,' Alexei said quietly as he placed a hand to the back of her waist. 'Please, sit down.'

She sank into the chair and a faint frown creased her forehead. 'There's no meeting?'

'Not tonight.'

'Then why are we here?'

It was difficult to read his expression, and her eyes widened as the lights brightened a little, and another waiter appeared bearing an ice bucket holding a bottle of champagne.

For a brief second she thought she got it...only to dismiss the possibility as a flight of fancy. Until the waiter popped the cork and poured a measure of champagne for

Alexei to savour and approve…a mere formality, given the exclusive label…before carefully pouring a quantity of the sparkling liquid into two crystal flutes.

Alexei lifted his flute, touched its rim to her own, and gently named the toast… 'To us.'

Natalya's lips parted, but no words emerged.

Light muted music wafted from hidden speakers, and a waitress appeared with a silver platter, on which lay a single red rose and a personalised card.

Natalya simply looked at him as he removed both and placed them in front of her.

'I planned a surprise evening five years ago…champagne, food,' he revealed quietly. 'A ring to seal our love.'

Her lips quivered a little, and there was nothing she could do to prevent the single tear escaping to slowly trickle down one cheek.

He leant forward and carefully brushed it away. 'I love you. For the beautiful woman you are, in heart, mind and spirit.'

Her heart stopped beating, then quickened a little as she attempted to say the words caught in her throat, only to feel the press of his finger against her lips.

'Last night…'

Natalya's eyes softened as she resisted the temptation to interrupt him. Was it asking too much to want to hear the words?

'Will you marry me? Please.'

It was the *please* that did it for her. 'Yes.'

He rose to his feet and caught her close, his mouth on hers as she clung to him. Unaware of time or place…until he gently released her, and the restaurant, the importance of the evening returned to focus.

'There are words,' she offered quietly, 'written, said, for momentous occasions such as this. Poetic prose escapes me...you're my only love. *Yours*, for as long as I draw breath.'

Alexei's eyes darkened with slumberous passion. 'I'll hold you to that.'

It was her turn to tease him a little. 'I'd hoped you might.'

He drew her apart a little and reached into his pocket, withdrew a ring, took hold of her left hand and slid a magnificent solitaire diamond onto her finger.

For a breathtaking few seconds, she couldn't find the words. 'It's beautiful,' Natalya accorded with quiet reverence. *Stunning*, she added silently. A visual testament to his wealth and power.

'But?'

'The ring you bought five years ago,' she began. 'Do you still have it?'

'Why do you ask?'

The thought he might have kept it held such meaning. Bought with an emotion-filled heart...a symbol of everlasting hope, love, and the intention of them spending their lives together.

The ring he'd placed onto the third finger of her left hand flashed brilliant fire as caught by the steady flickering candle. Magnificent and ruinously expensive.

'It represents the love we shared at that time.'

'And that is important to you?'

There were words she could say, a few of which she had already expressed. 'Yes.'

A warm smile curved his lips. 'Are you going to tell me why?' A diamond worth little in comparison to the ring which now replaced it.

Natalya lifted both hands to frame his face, her expression soft with emotion, and incredibly beautiful. 'You need to ask?'

No, he didn't.

'Will you mind if I accept this ring as a commitment gift representing everlasting love throughout all the years we'll share together, and wear it on the third finger of my right hand?'

Alexei shook his head and offered a quizzical smile. 'And the original ring?' he teased.

'Suspended on a gold chain close to my heart.'

She was something else. 'If it pleases you.'

'Thank you.'

He gave a soft laugh. 'I'll commission the jeweller to craft a wide wedding band.' Encrusted with diamonds, he added silently.

He knew her so well, her values, ideals...her generous loving heart.

His for ever...all the days and nights of his life.

She reached up and kissed him. 'Perfect.'

So too was the evening.

The champagne, the food, ambience...a special memory that was theirs alone.

One, Alexei determined, they would celebrate each year for the rest of their lives.

The next thing on their agenda was to inform Natalya's parents before the ring on her finger resulted in a media article citing rumour and supposition. Even if the ring didn't appear on her left hand, the mere sight of it would draw comment, assumptions would be made...and Ivana deserved better than to hear such important news second-hand.

It was okay to be cool-headed in all things business... inviting her parents to dinner to formally announce an engagement, followed by a wedding, was something else.

Alexei and Roman in the same home, the same room?

'You're stressing too much,' Alexei chastised gently. 'Ivana will be delighted.'

'Perhaps I should pre-warn her?'

'In order for her to pre-warn your father?'

He read her too well. 'Something like that.'

Alexei touched a light finger to her cheek. 'I'm sure Roman will be the consummate guest.'

If not, he'd deal with it.

Natalya planned the menu with care, choosing each course with her parents in mind. Cuisine was one of her skills, and she made lists, selected the best ingredients, took care with the dining room setting, using the finest linen inherited from her *babushka*, a favoured dinner set, fine crystal, and silverware. Faintly scented candles.

A double-check, a change of clothes to pencil-slim linen skirt with matching silk top, make-up, hair…done.

'What do you think?'

Alexei crossed to her side and laid his mouth to the sweet hollow at the edge of her neck. 'Amazing.'

He was her rock, the love of her life…everything.

Designer black trousers, a pristine white shirt unbuttoned at the neck, the shadowed designer stubble…eyes so expressively dark as he smiled.

Hers. Truly hers…as she was his.

Together again, as they were meant to be.

Not by luck…*faith.*

'It's perfect,' he accorded quietly. 'So, too, are you.'

'Don't make me cry, or I'll have to…' she caught the musing gleam in his dark eyes '…go fix my make-up, and leave you to greet the parents.'

'For a moment I thought you might be considering an interesting diversion.'

She trailed light fingers down his cheek, the soft designer stubble to the edge of his mouth. 'Later.'

'I'll hold you to that.' He lowered his lips to her forehead. 'You're my love, my life.'

'Same goes.'

At that moment the external buzzer sounded, and she watched as Alexei crossed to release the gate mechanism.

There were hugs, a mutual handshake between Alexei and Roman, who expressed his appreciation for the invitation, while Alexei attended to serving drinks in the lounge.

Ivana's delight, her appreciation of Natalya's ring.

Warm, friendly…even Roman appeared to behave himself, and it became easy to relax a little.

Fine wine preceded the starter, followed by the main course, eaten in a leisurely fashion. Conversation flowed, as Roman made an effort to engage, sans his usual bonhomie. Dessert was a pavlova variation created by Natalya's grandmother…crisp meringue, soft on the inside, covered with whipped cream and drenched in fruit and their juices.

'Perfection, darling,' Ivana complimented, adding to Natalya's pleasure, 'Let me help you in the kitchen while Roman enjoys his customary after-dinner cigar.'

A familiar ritual following a lifetime of family lunches and dinners for as long as Natalya could recall.

Alexei stood to his feet. 'I'll join you.'

This evening's short sojourn would hopefully create an emerging bond of sorts between Alexei and her father. Each had issues to be resolved, and although the timing wasn't perfect…at least it might help both men to move forward.

Natalya waited until the men had moved out on the back terrace, and spared her mother a quick glance, received a reassuring smile. 'I'll be okay.'

Alexei closed the door quietly and indicated the decorative gazebo at one end of the terrace, waited until they reached it, and they stood facing each other while Roman extracted a cigar, expertly clipped the end, then his lighter flared, and he took the first draw.

Alexei kept it brief, merely the bare facts, and lowered his voice.

'Five years ago you went to extraordinary lengths to separate me from Natalya. You deleted text messages from Natalya's cell phone, wiped her answering machine clean and misappropriated her mail. Information I imagine you'd prefer to remain buried?'

'Are you threatening me?'

'Not at all. Merely assuming you'll want to attend your daughter's wedding and share a part in your future grand-children's lives?'

Roman closed his eyes, then slowly opened them again and inclined his head. 'Yes.'

'Then we understand each other,' Alexei extended his hand, which Roman shook, then Alexei indicated the night-scape, the sprinkling of electric lamplight in the distance, the moving vehicles along major traffic roads, and the darkness of the ocean beyond. 'An attractive view, by day or night.'

'Yes. The home which once belonged to Ivana's mother.'

'So I understand.'

'A hardworking feisty lady,' Roman imparted. 'Who spoke her mind.'

'Of whom Natalya was very fond,' Alexei reminded, which drew a nod in silent agreement.

'Shall we return indoors? Share champagne, raise a toast to the future…and family.'

In hindsight the evening proved a pleasant one, as Ivana suggested lunch to initiate pre-wedding plans.

'I don't want to diminish your enthusiasm,' Natalya offered with gentle affection. 'But we haven't discussed the when or where of it yet.'

'It's every mother's dream to help plan a daughter's

wedding. The dress, the venue, flowers…all of it.' She caught hold of Natalya and whirled her around full circle.

'Okay,' Natalya protested with a light laugh. 'I totally get it. But let me talk to Alexei first.'

There was coffee, thick, black, aromatic to provide a finishing touch to the evening, and there was time to relax a little before her parents took their leave.

'Our time, I think,' Alexei decided as he drew Natalya into his arms. 'Ivana is in her element.'

She turned her face up to him, and trailed her fingers down his cheek. 'Prepare yourself for bridal magazines, material swatches…everything that goes towards a wedding. Which we need to discuss.'

He wanted to indulge her, run the shower, share it with her, and help ease the tense muscles formed from a long day. And he would, soon.

'How do you feel about a private family-only civil ceremony, a relaxed tropical island honeymoon, followed by a formal church wedding for family and friends?'

Natalya closed her eyes, then opened them again. 'Two weddings? Are you kidding me?'

'Think about it.'

'I'm endeavouring not to.'

'Your parents, a few close friends. No fanfare, followed by lunch, or dinner if you prefer…then we fly out for a week of rest and relaxation. A private island, no tourists. I know someone who owns the perfect place.'

It sounded appealing…becoming more appealing by the minute. 'And do it all over again in style…when?'

'Six, maybe eight weeks later.'

'I think that could be a plan.' She uttered a faint shriek as he lifted her into his arms and headed for the main bedroom, helped discard her clothes and his own, then he took her to bed.

It was bliss…utter bliss, as he massaged out the kinks in tight muscles, *more* as his hands shaped her body, lingered a little, then he took her to bed…to sleep curled close in against him.

Discretion was key in planning a private wedding.

Subterfuge a given.

What should have been simple in arranging a very private wedding ceremony took effort in a bid to avoid media attention.

The preferred setting narrowed down to two venues… The gardens at Ivana's home, or the grounds surrounding Alexei's home.

Alexei's Seaforth mansion proved the ideal choice, followed by a celebratory lunch prepared by Lisette.

'I'm calm,' Natalya assured Ivana as she put the finishing touches to her make-up.

Words, which didn't hold much weight, evidenced by the slight tremor in each hand as she tended to her hair.

There was a brief tap at the door as Lisette entered carrying a tray. 'I thought tea might be a welcome distraction.'

'How kind,' Ivana assured her with a smile. 'Will you join us?'

A small window of light relief helped ease the increase of nervous tension…which was crazy.

She loved Alexei with every cell in her body, every beat of her heart. *Sure*…as every breath she took, that his love for her was absolute.

Ivana offered a faint smile in silent understanding, almost as if she knew the train of her daughter's thoughts, and Natalya returned the smile, sipped the tea, then she discarded the silk wrap-around, and selected the white fine linen mid-calf dress overlain with guipure lace, elbow-length sleeves and a wide scooped neckline, stepped into it, stood still as Ivana slid home the long zip, before stepping back to offer a smiling nod of approval.

White stilettos, a wispy white confection of a cocktail hat, completed the outfit, Ivana handed her a bouquet of white roses culled from her own garden…and it became time to join Alexei waiting in the formal downstairs lounge.

Alexei cut a resplendent figure in a dark suit, white shirt and dark silk tie.

Ivana shared the role of matron of honour and mother of the bride. Roman gave the bride into Alexei's keeping, and Cristos, who'd flown in from New York, took the part of Alexei's best man.

A simple, heartfelt ceremony conducted by a celebrant…touching in that Alexei caught hold of her hand as she reached his side and lifted it to brush his mouth to her fingers, offered a deep emotive smile, then lowered his head to take her mouth with his in a soft lingering kiss.

It added to the informality, and brought a smile to those present.

The exchange of rings, hers a magnificent wide diamond-encrusted band, while Alexei had chosen a plain gold ring.

The kiss sealing their marriage was more evocative, loving, and tears shimmered in Natalya's eyes as she whispered, 'Love you.'

Lunch was a delight, with love, laughter…laid-back and incredibly personal.

Lisette had excelled herself. Roman remained quiet, reflective, while Ivana appeared relaxed, delighted her daughter had found everlasting happiness with her first and only love.

Not journey's end, she perceived.

A beginning.

* * *

The choice of a tropical island paradise became their personal honeymoon destination.

Owned by one of Alexei's friends, it was off the tourist tracery of holiday island venues.

Small, unique, with live-in staff to cater to the smallest of any guest's whim. There was an indoor pool, private, with an electronic roof to let in the sun…if desired, or not. A lanai…with cushioned cane chairs overlooking an outdoor pool that appeared to meld into the sapphire blue ocean. A motorised yacht moored at the end of a long jetty.

Indoors a large central lounge, a home office, three large luxe bedroom suites each with an en suite bathroom. A games room, set up for billiards, table tennis. A sauna.

Together with a rich man's necessity…a heliport complete with helicopter.

Perfection, luxurious, a haven from the hi-tech world of international business. Yet everything on hand at the push of a button, if need be.

Staff quarters situated at one end of the island housed a married couple employed as caretakers, their eldest son who acted as chef when the owners or invited guests were in residence. A younger son who piloted the motorised yacht and helicopter, and a daughter who assisted with household chores.

It was divine, an experience to remember…infinitely special—as Natalya evinced at the end of their stay.

'We can always return,' Alexei assured as they boarded the helicopter for the return home.

It was the caretaker's youngest son who took the pilot's seat, and set the engine in motion.

'Something to look forward to,' Natalya said with a whimsical smile. Maybe in a few years, with a young child to laugh at puddles, make sandcastles, enjoy the sunshine unfettered by the rush and bustle of city life. Playschool, kindergarten...

It was good to be home, to complete the final move of her belongings to Alexei's mansion. To make decisions to lease her own apartment, interview prospective tenants... only to discover Ben had a friend who was looking for an apartment, possessed of impeccable references, solid employment, whom she had already met, knew, and without hesitation she offered a lease, stored her furniture, and was grateful for the done deal.

Work proved intense during their first week, with Alexei taking up the slack from their absence, involving long hours...evenings when it was almost midnight before they each hit the shower and fell into bed.

Only for life to settle back into a reasonably familiar routine...if you factored in a formal wedding to be held with Alexei's family as guests, close friends, ADE's office staff together with top personnel from ADE's industrial plant.

A wedding planner took care of the details, liaised and approved the caterers' menu...ensuring everything went as smoothly as possible.

Eight weeks after their intimate wedding, they enjoyed the best of the best...both families together, guests they'd requested to attend, a beautiful church favoured by Ivana's mother during her lifetime, and a stunning venue for the wedding breakfast.

The bridal gown surpassed Natalya's dreams, with an exquisite bodice of intricate lace moulded to showcase her upper body, a sweetheart neckline, three-quarter sleeves in lace, with layers of silk falling from the waist beneath pale ivory silk to boost the skirt's volume a little so the hemline touched the tips of ivory stilettos. A floaty veil completed the bridal gown, and only she and Alexei knew the slender gold chain at her neck held his original gift of the simple diamond ring nestling deep within the V between each breast. On her right hand she wore the magnificent solitaire diamond Alexei had gifted her, and which she'd worn as a betrothal ring at their private wedding.

Soon he'd place the wide diamond-encrusted wedding ring on her left hand, and they would formally be named husband and wife before a church filled with family and guests.

'Tilt your head a little. I need to blend the eyeshadow just a touch more.'

Natalya obeyed, and shot Anja a faintly wry smile. 'Tell me again why I agreed to do this?'

'Ivana,' Anja reminded her gently. 'Your mother is in her element. Her smile, the soft laughter, her bond with Alexei's mother and family is a beautiful thing to witness.

'Then there's Alexei, the gorgeous man you're already married to…'

'I get it. I really do.'

'So hush… It's a lovely day, the sun is shining, the wedding planners have achieved a magnificent setting. The photographers are due to arrive any minute. Each mother of the little flower girl and pageboy have everything in hand.' She tapped a light forefinger to the tip of Natalya's nose. 'Relax.'

She was tempted to roll her eyes, and refrained…barely. 'I am perfectly relaxed.'

'Uh-huh,' Anja responded, *sotto voce*. 'Perfectly.'

'Am I permitted to say I preferred my first wedding?' It had been so intimate, so laid-back. *Special.*

'Of course. But only to me.'

Her mouth curved into a genuine smile. 'Thanks for being here. For doing what you do best. Friend, the sister I never had. All of it.'

'You're welcome. And for the record…right back at you. What you said, and more.'

It became time to shed her wrap, and step into her wedding gown…exquisite, delicate, perfect.

'You look so beautiful,' Ivana complimented gently, almost on the point of tears.

Natalya caught her mother close. 'Please don't cry.'

'I'm so happy for you…both of you.'

A special moment, encapsulating the now, the promise of the future.

'I know,' Natalya said gently. And she did. 'Thank you for everything. All of it, for as long as I can remember.'

Her childhood, the happiness, laughter, and memories of three generations…the special times influenced by a different culture from a different country.

Ivana and Natalya drew apart, smiled, touched a hand to each other's cheek…and stepped out into the sunshine together where three limousines waited to transport the bride's parents in one, Anja with the two small children in the second, and the bride with Paul at the wheel ready to complete the procession.

This was the moment, Natalya reflected as the limousine travelled the suburbs en route to the beautiful old church her darling babushka had adored. Settled back from the road and accessed via a long curved driveway shadowed by trees, it captured a timeless era of tradition, faith and something more…almost indefinable. And familiarity, for all the occasions she had attended there with her grandmother and mother.

A year, even six months ago, she could never have envisaged she would be attending her own wedding. Or that Alexei would be waiting for her at the church.

A broken dream, never imagined to be realised.

Yet there were occasions when dreams shifted, reassembled and were resolved. As hers had been...by the hand of Fate.

Paul slowed the limousine to a crawl prior to making the final turn to the street where the church's entrance lay, and slowly travelled the gently curved tree-lined driveway, where a team of photographers captured the moment of the bride's parents' arrival, immediately followed by Anja and the two children...and minutes later by the bride.

Flashbulbs popped, almost blinding as they melded with the sunshine, and the media were there to record the scoop of the day that would feature in the evening's newspapers, and probably occupy a small segment on the TV news.

As a notable event, the wedding would attract attention...and better an organised compliant willingness to share, than have the gutter press issue their dubious take filched from supposition and unsubstantiated fact.

Consequently there had been a private interview with the press, vetted and approved prior to publication. Also a sanctioned photograph...both of which had been released prior to the wedding. Now it was time to seal their love sanctioned and blessed in the church of their choice.

Today would feature a touch of grandeur, of love, light and happiness...genuine, even to the most critical eye.

Nervous, much? A little, Natalya admitted as the limousine eased to a halt outside the main entry. She knew enough not to look directly at the flashbulbs, to smile, and appear composed.

To pause long enough for Ivana and Anja to straighten her veil, ensure the gown's hemline wasn't caught up, and surprise both women with an impromptu kiss to her mother's cheek, before bestowing a similar salutation on Anja.

'My only wish is for you to be happy,' Roman said quietly as they took the first steps down the aisle.

There was a time to put her father's transgressions in the past, to move forward with the future...and this appeared to be the appropriate moment.

Natalya turned her head to offer Roman a winsome smile. 'I am...very happy,' she assured him gently.

Then she took her father's arm, leant forward and said quietly, 'Let's do this.'

The aisle seemed long, and she took the first step, then another, looked up and saw Alexei ignored tradition and had turned to watch her progress.

Natalya simply focussed on his expression as she slowly closed the distance to his side, saw the way his mouth curved into a smile, the light, the love in his eyes...for her. Only her.

And her head lifted a little, her smile faintly teasing as they shared a silent promise mere words could not convey.

Perfect, so incredibly right as she drew to a pause at his side...totally unprepared as he lowered his head and bestowed a gentle lingering kiss, sensed her response, only to reluctantly withdraw and clasp her hand within his own as they both turned to face the beaming minister, oblivious to the light laughter of the guests.

Oh, my.

Natalya was conscious of the vows spoken, the solemnity of the service, the faint tightening of Alexei's hand as they were pronounced husband and wife.

The kiss was a mutual benediction, and they turned to face the guests, to the hand-clapping and the smiles as they slowly stepped forward, paused for Anja to set the flower girl and pageboy in their positions, then began the slow walk down the aisle…only to hear a child's startled cry, and turn to see Gigi had tripped and become momentarily disoriented, bent on ignoring Anja's soothing voice and helping hands…as the little girl turned and ran towards the closest person she recognised… Alexei.

Without hesitation he scooped her into his arms, soothed her tears, and touched his lips to her small forehead as she curled her arms round his neck.

Xena rushed from her seat, only for Gigi to shake her head and cling to Alexei.

'It's okay,' he offered gently as Xena looked distressed.

And it was. Gigi simply buried her head against Alexei's neck, and didn't lift it until they reached the vestibule where Cristos waited to extricate his daughter.

Natalya felt her heart melt at the sight of Alexei cradling his niece as if it was the most natural act in the world.

Aware he would do the same with their own children, be a hands-on father who would gift his heart, everything he had, to the well-being of his children…and for her.

There, whenever, wherever he was needed.

Because it mattered. As she mattered.

Evident in everything he did, the words said and those not needed to be voiced.

Love. Theirs alone.

Now, she waved aside Cristos's attempt at an apology. 'It was delightful,' she assured him with a genuine smile.

It became a talking point among the guests, who collectively accorded it a touching moment.

There were photographs, professional, the media, family, video cameras recording the ceremony, before and after wedding snaps, laughter, smiles, the beautiful bonding between Calista and Ivana.

It was, in retrospect, a very special wedding. A blend of grandeur and contemporary…of love, family and friends who each came together to celebrate the joining of two people who had loved, lost, and found each other again.

The moment when Natalya and Alexei were alone, Alexei took hold of her hand and lifted it to his lips, then kissed the tip of each finger in turn.

It was the wedding waltz which almost brought her undone as she circled the floor in Alexei's arms. The lowering of his head as he brought his lips close to her ear and said, 'You're the love of my life. You…only you complete me.'

Uncaring of time or place, she reached up and touched gentle fingers to his cheek, caressed the groomed stubble, and rested fingers to the edge of his mouth.

'There are the words I could say,' she said quietly. 'And I will, because I need you to hear them. I want to touch you, to show you you're the other half of me. My love, soul-mate…my everything.'

He pulled her close against him, held her there…his arousal a potent force. 'Let's get out of here.'

It was easy to smile, to tease a little. 'It's our night. We get to choose.'

They finished the bridal waltz, circled the room with unhurried steps, pausing to thank their guests individually for attending the wedding celebration, spent a little time with each of their parents and family, then slipped away from the venue to a waiting limousine with Paul at the wheel. For he, too, had been a valued guest.

'Home?'

'Yes. Please,' Natalya added, as she nestled her head into the curve of Alexei's shoulder. Perhaps the best gift she could give him was the one she'd been waiting days for the right moment. When would be better than now?

There was more. Just a few words, and she offered them

later…much later after they'd made love, tears gathering at the edge of her eyes as she relaxed in his arms.

'This morning I took a pregnancy test.'

She didn't make him wait.

'It was positive.'

EPILOGUE

LIFE WAS GOOD, Natalya reflected as she carefully eased the sated babe from her breast. The night was still at this pre-dawn hour.

'There we go, my little darling,' she murmured with a loving smile as she hugged Nikos close and brushed soft lips to his forehead.

This was their time, so precious and special, and she quietly began singing a soft lullaby of a small babe falling asleep in a cradle as she gently rocked him in her arms, smiling at the sound of his customary burp.

She wanted to hold him a little longer, to stroke light fingers over his soft cheek, and to give quiet blessings for the miracle of life. And she did, silently, with all the love in her heart.

Then she carefully placed him into his crib, reached out and lowered the baby night lamp, paused to double-check he was sleeping, then she turned to leave the nursery…and saw Alexei's tall frame leaning against the door frame.

'How long have you been standing there?' Natalya queried quietly as she drew close, and in the dim light she caught his slow smile.

'A while.' He lifted a hand and curved it beneath her chin. 'I like to watch you both together.' He pressed his thumb-pad to her lips. 'Share the bond between mother and child.'

A lump rose in her throat, and she swallowed it down. 'You're a great father.'

A wonderful support during the initial few months of her pregnancy, when he took time out to accompany her to every appointment—there at her side through every injection, each examination. Marvelling at each sonogram as they watched their son develop in the womb. Counting fingers and toes, the moment when it appeared the unborn babe turned and appeared to look at them.

Choosing a name, agreeing on his late grandfather's name… Nikos.

Alexei touched his mouth to hers, gently at first, then he curved an arm around her shoulders.

He was a good babe, suckled well, only woke once through the night for a feed, then slept until the early pre-dawn hours. He tended to smile…although Natalya felt sure it was simply wind.

Natalya cast Alexei a musing glance. 'This is one of the best times of the night. The day is done, Nikos is sleeping, and…'

'It's our time,' he assured her quietly and pulled her into his arms and deepened the kiss before raising his head to touch his lips to her temple. 'I love you.'

Her eyes filled, and she blinked to hold back the tears. How could she not know?

'You touch a hand to my cheek, and my heart begins to dissolve,' she said gently.

'You're the other half of me.' His lips traced her own, nibbled a little, then soothed. 'I sense every move you make during the night, and draw you close.'

She held back the threat of tears. 'Returned in kind. Every word. All of it.'

How could she not, when he'd read everything available

on pre-natal care, gowned in the operating theatre during the caesarean section?

His was the first face she saw after the birth. The gentle kiss he bestowed as she offered him a wondrous smile as she was given their son to hold for the first time.

Now, she reached up to cradle her husband's face. 'Let's go to bed.'

His smile almost undid her. *Love*…all of it, and more, clearly evident. For her.

'You need a few hours' sleep before Nikos will want his next feed.'

'Uh-huh.' Natalya pulled his head down to hers. 'And I'll have them.'

A touch, the light drift of fingers over sensitised skin.

All consuming, captivating as the senses coalesced in the joining of mind, body and soul.

The completion of the circle of love. Sensual magic.

'But first,' she teased gently, 'I want to make love with the main man in my life.'

Alexei smiled in the dim moonlight filtering through the shuttered windows. 'I have no problem with that, *agape mou.*'

* * * * *

'The baby changes nothing, Max. We should never have married.'

'But we did,' he said, and he put down the pen and stood tall, his arms folded across his chest. Anything to stop himself from going to her, from trying to kiss some reason into her. Lisa was his wife and the thought of her moving on, meeting someone new, lashed at him like icy rain.

'I don't want a reluctant father for my child, Max.'

He drew in a deep breath as her words hit at his biggest insecurity. 'Then we agree on that, at least, because I want to be there for my son or daughter all the time. Which is why I am not signing these papers—at least not until we have given our marriage another chance.'

'We already know we don't work. Just sign them, Max. Please.'

'I'll make a deal with you, Lisa. We give our marriage one last chance. We live as a married couple for the next two weeks, and if by New Year's Eve you still feel the same I will sign the papers and we can both start our lives again.'

Introducing a sizzling and sexy new duet
from Rachael Thomas

Convenient Christmas Brides

Estranged brothers Raul Valdez and
Maximiliano Martinez are about to unlock some
dark and hidden secrets. But with Christmas
around the corner first comes seduction!

Lydia Carter-Wilson finds herself blackmailed into
an engagement by Raul Valdez in

Valdez's Bartered Bride

Maximiliano's life is turned upside down when his
estranged wife announces she is carrying his heir in

Martinez's Pregnant Wife

Available now!

MARTINEZ'S PREGNANT WIFE

BY
RACHAEL THOMAS

First Published in Great Britain 2017
By Mills & Boon, an imprint of HarperCollins*Publishers*
1 London Bridge Street, London, SE1 9GF

© 2017 Rachael Thomas

ISBN: 978-0-263-93514-1

Our policy is to use papers that are natural, renewable and recyclable products and made from wood grown in sustainable forests. The logging and manufacturing processes conform to the legal environmental regulations of the country of origin.

Printed and bound in Spain
by CPI, Barcelona

Rachael Thomas has always loved reading romance, and is thrilled to be a Mills & Boon author. She lives and works on a farm in Wales—a far cry from the glamour of a Modern Romance story, but that makes slipping into her characters' worlds all the more appealing. When she's not writing, or working on the farm, she enjoys photography and visiting historical castles and grand houses. Visit her at rachaelthomas.co.uk.

Visit the Author Profile page
at millsandboon.co.uk for more titles.

PROLOGUE

Two months ago...

MAXIMILIANO MARTINEZ OPENED his eyes, the uncustomary warmth of someone next to him in bed shocking him. Memories of the previous night, of talking and drinking wine with Lisa, flashed through his mind. As if roused by those same memories, she stirred and moved against him, her naked body almost too much to resist. He gritted his teeth, trying to ignore the stab of desire rocketing through him, preferring instead anger at having given into that weakness last night. It had been the same weakness that had made marriage to Lisa the only option.

To wake up with Lisa next to him each morning was what he would have had if he'd been able to honour his wedding vows, if he'd been able to let go of his past and love his wife. But he hadn't. He'd thought he'd banished those memories from the past, thought what he and Lisa had would mean the past could be hidden, forgotten, but he was wrong. Very wrong. His past had reared up like an angry stallion, mocking him, reinforcing what he'd been trying to escape—he wasn't capable of love.

Never had been and never would be. That was why he'd set Lisa free. Just months after they'd married, he'd left.

For the last six months they had maintained a professional distance despite working together. He knew full well it was avoidance on her part but he couldn't really blame her. He'd hurt her.

So what the hell was she doing in his bed?

Lisa put her arm across his chest, sleep still clinging to her, but the action made the contrast between his mind and body polar opposites. His body wanted her, wanted to make her his again and never let her go, but his mind knew that whatever had happened last night was already mistake enough. He might not be capable of loving his wife, but he didn't want to hurt her. That was why he'd walked out on the marriage. To save her from the heartache a man like him would inflict on her.

He gently moved her arm from his chest, fighting against primal urges as she sighed softly and very sexily. He looked down at her, at the long lashes splayed over her pale skin, and knew he was doing the right thing, even if he hadn't last night; now he did he would do exactly that. He slid from the tangle of Lisa's long legs and sheets before his body won the battle of desire.

'Where are you going?' Lisa's voice was husky and so damn sexy. Sleep lingered in every syllable and for a moment he froze, unable to move or speak. This wasn't a casual one-night stand with a woman whose name he barely recalled. This was his estranged wife.

Before he'd met Lisa he'd always been strong, able to resist the lure of desire, but then she'd always affected him in a way no other woman had. How the hell had they gone from business talk to bed? It should have been a meeting about the players of the latest football club he'd bought and how he wanted her to continue working for him and be the club's physiotherapist.

Because she's the woman you wanted to love.

He looked at her again, the tug of desire strengthening. But so too were the ghosts of his past.

Last night they had drunk far too much wine and his head began to thump in protest. He must have been mad to have thought he could talk over dinner with Lisa and not give into the desire, the need to touch her, kiss her and make her his again.

If he didn't remove her from his apartment, his bed, he'd be in danger of giving in once more. Whatever spark had brought them together was still there and it was past time he snuffed it out. For good.

'I have an important meeting in an hour.' He growled the words out as he pulled on his clothes. The only meeting he had was with several strong cups of coffee and painkillers. When he turned to look at his wife, red hair tumbling around her shoulders, he knew he was hurting her. Again. Yet the aggressive words rushed from him regardless. 'You need to go.'

'But...' she began as her eyes implored him to soften his mood, to look at her without the icy spark in his eyes or the anger in every line of his body.

He wasn't going to be drawn. 'No buts, Lisa. Just go.'

'But last night...' she tried again, sitting up and clutching the white sheet against her in a show of modesty, or maybe protection. Either way, it failed as one full breast became exposed, snagging his attention. He strengthened his resolve.

'Last night should not have happened. Hell, Lisa, we agreed. Our marriage was a mistake.' He pushed his fingers roughly through his hair and turned away from her, not wanting to see the hurt in her eyes, the pain on her beautiful face. He swore in his native Spanish, his first language ruling the moment, despite his having lived in London since leaving Spain as a teenager.

Lisa threw aside the sheet and got out of bed, her movements fluid and graceful but also showing him how angry and hurt she was. She pressed her fingers to her forehead for a moment as she stood there, invitingly naked. He wasn't the only one who was suffering from indulging in too much fine wine last night.

'We agreed to keep things professional.' He looked at her, wishing things had been different, wishing that his past didn't haunt him, making any kind of emotional commitment impossible. When she began to dress, to hide her sexy body, his control slipped back into place. 'We agreed we could work together. Just as we did before we were married.'

'We are *still* married.' Her frosty look couldn't hide the hurt in her eyes as her fingers fumbled to hastily fasten the buttons on her blouse. 'You admitted it was a mistake but you haven't done anything about it.'

Was Lisa right? Was he too weak to admit a mistake? Or was it that he still wanted her?

But you can't give her what she wants.

Her neat brows furrowed together and hurt showed in every pore of her delicately pale face. 'So what was last night? A casual fling? A big mistake?'

'*Sí*, a mistake. One that should not have happened.' He stood firm. He wasn't the man for her. Lisa wanted to be loved and to love in return and had never made a secret of that. This was his issue. He couldn't accept her love, couldn't take that from her when he knew, without a doubt, he could never love her. Not that he hadn't tried. He'd even married her in an attempt to unshackle himself from the chains that cut off his emotions, that held him firmly in the past. But to no avail.

She gasped, her eyes widening, and he knew he was hurting her. He had to do it. Had to make her see they weren't right for one another, to save her from even greater hurt. Despite the sparks of passion that had fired instantly between them last night, as if the six months apart had never happened, they weren't suited. Surely she could see that.

'I hate you,' she snapped at him and he knew it was anything but. He knew she had once loved him, but he wanted her to hate him, wanted her to despise him and find someone who could give her what she needed, what she deserved. If she could say she hated him, then soon her heart would feel the same.

'Then we are doing the right thing.' Deep inside a small part of him withered and died at the thought of her hating him. But it had to be that way.

'Damn right we are. Last night was a massive mistake.' She threw the words at him like daggers, snatched her purse and jacket from the armchair where he now vaguely recalled her tossing them last night and marched to the door. 'I want a divorce.'

The door slammed hard behind her and he stood in the heavy silence and glowered at the door, as if it were responsible for shutting her out, but he'd done that. It was for the best, but it sure as hell didn't feel like it right now.

CHAPTER ONE

LISA MARTINEZ TOOK a deep breath, trying to ease the nausea that had just started to become a normal part of her morning. She couldn't put it off any longer. She had to tell him.

She was pregnant—expecting the baby of a man who wanted neither her nor any sort of commitment in his life. Icy fingers of dread slithered down her spine. What on earth was she going to do?

All she knew was that she had to tell Maximiliano, the man she'd fallen head over heels in love with from the moment their eyes had first met. The man she'd married, sure her love could bring them happiness. The man who'd walked out on her within months of exchanging vows. He was also the man she'd hurled the angry words *I want a divorce* at when the passion of their recent one night together had been extinguished by the cold light of day.

She knew exactly where Max would be right now. Ensconced in his office, chasing the next big deal, the next football club to drag up from the lowest league and make it great. It was his way of proving he could succeed, could still be something in the world of football despite the car accident that had cut short his career.

Lisa fought against the flurry of nerves that added to the nausea she'd been trying to shake off since she'd finally had the courage to see her doctor. There was no getting away from it now, no way she could deny it and no way to avoid telling Max. To do that would be to go against everything she believed in. She had to tell him that their night together two months ago had lasting consequences and before anyone else they worked with guessed. He might be her boss at the football club where she was a physio but he was still her husband, despite the divorce papers she knew the court had sent him. Max had to hear this from her.

She took a deep breath and then blew it out in an attempt to regain her composure, Max's closed office door suddenly seeming more like the highest mountain on earth. She knocked and opened the door, stepping warily inside the masculine space. The room was empty. As she stood on the threshold, her hand still holding the door open, footsteps sounded in the corridor and she turned, knowing it wasn't Max. Relief and annoyance rushed through her. She wanted to get this over and done with. Only then could she move on and leave this part of her life behind.

'He's not there,' Max's PA informed her as she slipped past her and put some files on the desk. 'Probably gone for his usual coffee fix. Although he wasn't in a good mood.'

'He wasn't?' Lisa's confidence began to erode like a cliff face pounded by an angry sea.

'No. Far from it,' his PA said as she ordered the files on his desk. 'Very distracted.'

'Thanks.'

Before she became further embroiled in conversation, Lisa turned and made her way out of the modern building that served as the headquarters for Max's various business ventures. It was also the head offices of the latest struggling football club whose fortunes he was intent on turning around. The cold December air snatched her breath away as she walked toward the very place she and Max had drunk far too much wine two months ago during an evening that had been meant to be for discussing business.

That night should have been about her as the club's physio and him as the club's owner. Nothing more. Instead it had turned into being about each other, their marriage and the events that had led up to him walking out on her. Worse than that, it had soon become about the passion that still sparked between them, the consequences of which now linked them more closely and permanently than any marriage certificate ever could.

She stopped walking. She couldn't do this. How could she tell the man who regretted marrying her that he was going to be a father? Maybe she should wait until after Christmas? It was tempting, but the thought of whispered gossip reaching him before she did pushed her back on course and she walked on, her boots sounding hard and loud on the pavement, tapping out a rhythm of determination she was far from feeling.

What was the worst he could do? Tell her he didn't want anything to do with his child? That response was exactly what she expected and it certainly couldn't be worse than his admission that he didn't love her. The pain couldn't be any harder to bear than that of losing the man she'd fallen in love with.

Two months ago, after doing her utmost to keep out of his way at work, at least until she'd found a new position, she'd allowed her heart to rule her head and had given into Max's lethal charm. It had been the most foolhardy thing she'd done and now, with their baby growing inside her, she couldn't afford to make the mistake again of fooling herself that he cared. Her head had to be well and truly in charge, keeping her heart locked away. This was not a time for sentimental dreams of love and happy ever afters. Such a thing would never be possible with Maximiliano Martinez. She knew that now.

She pushed open the door of the bar Max always favoured, the blast of warm air from the overhead heaters notching up the nausea as she walked in. The place was decked out for Christmas but at this hour of the morning it was practically deserted. She glanced into the dimness of the room and saw Max straight away, sitting with his back to her, staring ahead of him, seemingly oblivious to anything else.

His PA was right. He wasn't in a good mood.

Her heart flipped over and tugged at the emotions she was desperate to keep under control. So much for being strong, for locking away her feelings. They were pouring from her like a torrent of rain, all jumbled up and veering from one extreme to another. She couldn't decide if she was angry or nervous or even if she was doing the right thing as she stood looking at the man she knew she couldn't remain married to, the man whose child she now carried.

The tension in Max's broad shoulders was all too obvious as he sat, elbows on the table and hands clasped tightly and pressed against his chin. She walked slowly forward, coming round to his side, but still he didn't see her, didn't hear her. He was lost in thought.

Why was he so unreachable? She'd known he kept his emotions well-hidden even as she'd said *I do*, but had thought she could change that—change him. She'd thought she had love enough for them both and, after the hard upbringing she'd had, it was just another gamble in life she was prepared to take. But she couldn't gamble any longer, not now there was a baby on the way.

Now she had to be mercenary. She didn't want her child growing up as she had, feeling unloved, unwanted. She'd dreaded the days her father had turned up, demanding to see his *little girl*, not out of any kind of love, or even duty, but out of spite. She'd been the weapon he'd used to get at her mother and that would not be happening to her baby.

Planned or not, she wanted this baby, wanted to provide a happy and loving home, one free of any worries for her child, and after her childhood she knew that could only be achieved either entirely on her own or with the full support of a man who loved her and wanted the same. Max did not. He hadn't even been able to commit to marriage so how could he possibly be there for his child? That left only one option. To get the divorce papers signed and end that chapter of her life so that she could raise her child alone. First she had to tell him. He had a right to know even if he never wanted to see his child.

'Max.' She put aside her past together with her future worries and focused on the present. She said his name softly as she moved toward him, but he remained still, lost in thought. She tried again, firmer this time. 'Max.'

He turned and looked at her, his handsome features she knew and loved marred by an expression that struck dread into her heart. Had he already heard? Was it possible someone had already given away her secret?

'What are you doing here, Lisa? Come to make sure I sign the divorce papers? Maybe you have found someone new and want to move on?' His accent was more pronounced than she'd heard for a long time and anger glittered in his eyes. The heavier than usual shadow of stubble on a man who demanded nothing but perfection notched up her nerves. Something was seriously wrong. He must know. Was he now toying with her? Seeing how long she'd hold out on him?

Well, she wouldn't give him the satisfaction. She would tell him before he could challenge her.

'I have something to tell you.' There was a waiver of uncertainty in her voice and, judging by the slight narrowing of his inky black eyes, he'd detected it.

'Nothing I don't already know. You are a bit late to the party, Lisa.' The venom in his words sent her heart into freefall as panic raced around her. How could he be so callous about the baby? His baby. Even if he'd found out from the malicious whisperings of the club's gossips, it was still his baby.

She lifted her chin and glared angrily at him. He wasn't going to reduce her to a nervous wreck. She had to be strong, had to say what she needed to and then go—leave him to his foul mood. 'I wasn't aware such news required a party.'

He stood up, his height suddenly dominating the air she wanted to gulp down in order to remain calm. As always he wore a dark suit, tailored and very expensive, which fitted him to perfection and she couldn't help but allow her eyes to travel down his long legs. The part of her that loved this man fought for supremacy, not wanting to freeze him out of her life. But hadn't he already done that when he walked out on her so soon after vowing to spend the rest of his life with her? Then again the morning after that night, when he'd told her to go?

He moved closer to her. Too close. 'Since when have you known?' The feral growl of his voice warned her that his anger was running on a short leash, desperate to break free. The day he'd walked out on their marriage he'd made it clear he'd never wanted to be married and most certainly had never wanted to be a father. She'd been convinced it was her casual mention of children that had tipped him over the edge. Now he glared up at her, as if to reaffirm all he'd said that day. As he glared up at her she was shocked by how anger glittered dangerously in his dark eyes.

'About two weeks.' As soon as she'd said it she knew it was a mistake. His eyes darkened to glacial black and his lips pressed into a firm line of fury.

'Two weeks?' The words echoed around the empty room and he looked directly into her eyes, so intimidatingly close. She'd never seen him this angry. 'And you thought now was the perfect time to tell me what you knew? More to the point, how the hell did you find out?'

'Find out?' She stumbled over the answer, not understanding the question, but stood tall before him, refusing to be intimidated by his black mood. 'I wanted to be sure.'

'Be sure of what?' He sat back and looked at her as if seeing her for the first time and a flutter of doubt crossed her mind. Was it possible he didn't know? That she'd wrongly assumed that he did? Were they talking about two entirely different subjects? If so, what was so bad it had made him this angry?

There was no escaping it now, no easy way to break this. She had to tell him—right now. The suspicion in his eyes warned her of that.

'Be sure of what, Lisa?' Max demanded, the tension in the air ratcheting up, almost suffocating her.

'I...' She tried to form the words, but his jaw clenching in anger snared her attention and her words dried up.

'What, Lisa?' His voice thundered and inside she jumped as he stood up, tall, powerful and demanding.

The words failed her as she looked up at him, her heart thumping hard in her chest. She tried again. 'I'm pregnant.'

Max's world rocked violently. Not for the first time today he was unable to utter a single word in either English or his native Spanish. He'd thought she'd come to ensure he would sign the divorce papers, to tell him she'd moved on, had a new lover, but her words still ricocheted through him. Lisa was pregnant? His estranged wife, the woman he'd turned his back on, was carrying his child? A child he hadn't wanted, a child he wasn't ready for, not when everything from his past was thrusting into the present with the force of a tidal wave.

He focused his attention on the woman he'd married, the woman he'd never be able to love after learning at a young age that such emotions hurt. His mother had loved his father and that had hurt her—badly. He'd loved his father and when he'd walked out it had almost ripped him apart. He could still hear his harsh parting words echoing from the past, taunting him with the one thing he'd steadfastly refused to acknowledge since that day.

Never forget you have Valdez blood in your veins.

Ever since then he'd tried to forget. He'd been resolutely determined to have nothing to do with the might of the Valdez banking family. He'd been entirely successful until a lawyer had contacted him, informing him of his father's death. Then his half-brother had done the same and now the whole sorry mess was splashed over every damn newspaper.

He pushed his childhood memories back, but didn't take his eyes off Lisa as she stood there, holding her nerve, those green eyes locked with his. She was more than a match for him. The only woman he'd ever known who didn't hang on his every word, didn't simper and giggle in an act of coyness. Lisa was real and honest. She'd grounded him, made him believe he was worthy of more than one-night stands. Then she'd told him she'd had a job offer in America and he'd known he couldn't let her walk away, that he had to try and open up to her, to love her.

That was why he'd married her, but very quickly he'd realised that had been a mistake. A big mistake. They didn't belong together, they should never have married and he cursed the weakness of his desire for this redhead, which had driven him to make her his wife.

Finally he found his voice. 'Pregnant? What about the pill?'

He couldn't be a father. He didn't want to be a father, didn't want to take the risk that he'd be the same as his father, that the Valdez legacy would rear its ugly head. Now it had. In more ways than he could believe possible.

Lisa was pregnant. From one careless night. How could she calmly stand there and tell him as if it were just one of those things that happened?

'I think you have some explaining to do.' He growled the words at her, annoyed at her reluctance to say anything else.

She pulled out a chair and sat wearily at the table and he could clearly see just how pale she was beneath her make-up. Unease and worry threatened but he pushed them savagely away, along with the fear of the past, as he sat opposite her. She clasped her hands in front of her on the table. His gaze lingered on her long slender fingers and the glitter of the diamond engagement ring and band of gold he'd placed on her third finger over a year ago. She still wore his rings? Why, when the divorce papers he hadn't yet signed were on his desk at home? Had she put them back on once she'd realised she was carrying his child?

'We had a lot of wine that night, Max. I guess suffering the after-effects of that had an effect.' She paused and looked at him. 'It wasn't something I even considered until I realised that I could be pregnant.'

Did she seriously think he'd buy that? Too much wine? 'A few glasses of wine?'

'It was more than a few and you know it.' Her hot retort fired back at him, much more like the Lisa he knew, then she blushed, the colour bringing life to her cheeks. 'I was ill after I left.'

He narrowed his eyes as he replayed that night in his mind and then the morning after. He recalled how his head had been splitting in two, how every noise had made him wince, especially the slam of the door as Lisa had left. He'd made several cups of coffee that morning before finally being able to drink one. She was right. They had drunk far too much wine. Or had that been a cover up for the sudden defrosting of his estranged wife? After all, she hadn't needed much persuasion to return to his bed.

Max put one elbow on the table and pressed his hand over his eyes. Could life get any worse? He'd discovered a family he'd never known of, or even had any desire to know, after his father's death. Now it was being played out through newspaper headlines, but, worse than any of that, he'd created a new generation to add to the Valdez family. One he did not want.

He looked down at various copies of today's newspapers spread out on the table before him. Each headline different, but saying the same thing. He looked again at the newspaper on the top. His throat tightened as he read the headlines again. Bold black words screamed from the page, hurtling him into a past he'd rather forget, colliding wildly with a future he didn't want.

Billionaire's Illegitimate Heir Found!

'Max?' Lisa's question sounded far off and he fought to get himself back under control, to be in charge of a situation that was escalating with alarming speed.

He couldn't speak, couldn't say anything to her, not after the way she'd deceived him—tricking him into being a father.

'Max? What is it?' She reached out and slowly pulled the newspaper round so that she could read it. He looked up and watched her lashes lower as she read the headlines, annoyed that his thoughts rushed back to the times he'd watched her sleep. To the morning, just moments before she'd left him. How could such a beautiful and beguiling woman be so deceitful? How could she do this to him? And why now?

She looked up at him, her soft green eyes full of shock. 'This is about you. You have a brother?'

He pressed his lips firmly together. 'A half-brother.'

In the same day he'd found his connection to Raul Valdez, the billionaire banking tycoon, had been plastered everywhere, he'd been told he was to be a father. Was he in the middle of a nightmare? If he opened his eyes would it all go away?

'And you never knew?' Lisa looked at him and he was certain she hadn't known any of this. He could see so many questions in her eyes but was grateful that she didn't ask them now. Hell, he didn't even know the answer to any of them himself. All he could think about was that he'd done exactly what his birth father had done. He'd created a child he didn't want.

'No, but that is not important now. We need to discuss the baby.' Saying that word made it so real it came out in a growl of harshness and he saw her sit back away from him as if he were the devil himself. He hadn't wanted it to sound so cruel.

'There is nothing to discuss.' She pushed back her chair and stood up, forcing him to look up at her. 'I'm going to have your baby, but you needn't worry, I won't make any demands on you whatsoever. You made it very clear when you walked out on our marriage that any kind of commitment is very much off the agenda for you.'

'Sit down, Lisa.'

'No.' She buttoned up her coat and he knew if he didn't get this right, didn't say the right thing she would walk out on him—again. Only this time she would take with her his child, a child that would grow up wondering where in the world its father was and why he didn't want them in his life. He knew only too well what that was like and didn't want that pain, that rejection for his child.

'We need to talk about this. Sit down, Lisa.' Anger simmered in his voice and he bit down hard, stopping himself from saying anything else. Something that would make this even worse than it already was. He needed to sort things with Lisa, then he could deal with the other avalanche that had crashed into his life. His brother.

'Why? So that you can tell me it's not what you want and walk away from me again?' The truth of her words stung. Just as the truth of the headlines smarted like salt in an open wound.

He wanted to demand to know why she'd let this happen, why after living apart yet working together professionally she had agreed to have dinner with him, turning it into a date, then a one-night stand. Inwardly, he savagely cursed. He'd been the one to invite her to dinner, the one to suggest that avoiding each other wasn't professional. After all they were both shareholders, both had a stake in the club. Neither of them could just walk away.

'I don't want children and this is why.' He picked up the newspaper and shook it, anger making his movements sharp. 'It's all here.'

'You are not the only one to have had a bad childhood, Max.' His gaze snapped to hers and the one and only time they'd discussed her childhood surfaced from his memory. The way she'd told him she'd hated the family arguments, especially at Christmas.

'My point exactly.' His reply was swift.

'I am having this baby, Max, and, as I said, I expect

nothing from you.' Her chin lifted and her eyes glittered with defiance.

'So you think you can just arrive here, today of all days, and tell me I am to be a father then walk away?'

'The timing is bad, I admit.' Her voice softened slightly, snagging at his senses, pulling at his conscience. 'But I am having this baby, Max.'

'And I intend to be there for my child, no matter what. It will not grow up thinking I cared so little I walked away.' As he spoke he knew that it was the one and only thing he was certain of at the moment. If his brother wanted nothing to do with him and Lisa hated him, it didn't matter. All that mattered was to be a part of his child's life. But to do that he would have to be a part of Lisa's life. He pushed the paper at her, stabbing coldly at the image of the father he could barely remember. 'I will not be this man.'

'No, Max, it's not possible, not when you have already made it clear you don't want me in your life.' Lisa stepped back from Max, away from the temptation of reaching out to touch him, to go to him and soothe his pain. He was dealing with two life-changing things in one morning, but, from the cold expression on his face, neither had made any great impact other than to make him angry. He didn't want a brother or a baby.

'There wasn't a baby involved then. My baby.'

'And that changes things?'

'You're damn right it changes things.'

He glared at her and the sensation of being in control, of being able to drive the situation how she wanted, vanished as he looked at her. Only a small distance separated them but right now it felt like an ocean. Deep and unnavigable.

'No, it doesn't.' Her life-long instinct to protect herself and stand up for herself, to fight her corner, kicked in. 'I'm doing this on my own.'

'No.' That one word thundered around the room and she blinked in shock. She'd never seen Max so angry. Would she have told him about the baby if she'd known his reaction would be this bad? Yes, the answer fired back into her mind. She didn't want him turning up when the child was older as her father had done, creating hell in an already dysfunctional family and giving her false hope of being wanted, of being rescued from the latest stepfather, a spiteful older stepbrother and uncaring mother who seemed only to want to make her feel useless.

'What do you mean, no?' she demanded hotly, the pain of her childhood almost too much in the emotional state she was in.

'I mean we will remain married.' He paused as his expression hardened further and she braced herself against what was to follow. 'And we will live as a married couple.'

'No. I don't want to.' Anger made her irrational. 'I want a divorce.'

'Divorce is not an option now, Lisa.' His words had calmed, become laden with iciness. His expression was severe, his eyes dark and watchful.

She lifted her chin. 'It is the only option for me.'

'Not for me.' Those words were hard and forceful.

'Why?' The response blurted from her as if it had been catapulted across the room. He didn't flinch at the accusation firmly loaded within it.

'Because I will not be the man my father was.' His mood softened and he moved toward her, the man she'd fallen in love with showing through the tough façade like an echo of a ghost. 'I will not abandon my child because it doesn't fit in with my life.'

All her past pain from her childhood melted away and her heart went out to him; the pain was so clear in his voice. Whatever had happened she'd loved this man, even if he'd destroyed that with his coldness that morning two months ago. She had once loved him enough to marry him and promise to be there for him in good times and bad. Didn't that count for something?

Marriage for ever was something she'd dreamt of as a young girl, yearned for as a young woman, and then she'd met Max. He'd swept her off her feet, made her feel special, wanted and very much desired. He'd never told her he loved her, no matter how many times she'd said it to him, but when he'd asked her to be his wife, that hadn't mattered. She'd had enough love for both of them.

Only she hadn't, she thought as she watched him press the pads of his fingers over his eyes in an uncustomary display of inadequacy. Her heart lurched as she weakened. This was her baby's father, the man she'd fallen in love with, the man she'd married.

'I understand why you are saying that,' she said more softly now as she moved closer, physically bridging the gap if not emotionally. 'But we shouldn't make any decisions now. Not until you have met your brother. This is too much to deal with in one go.'

'You're right,' he said firmly and looked up at her. 'First I will meet my brother and then we will sort this out.'

He made their baby sound as if it were a little mistake that could be swept to one side, but she kept her nerve, hid her pain and looked him in the eye. 'So when are you going to meet him?'

'He's here now.' The curtness of his reply shocked her as much as what he'd said.

'Here?'

'No, in London. We have a meeting planned for today.'

'And he thought it would be a good idea to blast it all over the British papers on the very same day?' Furious loyalty suddenly sprang up inside her and she couldn't keep the spike of venom from her voice. What kind of man would do such a thing?

'I've read it over several times and I don't think he is responsible. He would be dragging his own name through the dirt too. He's been accused of blackmailing a woman into an engagement. Maybe by meeting him I will discover just who is responsible for this.' He picked up the newspaper again and glared at it.

'So you are going?' She frowned at what he'd just told her, the puzzle over who would gain from leaking such a story taking her mind from her own problems.

'Yes, but first we have things to sort out.'

'What things?' She curled her fingers together; the engagement ring she'd picked out with such enthusiasm and hope for the future cut cruelly into her palm as it turned on her finger. Was that a sign they were doomed? Whatever duty and honour kept them together?

'Our marriage. How we are going to make this work.'

'Our marriage is over, Max.' She didn't dare mention that once she'd loved him so much she'd thought nothing could ever change that. If she mentioned the word love now it would push her over the edge, even if it didn't do that to him.

'Not until I return the signed papers saying I agree to the divorce and right now I have no intention of doing that.'

CHAPTER TWO

'YOU HAVE TO AGREE.' There was a hint of panic in Lisa's voice and Max realised how much work he would have to do. Whatever Lisa had once felt for him, it was gone. Maybe she even hated him. But what of the passion of that night two months ago? Didn't that count for something?

'You are expecting my child, Lisa. What kind of man would I be if I didn't contest the divorce?' The words were out before he'd had a chance to check them, to rationalise the deeper level they came from.

The door to the bar burst open and a group of office workers entered on a rush of cold winter air, their revelry matching the season but not his mood. He glanced one last time at the newspapers, the image of the father he hadn't seen for years and that of the brother he'd never met staring up at him. That particular problem would have to wait.

He pulled his heavy wool coat on, his eyes meeting the question in Lisa's green ones. 'We can't talk about this here.'

'There is nothing else to talk about.' The passionate retort fired hotly back at him as the group of men and woman laughed loudly at their private joke. This was not the place to have such a discussion.

Max moved toward her, inhaling her perfume, its light floral scent taking him far from the coldness of winter in London. The determination to do what was right by his child made his words sharper than he intended. 'That is where you are wrong, Lisa. We have a child to talk about. Our child.'

'A child you don't want.' This time her hot words were barely above a whisper.

He looked at her, the rising noise levels of the lunchtime crowd now arriving only increasing his anger, his frustration that she was so hell-bent on pushing him away, out of his child's life. 'A child I hadn't planned on ever having, but that will not stop me from being a father.'

Anger at the way his father had so willingly turned his back on him rushed from the past, threatening to drag him back into the pit of hell he'd lived in as a teenager. All those doubts, the questions, the hatred and the overwhelming sense of worthlessness swirled around him. In one breath it made what he had to do completely clear and in another it clouded it completely.

'Let's get out of here.' He took Lisa's arm, ignoring the startled look she shot at him as he propelled her toward the door.

Outside the cold winter wind, as it whipped wildly around them, the hint of snow wrapped up in it, matched his mood. He sucked in a deep breath and, still holding Lisa's elbow, marched across the car park toward his car. He pressed the remote and the orange lights flashed as the car unlocked.

'You can't just march me out of here and bundle me into the car like a troublesome package.' She lifted her chin and looked at him, the wind snatching at the glorious red hair, reminding him yet again of the morning two months ago when he'd woken to find her in his bed.

Why the hell had he given into lust then? Why hadn't he been able to control the wayward desire and walk away before things had got heated?

Because it was Lisa.

'So you'd rather discuss our marriage, our child, against the backdrop of an office Christmas lunch?' He let go of her arm and shoved his hand deep into his coat pocket, taking away the temptation to prevent her from leaving. If she turned and walked away, left him standing here like the young boy who'd watched his father leave, then he'd know it was all over. He'd know that there was no point.

Lisa didn't move. She stood proudly looking up at him, a haughtiness that was born out of the hurt he'd caused her when he'd told her their marriage was over, that he didn't love her. 'So where are we going?'

'My apartment.'

He saw the shadow of doubt enter her eyes, obliterating the angry spark, then her delicate brows lifted gently. 'Your apartment? Can't we talk here?'

'In this freezing wind?' He opened the passenger car door for her then stood back. 'We need to sort things out, Lisa.'

'Very well, but nothing is happening between us again.'

Her insistence almost made him smile. 'I think enough has happened already, don't you?'

As she slipped into the low sports car he tried to

eradicate the memory of those long legs wrapped around him. Now was not the time to be carried away by lust, but he would have to be careful. As he manoeuvred the car out of the car park and onto the road, joining the busy afternoon traffic, he ignored the fact that Lisa was the only woman who'd made such control impossible. The only woman who had affected him like this.

Lisa looked around the apartment she hadn't been in for months, the memories of her foolhardy expectation of love and happy ever afters almost mocking her from every corner. It felt strange to be here, to be following Max across the polished wooden floor as if the last year hadn't happened.

But it had.

Nothing could erase those words he'd said to her, the admission that he didn't love her, never had and never would. Just as nothing could erase the fact that after one reckless night they had created a new life. A baby that would join them together for evermore, whatever the outcome of this discussion he was so insistent on.

'I should have thought,' he said as he turned from hanging up his coat, waiting to take hers. 'This maybe wasn't the best place. I could have been a little more sensitive.'

She frowned at him, knocked off balance emotionally by the sudden show of consideration. Was it possible that he cared for her still?

'This is far from neutral territory and not the best place to make a deal.' The hint of his Spanish accent had deepened. It tugged at her heart, unleashed memories of happier times and she instantly went into defensive mode.

'We are not making a deal, Max. Our child is not something that can be bartered over.'

'I'm aware of that.' He took her coat from her, the warmth of his fingers brushing against hers, sending a shock wave of heat through her. He'd felt it too, she was sure. His eyes had widened, the darkness of his eyes holding hers. Tension had stretched between them, only breaking when he once again spoke. 'But this has to be settled.'

'We both know we can't remain married, so I don't see any other option but divorce.'

He turned and walked away from her and she watched him, watched the rigid line of his shoulders as he looked out over the river Thames. She couldn't move even though somewhere deep inside her she wanted to, wanted to go to him, tell him she loved him that it was enough for her. But it wasn't. She'd tried that.

'I grew up in Seville.' He turned to face her and she wondered where this was going. They'd never really discussed their past, their childhood. They'd always lived for the moment, which had suited her perfectly.

'So how—?' She stumbled over the question that came to mind after having read the story in the newspaper. 'Your father?'

'How did he have two families and neither knew about the other? Because my mother and I were in Seville and his other family, his wife and legitimate son, were in Madrid. It's only now I realise why we moved to Madrid when I was a young boy, why my mother thought it best to leave behind her family and follow him—my father.'

She blinked a few times and took a deep breath as a

wave of nausea threatened. 'I hope my child never goes through anything like that.'

The words were out before she could stop them. The pain of her childhood blending with the hint that his had been far from filled with love and happiness.

'Then we want the same things, Lisa. A happy home for our child.'

She turned from him, frowning as questions cascaded over her like a torrent of floodwater. He made it sound as if he wanted to give them a chance, to build a happy marriage for their child, but how could that be when she knew he didn't love her and, worse, that he didn't want to be loved?

The heels of her boots made a soft tap as she walked away from him, excruciatingly aware of his gaze following her, taking in every move she made, as if he could read every question, every doubt she had and was preparing his answers, his arguments.

She turned and looked at him. 'We don't have to remain married to give a child that.'

He walked toward her, long strides that brought him far too close to her. 'We owe it to our child to try.'

Her heart ached. He'd said nothing about them. She shook her head slowly. 'No, Max.'

He touched her cheek, the palm of his hand warm, and she sucked in a deep breath. 'We had something good once, Lisa, something that brought us back together and created a child—our child.'

Her heart thumped. Stupidly she thought he was referring to love and to her dismay her eyes fluttered closed, hope filling her.

'That passion is still there, is it not?' Her eyes flew open, not because of the heavy accent of his words, which reminded her of those intimate moments when she could easily fool herself that he loved her, but because of what he considered to be between them.

'Passion isn't enough.' Her hot retort did little to deflect the charm that this man was renowned for.

'But it's something.'

She looked away, desperate to break the heady contact of his dark eyes. Beyond the small but well-equipped office she looked through the window and out over London lying beneath dark heavy clouds. She was about to turn back to him, to tell him that maybe he was right, when papers on his desk caught her attention.

The petition for divorce. On top of the acknowledgement form lay a pen, as if he'd been interrupted in the process of signing it.

Max followed her gaze and looked at his desk, seeing a story he knew she would quickly piece together. The pen lying where he'd dropped it as he'd answered the phone call from his half-brother, Raul, which had thrown everything into disarray—and that had only been the beginning.

Then he'd been poised ready to sign the papers, to end a marriage he'd made in haste, but even before the ringtone of his phone had slashed through his thoughts he'd been unable to do it. Unable to make it so very final.

'You were going to sign them,' Lisa said softly as she looked back to him, and the pain in her eyes clutched at him, stabbing his conscience.

The truth of it all was that even before the phone call his hand had hovered over the form, ready to sign but not able to. Still the shock of receiving them cut deeply.

He'd failed. Just like his father, he'd been unable to be the man he'd promised to be.

'Isn't that what you wanted me to do?' He deflected her question, throwing one back at her, and he knew that if he stood any chance of being in his child's life he had to get Lisa to understand that they needed to remain married.

'Yes,' she said, but the hint of hesitation told him he was finally winning. 'It was.'

'And now that you are carrying my child? Do you still want me to sign them?' He moved away from her, wanting to give her space to think but more importantly to take away the temptation to kiss her.

He looked out over London, the tension in the room notching up as her silence lengthened. He went to his desk, turning the papers round to face him and picked up the pen.

He looked at her, saw the way she bit at her lower lip, her focus on his hand. 'The baby changes nothing, Max. We should never have married.'

'But we did,' he said as he put down the pen and stood tall, his arms folded across his chest. Anything to stop himself from going to her, from trying to kiss some reason into her. She was his wife and the thought of her moving on, of her meeting someone new, lashed at him like icy rain.

'I don't want a reluctant father for my child, Max.'

He drew in a deep breath as her words hit at his biggest insecurity. 'Then we agree on that at least because I want to be there for my son or daughter all the time. Which is why I want to give our marriage another chance.'

'We already know we don't work.'

'I'll make a deal with you, Lisa. We give the marriage one last chance. We live as a married couple for the next two weeks and if by New Year's Eve you still feel the same, I will not contest the divorce and we can both start our lives again.'

'Why?' she asked, her brows furrowing in suspicion. 'You don't love me. You told me that in no uncertain terms.'

Lisa looked at Max as his eyes met hers across the small space of his office. Her heart flipped over and her stomach fluttered just as it always had done when he'd looked at her like that. For her it was all about being in love, but for him it was something different.

'Because we have created a child, our child, and we owe it to that child to at least try.' His words confirmed her thoughts. This was about his conscience, about doing the right thing.

She'd never wanted a divorce. Not because she couldn't admit they'd made a mistake, but because she still loved him. It had been his cold and cruel words after their passionate night that had prompted her to tell him that morning she wanted a divorce and the pain had stung long enough to ensure she'd eventually seen it through.

'Our night together should never have happened.' She turned and glared at him, pushing down her softer side, the one that wanted to fall into his arms and take anything he was offering. She might have been able to do that once, but not any more, not now she had a child to think of.

'So why did it, Lisa?' His voice was deep, gravelly and very sexy.

She bit down hard, keeping the truth inside. There was no way she was ever going to let him know she still loved him. She'd thought her dreams had all come true at once when she'd first met Max and giving up on her dreams was hard. Too hard.

'Far too much wine.' She snapped the words she'd used earlier and turned, leaving the small office and the air that was full of the scent of Max. She couldn't stay here any more, not when every word, every look, made her remember all she'd lost.

'Nothing else?' He taunted her and she stopped, her breathing deep and fast as she looked steadfastly at the door of his apartment, her escape. She wouldn't turn round, couldn't look at him.

'No.' She shook her head and took the final steps to the door but before she could open it Max was in front of her. 'Nothing.'

'But there is something now,' he said all too calmly. 'Our child.'

She clutched at the first thing she could think of to change the subject. 'What about your brother? Aren't you intending to meet him this afternoon?'

'I am meeting my brother...' he paused and lifted his arm to look at his watch, the movement exposing his tanned wrist and, try as she might, she couldn't tear her gaze away '...in one hour. Which means, we will have to continue this discussion later.'

'In that case, I'll go home.' Her blasé reply made his brows rise in a suggestive and incredibly sexy way and she drew in a deep breath.

'You will come with me, Lisa, and afterward, we will call at your apartment to collect all you need to move back in here while we sort things out.'

'Are you mad?'

'Quite possibly.' He smiled, the kind of smile that left her in no doubt he was sure he held all the power. 'But I am not about to allow you to walk away with my child.'

'A child you've never wanted.'

'That may have been the case once, but not any more.'

CHAPTER THREE

MAX'S MIND HAD been a turmoil of thoughts as he and Lisa had made the journey across London to the hotel his brother had suggested for their meeting. One minute he'd been thinking of his brother and how finally meeting him would affect him, and then his thoughts had gone to the child he was now responsible for. How could he be a father when he was the son of a man who'd led a double life, effectively having two families simultaneously?

He looked at Lisa as she sat down in one of the cosy-looking armchairs in the hotel foyer. A wave of unease washed over him as he noticed she was still pale beneath the heavy make-up she nearly always wore. It was her armour, her wall to hide behind. He knew that much at least, although not why. In fact he knew very little about her past. Nothing else had mattered at first because he'd seen the real Lisa, had loved the real Lisa— at least physically.

Then he'd broken her heart because his past meant he couldn't open his heart to hers. He couldn't let himself love her. It was an emotion he wasn't capable of. His father's sudden abandonment had seen to that, not that he'd been around much before he'd walked out for

good. Max had never known where he went for weeks
at a time, but now, finally, he did. He'd gone to his other
family, to his legitimate son and legal wife—leaving
his mistress and his illegitimate son behind.

A stab of hurt pierced into him. He had been nothing more than a bad secret to be swept out of sight. A
child to be avoided, forgotten, not loved and finally
knowing why only intensified the pain. The shadows
cast by his past reached far into the future, destroying
everything. If he hadn't been able to love Lisa, how
could he love his child?

Hell, he really didn't need this guilt now. Not on
top of recent revelations and now today's headlines,
which played to the one thing he hated—being illegitimate. The bastard child of the man who'd broken
his mother's heart and wrecked their lives without so
much as an apology and definitely never an explanation. He'd walked out one night and never come back.
Max had tried to console his mother, but, at eight, that
had been a tall order and yet another failure as far as
he was concerned.

Now he had to face that man's legitimate son. The
son he must have really wanted. His true heir. His half-
brother, Raul, had only said that as part of his will his
father had wanted him found and brought into the family business. So what was this all about? His father's
pathetic attempts to make peace?

He moved away from Lisa and all the complications,
wanting to get this meeting under way. He paused outside the restaurant, took a deep breath and then opened
the doors and walked in. It was empty of anyone except a couple who were locked in a heated debate. They
were lovers, of that there wasn't any doubt, lovers who

hated and loved with equal passion. Neither was he in any doubt that he was looking at his brother.

For a moment Max waivered. If he couldn't do emotions, could he be any kind of brother? Savagely he pushed the thought aside. He'd do this to show his father he wasn't completely cast from the same mould as him.

Lisa's nerves were so taut she could hardly sit still, the events of the day, which had unfolded at breakneck speed, only adding to her nausea. Raised voices had come from the room and the hasty retreat of another woman had made her more anxious. It had all gone quiet now. Too quiet.

'How did it go?' She jumped up from her chair as Max pushed open the door. From the look on his face she already knew the answer to that. She also had so many more questions to ask, not least who was the woman who'd fled the room, almost in tears. What had happened in there?

'As well as such a meeting can go.' He fired the words back at her, his jaw firm and hard, and a tremor of fear slithered down her spine.

'That's it?' Lisa could see the defensive wall being built around him. He was shutting her out, keeping her away from him, from his emotions, just as he always did. Her heart softened. She'd picked the wrong day to tell Max he was going to be a father.

'For now, yes,' he said, but from the frown on his face, the tight set of his jaw, she knew things were far from right.

'Will you see him again?'

Finally, Max looked at her properly, as if he'd buried all the hurt that must have come from meeting a brother he'd never met. 'I will, yes. We have agreed not to let the past cloud the future. In light of the press headlines we will present a united front, but now it's over I can deal with other problems.'

That fear turned to ice, draining any warmth from her body. Was she just another problem to be briefly addressed then pushed aside to be forgotten? 'What other problems?'

'Don't play the innocent with me, Lisa. You know as well as I do that your news this morning is a problem.'

Was he blaming her? The accusation in his dark eyes and laced into every word certainly made it feel like that. Anger fired through her, its heat chasing away the chill of fear. 'One you no longer need to worry about.' Sickness filled her stomach, but she remained strong as she turned to walk away from him, in disbelief as he said nothing to stop her. He thought that little of her and the baby he was letting her simply walk away. She bit down the cocktail of anger and disappointment and continued walking, each step almost killing her.

Max caught up with her and took hold of her arm, bringing her to an abrupt stop. 'Where the hell are you going?'

She whirled round to face him, freeing herself from his grasp. 'As far away from you as possible.'

He looked at her, a frown of worry creasing his brow. 'That will not be possible. You are coming home with me.'

Lisa looked at him with total shock. 'I am not going home with you.'

'We agreed.' His lips pressed into a firm line, but she was too angry, too irrational to care what he thought.

'You agreed and you can't make me.' She knew she

sounded emotionally unstable, but she couldn't help it, not when her body was full of pregnancy hormones, which flung her from highs to lows in just a few seconds. Or was that Max? Was he the one turning everything on its head?

'You are coming home with me. You are my wife.' The feral growl of his voice served only to spike her mutinous anger even higher.

'Only when it suits you, it seems.'

'Don't challenge me now, Lisa. You have just told me you are expecting my child. And that changes everything. We are married and will remain married— living under the same roof.'

Like an angry lion he stood and almost snarled out his demands and instantly she became the defensive woman she'd grown up to be. The need to fight her corner, to stand up for herself and be heard, dominated all her thoughts and she lashed out verbally.

'You might have watched your father walk away but I will not allow that to happen to my child, not when I know what it's like to be despised by my own father and then stepfathers.' She hadn't meant to let the past creep out, but as he took a step toward her, towering over her, she stood steadfast, refusing to be dominated. Ever. Not by anyone, least of all the man she'd married.

'I'm not the only one with a past to hide, or hide behind, am I, Lisa?'

'No, you're not,' she raged against him and the past she'd been trying to escape all her life. She'd thought marrying Max had finally meant that she could put all that behind her, that she could finally settle and make a home, but how wrong she'd been. The situation she had been plunged into meant she had to face that head-on. 'But I'm not the one still running.'

The barb, laced with recrimination, hit its mark. His eyes glittered with anger but she matched his with her own. Being brought up on the wrong side of town had made her always ready to leap to her defence with anger. She didn't need him—or any man. She was more than able to look after herself and now she would do the same for her baby, just as her mother had had to do. But with one difference. She would not be inflicting a constant stream of father figures on her son or daughter. She'd rather do this alone than risk that.

'You think coming here today, meeting a brother I never knew I had, is running away? You think saying we will remain married—living together for the sake of our child—is running away?' He moved closer to her, his intoxicating presence making her head swim, increasing the nausea, but she remained, tall and strong.

'It is not a physical presence that counts. It's more than that and it's something you have already proved you are unable to do when you walked out on our marriage. I'm not going anywhere with you.'

As the words flew like accusing bullets from her lips the nausea took over, weakening her body. The luxury of the hotel foyer blurred and the last thing she could focus on was the Christmas tree, resplendent in gold, its lights twinkling like a thousand stars. She couldn't hold on any longer and slipped into the bliss of soft darkness and the sanctuary it offered.

'Lisa.' She heard Max say her name and smiled weakly. She'd always loved the way his accent lengthened her name, made it sound so exotic and sensual, but this time there was a hint of panic.

In the depths of darkness, she was aware of her body beginning to fall but before she reached the floor Max's arms were around her, his strong and muscled chest now a cushion for her head. She leaned against him, finally finding the will to fight the blackness as she inhaled the scent of the man she loved. The only man she would ever love. A man, by his own admission, incapable of love.

That last thought lingered in her mind like the frost that had covered the ground this morning; its chill revived her mind, her body, bringing everything once more into stinging focus.

'I'm okay.' She pushed against him, but his arms held her tightly. Weariness and confusion muddled her mind.

'Is she all right?' Another male voice, one as strong and commanding as Max's, forced her to open her eyes.

She looked into a handsome face, one so familiar to that of the man whose strong arms now carried her to the chair she'd been sitting in only a short time ago. His brother. Her mind processed the information slowly but she knew that there could never be any doubt about that fact.

'This is my wife, Lisa.' She looked up at Max as his arms slipped from her, allowing her to sit in the chair again, but he stayed, crouched low, at her side, lines of anger on his face, and she wished he could look as concerned for her as his brother did. 'Pregnancy is not agreeing with her.'

Not agreeing with her. How very dared he? *He* was the one who found this pregnancy disagreeable.

'You should take her home. Call the doctor.' The dominating male voice of Max's brother spoke again and she looked up at him, standing over them like a demon.

'That is precisely what I intend to do.' Max stood up, matching his brother's height, and Lisa watched as a silent challenge passed between them, spiking the air with tension. 'I suggest you leave me to my wife and deal with your own issues.'

'My issues?' Even his voice was similar to Max's. The same strength, the same determination. The same icy control.

'She was crying,' Lisa said without thinking, knowing they were referring to the woman who'd fled the restaurant earlier, and both men looked down at her. 'One of you must have said something terrible because she couldn't get out of here fast enough.'

Max looked at his brother. 'As I was saying.'

Raul looked first at her then back to Max. 'I will call you later, to see how your wife is.'

A little flicker of hope leapt to life inside Lisa. Did this mean Max and his brother were to begin building a relationship? Would it prove to Max he did deserve to be loved? It might be enough to bring back the man she'd married, the man who hadn't been afraid to feel her love even if he'd been unable to show any in return. She'd hoped it would be just a case of needing time, but time had only closed him off from her. It had built an impenetrable wall around his heart and locked her out.

'I'm fine now,' she said, and looked into his dark eyes, so like Max's.

Without another word to her or Max his brother turned and strode from the hotel; the sound of London traffic rushed in briefly as the doors opened. Then he was gone and she looked up at Max and knew that the meeting with his brother had changed him, but, from the expression on his face, it wasn't the change she'd briefly hoped for. He was colder and far more distant than ever before.

Max watched his brother walk away. He had looked him in the eye, had assessed him and known without a doubt that his brother was as commanding as he prided himself on being. Raul Valdez possessed the same kind of character, the same depth of determination. The similarities already went much deeper than their physical likeness, of that there was no doubt.

He pushed the jumble of emotions to one side and pulled out his phone and dialled, still unable to believe he'd been told what he should do by the brother he'd only just met. He did, however, agree with him. Memories of his mother and all she'd been through while pregnant with his little half-sister, Angelina, rushed at him. Lisa would see a doctor, his doctor, and then he intended to take her to his home in the suburbs of London, even if that meant dragging her kicking and screaming.

The call connected. 'I'd like to make an appointment for my wife, who is eight weeks pregnant and feeling unwell.'

He saw the confusion and shock on Lisa's face as she registered what he was doing, but right now he didn't care what she thought. All he wanted to do was ensure she was well, that the symptoms were nothing more than to be expected in the early stages of pregnancy.

The very word, pregnancy, struck through him like a sword of fear, reminding him he would be responsible for another human being for evermore, that he would have to somehow find a way past the hurt his father had inflicted on him and connect with that child. But would it be enough? Would his child grow up resenting him as he had his father?

'I don't need to see anyone,' Lisa protested as an appointment time was given to him for later that afternoon.

He ended the call. 'You will see a doctor this afternoon for a scan and that is not negotiable.'

'Why are you doing this?' Lisa looked at him, sparks of anger in her eyes. 'What are you trying to prove and to who?'

'I have nothing to prove, other than to you, it seems. You are my wife, Lisa, and now you are carrying my child so we shall live together once more. We crossed the boundary of professionalism and must now deal with the consequences.'

He watched as a myriad emotions danced across her face, sending a stab of guilt through him, but this wasn't about the two of them any more, this was about a new life—his child.

'I can't do that, Max, not after you walked out on me. What happens when you feel the same again? Am I to stand by and watch you hurt our child? You of all people should understand that.'

The pleading in her voice only increased the fury that erupted like a volcano around him. Was she saying he wasn't capable of being a father? He bit down hard on the bitter taste of the truth, knowing that was exactly what he himself had thought. There was no way he would allow Lisa to know his uncertainties.

'We should have thought about that before spending

a night together.' He was angry at her, at himself. 'But fate has seen fit to bring us together once more and this time it will not be so easy for either of us to walk away, not when our child needs us—both of us.'

If only his father had had those thoughts before he'd indulged in the affair with his mother, before he'd sired two sons within months. *If only* wouldn't help and he was damn sure he wouldn't be like his father. Whatever it took, he would be there for his child and right now that meant taking Lisa to see a doctor and reassuring himself that she and the baby were well.

'Why don't I believe you?' Her voice had softened and he sensed she was giving in.

'Whatever happened in our past has to be put aside, Lisa, for our child's sake.' He lowered his voice and moved a little closer to her, pleased she was no longer standing rigid as if preparing for battle. If anything she looked as if she wanted to be kissed, to be reminded of the passion that had brought them together so spectacularly in the first place.

'But can you really do that for a child you so obviously don't want? Can you rise to the challenge of fatherhood?' She looked up at him and her eyes glittered, not with the anger of earlier, but if he wasn't mistaken with unshed tears.

'I am not going to deny that it will be a challenge, that it is the one thing I never wanted,' he began, choosing his words carefully, just as she had. Using the word challenge had been strategic to say the least and now he would take on that challenge. 'But I will be there for my child, Lisa.'

'And what about me, our marriage? Us?' He refused to be slain by the guilt her words propelled at him and instead reached out to push her hair back from her face, allowing the backs of his fingers to brush down her cheek. Her lashes fluttered and very briefly her eyes closed. Then the moment was gone. The in-control Lisa was back in play. 'There is no us.'

'Once there was and there will be again, for our child's sake. We should spend Christmas together.' He looked into her eyes as he spoke, recalling all the plans they'd made during their first Christmas as a married couple when they had been on honeymoon in the sunshine. He'd learnt his new bride longed for a traditional Christmas in a cottage complete with log fires, but he'd never envisaged spending their next Christmas like this.

She stepped back from him and his touch, determination in her eyes. 'I will give you until New Year's Eve, by which time I am sure you will be asking, no, demanding that I leave—and I will.'

There was fierceness in her voice, but it matched the strength that ran through him. She'd laid down the gauntlet, challenged him to be the one thing he'd never wanted to be. Was she pushing him, using tactics to force him to look his past in the eye and own it?

'New Year's Eve?'

'Yes,' she said firmly.

'Very well, we have a deal. We will remain man and wife—until New Year's Eve.'

CHAPTER FOUR

FOR THE LAST two days Lisa had followed the doctor's advice and had rested. She'd given into Max's demands and stayed at his apartment, the one they'd lived in as a married couple, which played more than she cared to admit on her nerves. Max had veered from being tense, more like an animal confined to a cage it didn't want to be in, to showing concern for her. Today, with just two more days until Christmas Eve, Lisa was beginning to regret agreeing to stay until New Year's Eve. It seemed so far away.

She knew Max wasn't going to change. He didn't have any feelings for her. Never had. That was why their marriage had failed. He couldn't give her his love so would he be able to love his child? She really hoped he could after he'd given her a small hope that they could be the perfect family she'd yearned for since she'd seen how families really lived, and loved, when she'd gone to stay with her best friend at school.

Memories of Max's words, just six months ago, took her back to the day those dreams had crashed around her. It had been at a glamorous summer party in the grounds of a sumptuous house and they had been talking with friends. Friends who had casually dropped into conversation the question of children. As they'd walked away she'd turned and smiled up at him, but the dark look on his face had halted any words.

He'd stood there, with clenched hands and glittering dark eyes. 'I can't give you what you want, Lisa.'

'What is it I want?' Instinct of self-preservation had as usual kicked in and she'd instantly hidden away behind her defence wall.

'Love and happy ever after.' The words were forced out between gritted teeth. 'That's what you want, isn't it?'

'Of course it is.' That had been her response then and it was still the same now.

'I want love, Max, and a happy ever after, which now includes children, and it seems that you are not the man to live this dream with.' A spike of hurt charged through her, but she kept her righteous stance. 'You were right. We should not have married.'

Fog clouded over the memories of the day her world had fallen apart and, fed up with resting, Lisa got up from the chair and picked up the scan image that Max had barely looked at before leaving it on the coffee table. That cursory glance had been as hurtful as his cold and unyielding face the moment the image of their child had appeared on the screen at the private clinic he'd insisted she went to.

What was she going to do? How could she have allowed herself to be talked into this charade, this pretence that everything was going to be just fine? As the questions flowed through her mind in a turbulent rush the nausea returned, bringing with it this time sheer panic.

'You should be resting.' Max's accented voice cut through her thoughts and she looked up at him, the image he created as he dominated the entire room, and as usual made her heart skip a beat. She didn't want to feel anything for him. That would only lead to more disappointment and pain. For her and her baby.

'I can't do this any more, Max.' The words rushed out, desperate to be heard, believed.

'I'm not having this discussion now. You need to rest.' The tension in his body was palpable, but she didn't heed its warning.

He'd confessed that love and happiness were not on his radar, so what else could be making him so cold and distant? News of his brother? Her conscience reminded her that the very same day, even the very same moment she'd told him he was to be a father, he'd seen the true extent of his father's treachery emblazoned across the headlines. Wouldn't that be enough to make any man fear the idea of fatherhood? Well, there was no way she was going to give him the satisfaction of beating down her dreams, of accusing her of things she didn't do— would never do.

'I'm pregnant, not ill.' The fierceness of her voice surprised her as much as it did Max if the quick rise of his brows was anything to go by. 'I should be at work.'

The distance between them seemed to open up and the luxury of his living room became a vast ocean. One she no longer wanted to cross, not when she had no idea what waited for her on the other side. He was the one holding out on her, holding back his emotions. If he forced her to stay she'd keep up the pretence of cold indifference, guard her heart well, until New Year's Eve and then she would leave. At least she could never be accused of not trying to involve him in his son or daughter's life.

'No, Lisa, you should not. If you return to work, it will not be until after New Year and only when I am satisfied you are perfectly well.' The command and control in his voice were clear and she tried hard to fight the need to rebel, the need to revert once again to the capricious teenager she'd hidden behind.

'I can't stay here like a pampered princess. That's not me, Max. I need to be out doing something.' She swung round and glared at him, instantly regretting the fast movement as her head spun. 'Like buying a Christmas tree.'

'A Christmas tree?' He looked perplexed and if she weren't feeling so headstrong she might have laughed at him then kissed him. But that was before she'd discovered who he really was. Actions such as those belonged to the short and very false marriage they'd shared.

'Of course, a Christmas tree. It's only a matter of days until Christmas and there isn't one bit of sparkle and cheer in this apartment.'

'I don't do Christmas.' He glowered at her.

'Too emotional for you?' She prodded him, like the mouse that just couldn't leave the sleeping cat alone. 'What about visiting family? Do you indulge in that?'

The thought of staying here locked away in an apartment that didn't have any hint of Christmas in it was too much. She loved Christmas. It was the one time of year she felt hope, felt that dreams could come true. She loved the magic of the season even though it had never reached inside her childhood home. Now she was trapped here with a man who didn't believe in love or the festive season. How had she ever fallen for a man so opposite to her?

Because he never revealed his true self.

'Visit family?' He crossed the room toward her and even though they were physically closer the distance between them seemed as vast as it had when he'd walked into the room. 'Do you need to visit your family?'

Shock hit her like icy water. Visit her family? She wished now they had talked more before their short marriage, wished that she'd confided in him about her past, one she'd always strived to hide. But she hadn't been able to tell him how much she resented her mother for the unsettled childhood she and her older stepbrother had experienced. How she now blamed her mother for all the trouble he had got into? She hadn't wanted to taint what she and Max had found by sharing the darkness of her childhood with him. Better it stayed hidden away.

'No, I do not.' She snapped the words out as emotions cascaded over her. Whatever was the matter with her? Was it simply pregnancy hormones that made her so sensitive, so very emotional, or was it being forced into close proximity with the man she'd once loved with abandon, hoping it would be enough, that one day he would love her too?

She moved to the window and focused her attention on the view of London beyond the apartment, thinking of her mother and older stepbrother that'd made up the mainstay of the dysfunctional family she was part of. The constant visits by the police looking for her brother and the ever-changing partners in her mother's life were exactly what she'd hoped to escape when she'd married Max. How very wrong she'd been. Now her child seemed doomed to be part of a family where broken promises and part-time fathers were normal. It was the last thing she'd ever wanted and not at all what she would have chosen.

'Then I want you to rest as the doctor suggested—especially as we will be travelling to Madrid tomorrow.' Max's words snapped her back into the moment, but the fizz of anger didn't abate.

She turned to look at him, frowning in confusion. 'Madrid?'

'*Sí*, Madrid. Raul and Lydia are getting married.' There wasn't a drop of emotion, good or bad in his words. Did he still resent his brother?

She kept her thoughts to herself. Safer to stay on the topic of discussion. 'On Christmas Eve?'

'*Sí*, on Christmas Eve.' He crossed the room and joined her at the window. His profile was stern as he looked absently out over London. 'And I have promised we will be there. He is my family.'

The pointed remark to their discussion of moments ago wasn't lost on her. Did he really consider Raul Valdez as family? She wasn't entirely convinced a man who rebuffed emotions as if he had a bat in his hand could suddenly become sentimental over a brother.

Max glared at the skyline of London and tried to push down the annoyance of what he'd learnt of his brother's impending nuptials. He felt a failure in the shadow of the love Raul had admitted he had for Lydia, the woman who'd been at their first meeting for a short while. As he stared unseeingly at London, beneath a winter-grey sky, he became acutely aware of Lisa's questions as if she'd spoken the words aloud. Was Raul his family? Did he belong or deserve to be named as such when the only other person he thought of like that was the mother he'd lost when he was fourteen and his little sister, now almost twenty-one and living her own life.

'It was obvious there was something between them from the very first moment I saw them, but I did not expect this.' He tried to divert the attention from himself, from what was happening here between him and Lisa. As his wife, wasn't she his family too?

'Didn't you expect it, Max? Do you think all men should be so against committing themselves emotionally—for life?'

Her green eyes fired her anger at him, anger he knew would take a long time to cool, unless his rapidly forming plans would salve it. He had no intention of pretending that all was okay. He knew she still wanted that happy-ever-after nonsense and that his mixed messages, thanks to his wildly changing emotions, were making her colder toward him. Angry, even, and he had no intention of arriving in Spain with a wife that was obviously angry at him. He didn't want Raul to think he had triumphed where his new older brother was failing—completely and utterly failing.

'I didn't expect Raul to rush into marriage, not when they were so obviously poles apart the day I met him.'

'Some couples fall out and make up, Max,' Lisa insisted, with a jaunty rise of her brow, just as she had done that night when a business dinner had become a night of explosive sex. 'It's part of the fun of being a couple, being in love.'

'That's not love, that's just sex.' The words were out before he could stop them, the anger in them clear.

Lisa looked at him, not saying a word, and the tension in the room became unbearable until she moved away from him, giving him some sort of relief from having her so close. So entwined in his life when he'd already proved and she'd admitted that he wasn't the man she needed, the man who could love her unconditionally.

'Maybe it's something you should attend on your own.' Her words were soft, almost wistful, but beneath that he could detect the steely hardness she used to deflect the world and anyone who threatened to hurt her. He'd never found out why, content that she wanted to keep the secrets of the past as much as he did. It suited him well, as did the hot passion they'd shared. But things had suddenly changed—too much.

'Oh, no, Lisa, that is not about to happen. You and I will go together—as husband and wife.' He moved toward her, saw the surge of defiance in her eyes, which sparked angrily at him, a stark contrast to her pale face. He would have to calm his anger. He might not have wanted to create a child, but he had and he wouldn't now do anything to jeopardise his baby or Lisa.

He hadn't decided if taking Lisa to Madrid was an excuse to keep her close or the competition of being the better brother, but all he knew was that she had to be there with him. He needed to see for himself that she rested, that she was taking care of herself as the doctor had instructed. Just as his mother should have done. He was adamant that they would remain married and very sure that he would do anything necessary to make her want to stay with him beyond New Year's Eve. He wanted to be the father he'd never had. He just wasn't sure if he could.

'What, to show we are so happily married?' The accusation was stinging—and true as her words flew at him, dragging him back from thoughts that would only lead to the past, to the pain of losing his mother so soon after his baby sister was born. He might only have been a teenager then, but he wasn't about to take any chances with his unborn child. At least not until he was sure everything was as it should be.

'Happily or not, we are married, Lisa, *and* expecting our first child. That at least you cannot deny.'

Her anger sparked across the room like lightning and he pushed down the irrational guilt. He wasn't the only one who'd walked out on this marriage. Lisa had done the same the morning after the night that had changed their lives. Had she come to find him, tell him about the baby because she'd already known his world was falling apart around him?

It wasn't the first time such a mutinous thought had occurred to him. He knew that Lisa had married him because she'd loved him. She'd told him often enough, but his constant silence had not been what she'd been looking for, what she'd wanted to hear. He didn't tell lies, he'd had enough of those in his childhood to know how destructive they could be, but his reluctance to say those three words she most wanted to hear had finally made staying with her impossible. Walking out had been the only option, before he hurt her any more than he already had done. Was this all about revenge, about making him feel the same pain?

'No, I can't, but I wish I could walk away from you, this time for ever. I know what it's like to have a part-time father, then stepfathers drifting in and out of my life when it suited them—or my mother.'

An unwanted wave of sympathy washed over him after his angry thoughts about her motives and he moved toward her, wanting to offer comfort, reassurance—anything to make her feel better. This was the first time she'd allowed him to see into the window of her childhood and he guessed it wasn't the happy picture she'd always tried to portray or hide behind.

'So, it seems we both have our own motives for remaining married.' He locked away his emotions, becoming the cold, detached businessman he'd been since a car accident had halted his footballing career five years ago.

'It looks that way. When do we leave for Madrid?' She was as cold as he was, proving, if nothing else, that any of those softer and sentimental emotions she'd once had for him had well and truly been buried—and it suited him perfectly. Emotions complicated things. Emotions only led to pain.

'I have chartered a private jet to ensure your comfort. We leave tomorrow morning.'

Initially, he thought she was going to challenge him, but after a moment of those green eyes scrutinising him, she nodded. 'When do we return?'

'As soon as the wedding celebrations are over. I have plans here in England for the festive season.'

Now he felt the full force of her suspicion. 'What plans?'

He wasn't about to reveal anything yet, but her talk of wanting a Christmas tree reminded him of the one occasion they'd talked about anything to do with their past. She'd told him how her family had never had time or the inclination for festive celebrations, that Christmas was something she'd missed out on as a child. He might not be able to feel love, but he wanted to make her happy, prove he could enter into the façade of family life being forced on him, even though he had no intention of engaging his emotions. With this in mind, he'd put in motion arrangements for the kind of festivities his mother had loved—the kind he'd never had since her death.

'Plans that will prove to you we can bring our child up together. Offer it all neither of us had. You gave me until New Year's Eve to prove that our child will be better off brought up by married parents and not divorced parents and that is precisely what I will do.'

Lisa swallowed down the bitterness of the truth of what he'd said. Max was right. They needed to find common ground, find a way to remain married and bring up their child, but the little girl who'd watched her own father leave, only to see her mother replace him with a new one, then others as the years went by, didn't want to muddle through her marriage and parenthood. She wanted to be a happy, loving parent with Max, create the solid foundations for the kind of life she'd never had. The other option was to raise her child alone—completely—unlike her mother who even now couldn't face life alone, constantly searching for the next man to live with for a year or so.

As far as she was concerned, Max would either be a full-time father or a permanently absent one. For her there were no halfway measures, not when she knew the effects of being brought up like that. She knew only too well what it was like to be that child, to blame yourself for your father leaving, to wonder what you'd done, never thinking it had been something totally unconnected with her. She also knew what it was like to have a stepfather who bullied her into submission. Not that he'd ever laid a hand on her, but there was more than one way to bully someone.

'Can you do that, Max?' she challenged him, all thought of Christmas and New Year evaporating. 'Can you be in your child's life all the time when, judging by your reaction to the news, fatherhood is not something you want?'

He came toward her and she looked at him, her challenge still lingering in the air. 'My reaction, as you so nicely put it, was due not only to being told you were pregnant, but to the headlines about me and my brother—and, if I am honest, the initial thought that you had known about that and hadn't told me.'

'But you still wouldn't have been overjoyed.' Lisa ignored the reference to that moment when she'd realised they had been talking at cross purposes, determined to keep the focus on what was important. The baby. After several meetings over the last few days he'd sorted things with Raul and now it was time to sort things with her. Deep inside her, she hankered after the man who'd melted her with just one kiss, the man who'd loved her physically with a passion so intense it still burned in her memory. She wanted that man now, but each time the baby was mentioned the chances of that seemed to slip further and further away.

'No, I would not.' The truth lashed at her like icy rain and she steeled herself against it, but the onslaught continued. 'Our marriage broke up because we are too different. You wanted love from me and children too. The truth is, the only thing that ever existed between us was passion. It's what brought us together and ultimately what pushed us apart.'

For him that was true, but she couldn't say that now.

If she did she'd be admitting she'd had feelings for him, deep feelings of love that she knew he could never return. It was that realisation as she'd watched him get dressed that morning after their night together that had made her see that. It had only ever been about passion—or was it merely lust? Whatever it was, love had never entered into it for him. She had just become another of his deals, his challenges to master and command.

In total contrast to everything she wanted to feel, her body heated with something distinctly like lust as he moved very close to her, his dark eyes full of unveiled desire. Her heart almost stopped beating as he reached out and lifted her chin slightly with his thumb and finger. 'I also think that passion still exists, that, however much you glare at me with sparks of anger in your sexy eyes, you want me as much as I want you.'

Why was he doing this? Why was he torturing her so?

'That's absurd.' It should have been a hot denial, but the husky undertone to her voice said far too much about the effect he was having on her. The light touch of his thumb and finger on her chin was pure torment but she couldn't step back, couldn't move away. She wanted him, wanted his touch that could lead to a kiss so powerful that it would render her unable to fight him at all.

'Is it?' His voice was far too sexy but she refused to give into the urge to close her eyes, to surrender to his touch, his will.

'Of course it is.' She'd wanted to snap the words out, to make it very clear how cross she was, how she hated what he was doing to her, the power he had over her, but they came out as a ragged whisper.

'I disagree,' he said softly. Too softly. 'Passion is

what brought us back together two months ago, Lisa, and it's what will keep us together.'

He had that look in his eyes, that sexy come-to-bed look that she'd never been able to resist but this time she would. This time, she wouldn't fall for it or him and she most certainly wouldn't be falling into his bed.

'No way.' She stepped back from him, noticing for the first time that the apartment was now much darker, that the light outside had faded, creating a very different ambiance from the one she'd felt as she'd walked through the door of his apartment a few days ago.

'No way, what, Lisa?' he teased.

'No way am I falling back into your bed—ever again.'

To her horror he moved closer, closing the distance between them. His eyes were so dark, so heavy with desire and she couldn't help the leap of need that jumped into life within her, defusing the anger she'd been harbouring all afternoon.

'Are you quite certain about that?' His husky voice and heavy accent left her in no doubt that passion and desire were fighting for supremacy within him too.

'Yes.' The whisper was barely audible, but he'd heard it and she wondered if he could hear her heart thumping too, hear the beat so loudly, calling to him.

Max gathered her unresisting body against his, the masculine smell of his aftershave doing untold things to her senses, making her want him, want to be in his arms, to feel his lips on hers. But she had to resist, had to hold onto her control, her sanity.

'Very sure.' She pushed at his chest, trying hard to ignore the muscles beneath her palms. 'Just as I am about the fact that by New Year's Eve you will have tired of me, of being the expectant father and maybe even playing the role of diligent brother, which will leave me free to return to my life.'

'So I have until New Year's Eve to prove this theory of yours wrong?' The velvet edge to his deep voice sent tremors of awareness over her and she fought to remain rigid and still as she glared at him angrily—although that anger was directed as much at herself as at him.

'But you won't prove anything, Max.'

'Are you quite sure about that, Lisa?'

She wanted to shout at him, to rail against the way her body even now wanted to feel his touch, his caress. Instead she stepped calmly away, accepting that distance was her only defence right now.

'Absolutely sure.'

He smiled. 'Then I look forward to attending my brother's wedding with my wife at my side.'

'That will only be temporary. I know you don't want to be married, much less a father.'

'But we are married, Lisa. And I am going to be a father to my child. A proper father.'

CHAPTER FIVE

IF LISA HAD thought being in Madrid with Max at Christmas might soften his hard mood, she was quickly realising that was not the case. Since their arrival yesterday he'd been courteous yet as distant as a stranger. That last night in London he'd just been proving his power over her, proving that desire and passion still simmered between them—waiting.

They had left their hotel early that morning and now Lisa found herself shivering against the unusually cold winter winds, in a much less salubrious area than that of the hotel. The kind of area she'd grown up in. Surely Raul Valdez, with all his millions, wasn't getting married anywhere near here.

'What are we here for?' she asked tentatively, pulling the collar of her coat tighter around her neck.

Max seemed impervious to the cold, his attention focused on the shabby apartment buildings and one in particular. 'This is where my mother and I lived after we left Seville.'

Lisa's mind reeled. Max was a billionaire in his own right and his stepfather was well known in the world of football. She'd never for one moment considered that Max knew what it was like to live on the wrong side of town.

'I never knew.' Her voice was soft, full of thought as she looked around her, turning to see a football ground beyond. It was very different from the grounds of the clubs that Max invested in. 'Did you start your football career here?'

Finally, he turned to look at her and for the briefest of moments she thought she saw sadness in his eyes. Then he blinked and the usual, ever-present guard was back in place. The protection he always wore.

'My mother moved us to Madrid soon after my father walked out. I thought at the time we were just making a new start, now I know she was hoping that, by being close to him, she could change his mind.' His jaw clenched as he turned to look once more at the three-storey apartments. 'And yes, I started playing football here seriously. It's also where my mother met my stepfather, when she would stand on the sidelines cheering me on, trying to be the father figure I was lacking.'

Lisa's heart wrenched as she thought of the young boy he'd been. 'Maybe your father did a good thing leaving you both to build a new life.'

She was talking from her own experience, from the heartache of being stuck in the middle of warring parents, but the deep inhaled breath that prevented Max from saying anything warned her that was not what he thought at all.

'I'm sorry.' She stumbled over her words. 'I didn't mean it like it sounded.'

'We should go,' he said and turned to walk back to the waiting car, the driver having kept the engine turning over.

As the car negotiated the busy streets, past landmarks she longed to stop and see, Max sat coldly beside her and that coldness continued after they arrived at the wedding venue. There wasn't even the smallest amount of tenderness from him, not this morning when her pregnancy had left her nauseous and he'd rushed her out early, and definitely not now as she stood waiting, the cold making her shiver again. Or was it the revelations of this morning? Either way, nobody could have ever guessed they were a married couple, least of all the few assembled guests awaiting the arrival of Lydia, Raul's bride.

Lisa pulled the softness of her black coat around herself and tried to focus on what was going on around her. Expectation hung in the air of the old town hall as the few assembled guests awaited the arrival of the bride. She glanced at Max as he sat at her side and then at Raul, who waited calmly for Lydia's arrival. Had Max been as calm the day they'd married?

The sun had shone that day and she'd thought she was the luckiest woman on earth. She was so in love, so full of the promise of her happy ever after, yet within a few months all that had crumbled away with Max's admission that he couldn't love her.

Lisa pushed the memories aside as her doubts began to build, increasing to such a level she could barely sit still. Why was she even here? As the thought careered around in her mind like an out-of-control horse, the bride made her entrance. Lisa had always loved attending weddings, loved to admire the bride, but this time her focus was on the groom. Although she'd met him briefly after that first meeting, she hadn't been feeling well. He was so like Max they could be twins, not mere half-brothers.

It was the love in Raul's eyes as he watched his

bride come nearer that had her so transfixed she could scarcely breathe. There was no doubt that he loved her—completely and utterly. The smile on his lips held a secret message, known only to the bride and groom. Her heart ached and began to crack into pieces. Max had never looked at her like that and certainly not on their wedding day. He'd never shown any sign of love because he couldn't.

'I can't love you, Lisa. I can't love anyone.'

The words he'd cruelly delivered just months after they'd exchanged vows still cut deep. She'd been so in love with him, so sure he'd come to love her, she'd clung to the hope, like a thirsty woman in the middle of the desert, that one day he'd love her as she did him. That had never happened. To him it had been only lust. Nothing more than undeniable passion, which had blazed between them since they'd first met.

She moved, physically shivering as the icy memories invaded the present, desperate not to allow her emotions to get the better of her, but in doing so she brushed against Max. He stiffened instantly beside her and she risked a quick glance at him. His profile was stern, his focus on his brother as Lydia joined him. Then he looked at her and the steel in his eyes turned her and her battered heart to stone.

'I would never have guessed.' His whispered words held a feral edge, as if he were a wild animal afraid he'd be cornered at any moment. She knew exactly what he meant. She'd seen the love there, the very emotion he couldn't feel, couldn't give.

'That they could be so in love?' She goaded him, wanting some kind of emotion from him. Even anger was better than this distant, cool reserve.

The sound of his breath being sucked in made a few heads turn their way, but the fierce connection his eyes had made with hers was too strong to break. 'That the might of Raul Valdez would be so weak. He must be doing what is expected. Going through the motions.'

'Faking it?' Her gasped whisper once again made heads turn their way, but she wasn't going to let this go now. Not when she was finally getting somewhere, finally able to talk about the emotions that had made him marry her, then walk away. 'Like you did?'

'*Sí.*' His eyes hardened, challenging her to say more, and she wished they were alone, that they were anywhere else. But this was Raul and Lydia's day and she wasn't going to spoil it and, damn him, he knew it too. She glared back at him, matching his challenge, his anger. She held his gaze for several long seconds, then turned without a word and focused once more on the bride and groom.

Raul was the epitome of command as he stood, resplendent in a black suit worn with a pale blue tie, and even though it was Max who had stolen her heart she had to admit his brother was strikingly handsome. Lydia wore a white cape, the hood trimmed with fur, over her wedding dress, looking every bit the winter fairy-tale bride.

Lisa watched stoically as they exchanged their vows, their rings and then kissed one another. They didn't take their eyes from each other as they stayed locked in their world of love.

Max had done all that with her. The vows, the rings exchanged, the look and then the kiss, but none of it had been for real, none of it had been love. She clamped her teeth together against the threat of tears, cursing the pregnancy hormones that seemed to make crying her default emotion right now. No, she would not cry. She would never let Max know how much he'd hurt her—or that she cared.

She kept up that pretence as the guests assembled for the wedding breakfast, hardly daring to look at how happy and radiant the bride looked. It was hard to believe she was the same woman Lisa had seen leaving the restaurant in London so hurriedly just a few days ago. Did that mean there was hope for her and Max? That they could put aside their differences and fall in love again?

Again? Who was she kidding? Max had never loved her. That was the one difference. Raul had obviously loved Lydia despite the fallout that must have happened, probably all due to the stress of discovering and meeting his brother.

Beside her, she felt Max inhale deeply as an older woman talked with Raul, looking at them, and then she walked toward them. Instantly on alert, Lisa guessed this must be Raul's mother, the woman his father had left Max and his mother to be with all those years ago. As she tried to process this, the woman spoke to Max in Spanish and, judging from his curt and brief response, it wasn't good.

She risked a glance at Max to see his jaw was set in that stubborn way she knew only too well and she wished she understood what the woman had said, and if it was even Raul's mother.

Then the older woman looked at Lisa and spoke in heavily accented English. 'I am happy that my son has found love, but it is strange, is it not, that both the Valdez sons have taken an English bride?'

Her voice was warm, friendly. She wasn't merely making a comment, it was accepting Max, a way to bridge the gap between them. She didn't have to do that. It must be the hardest thing to face the son of your husband's mistress. Lisa smiled at her, but she could feel Max's anger, feel him bristle with indignation. She didn't need to look at him to know that.

'I am *not* a Valdez.' Max's response was harsh and razor sharp.

Raul's mother looked at him and continued in her accented English, obviously wanting Lisa to understand. 'You may not like to admit it, but you are. More than you will ever know.'

'I think not.' The growled response was fierce, full of denial.

'You are, Max. There is no doubt that you are Maximiliano's son and it is far more than good looks which makes me say this.' Raul's mother looked into his eyes and Lisa could see her expression soften. This was a woman who didn't blame him, didn't hate him and was extending the hand of friendship. Maybe she knew he'd lost his mother as a teenager and all too soon after losing his father.

Further thoughts were cast aside as Max cursed in Spanish. 'I have no wish to be like my father.'

Raul's mother turned and looked back at her son and Lisa wondered how this was all really affecting her. Then she turned her attention back to Max and touched him gently on the arm. Max looked down at her hand, a stark contrast to charcoal grey of his suit. She saw Max swallow, as if he was trying to gulp down the pain of the past, and Lisa realised she knew very little of it—just as he knew very little of her.

Finally, after what seemed like an eternity, she spoke in a hushed tone, but still in English. 'There is no denying you are his son, just as there is no denying you are Raul's brother. Don't run from the truth, Max, face it. Own it. Make it your friend, not your enemy.'

Lisa frowned. What was this woman talking about?

'Thank you for your advice, *signora*. I will give it some thought, but right now my wife and I need to leave.'

'We do?' Lisa sensed there was more to this conversation if only he'd participate in it, but she also knew Max and pushing him to do anything he didn't want to do was useless.

He put his arm around Lisa in a show of affection she knew wasn't real, pulling her close, and that instant spark of heat surged through her, much to her annoyance. 'We are returning to England for Christmas.'

'How romantic.' Raul's mother smiled at her. 'It looks like you don't need my advice after all.'

Lisa hid her confusion behind a bright smile of her own. What was he talking about? Christmas in England? With Max?

Max looked at Raul's mother, questioning if the genuine warmth in her voice and soft brown eyes was really directed at him—her husband's secret love child. A stab of something approaching jealousy pierced him as he thought of his own mother, her unhappiness after his father, this woman's husband, had left. He recalled the defeat in everything she'd done since that day. Even though she'd found a gentle and loving man in his stepfather, she'd never had the will to properly fight her can-

cer and by the time Angelina had brought a smile back
to her face, it was too late to win that particular battle.

Life had been cruel and hard for his mother. When
her cancer diagnosis had been confirmed she was pregnant and her choice at that time was to delay treatment
and save the baby. She only got to spend a few years
with her new daughter. Max hated the memories from
those dark days. He'd ignored his sister once he'd been
told the full truth of her illness, but his mother had
talked him round, made him see it had been her choice
and then extracted his promise to look after Angelina.
He was now her fiercest protector, although he knew
she thought of him as nothing more than a tyrant big
brother. At least it didn't involve emotions that way.

He refocused his mind, determined not to get sidetracked by the past. 'Lisa and I spent last Christmas in
the sunshine for our honeymoon. I intend to give Lisa
the Christmas she has always dreamed of.'

'Very romantic.' Raul's mother smiled at Lisa and he
felt her body freeze next to him, as if the hardest frost of
the winter had descended. Lisa obviously had no intention of being romantic with him, but would his planned
surprise soften her? Would it show her he could play
the role of dutiful husband and protective father without the need for love to complicate it all?

'It will be fun, if not romantic,' Lisa said resolutely,
looking anywhere but at him. She might have missed
Raul's mother's frown, but he didn't. Life had taught
him to look beyond mere words, to look for more in a
person's actions. It was the only way to safeguard himself and those around him from dangerous emotions
that only caused upset and pain. The kind of emotions
he would never expose himself to again.

Raul's mother reached out and laid her hand on his arm for a second time. This time he had to fight hard against the instinct to pull away, avoid any kind of contact. It was his default setting, but somehow he managed not to. Instead he looked at her, trying to decipher what was really going through her mind.

'I don't blame you for any of this,' she said, looking directly and earnestly into his eyes, just as his mother had done the day she'd told him the truth about his father, knowing she didn't have long. Savagely, he pushed that to the back of his mind. 'And neither must you blame yourself.'

'There is only one person to blame and he is no longer with us to accept that blame.' The harsh words rushed from him in an uncustomary display of hurt. He took a deep breath, determined to lock himself back behind his barrier, his wall of protection. She was getting too close. The only other woman to have got that close to his emotions since his mother had died was Lisa. And that had done neither of them any good.

Raul's mother spoke again, this time in fluid Spanish. Was it because she didn't want Lisa to know or was it because it was truly meant? But as he watched her turn and walk away, mingling with other guests, the pain of his childhood began to resurface.

'I'm guessing that wasn't good.' Lisa's voice jolted him back to the present, thankfully shutting away the past, the pain and knowledge that he didn't deserve the kind of happiness she'd been looking for when they'd married.

'Apparently I am like my father, but I don't have to be.'

Lisa's perplexed expression reassured him that he

wasn't the only one who was unable to decode whatever message was within that statement, but her next words threw that into disarray.

'You are also like your brother,' she said tentatively, her green eyes ever watchful.

Was she still holding out for love and happiness, the kind that sparked around the bride and groom? Raul had confessed on their very first meeting in London that he didn't do emotions and that had been the fine thread that had pulled them together, allowing them to bond. Two brothers rejected by the same man. Either Raul was a liar or a very good actor.

He shook his head in denial. 'We might look similar, but that is where it ends.'

He looked over at Raul as he lowered his head to kiss Lydia and even he could see the love between them. From the other side of the room he could feel it, heavy in the air. The man was a liar. A damn good one. He did do emotions and the most painful one of all.

'Are you sure?' Lisa's breathy whisper irritated him, sure as he was that it was intended to evoke emotions from him. What was she pushing him to admit? That he loved her, that they too would find the happiness Raul and Lydia had? Well, she'd be disappointed.

'Absolutely, now if we are to arrive in England on time, we should leave now.' He changed the subject, diverted her attention, hoping to distract her from the destructive course the conversation had veered to after Raul's mother had left them.

'They have only just said their vows,' Lisa implored, her green eyes full of confusion. 'We can't leave now.'

'We can and we will.' He put his arm in the small of her back, ignoring the jolt of heat that rushed through him, and gently but firmly propelled her through the guests. 'After we wish the bride and groom well.'

Before Lisa could process what was happening, a radiant Lydia was smiling at her. 'I hear congratulations are in order, that you are Max are going to be parents.'

'Yes.' This was the hardest bit of acting she'd done since arriving in Madrid.

Raul and Max were suddenly deep in conversation, turned slightly away, and Lisa had never felt so excluded. Lydia must have noticed. 'They are talking about their father's will. It seems he'd had help all along from one very corrupt member of the board, but I bet he never expected Raul to find his brother and welcome him into the business *as well as* get married.'

Lydia's light laughter didn't quite disguise the undercurrent of seriousness of her words and Lisa vowed to ask Max about it later. In fact, maybe now would be a good time to find out more about the man who was her child's father. But that would mean revealing more about herself, her childhood brought up on the wrong side of town where police visits to her house happened with alarming regularity.

'Lisa and I will look forward to seeing you in London for Angelina's twenty-first birthday party.' Max's words dragged her mind back from the brink of those dark days as he pulled her close against him in a pretence of affection.

'We wouldn't miss it.' Raul's deep and accented voice was so like Max's it was hardly believable.

'You're not going on honeymoon?' Lisa asked before giving it any thought.

'My wife is a romantic,' Max said quickly as if it was

something to apologise for, the sting of hurt bringing heat to her cheeks.

'Then you are very lucky,' Raul said as he looked into his wife's eyes, making a connection that almost excluded her and Max. 'And so too am I.'

'I think we should leave you two alone.' Max's stern voice hardly dented the aura of love in the air and the newly-weds barely noticed. 'Especially as I have *romantic* plans in England.'

Lisa had resisted the urge to ask any further questions as the small jet plane had flown to England. The dark and brooding scowl on Max's face had been enough to see to that, but with each passing hour his mood had deepened and she was beginning to feel he was further away than ever from her. Unreachable.

She'd never imagined Christmas Eve would be like this. It had gone from the wonderful moment of seeing two people in love say their vows to a cold and stony silence that was frostier than the weather they'd returned to. That silence had deepened, becoming more Arctic as a sleek black car had pulled up at the steps of the plane and Max had ushered her into the passenger seat and then settled himself in the driver's seat. They had left the airport and driven, not toward his London apartment as she'd thought, but out into the darkness of the countryside.

'This is where we will be spending Christmas.' His deep and all too sensual voice shocked her as he spoke in the darkness of the car. His gaze was firmly fixed on the road ahead, lit by the strong beams of the car's headlights, as he manoeuvred his sleek sports car off the main road and onto a smaller one. Around them was nothing but darkness. She had no idea where they were. All she knew was that they'd left London behind over an hour ago.

'Where are we?' The mystery was too much for her tired mind, but as the car turned another corner, a cottage, festooned in festive lights, sprang from the darkness of the countryside. The yellow glow of lights from the windows warned her they were arriving at someone else's home. One very much occupied.

'You wanted Christmas and if my memory serves me right, your idea of Christmas, something like this.' There was the faintest hint of amusement in his voice, but she wasn't going to be fooled or lulled into a false sense of security, not after the hard and cold mood he'd been in all day.

'But I told you that a long time ago. Before we were married.' Inwardly she cursed herself for saying that word, for reminding them both of the issues that lay between them.

'You did. You said you'd always imagined spending it at a cosy country cottage, complete with Christmas lights and a log fire.' He moved toward her in the darkness of the car, the leather of the seat scrunching softly above the subtle hum of the engine. Her heart leapt as she inhaled his scent. Why did she have to react so acutely to him?

'I never thought…' Her voice trailed off in a whisper. He'd done this for her?

'I give you exactly that.' He looked over at her as he turned off the engine stopped and an expectant silence filled the car, wrapping around them. 'Christmas in a country cottage.'

'But whose cottage is it?' It was late on Christmas

Eve and she wanted to know just whose Christmas they would be descending on.

'Ours—for Christmas, that is.'

'And you did all this?' He'd remembered all she'd said when they were dating, how she'd never had a Christmas that had been special, how she'd wanted the tree, the trimmings, the lights and champagne in front of an open fire. Didn't that mean something? That he cared?

'You doubt that I could be a family man, one who cares, and this is my way of showing you otherwise.' A determined firmness entered his voice but she refused to spoil the moment by thinking too hard about what he'd just said. She didn't want to acknowledge the true implications of this. She just wanted to enjoy this special moment, imagine this was how they really were.

'I can't believe it,' she said as she opened the car door and got out, smiling at the traditional wreath hanging on the green-painted door. It was her dream Christmas and the man who claimed not to be able to love her had brought her here.

The night air was cold and crisp. Exactly what she'd always imagined in her idea of a perfect Christmas. The only glitch was that she'd imagined spending it with the man she loved, one she'd foolishly thought had loved her too. If she put that notion to one side, she could make a memory to hold onto, one to cherish when the clock struck midnight on New Year's Eve and all this pretence of affection, of wanting to be a father, came crashing down.

'I hope you like it because we are here until we return to London for Angelina's birthday party and then there will, of course, be the New Year's Eve party.'

His breath hung in the air, clouding around her, and she smiled up at him. Surely it meant something? He wouldn't have gone to all this trouble otherwise. The pain and anger which had built up since they'd gone their separate ways thawed even as the night air chilled.

'I won't know until I see it,' she teased him, anxious now to see what his idea of the perfect Christmas cottage was like inside and trying hard to stifle the hope that he really did want her and the baby in his life. To allow that hope to grow would be foolish.

He smiled at her. Warmth filled his eyes that she hadn't seen for a long time and her heart constricted with the effort of not letting her love show. She wanted to reach up and kiss his lips, to snuggle against him and be held in his arms.

'Very well.' He took out a key from his pocket and opened the door, the old key turning in the lock, sounding loud in the dark stillness of the winter night.

She pushed open the door and the heat from inside the cottage rushed at her. The scent of Christmas filled the air as he followed her in, but having him standing so close behind her made her feel weak as her legs trembled. She tried to ignore it, looking around the festive feast of decorations in the room, of which a real tree was the centrepiece.

It stood beside the fire, which glowed with orange warmth, creating the perfect scene. Beneath the tree were presents and its branches were heavy with coloured baubles and lights. How had he managed to arrange all this? The fact that he had even thought of it infused her with hope. Maybe he wasn't so immune to her or the idea of fatherhood. Maybe there was a future for them.

'I love it,' she whispered as she pulled her cashmere scarf off and walked into the room. 'But how did you manage all this when we were in Madrid?' With arms wide she gestured around her. The whole room looked as if the owners had just stepped outside for a moment.

'I rented the cottage and specified exactly what I wanted, even down to the mistletoe.' He moved closer to her and pulled her toward him and under the piece of mistletoe adorned with white berries. The darkening of his eyes left her in no doubt that Christmas decorations were the furthest thing from his mind right now and her resolve to keep her distance melted like ice in front of the fire.

'Thank you.' She moved toward him, wanting to make the most of the change in him. It must have been Raul and Lydia's wedding that had been darkening his mood over recent days, not impending fatherhood as she'd thought. She'd been too sensitive—too emotional. 'It's beautiful.'

'As are you.' The deep tone of his voice and heavy accent left her in no doubt where this was going to lead. A sliver of doubt crept in, threatening to spoil the moment, but she pushed it aside. It was Christmas Eve and didn't wishes made on Christmas Eve come true?

'Max,' she said as he took her in his arms, pulling her against the hardness of his body. She could feel his warmth through the heavy coat he wore and her heart somersaulted just from being in his arms. 'Is this really what you want?'

He looked at her, dark eyes hooded with building desire. 'We had something good, Lisa, and I have every intention of finding it again, especially as it is Christmas.'

Before she could protest or ask him just what he

meant, his lips brushed teasingly over hers. Her resolve didn't melt. It blew apart into millions of pieces and she wrapped her arms around him, pulling herself closer. Right now she didn't care what he meant. She just wanted to feel the passion, the desire that this man, the man she loved, evoked in her.

'Here?' She breathed the word against his lips, pleased to hear the feral growl her whisper created.

Never in her life had she been so bold, so empowered. Her love for him changed her, made her a different woman. A real woman. She took hold of the lapels of his coat and kissed him, letting every bit of desire in her show. Then, with purposeful intent, she slid her hands inside the coat and up to his shoulders before pushing off the heavy fabric. All the time her eyes held his, daring him to want her—daring him to stop her.

'I have been reliably informed that every room in the cottage has been prepared for Christmas. Maybe now would be a good time to see what the master bedroom has to offer.'

CHAPTER SIX

MAX LOOKED DOWN into Lisa's face, the sensation of losing control, of slipping once more under her spell, was so powerful that for a moment he couldn't say anything. He wanted her as he'd never wanted her before.

'I think that is a perfect idea,' she whispered and reached up to kiss him once more. He should resist, keep himself distanced and prove they could live together without the added complications of passion, but he'd never been able to resist Lisa.

He kissed her back as a fierce and insistent desire began to beat like a drum around him. She responded and the gentle kiss became deep, hard and explosive. Every nerve in his body called for hers, called for the satisfaction that only she could bring, the pleasure and pure torment of her touch, her caress and kisses—his possession of her.

When she pulled back from him, her eyes were heavy with desire and, without another word, he took Lisa's hand and led her away from the warmth of the log fire. Her hand held his tightly as they climbed the narrow staircase of the cottage and when they reached the top he was pleased to see his instructions had been followed to the very last detail.

The door of the master bedroom was open and the soft glow of lamplight shone from within. The gift shopper he'd hired online to give Lisa her perfect Christmas had excelled herself; her touch was so personal, he briefly wondered if she was still here. Not that she should be. He'd paid her well, extremely well, for this special gift. It was a gift to disarm his wife, to allow her to see that they could be together and raise their child without the complication of love and unnecessary emotions.

He knew well enough that when he opened up and loved someone, let them into his heart, it all went wrong. His father had left him and his mother had taken a choice that had led to her leaving him. Then, as his career as a footballer had taken off, plunging him into the spotlight of the sports world, a freak accident had taken all that away too. There was only one person who'd been steadfast in her affection for him and that was his sister, Angelina, although he didn't deserve any from her, not when he never allowed her close, when he always wore the armour of dominating older brother.

'I can't believe you've done this—for me.' The disbelief in Lisa's voice was clear, as was the wonder of the whole setting. He'd been sceptical at first, when the gift shopper had suggested a romantic cottage decked out for Christmas instead of a grand country spa hotel, but now he knew he'd made the right choice. This was far more personal and, judging by the wistful look on her face, far more what Lisa would have chosen.

He turned to her, pulling her into his arms as they stood on the landing, the soft light spilling from the bedroom. Her body softened against his, the resistance she'd been putting up over the last few days gone and in its place burning passion and desire. 'You wanted Christmas and so I ordered it for you.'

'Ordered it?' She frowned up at him then smiled shyly and he knew he was finally cracking through her hardened barriers. The same as the ones he'd created when he'd walked out on her and their marriage so soon after saying I do.

This romantic setting would definitely prove they should be together, that they could raise their child together. That despite their short-lived marriage and the fact that he'd openly admitted he could never allow himself to love anyone, they could make this work. For their child's sake.

'I wanted to prove to you we can be together, despite our time apart.' He stroked the backs of his fingers down her cheek, a sense of satisfaction rushing through him when she closed her eyes briefly, those lovely long lashes lying on her pale skin.

When she opened her eyes and looked up at him the green of her eyes was so vivid, so bright he was dragged into her soul, into her heart. He knew then that her feelings for him hadn't changed. She'd told him more than once she loved him until one day, unable to tolerate it any longer, he'd thrown it back at her before walking out on his new marriage. He'd done it to save her pain, to save her heartache, but instead he'd created more. Now was a time to be honest, to tell her he did want to be in his child's life, in her life, but he knew that he couldn't allow himself to love her, not in the way she wanted. He owed it to her, to his child, to be honest.

'And that's all?' The hope in those whispered words tugged at his conscience like a gale-force wind rushing in off stormy seas, but he couldn't yield to it, couldn't let it affect him. Not when his childhood had taught him that those he loved always left him, making him lock his heart away. He didn't deserve the happy ever after Lisa craved so much.

'We had a good marriage, Lisa. We had passion— lots of it.' He lowered his head and brushed his lips over hers; the soft sigh of desire she made only heightened his own, his need for her. 'I warned you I didn't go in for love and romance. You knew that before we married.'

'I just thought...' she said softly, the words dying on her lips as her eyes met his.

More than anything he wanted to kiss her again, to claim her as his once more, to show her that even while he couldn't say words of love to her he desired her, wanted her in the most primal way a man could want a woman.

He shook his head. 'Don't overthink things, Lisa. We married because we couldn't get enough of one another and now we will remain married because of our child. A child created with desire and passion so strong that neither of us could deny it then—or now.'

Lisa's heart thumped so hard in her chest that she was sure it was echoing around the cosy cottage he'd presented her as a Christmas gift. Did he know that he was playing to her childhood insecurities by doing that? Did he know that in this house was all she'd ever wanted? Even the handsome man to live happily ever after with?

'So this is all because I am carrying your child?' The words sprang from her before she had time to think, time to work out this bizarre situation. The passion in the air around them evaporated and she was glad of that. Just now, kissing him under the mistletoe had been a mistake, one that had very nearly made her forget everything.

'In part, yes, but also to show I can be in your life—in our child's life.' He touched her face again, sparking up the intense heat of passion. She wouldn't be able to resist him, she knew that without any doubt, and before she ended up exactly where she'd vowed never to be again—in his bed—she wanted to clear things between them.

'Is that to show you or me?' A spark of defiance raced through her.

He frowned slightly, but the darkness of his eyes remained full of desire. 'I deserve that.'

The moment of honesty almost fooled her, but she had her own honest moment to deal with first. 'I never knew about your brother, the headlines. I wouldn't have added to it all on the same day if I had.'

He sighed. 'I just couldn't think straight. So much was happening, so fast.'

A wave of sympathy curled through her. He'd had more than most men to deal with in recent weeks and she knew better than most what the past could do, how it could haunt you, colour your views and follow you through your life.

'I have always wanted children, one day, although I am only too aware you don't feel the same. I could never subject a child to the kind of childhood either of us experienced, but the fact is that I am pregnant and you made me feel that it was all my fault. We both drank too much wine, Max, both allowed ourselves to forget all we'd agreed on about being professional.'

'More than a little wine.' He smiled and her relief must have shown on her face. 'Do you forgive me?'

He pressed his lips lightly on hers, testing her reaction.

'Give me one good reason why I should,' she teased, thankful the mood had lightened, the heady passion returning. All it took was one light kiss, one gentle touch, one desire-filled look and she was lost.

'Because it's Christmas Eve.' He said the words between light kisses and she closed her eyes to the sensation of fire on her skin.

'And?' Her teasing became bolder.

'And because I desire you more than any other woman.' His eyes were darker than ever, the message of promised passion within them unmistakable. And didn't she desire him too? Want him with a passion she'd never known possible until he'd come into her life?

'And if I don't want to be that woman?' She challenged him, hurt blazing a trail through her as she remembered the time she'd first said words of love to him, fooled by their desire into letting him know that she was emotionally committed to him in a way he'd later made clear he didn't want.

'I think that you do.' He brushed his lips over hers again and just as moments ago a soft sigh escaped her. She didn't want to respond, didn't want to convey her compliance with his wishes to him quite so emphatically, but she couldn't help herself. The bold, teasing woman was gone, the passionate woman who loved him had returned. Whatever it was between them was still there, so didn't that make staying married for the sake of the baby easier? If passion had once brought them together could it now bind them once more?

'I'm not so sure,' she said in a soft provocative whisper and smiled at him. 'I think you might just have to prove that to me.'

It was just like that night two months ago, the night her baby had been conceived, all over again. One kiss, one caress and she became a melting puddle of need at his feet. She hated herself for wanting him, for wishing it could be more, but surely two parents who got on like this would be better than a family torn apart, living very different lives. Her own childhood had been like that and she didn't want the same for her baby.

'I do, do I?' He laughed softly, a sexy deep sound that didn't quite mask the words he'd just said to her, words he'd said once before but hadn't truly meant.

'Yes, you do.' She pushed all her misgivings to the back of her mind. They had agreed on being together until New Year's Eve and maybe that was just enough time to convince him there was more to their marriage—more to them—than passion.

'In that case...' He swept her from her feet and headed for the bedroom and the excitement in Lisa's body intensified. She loved this man, wanted him with a passion, and all she had to do was break through his barriers and make him see that, make him feel it.

She looked around her as he placed her on the large bed covered in a festive throw and on the wall above it a trail of twinkling lights. Parcels done up with bright red ribbons adorned the window sill and beyond the cottage the darkness of the night was sparkled with stars. It was all so perfect, so romantic and she couldn't help but lose herself in the moment. There might never be another like it, not with this man, the man she'd given her heart unconditionally to the day they'd met, the man who even now still held it—and always would.

She looked at him, deep into his eyes. 'It's Christmas Eve, Max. I want to forget everything else, to enjoy the magic that's here in the cottage. Tonight all I want is you.'

'How can I resist that?' The feral tone of his voice left her in no doubt that he wanted her too.

'Then don't.' She reached up and touched his face, belatedly realising what a loving gesture it was and sliding her fingers into his hair instead. To hide the rising emotions within her, she kissed him. Hard. Demanding his response. When it came, it took her breath away.

'Never,' he said against her lips, sending her heart-rate soaring. His arms pulled her close and, to cover up the love that was threatening to erupt within her, she slid her hands down his chest, to the suit jacket he wore, and pushed it off his shoulders as she had done with his overcoat.

This time, the heat of his body scorched her palms, pushing her on in the increasing heat of the dance of desire. As she kissed him, her tongue entwining with his, she pulled off his tie and opened his shirt buttons, until her hands touched the firmness of his chest.

He broke the kiss, with words of Spanish she didn't understand, but she couldn't allow him to see her face, couldn't allow him to look into her eyes, not if she wanted to conceal the truth of her feelings for him. Whatever else happened tonight, he must not think she still hankered after love and happy ever afters with him. Keeping that to herself would give her strength and badly needed control.

'I have no idea what you just said,' she teased as she pulled back from him, glancing briefly into his desire-filled eyes before she pressed her lips to his chest.

'That you are a temptress and, I might add, you are wearing far too many clothes.' The deep guttural sound of his voice sent razor-sharp pins into her heart and at the same time set loose the heavy throb of desire from deep within her.

'In that case…' She moved back, flirting wildly with him. Anything other than let him see what she really felt. Then with a coy smile at him, she undid the buttons of her cream silk blouse. She could feel his eyes on her, feel the heat of his need coming from him in an electrifying mix of desire and command.

It gave her power. Power to hide her love. Power over him.

Max could barely contain himself as Lisa let the cream silk of her blouse slip to the floor, revealing the lacy cream bra that did nothing to conceal the peak of her nipples. His body hardened even more in response. Hell, he wanted her as he'd never wanted any woman before. She was his wife.

He watched as she slipped off her heels and then unzipped her skirt. The sound of the silky lining as it slipped to the floor around her feet was so loud in the charged atmosphere of the bedroom it raised the tension to almost explosive levels.

'Stop,' he said and moved toward her as confusion rushed over her face. 'That's enough—for now.'

Before she could remove her underwear he took her in his arms, pressing her near nakedness against his bare chest. He could feel the flatness of her stomach, where concealed within was his baby. The child he would do anything for.

Whatever happened, he had to win Lisa round, had

to show her he could give her and the baby so much, that he would be there for his child in a way he himself had never known when he was younger.

'For now?' She breathed the question against his lips.

He pushed her gently back onto the bed. She didn't resist and neither did she take her gaze from his. 'I want to kiss you all over, to caress every bit of you. I want to show you how good we are together.'

'But...' she whispered and then hesitated.

'Do you really expect me to walk away from you, Lisa, when you are carrying my child?'

Her green eyes filled with the sparkle of tears, but he knew he had to set things straight between them, do what he hadn't done before they'd got married.

'It's not what you wanted, is it?'

'No, but now that you know more of my past, maybe you can understand my reaction, understand why I feel I can't be a father—a good father—to my child.'

'Feel?' Her lips trembled and he wished he had chosen another time to have this discussion. It was spoiling all he'd achieved with his Christmas gift. 'You make it sound like it's still that way.'

'My past has shaped who I am, Lisa, determined who I can be. Do you really want that for your child?' The pain of his father's rejection was unstoppable.

'What about a mother who has never known a happy childhood, who ran with the wrong crowd as a teenager in order to hide from her past? One who grew up in a bad part of town? Do you want a mother like that for your child?'

The passion and pain in her words reached him on a level he thought impossible. He wasn't the only one unable to stop the secrets of the past from intruding. 'That was your childhood?'

'Yes.'

He'd never have guessed, never have known she'd led anything other than a happy life. She seemed so calm, so in control of herself. Words, he decided, were not enough and he joined her on the bed, wrapping her in his arms, pulling her close in an attempt to show her he understood. The heat of her near-naked body transformed that understanding into passion and he claimed her lips, demanding a response from her.

She kissed him so hard it was intense and fevered. It heated him to the very centre of his darkened soul, dragging every tiny bit of emotion he'd ever hidden away out. Her fingers were pressed deep into his hair, her lips pressing against his. It was powerful, intoxicating. It was something he'd never felt before. As if they were kindred spirits, both wounded and hurt from life, both needing one another.

He pulled back from her, his breath coming hard and fast as he looked at her, saw the wary expression on her face despite the flush of desire on her pale cheeks.

'I want you, Lisa, like I've never wanted you before.'

Rebellion surged forward and Lisa held her breath, fighting it back. She didn't want to spoil this moment and all he'd done for her, but she wanted more than just knowing they would be good together, more than just being told he wanted her. She wanted the one thing that had been missing in her childhood and the one thing Max had already confessed to being unable to give. She wanted love.

Did that mean they were doomed? Even now?

Max braced his body above hers, his arms either side of her, and looked at her, his eyes swirling with desire. 'I want to find what Raul has found with Lydia. I want that with you, Lisa.'

Hope surged through her. He wanted love? There was hope.

'I want that too, Max.' With her hands still entwined in his hair she pulled him down to her and kissed him with all the love she'd been hiding from him. Would that be enough to open his heart to her?

Without giving her doubts any more attention, she kissed him seductively, daring him to love her with his body if not his heart. His lips left hers and scorched a trail of heat down her throat as she let her head fall back against the softness of the pillow, giving herself up to his kisses.

He spoke soft Spanish words she didn't understand, but she fooled herself into thinking they were words of love. Then the trail of kisses moved lower and she arched herself as he kissed between her breasts. Max moved, his body pressing against her legs, leaving her in no doubt that he was as aroused as her. He kissed over the lace of her bra, his tongue finding her nipple through the lace, teasing her mercilessly.

'Max,' she said as she gasped air into her lungs, forcing her eyes open to look at him. His gaze met hers and for the briefest of seconds she thought she saw hesitation, then it was gone as he moved lower, kissing his way down her stomach.

Again he paused and looked at her. This time she held her breath, then he lowered his head and kissed her stomach and his child within. Was he finally warming to the idea of fatherhood—his child?

He spoke again in Spanish. Soft gentle words.

'Max?' She couldn't keep the question from her voice, had to know what he was thinking, what he was feeling.

'My baby is here,' he said and once again kissed her, sending a flutter of butterflies all over her. 'And I will be there for my baby—always.'

Elation tore through her, mixing with the desire and passion of being partially clothed as the man she loved kissed her. 'No more words,' she said softly. 'Just make love to me.'

His eyes became as black as the midnight sky as he looked at her, then with a frenzied passion he levered himself from her, discarding the remainder of his clothes before pulling her lace panties down her legs, casting them carelessly aside.

A fevered passion took over her, so great she could barely think. All she wanted was to feel him deep inside her, to be claimed by him, loved by his body. In one swift movement, with a determined edge to his expression, he moved over her, pushing her thighs apart with his legs.

She didn't need any more encouragement and wrapped her legs round him, drawing him into her, needing the heights of desire only he could give her. He resisted, and she wondered if he was wishing he hadn't done this, hadn't got involved all over again, but as that thought slipped through her mind he claimed her once more.

She clung to him, her fingernails pressing into his back as the tide of desire increased. She moved with him, taking him deeper, wanting more, and when he spoke it was words of Spanish. Not soft gentle ones like earlier, but a harsh, gravelly sound full of passion.

'Max, I—' She started to tell him her innermost feelings, to tell him with words as well as show him with her body just how much she loved him, but before she could finish he claimed her lips in a demanding and hard kiss, which silenced those all-important words.

The wave of desire crashed over her and she clung to him, shaking with pleasure as he too found his release. Slowly her breathing returned to normal and her body cooled as Max rolled away from her.

'Max.' She said his name softly and he turned to look at her.

'Don't.' That one word was a feral growl and she looked deep into his eyes, wondering if he was teasing her. The glittering hardness within the depths of his eyes scored her heart, singed her love and sent a shiver down her spine.

'But…' she began again.

He turned and lay on his back, his hands behind his head, his biceps tense and solid as he looked up at the ceiling. 'Don't say anything, Lisa. It's better that way.'

Better for whom? she wondered and hid her confusion by moving close to him, laying her arm across his chest and pressing her body against his. She trailed her fingertip lightly over the defined muscles of his abdomen, desperately fighting to control her emotions, to become as detached as he was.

'You're right,' she whispered as she kissed his chest. He lifted her face up, forcing her to look at him. She smiled as power slipped into her domain. 'It's better this way.'

CHAPTER SEVEN

LISA OPENED HER eyes and looked around the dimly lit room, acutely aware of Max's body wrapped around hers as she lay with her back to him. She knew without a doubt that she still loved him. There had been a moment last night when she had briefly thought he was fighting it too, trying not to admit he felt the same way, but those hard words after the first time they'd made love had chilled that notion. Yet still she hadn't been able to resist him. How could she when he was the father of her child and the man she would always love, no matter what?

She stirred against the warmth of his body and hers leapt to life once more. The hungry longing within her for him was far from sated. Last night's lovemaking had only intensified it. As the lateness of Christmas Eve had slipped into the early hours of Christmas Day they had alternated between making love and sleeping. Now the grey light of a winter's morning seeped around the edges of the thick curtains Max had drawn across the small window of the cottage late last night.

It was Christmas morning and she'd never expected to be waking up in Max's arms or in such a wonderfully festive cottage. Suddenly her excitement couldn't be contained any longer. Fate had brought them together and he'd given her the kind of Christmas she'd always longed for and she wasn't going to ruin it now by dwelling on what was or wasn't between them, trying to give it a name. She turned and faced Max in the bed, the covers sliding from her as she did so.

'Happy Christmas.' His eyes opened as she whispered the words.

'Now I know what would have been missing from my Christmas morning.' His dark eyes held the promise of more passion as he pulled her closer to his naked body. 'You.'

'But you don't like Christmas,' she whispered as memories of how this time last year, he had suggested they delay their honeymoon several weeks to avoid the festivities, convincing her that he wanted only to be with her. Instantly she regretted saying anything as the shutters of steel came down over his eyes, suffocating the passion she'd seen brewing there again.

'I was simply referring to the fact that Christmas morning isn't the same in Spain. We traditionally give gifts, but on Fiesta de Los Tres Reyes early in January. Twelfth Night here.' She knew he was hiding something, holding back on her as he'd always done. Everything he'd just said was a cover for what he was really feeling—or not.

'So why have you done all this?' She looked around the room, at the subtle decorations that left her in no doubt she was in a cottage decked out for Christmas. She'd thought he'd done it to bring them together—and it had achieved that in the most spectacularly passionate way—but not in the way she really wanted. Perhaps she should do as she'd thought last night and accept that the man whose child she carried wasn't capable of emotions and that nothing would change that, just as he'd told her when he first walked out on their new marriage.

He hadn't wanted her to say what she felt, hadn't wanted to hear those words spoken aloud.

'Because it would make you happy, because even though I can't say what you want me to say, I care about you.'

It wasn't what she wanted to hear right now, but she certainly wasn't going to spoil Christmas Day. Not when the things he'd done, the way he'd been last night, gave her hope.

Max could almost hear a pin drop in the room as Lisa listened then thankfully accepted what he'd said. He got up, enjoying the way her gaze lingered on his body, which still wanted her despite their night of passion.

He pulled on some jeans and a sweater. 'The surprises aren't over yet.'

'They aren't?'

'No, I have arranged for us to have Christmas dinner at a nearby hotel, where, I'm reliably informed, we can relax afterward in comfort in front of a large open fire.'

She smiled at him, a smile full of genuine warmth and pleasure. Finally he was uncovering the real Lisa, breaking down her barriers. She'd tried to do the same to him, but over the years he'd made his defence impenetrable. Would she tell him what it was that had happened in her past to have made Christmas a bad time for her and her family?

'What happened?' he asked, knowing full well he was taking advantage of the unspoken truce between them, but if they stood any chance of building some kind of future together for their child he had to know.

'Happened? When?' She stood by the bed, wrapped in the faux-fur throw from the end, looking deliciously sexy but also very scared. He was intrigued and now he had to know.

'When you were a child? To make you miss out on Christmas?'

'I think that is a question I should be asking you.' She smiled at him, but he could see the defence barrier beginning to slip into place again. 'You are the one who doesn't like this time of year. I've just never experienced it like this.'

She was right. He was also well aware that if he wanted to find out what it was she was hiding from him, keeping locked away, then he too would have to reveal who he really was.

'I have a very good reason for not liking this time of the year.' How had this been turned around to be about him?

Lisa sat down on the side of the bed, her long legs on display as she snuggled in the throw. Her red hair was tousled and she looked as sexy as she ever had. But there was something different about her. She looked vulnerable in a way she'd never appeared before. He'd always thought she was tough, the kind of woman who never let things get to her.

As he stood there, looking at her, he knew it was time to be honest, to let her know exactly who he was, the kind of man the father of her baby really was. She'd made it very clear she wanted a full-time father for her child, not one who visited every month or so, and he still didn't know if he could be that man, but he'd damn well try. He certainly didn't want to be the same as his father.

He turned and looked out of the window at the white frosted grass of the cottage's garden. 'Everything bad that happened in my childhood happened around this time of the year.'

'Your father?' Her voice was soft and he could hear her get up and move across the room toward him. He braced himself for her nearness. He wasn't ready for that kind of sympathy yet.

'He walked out just weeks before Christmas. I was eight years old and convinced he was punishing me. I had no idea he had another family—another son.'

He could feel her warmth, smell her perfume as she moved closer to him. It grounded him, kept him in the present instead of being dragged back into the past. 'Did you ever see him again?'

'No.' He couldn't stop it and slipped back to that moment. He'd watched as his mother had stood proudly in the middle of the room and his father had opened the door of the apartment and looked back at her. She'd kept her chin up, defiance and anger in her stance that he'd recognised as pain, even as the young boy he'd been.

They'd said nothing to one another. All that had been done with an angry argument that he'd witnessed as he'd sat on the cool marble staircase, wishing they would stop, wishing it didn't sound as if they hated one another.

He had come to stand by his mother, knowing even at that age that this was very real, very permanent. His father had looked at him for the briefest of seconds and the annoyed disgust in his eyes that day still haunted Max now, still made him feel insignificant and totally despised. He'd glared angrily at his father and now he knew that had been his first step toward becoming a man—challenging his father.

'I wished mine had never come back, never used me as a weapon against my mother.' Lisa's words rushed him back to the present, away from the dark memories he'd successfully locked away until the newspaper headlines had freed the skeletons from the closet, allowing them to run wild. Uncatchable and untouchable.

He turned and looked down at her, but she was staring out at the frosty countryside, although he knew it wasn't what she was seeing. The past had a hold on her too. It was pulling at her just as his was.

'He left when I was five.' She spoke softly, her voice almost a whisper but there was an undertone of anger swirling through it. 'And I didn't see him for two years. Two years of my mother struggling to make ends meet. Two years of wondering why, of blaming myself. I didn't know the reasons at the time, of course, I just wondered why she was sad. Then he came back.'

A heavy silence fell in the room, as if snow were falling around them, covering everything, hiding the present so that only the past was there—for both of them. Max could feel her pain, her sense of rejection. He'd been a bit older, but it had still hurt and as a boy he'd had to be tough, had to man up and be there for his mother.

'What happened then?' He tried not to think about his past, how in some ways it mirrored Lisa's, how they'd both tried to hide from it but for very different reasons.

'He wanted to see me, wanted to play happy families and take me out.' She turned from the window and he watched her as she walked back to the bed, sat down and drew her knees up to her chest, hiding her body from him with the throw, hiding from her past.

'That was good,' he said, but as she looked up at him, sadness in her eyes, he knew it wasn't.

'Not when you are a young child being used as a weapon to cause hurt and pain.' The answer flew at him, the pain of her past echoing in each word. 'He didn't want me any more than my mother did. I was just an inconvenience, but when it suited them I was their weapon of choice. Other than that, they didn't give a damn.'

'Surely your mother—' Max began, realising how lucky he was to have been kept out of his parents' arguments apart from that very last day.

'My mother didn't want *me*, the baggage from her bad marriage, and my father walked out.' Lisa wrapped her arms tighter around her and something clenched in his heart. She looked so lost, so vulnerable and now he was adding to her pain because of all that had happened in his past.

He wanted to go to her, to hold her, to make her feel better, to put everything right. How could he when he was in the same dark place, haunted by the rejection of his father?

'At least he came back,' he said as he sat on the edge of the bed, physically close to her but so far away. 'At least he wanted to know you, see you grow up.'

The green of her eyes flared so bright with anger as she looked instantly up at him that he leaned back away from her. Her face was pale and he wondered if she was feeling ill because of what they were talking about or because of the pregnancy. Thoughts of his mother clouded in. She'd been ill carrying his little sister, Angelina. Very ill.

With a huff of angry irritation he pushed that thought away and marched back to the window. History wouldn't repeat itself. Would it? He couldn't take losing another person he was close to. That was why he kept himself as emotionally distanced from Angelina as he could. A tyrant of a brother, she'd called him last time they'd spoken on the phone, finalising the last-minute details of her party. What would she say to him about the baby? That he had no right to be a father when he was such a cold, hard brother? And wasn't that the truth? He had no right.

'So you would rather your father had never come back into your life?' The words were rough and feral as he pushed back all his past demons, determined to lock them away. It was Christmas Day after all and this wasn't what he'd planned it to be.

'You have no idea how much.'

He turned to look at her. How could she look so vulnerable and hurt, yet so angry at the same time? As she held his gaze, her eyes so vivid and green as she fought back tears he knew exactly why she wanted to walk away from him, deny him the chance of being a father. 'And that's why you don't want me in our child's life? Why you have given me such an ultimatum, demanding all or nothing?'

The fury in Max's voice cut through Lisa's heart, making her shiver as she realised her words had given everything away. She'd practically told him why she didn't want him in his child's life unless he could give her and the baby total commitment.

She looked up at him, unable to respond as she processed all they'd shared over the last hour. She'd never been able to talk to anyone about such things. Most women had good relationships with their mothers, were able to talk, but that had never been an option with her mother. Not when she was the unwanted child that had stopped all her partying and fun.

'It's Christmas Day, Max.' Finally, she could piece together a sentence. 'We shouldn't be talking about this now.'

He walked back toward the bed, sat down and looked straight into her eyes. After what they'd shared last night she wanted him to take her in his arms and tell her it was all going to be all right, that the past didn't matter, that she'd got it all wrong and he'd be there for her and the baby.

'We should and we will.' The firmness of his voice flattened any hope of that kind of sympathy. 'My father left when I was eight. I blamed myself but, worse than that, I couldn't help my mother. I couldn't make her smile again.'

'Oh, Max.' She reached out, the wrap slipping from her shoulder as she touched the side of his face with her palm. 'You weren't to blame. You were just a child.'

'I felt even more of a failure when she met my stepfather after we moved to Madrid. He brought the life back to my mother's eyes.' Lisa could hear the hurt in his voice and her heart went out to him and the eight-year-old boy he'd been.

'That was love that did that, Max. Your stepfather's love, but it would have been your love that kept her going, kept her strong.'

He sprang back from her, from her touch, his eyes so dark and so very hard. She was confused. What had she said that was so wrong?

'Love?' The word snarled out into the room as he once again paced to the window and she wished he could just sit and talk. Only then would she be able to break through the wall of pain he was barricaded behind. 'Not my love.'

'Of course it did,' she implored as she joined him at the window. How she wished they could go back to where they'd been when she'd first opened her eyes this morning. To the moment before their pasts had collided with the first Christmas that held the promise of something other than upset and tears.

He turned to her, towering over her, his anger taking her breath away, making her light-headed. 'Love didn't stop any of that for me and I'm damn sure it didn't help you either.'

'I-I,' she stammered and stepped back from his overbearing anger. 'I…no.'

The room began to sway and her body became heavy, making standing upright almost impossible. She stumbled back to the bed and flopped down on it, closing her eyes as everything began to spin and turn.

'Lisa,' Max demanded as he crouched beside the bed and looked into her eyes. 'Are you ill?'

If she wasn't mistaken his face was stricken, as if he thought she was really ill. For the briefest of seconds she wanted to smile and reach out to him, but the fury of moments earlier was still there in his eyes and the affirmation that he despised love and any sentimental emotions burned in her mind.

'I'm fine.' She forced herself to sit up, clutching at the soft faux-fur throw as if it were a lifeline. 'I think I just need something to eat.'

Relief rushed over his face and for a moment he

looked unguarded and she wondered what he hadn't yet told her. What it was that haunted him so much, because she was certain it wasn't just his father walking out, that it was more than that, much more.

He stood up slowly. 'Then I will fix you something light before we go out for dinner.'

'Thanks.' The moment of openness had passed. He was behind the shutters once more and even though she didn't want to, she could feel herself retreating there too. 'I'll have a shower then come down.'

Max sat in the kitchen, the tea and toast he'd decided would be best waiting as he heard Lisa come down the stairs. He watched her as she walked along the small hallway, looking about her like a child in a toy store at all the decorations, and he hated that things had gone wrong this morning. At least now he understood her reservations about him as a father. She didn't want her child to be emotionally messed around as she had been, never knowing if her father wanted her or not.

Anger simmered inside him as he thought of her being used that way by the very man who was meant to protect her from hurt—from anything. And then she'd married him, a man incapable of any kind of love or protection.

'Better?' He kept his voice casual as she entered the small rustic kitchen.

'Yes, thanks, and this looks good.' She sat with him at the small table and gingerly ate the toast and sipped at the tea.

'Do you feel well enough to go out for Christmas dinner?' Now he wondered at the wisdom of having arranged it. He hadn't given any thought to her condition. It was the very thing he'd avoided thinking about as it unleashed the past, the pain of losing his mother. The anger and injustice that she had chosen Angelina over herself—over him.

'You bet I do. I wouldn't miss this for anything.' There was a new lightness in her voice and he relaxed. Maybe all they'd discussed had cleared the air.

'Very well.' He stood up from the table and took her hand, pulling her gently to her feet. 'Then before we go, we have to see what gifts are beneath the tree.'

'Gifts?' She laughed lightly. 'You mean Santa has been?'

'If you like, yes.' With happiness he hadn't felt in a long time, he took Lisa into the living room. The fire he'd lit while she was in the shower now filling the room with warmth and the lights of the tree gave it all a surreal feel.

'Oh, but I haven't anything to add to this.' She looked up at him, genuine worry in her eyes. 'For you, I mean.'

He thought of his child growing within her as he looked at her gently. He must be going soft with all this Christmas stuff, because he wanted to hold her, to place his hands on her stomach and tell her that their baby was the perfect gift.

He shook himself free of such thoughts. 'So Santa didn't bring me anything, but he did for you. Shall we open them before we go out?'

Before she could get all sentimental on him he picked up a flat box, beautifully gift-wrapped. 'This is for you, as I have a suspicion you will need them over the next few days.'

She took the present from him and looked at him, as if trying to read his thoughts, find out just what this really meant. Then she sat down in front of the fire and slowly opened the wrapping, and lifted the lid on a large silver box.

'Oh, Max,' she said and he looked over the lid of the box, wanting to know if his instructions had been followed. 'It's lovely.'

She lifted out a black dress.

'For Angelina's twenty-first party.'

'There's more,' she gasped as she laid the black dress over the arm of the chair and picked up the green silk dress Lydia had assured him in their phone conversation would be perfect for her. 'It's beautiful, but how?'

'With a little help from my new sister-in-law,' he jumped in, suddenly feeling uncomfortable with the idea of clothing as gifts. He was far more used to a parting piece of jewellery. 'Lydia assured me you would look stunning in it on New Year's Eve.'

'We may not be together then.' She dropped the terse statement between them and he clamped his jaw hard together.

'After last night, I think that particular scenario is unlikely. I'm not letting you go just yet, not when you promised to be mine until New Year's Eve, which includes the party.' He kept his voice light, but from the uncertain look on her face he knew he hadn't fooled her.

'But what if we don't work this out?'

'We can only do that if we give it a chance.' He turned and picked up one more gift from beneath the tree, wanting to distract her. 'There is also this.'

She took the present from him slowly; for a moment he'd thought she wasn't going to take it. Then she opened it. First the ribbon, then the gold paper revealing a dark blue box. Cautiously, she opened it.

* * *

'This is too much.' Lisa almost dropped the box as she looked up at him. Why was he giving her such an expensive gift? It should mean that he loved her, but she knew it was far from that.

'Diamonds,' he said as she looked back down at the necklace, earrings and ring. 'To wear with the green dress.'

'But…' she said, her voice a hoarse whisper as she touched the coldness of the glittering necklace, lying beautifully against the blue velvet of the box. Her hand was shaking as she slowly moved it away from the dazzling jewels. This was a parting gift. It was the tactic she knew men like Max deployed when they wanted to sweeten a lover and encourage them to move on in life, move on from him.

'They will look amazing with the green dress,' he said, standing over her as if he thought she might just throw the box aside and bolt from the room, from the cottage and from him. 'Or so Lydia informs me.'

Lydia knew about these? Did she know how much trouble their marriage was in? Would Max have confided in Raul that he didn't want to remain married, much less be a father to a child he didn't want?

'She has wonderful taste.' Lisa's mouth dried as she looked up at him, seeing the satisfaction on his face. If he thought his plan had worked, he was very soon going to find out how mistaken that was.

'I wish my wife to be adorned with diamonds that will sparkle brighter than any fireworks on New Year's Eve.'

Why? To mark her as his or to ensure she quietly slipped away once the show of being together, because

of the media interest in them as a couple and Raul and
Max as brothers, had died down?

Could she continue with this and act the part of loving wife when his seduction last night had proved she
couldn't resist him at all? He was counting on that,
using it as a way of keeping her on display as his wife.

She closed the box and looked up at him. 'I don't
know what to say.'

'You don't have to say anything, just be at my side
when we attend Angelina's party and again on New
Year's Eve. Show the world we are a couple.'

Lisa tried to read what he was thinking but failed.
If she agreed, at least she could move on with her life
and know that she'd tried with Max, that she'd be able
to look her child in the eyes later on and say with honesty that she'd done just that.

'In that case I will be at your side and wearing the
diamonds as midnight strikes on New Year's Eve.'

CHAPTER EIGHT

As they had driven the short distance to the hotel, through frost-covered countryside, Lisa had tried to put all they'd just talked about from her mind. At least for now. Despite everything, she wanted to be able to enjoy her time with Max and the Christmas he'd arranged, although the real motives for that were now becoming clearer. It was all a façade, a show of being the man she needed him to be for their child, but why, when she was making it easy for him to walk away as he had done from their marriage?

The hotel was beautifully decorated for Christmas and the food had been amazing. Lisa felt like a small child as she sat on a large sofa in front of the heat of a log fire. All through her meal she'd been thinking about the gifts Max had given her, in particular the diamond jewellery. The diamonds were about not only showing he could, but showing that he held power over her, forcing her to accept his command, his control. It was the last thing she wanted. Power and command did not equal love.

'You're lost in thought.' Max's voice interrupted the circles her mind was wandering and she looked away from the orange flames of the fire and into his handsome face as he sat at the other end of the sofa. It wasn't that big, but he felt far away, isolating himself from her as much as he could. His long legs stretched out before him, snagging her attention, and he looked relaxed and at ease, but from the expression on his face she guessed this was not the case as he pulled at the berry-red tie he'd opted for with his almost black suit.

'I still can't believe how lovely it has been today. The meal, waking up in the cottage on Christmas morning and the gifts.' She wanted to ask him outright about the diamonds, ask him what he really hoped to achieve with them, but the day had almost been spoiled once by the conversation that had sprung out of nowhere that morning; she wasn't going to risk it again.

He put down his after-dinner coffee cup and moved toward her, closing the gap between them as if he'd read her mind. Had her thoughts been so blatantly emblazoned on her face?

She sucked in a deep breath against the tangy aroma of his aftershave, the unique maleness that was Max, shyly looking away, suddenly very self-conscious. Only Max had ever made her feel this way, like a lovesick teenager on a first date. How, after all they'd been through, all they'd learnt about one another, could he still have that effect on her?

His voice was low, deep and very sexy. 'You are my wife, Lisa, and this is the first time we are celebrating Christmas. I wanted to make it special for you because I remembered that passing remark about Christmas always bringing trouble and upset within your family. How it was never what others seemed to experience.'

She looked at him from beneath her lashes, desperate to hide her feelings and the way hearing that made her feel. She wanted to believe him, but she couldn't quite shake off the idea that he was just trying to disarm her—or the shock that it was working. 'Well, this is a pretty special place.'

She looked around the hotel lounge, with the small groups of comfortable chairs and sofas where families were now gathered, relaxing after Christmas dinner. The fire was warm and she could feel herself becoming less tense, less on edge, but after last night and then this morning's discussion, which had felt at the time like an opening of hearts, she was wary.

'This is my first taste of a British Christmas.' He smiled at her and her heart flipped over. How could he melt her so easily?

Because you still love him.

'Where do you normally spend Christmas?' she asked, before realising that once again she was tempting open the box he had clearly marked *do not disturb*.

'In Spain with my mother's family. We would usually be out walking now. Christmas Day is not such a big day in Spain.'

'A walk after Christmas dinner is pretty normal here too.' She laughed and relaxed a little. She'd probably been reading too much into everything, as usual. 'It would be nice to do that now. Is it too far to walk back to the cottage?'

The idea of being out in the crisp cold air of the afternoon was suddenly very appealing. She'd been inside for too long and needed the sense of freedom that came with a walk. It might also shake off some of the notions she was beginning to have that maybe Max did care, that he just wasn't able to put it into words.

'Are those boots up to the walk?' He looked down

at the long boots she'd put on with her deep burgundy dress, the only ones she'd packed, not being aware they were going anywhere else after Raul and Lydia's wedding.

'Of course they are, unless you aren't?' she teased, feeling the tension slip from him as she laughed at him.

'A walk home it is.' He took her hand and for a moment sat and looked at her, his dark eyes unreadable. She wanted to ask what he was thinking or, even more importantly, what he was feeling, but before she could form a sensible sentence he spoke again. 'Shall we?'

Max could hardly fathom that he found pleasure in the simple action of walking along a country lane with Lisa. As they'd walked down the hotel driveway, enjoying the views, he'd taken her gloved hand, smiling to himself when she hadn't resisted but had moved closer to him. He'd kept his pace slow as they'd continued the short distance to the cottage, despite the nearness of dusk, worried that anything faster would be too arduous for her in her present condition.

'I'm pregnant, Max, not ill.' She laughed at him in answer to his concern as they reached the gate of the cottage but her words took him straight back to the day his stepfather had broken the news that his mother had been told her cancer had returned and this time it was untreatable.

He remembered that day as if it were yesterday, felt the shock that he could lose his mother still icing his body. He'd looked at his stepfather and for the first time since his own father had walked he'd wanted to cry. He'd been barely a teenager and already he'd known the pain of watching his father reject him, reject his mother and walk away and now this.

'Is she going to die?' The forthright question had floored his stepfather, but he'd at least been honest in his reply. Too honest.

'It is not good.' Remembering the look of grief in his stepfather's eyes sucked him deeper into the memories of the past. 'She was diagnosed while she was expecting Angelina and refused any treatment until after she'd been born. She didn't want to risk your little sister. She wanted her to live.'

'But I don't want my mother to die.' The words had torn from him like the cry of a wolf calling to the moon and his stepfather had wrapped him in his solid embrace, trying to console him, trying to be there for him, but he'd had his own grief to nurse. Max had seen and felt how much love hurt, how much pain it caused when the person you loved left you, and had vowed then to shut that painful emotion out of his life for good.

'Neither do I,' his stepfather had said as he'd held him tight, being a better father than his real father had ever been. His mother had paid for the delay in treatment with her life. He wished he'd been told when she'd first found out, wished they'd considered him adult enough to know then. Maybe he could have talked her round, made her change her mind. By the time he'd finally been told the truth he'd formed a strong attachment to his baby sister, Angelina, and as much as he'd wanted to hate her he couldn't, but he'd pushed her away emotionally. What if something happened to her too just because he'd loved her?

As the English winter winds blew around him, he remembered more, could see himself at sixteen, see the moment he'd stood watching his four-year-old sister hugging a kitten her father had given her.

'Something for you to love, Lina,' his stepfather had said as he'd placed the mewling scrap of fur in Angelina's lap.

Max had looked at the kitten as it tried to nestle down on his sister's lap and that first wave of bitterness that shaped the man he now was, fuelled by anger, had crashed over him. Love wouldn't do the kitten any good, just as it wouldn't do him or his sister any good. Love set you up for disappointment, rejection and worst of all heartache.

He'd loved his father and then had been forced to stand and watch him walk away. He'd called after him as he'd marched to his car, but he hadn't looked back once. He'd just got in the car and had driven off, tyres spinning as he'd made his escape. Max had waited, hoped he would come back, but as his mother had veered from anger to crying and back to anger he'd accepted he wouldn't, that he now had to be the man of the house. After all, he loved his mother and she wouldn't leave him.

Then she had. Snatched in the cruellest way because she'd chosen her unborn baby over herself—over him.

Max shrugged the painful memory away. In rational moments he knew he would never have been able to help her. She'd had to make a terrible decision but done what any mother would and had protected her unborn child, but it still hurt like hell, that she'd risked leaving him—leaving his baby sister. Now here he was, a father-to-be, wanting to do anything that would make life better for his unborn child, including remaining married to a woman he'd once thought could change his life, change him. But no matter how hard he tried, he couldn't let go of the pain of the past and allow love back into his life.

'Women have babies every day.' Lisa's words hauled him unceremoniously from the past and he blew out a breath into the cold air, seeing it form a cloud before slipping away. If only his childhood pain could evaporate so easily.

'That may be so, but you must look after yourself.' It came out as an angry growl as he wrestled with the past, insistently pushing it back where it belonged. He wanted to look after Lisa but was well aware that in doing so it was giving her false hope of a loving marriage. How could he, the son of a man like Maximiliano Valdez, be capable of such things as love and commitment? Hadn't he already failed at that? He was certain Lisa wouldn't even be here with him now if she weren't carrying his child.

He took in a deep breath of cold fresh air and opened the gate, aware that Lisa was looking at him sceptically. Her cheeks were pink from the cold and the collar of her coat was pulled around her tightly, but all he could see was the image of her wrapped in the faux-fur throw as she'd sat on the bed this morning. Then it had slipped making her look so desirable yet so vulnerable and fragile that something had twisted deep inside him, something he'd never felt before. Something he didn't want to feel.

Now it was happening again. That same twist of pain and pleasure as he looked into her eyes, resisting the urge to pull her against him and kiss her until the pain stopped, until only pleasure existed.

Yet he couldn't do that. Too much had happened in

his life over the last week. First Raul, a brother he'd never known and the unexpected hand of friendship, then the baby. Both life-changing events and highly charged with the kind of emotions he avoided at all costs. It was as if fate was conspiring against him, forcing him to face, head-on, the one emotion he'd never wanted to feel again.

'I've seen my own doctor as well as yours, Max. There is nothing to worry about—unless you don't trust me to look after our baby.' Her eyes narrowed in suspicion as if this was the first time she'd had such a thought.

He trusted her, a hell of a lot more than he trusted himself. 'I'm not questioning that. I'm just worried for you—for our baby.'

'I'll be fine and so will the baby,' she said as she walked up to the wooden front door of the cottage. 'Now let's get in out of the cold. I might even need warming up.'

She turned to look at him, mischief on her face, and he knew right there and then he wouldn't be able to resist her. She'd cast a spell on him from the first day they'd met and it was as strong as ever. She made him believe he was alive, real, but, more than that, she made him *feel*.

Lisa's eyes locked with Max's as he shut the front door, enclosing them in the warmth of the cottage. The promise of passion blazed in his eyes and as he walked toward her she sucked in a deep and ragged breath. She loved him so very much. If only it were enough.

She pushed the thought aside. Until the clock struck twelve on New Year's Eve she was going to enjoy what was happening between them, she was going to allow her love to pour from her, drench him and hope that he'd see just how much she loved him. After all, only true love hurt this much.

In an attempt to delay the moment he took her in his arms, to make it last longer she walked into the living room where the lights of the Christmas tree twinkled in a festive display of colour. She frowned and looked at the roaring log fire. 'Someone has been in and seen to the fire.'

He'd followed her into the living room and now moved closer to her, the desire evident even as he smiled so very sexily at her. 'All part of the deal for the cottage.' His voice was deep and sexy even though he was talking mundane everyday things. She was suddenly and very acutely aware of every move he made. 'I have very serious plans for that fire this evening.'

Part of her was annoyed. He could buy anything he wanted. From a cottage that was invisibly staffed to her designer dresses and diamonds. The other part of her was overcome with the desire to be just that, to be his, to live in the moment of isolation from reality.

'And what might they be?' the teased and moved away from him with a provocative smile to stand on the soft rug in front of the fire, allowing its heat to warm her after their walk home. Not that she really needed it. One passion-filled look from him was enough.

He took off his coat, slinging it carelessly on the chair behind him and, with purposeful intent in every move he made, came to her, taking her hands in his. 'To take every piece of clothing from your sexy body and lay you down right here, with just the light of the fire, and make love to you.'

'That sounds like the perfect end to the day,' she breathed, her stomach flipping over and a shiver of pleasurable anticipation rushing through her. This was more intense, more wildly enticing than the night two months ago when they'd become lovers once again. She hadn't been able to resist him, had thought then, like now, that she would enjoy the moment.

'In that case we will start with these.' He lowered himself to his knees and she looked down on him, wide-eyed as he unzipped one long black boot then lifted her foot, pulling the soft black leather slowly from her. He looked up at her as his hands smoothed upward from her ankle, to her knee. She had to steady herself by reaching out and holding the mantelpiece, but he stopped just at the hemline of her dress and a ragged breath tore from her.

She couldn't speak. Every breath she took was slow and deep with expectation. She closed her eyes and he slid down the zip on the other boot, pulling it from her and then sliding his hands upward once more. This time he went higher, teasingly higher, and before she knew what he'd done he'd pulled down the thick tights she'd opted for that morning and discarded them with a mock look of disapproval.

'These have to go.'

The crackle of the fire was the only noise in the room as she looked at him, then as the tension mounted she laughed, shocked at the sexy giggle that sounded so unlike her. 'Not to your taste?'

'Absolutely not.' His hands caressed her thighs, teased around her lace panties, and she tried hard not to close her eyes, not to allow her knees to buckle with pleasure. 'This, however, is.'

'You are a wicked man, Maximiliano Martinez.' The unintended soft purr of her voice had an instant reaction on him and his grasp on her leg tightened.

'Very wicked.' He slid her dress a little higher and kissed a trail up one thigh and then down the other.

'Max,' she whispered, consumed by the rising tide of desire.

He paused and looked up at her. 'Come here.' There was unmistakable command in his voice but it was so sexy, so erotic.

She knelt down on the soft rug as his arms wrapped around her, forcing her to sit astride his legs as he knelt down. Her dress ruched high up her thighs as she followed her instinct and moved as close to him as possible. His hands slid up her thighs, pushing the dress up higher until his hands cupped her buttocks, pressing her intimately against his erection. It was reckless, it was amazing and it was what she wanted most—to be like this with him, showing him how much she loved him.

'Max,' she gasped and let her head fall back as pleasure rushed over her.

'Whatever else happens between us, we always have this, don't we, Lisa?' The words were heavily accented and husky and she didn't care what he meant, didn't want to think about that now.

She looked down at him, so close to him she could feel his breath on her face, feel that it was as ragged as hers. Words evaded her as his dark eyes, laden with desire, met hers. Words weren't needed now. She would show him what they had, that it could be more than passion, if he let it. Slowly and teasingly she kissed his face, anywhere but his lips, until he took hold of her face between his hands and kissed her so hard, so passionately she groaned with pleasure, the sound muffled by the pressure of his lips.

He stopped kissing her, looking deep into her eyes. Was he seeing her love? Could he feel it, taste it? Without taking his eyes from her, he lifted the hem of her dress and pulled it up as she put her arms up, allowing him to pull the soft knitted fabric over her head and off, leaving her wearing only her bra and panties.

He kissed her neck, her throat and the swell of her breasts. She clung to him as shivers of passion rocked her body. 'Your clothes,' she gasped as his tongue licked her nipple through the lace of her bra.

'You want me naked?' The teasing laughter in his voice was mischievous and very sexy.

'Oh, yes,' she said, taking on the role of seductress, raising her brows at him. 'Very naked.'

'As you wish.' The playful tone matched the look on his face as he allowed her to slide from his lap. She sat on the rug and watched as he began to take off his clothes, loving the firelight on his body, highlighting the muscles of his chest as he removed his shirt. Lust and a greedy need for him spiked through her as he finally stood naked and proudly erect in the firelight.

'That's better. Now come back here,' she demanded, loving this moment of control, even though she knew it was only because he was allowing it to happen. Just as he had that night two months ago. The night they'd conceived their child.

Within seconds he was over her, his strong arms holding his body off hers as his mouth claimed hers in a kiss so intoxicating her head spun as if she'd drunk champagne. As he kissed her he pushed her backward until she was lying on the rug, his body over hers, his erection pressing intimately against her. She moved against him, wanting him to possess her, wanting him to make her his again.

With expert ease he freed her first from her bra and then from her panties. 'This is what makes us good, Lisa,' he said as he looked down at her, raw, hungry desire in his eyes. 'This passion.'

She wanted to ask, what about love? But his lips claimed hers in a demanding kiss, quashing any ill-fated questions, and instead she gave herself up to the desire that raged within her brighter than the fire of the cottage.

Was it passion? Not for her, but all that slipped away as he entered her, making her his. She moved with him, wanting to be his in every way. As stars exploded around her, her body full of the pleasure of his, Max groaned out in Spanish as he too found his release.

Now lying together, naked bodies entwined, his touch made her tremble and his kiss made her head light. The warmth of the fire was dwindling, the logs becoming covered in a white ash, but she didn't move, didn't want to spoil any of this. What had happened in this cottage, the love she'd shown him, the passion he'd showered on her, would have to last her for evermore. But right now, none of that mattered.

He kissed her softly on her neck, nuzzling at her skin, sending a fiery trail of desire throughout her. She turned her face to him and he brushed his lips over her so lightly, so lovingly it was almost too much. Then he deepened the kiss, proving he still had plenty of desire raging in him. As she pulled away, taking in a deep breath of air, he smiled at her in that sexy way only he could.

'You are very beautiful, Lisa.' He trailed his fingers down her naked body, over her hip and down her thigh before creating the same torturous sensation back up her body. 'I love seeing the firelight cast a glow over you.

'This is all so perfect.' She closed her eyes as he kissed her softly again, but she couldn't keep it to herself any longer, couldn't hide her feelings behind the shield of lust for a second longer. 'I love you, Max.'

Her whispered words sucked the air from the room. Even the flames of the fire seemed to stop moving as Max stopped kissing her and looked down at her.

'No,' he ground out as he moved away from her. 'This is not love and it never will be.'

'But I love you, Max, why can't you let me in? Let me love you? Maybe then you can love me too.'

'Never,' he thundered as he got up, grabbed his clothes and left the room, his last word hammering at her heart, breaking it into thousands of pieces.

CHAPTER NINE

MAX HAD BARELY said a word to her the next morning, other than to insist they return to London. He had work to do and plans to finalise for Angelina's party, but she knew it was what she'd said. Why had she spoilt what could have been a perfect few days with those three words that Max couldn't say, much less be told?

She'd spent the day resting while Max worked, and as the afternoon had darkened into evening a light dusting of snow had fallen over London. She'd stood by the expanse of floor-to-ceiling windows and looked out over the city as the flakes had twisted downward in a crazy dance, feeling ever more confined, ever more trapped. Finally she couldn't tolerate it any longer, desperate to slip away for just a short time from the confines of Max's apartment, from the brooding silence that emanated from him louder than any thunderstorm.

She crossed the polished wooden floor of the living space toward Max's study. The desk lamp shone a bright circle of white light over the desk and onto Max. He hadn't noticed her and she used her brief advantage, taking in the dark hair, now reverted to its natural dark unruly curls. He sighed, dropped his pen onto the papers he'd been poring over and pushed his fingers roughly through those dark curls and her own tingled as she remembered doing the same at the cottage.

A dart of pain shot through her heart at the memory of the last time she'd looked into this room, of the papers he'd refused to sign to acknowledge the divorce she'd filed for the day of their first anniversary, unknowingly carrying his child. They seemed to be back at the beginning again, but she loved this man and after their special night together she knew she could never love anyone else. But her love wasn't enough and when she walked out of his life at the end of the year she knew that no other man could ever replace him, that she would be bringing up their child alone. That thought saddened her, not just for their son or daughter, but because something haunted Max, stopped him from caring, from loving. It hurt like hell to know that she hadn't been able to change that, to reach him.

'I'm going out for a walk.' That got his attention. He looked up from his desk as she stood in the doorway, not trusting herself to get closer as the need to stand behind him and wrap herself around his shoulders in a loving embrace surged forward.

'It's snowing.' The sharpness of his retort only fired the anger within her, but he hadn't taken his gaze from her. She could feel it burning into her.

'I'm not asking you to come, just telling you I'm going.' Instantly she became defensive. It was her default protection mode and right now she needed it more than ever. She needed to protect her heart.

Without another word she turned and left him to his brooding, grabbing her coat as her defensive barrier folded around her, around her heart. He might have a penthouse apartment with views of the Thames, but she needed fresh air and freedom. Was he this controlling with Angelina? As that thought settled in her mind like the tiny flakes of snow drifting in the air, trying hard to be something more than the light dusting of sparkly white on the ground, she burst out of the tall and commanding apartment block he called home and took in a big lungful of cold air.

'Damn you, Lisa, I haven't got time for this.' Max's curse sounded behind her and she turned to see him, buttoning up his coat as he walked toward her, looking anything other than happy to be out in the cold winter evening.

'Then don't,' she retorted hotly, adamant this was one thing she was going to get her way with. 'I grew up in London. I'll be fine.'

'I am not about to allow my pregnant wife to walk around alone in this weather. In the dark. What kind of husband do you think I am?'

'One who doesn't love his wife.' She threw the accusation back at him so quickly she didn't even have time to think it through first.

She didn't wait for a reply and began to walk along the embankment pathway, the trees twinkling with lights and the glow of lights from the city reflected in the water. Beneath her boots the snow was slippery and in her haste she briefly lost her footing and slid but quickly regained her balance.

Max was beside her in an instant, taking hold of her arm. 'I suggest you slow down if you must continue with this madness.'

She walked a few more steps and stopped, looking from the white pathway as it sparkled under the lamplight to Max. 'And what would that madness be? Taking a walk in my condition?'

He spoke over her before she had a chance to finish. 'Of course it would.'

'Or is that madness loving you?' The words came hurtling out, dragging out all her pain on a cold breath, which seemed to linger in the air between them, waiting for an answer.

'I have told you, Lisa, I can't love. It's not you, it's me.'

'Oh, isn't that the perfect excuse? One every man who doesn't want to be with a woman uses.' Anger sizzled in every word.

'It's not an excuse,' he said wearily. 'It's the truth.'

'The truth?' she fumed. Did he even know what that was?

He moved closer to her, his height towering over her, dominating everything. 'I don't want to be the man my father was. I don't want to risk hurting you—hurting our child.'

Lisa's heart thumped in her chest, so loud she was sure it was echoing around London, sure everyone would hear it. She'd found a chink in Max's tough armour and he'd let her slip through, opened up and was finally on the brink of admitting what his demons were. Demons that made loving impossible for him.

She moved closer to him. 'Just because your father did that to you, to your mother, it doesn't mean you will be like him.'

The softness of Lisa's voice nearly killed Max as he stood looking at her, vaguely aware of other people walking in the early evening darkness passing with a cursory glance at them but he couldn't take his eyes from Lisa's.

'This hasn't got anything to do with my father.' Even now when she was making it all so easy for him, he couldn't truly own his failings, couldn't admit that unlike Raul, who had found love and happiness, he never would. He was cast from the same mould as his father.

'You have to let the past go, Max. You can't live within its shadow for ever and I more than most know that. There are plenty of shadows in my past, plenty I'd like to ignore or run from, but I can't, because I love you.'

He moved away from her, needing the space to think, to gather the turmoil of emotions that had somehow escaped. He crossed the footpath to lean on the stone wall, looking out over the darkness of the moving water. 'You can say it as many times as you like, but it won't change anything, Lisa. I am who I am because of my past and I can't change that.'

She joined him by the wall, looking at him, trying to force him to look at her. He didn't want to, didn't want to look into her gorgeous green eyes and see the love in them. Keeping himself at an emotional distance had worked while he was bringing up Angelina. He'd never admitted to himself or his sister that he loved her. That was what had kept her safe, kept her in his life.

But Lisa wasn't Angelina. She wasn't the baby sister he so wanted to hate for being his mother's choice in a decision that she later paid for with her life. Lisa was his wife, the woman he'd thought he could enjoy passion and desire with, be a husband to, all without giving his heart. That fatal commitment that always made a person leave him, his life. He'd long since been secure in the notion that if he didn't engage his emotions he couldn't be hurt—couldn't hurt anyone.

'It doesn't have to define you, Max,' she said softly, too softly. He looked down at her, noticing she wore less make-up than usual. She'd stepped out from behind the façade of bright, bubbly and in-control Lisa to tell him how she really felt and he'd thrown it back at her—again.

'We never talked of our past before we married, did we?' He turned his attention back to the water and somewhere in the distance the eerie sound of sirens pierced the night, as if the truth of all she'd said was piercing his armour, cracking it open and exposing the young child who still lingered within, hurt and afraid.

'Maybe neither of us were ready to share those secrets.' She spoke so softly that he almost didn't hear her. He sensed her moving closer, felt her arm against his and he clenched his jaw hard as need for her began to bubble to the surface once more. 'But it's not too late.'

Was she right? Could he do that, tell her why he'd been a hard and dominating brother to Angelina and why he could no longer look his stepfather in the eye, knowing he'd been the one to stand back and allow his mother to make such a momentous decision? Could he tell Lisa that he wanted to love her, wanted to love his child, but that he didn't trust himself not to hurt her? That he couldn't stand it if she left him once he'd opened his heart to her.

'It won't change anything, Lisa.'

'But I'm willing to take the chance, Max—for our baby, not for me.'

He turned to face her once more. 'Why would you

do that? Why stay with a man who can't love you and maybe can't even love his child?'

'You know my past now, Max. You know why I want a father for my child, one who will always be there, not one who turns up and uses his child to get at me. I would rather be a single mother, completely on my own, than put my child through that.'

She was doing what his mother had done. Sacrificing herself, her needs for those of her child, albeit for very different reasons. 'Why? You saw where I grew up when my mother and I moved to Madrid after my father walked out.'

'It has nothing to do with where I'd live.' She looked at him, imploring him to understand. 'It's because I want to be a better mother than mine was. I want to care and love my child, to give it all it needs and that includes a permanent father. But only you know if I can manage that last part.'

He looked at Lisa, at the way her lovely red hair moved in the light wind, at the rosy glow the cold was bringing to her pale cheeks. He knew so little of her past. Was that where everything had started to go wrong? They'd allowed passion to rule, never words.

'You've never really mentioned your mother.'

'Because she never wanted me, never cared for me in any way. I was completely left to my own devices and if one good thing has come out of seeing my older stepbrother constantly being sought out by the police, it's that I decided to lift myself out of that rut. Not to be the girl from the wrong side of town. I studied hard at school and later got my degree with honours in physiotherapy. My mother hates that I did well in life. She is constantly looking for ways of bringing me back down.'

His heart ached for Lisa, who like Angelina hadn't known a mother's love, but it still didn't make it any easier for him to let go of his emotions, to feel love, much less show it. If anything the expectations she'd just heaped on made it harder.

'She would really do that?' He thought of the hard and unyielding woman he'd met just one week before he'd married Lisa and knew without a doubt that she was capable of that. Life had made her tough, taught her to inflict hurt, but how far would she go to teach her daughter a lesson for bettering herself? How could any mother want to do that?

'She would, but can we forget this now? All of it and move forward? We are having a baby together, Max, and I don't want to do it alone, but I will if I have to.'

He pulled her into his arms, sympathy rushing over him for the open vulnerability in her face. 'You won't be doing it alone, not while I have breath in my body.'

He meant every word. He would be there for her and for his baby. Lisa hadn't asked him now for love, hadn't said that was what she needed as he'd made his promise, one similar to that his mother had extracted from him. He'd promised his mother he'd look after Angelina and he had; for the last twenty years he'd been there for her, ensuring she had all she physically needed. He could do that for his child, couldn't he?

Lisa closed her eyes and sank into Max's embrace. He'd shared his secrets with her, opened up to her. Now, at last they could move forward, become a family and bring up their child together. It was all she'd ever wanted and with the exception of Max's love she had it all.

She looked up into his face and the sadness in his

eyes made him look so different—real. He'd lost that hard edge that gave him the command of total control. Was this the real man?

'It's cold out here.' She snuggled tighter against him, anything to stop herself saying something stupid, like *I love you*. She could never let those words past her lips again.

'Now you've noticed.' He laughed, looking and sounding more relaxed than he'd ever done. Was it because he'd unburdened his past, confided in her in a way she'd only ever dreamt possible? 'Shall we go back?'

'No, let's walk a while. The cold is invigorating.'

He kissed her so gently she was sure it tasted of love and as her body began to hum with desire she wished she'd asked him to take her back to his apartment, to his bed. The kiss intensified as the stirrings of passion began to boil higher and she kissed him back, deeply and passionately.

Inside her mind she was shouting to him. *I love you, Max, with all my heart.*

She continued the kiss, wanting to stop the words from tumbling from her mouth, and as the fury of passion threatened to spill over, like a dam about to be breached, she wanted to show him with the kiss how much she loved him.

He pulled away from her slightly, the cold night air tingling on her lips, still warm and bruised from the ferocity of his kiss. 'It's a damn shame I can't lure you into my bed instead of walking in this weather.'

Pleasure and heat rushed around her as his desire filled eyes that held hers, calling her into his bed in a way she was powerless to resist. 'On second thoughts—'

His brow raised in amusement. 'Yes?'

'That sounds a much better idea—and warmer.'

He took her hand and led her back along the embankment footpath, retracing their steps. 'I can guarantee it will be warmer—a lot warmer.'

Lisa woke late the next morning to find the bed cold and empty beside her, but memories from last night warmed her as the fire at the cottage had done. She'd poured all her love into last night's lovemaking, had tried so hard to show him what she wanted him to know without a word passing her lips. Were those three words really necessary?

If she could silence them, show her love with every caress and kiss, every gesture and thought, did it mean that Max was doing the same? Was her Christmas cottage a way of showing he loved her? What about the brilliant diamonds? Were they a token of his love and not the sordid conclusion she'd jumped to? Did he love her and not even know it yet?

Hope surged through her as she dressed and went in search of Max. He loved her and as soon as he'd wrestled the demons of his past into submission he would tell her as well as show her.

'How are you this morning?' he asked when she looked into his study, to find him busy with paperwork as usual. The concern in his voice touched her and pushed the hope a little higher as she walked in and stood by the window, looking out at London nestling beneath a toneless grey sky, where the promise of snow still lingered.

'Good, thank you. I seem to be escaping the sickness now.' It was the first time she'd thought about it, noticing that it was only when things weren't good between them that she felt ill.

'That's good to hear, because I'm looking forward to seeing you in that black dress at Angelina's party tonight.' He smiled wickedly at her, stood up and walked over to join her. Standing behind her, his arms winding round her, he pulled her against him, kissing her neck. 'And to taking it off again when we get home.'

'Maximiliano Martinez, you are unbelievably bad.' She wriggled round in his embrace and wound her arms around his neck, loving the intimacy of the moment.

He kissed her lightly on the lips, pushing her hair from her face until it fell behind her shoulders. 'Would you prefer I don't say things like that?'

She shook her head and he kissed her again, but this time the shrill ring of her mobile phone cut dead the rise of passion. 'That, I think, is your phone.'

'I will be back to finish this in a moment.' She slipped from his embrace with a smile on her lips.

'Promises, promises,' he called after her as she rushed to retrieve her phone from her bag.

The word *mother* flashed on the screen and with a sinking heart she answered the call.

'So you are back with Max.' Her mother's harsh voice shattered all the soft, gentle emotions the exchange with Max had just created. The warm sensation his words had stirred in her froze.

'Yes, Mother, I am.' Lisa bristled with indignation. Why couldn't her mother ever be happy for her? Why did every achievement she made, every choice she followed, have to be questioned and torn apart?

'I saw it all in the papers. He's now a very wealthy

man, heir to an impressively large fortune—no wonder you went back to him.'

'Mother,' Lisa snapped, and wished now her mother had had the nerve to say this to her face, to stand in front of her and accuse her daughter of being as shallow and mercenary as she herself was. 'I'm not like you.'

'No?'

'No.' Lisa walked to the windows that looked out over the dark, fast-moving waters of the Thames, not wanting Max to hear their exchange. After last night's discussion as they'd walked, the last thing he needed to hear was her cold anger toward her mother.

'Pregnant, then?'

Lisa couldn't answer and rested her forehead against the cool of the glass as the nausea she'd just thought she was avoiding came back at her with a vengeance. Her mother's vengeance.

'So, you are pregnant.' Her mother's jubilant righteousness echoed out of the phone.

'I haven't even answered you.' Lisa defended herself just as she'd always had to do when her mother was in one of these moods. The kind that usually ended up destroying everything she'd wanted or worked for. Well, it wasn't going to happen this time. This time she wouldn't try and keep anything a secret from her mother; this time she would tell her everything and hope that satisfied her.

'Your silence says it all, darling.' The endearment was said in a sickly tone, reminding Lisa of the wicked witches in the children's films she'd always loved to watch when she was younger. She'd never thought her own mother would take on that role though.

'Yes, I'm pregnant. Max and I are back together.

I've got what you have never had, Mother, or should I say what you've never respected yourself enough to hang around for.'

'So you still think a man like Max can love you, give you all those foolish dreams of happy ever afters, like those silly films you used to watch?' Lisa blinked in shock. Her mother had noticed that she had always been consumed by them as a child, before home life had got so tough, so miserable she'd been forced to roam the streets with a gang of well-known troublemakers.

'I love Max and that's enough for me. I'm not the same as you.' Behind her she heard a noise and turned, phone held to her ear, and looked at Max. She saw his armour reinforcing itself, saw him retreating from the place she'd finally made him reach, the place where her love could reach him. How long had he been standing there and how much had he heard?

She watched Max walk away, heard her mother's voice. 'Then I shall leave you to make the most of your love nest, because it won't last.'

'Goodbye, Mother.' Lisa ended the call and dropped the phone onto the smoked glass of the coffee table, the clattering noise an ominous sound. She wanted to go after him, wanted to find out what he'd heard, because a one-sided conversation would have sounded pretty damning. It would have made her seem as calculating as, only last night, she'd confessed her mother was.

She was walking after him even before she realised she was doing it and stood once more on the threshold of his domain.

'Save it, Lisa.' He glared at her and she knew he'd heard it all. 'I'm not in the mood.'

'No, Max, I won't.'

He drew in a deep, angry breath. 'Stop trying to force me to love you.'

'I'm not,' she said softly, knowing the last part of the conversation he'd overheard would have sounded exactly like that.

He stood taller, his glitteringly angry eyes fixing her to the spot. 'There will be no happy ever after here, Lisa, so stop looking for something that doesn't exist.'

'Damn you, Max,' Lisa hurled at him as the pain of his words spiked her anger. 'I already know there isn't such a thing, at least not with you. All I want is what is best for my child. And maybe that is not you.'

He moved from behind his desk and came so close she could smell his aftershave, but this time she fought hard not to let it unbalance her, to set off the sparks of desire. 'Then I suggest you leave.'

'Oh, I intend to.' She turned to walk away, anything to prevent the sting of tears from falling, but Max caught her arm.

'But not until our deal is over, Lisa. Not until midnight on New Year's Eve.'

'I'm leaving now. Right now.' She defiantly glared up at him.

'Angelina is expecting us at her twenty-first birthday party this evening and we will be there, Lisa—together.'

CHAPTER TEN

MAX STOOD AND watched Angelina and her friends as they laughed, toasting his sister with champagne. Tall and slender, with sleek dark hair just like her mother, Angelina looked exquisite in the cream silk dress Lydia had personally selected for him to give her as part of her gift. The other part, a central London apartment in one of the best areas, would give him peace of mind that she always had a place to go, a place to call home.

It was hard to believe his little sister was so grown up now and didn't need him any more. Now his child needed him and despite Lisa's act of loving him, the words she'd said as they'd enjoyed the most amazing sex, he wasn't at all sure his wife needed him. Her angry defiance just hours ago proved that.

'Angelina looks happy,' Lisa said as she came to join him, the black dress fitting her to perfection. The very same dress, before trouble had blown up between them once more, he'd envisaged taking from her sexy body before making her his again.

Lisa had sought him out after she'd seen him watching her talking to her mother, but he'd been too angry, too disappointed to say anything. Lisa's motives, her need for love and happiness, went far deeper, right to the very core of all the vulnerabilities he'd hidden well from everyone.

'And that makes me happy,' he said curtly, aware of Lisa looking up at him. He didn't look at her, but kept his focus on his sister, although he wanted to know if Lisa's beautiful face was tinged with sadness or if the anger she'd thrown at him still made her eyes spark.

'About earlier,' Lisa said and he swung round to face her, those expressive green eyes widening in shock.

'The conversation with your mother, where you told her you'd found a way to be better than she was?'

'That's not what I said.' She gasped and her acting skills surpassed any he knew as tears welled into her eyes.

'What I heard was exactly that, Lisa.'

'That's not fair, Max. You only heard what I said, not what she'd said to me.'

'It was enough.'

'Enough for what?' Lisa said the words slowly, intently looking up at him now, her silver earrings swaying gently against her neck, touching skin he'd kissed. Damn it. Why did she always do this to him? Always distract him from what was really going on?

'I will support you and our child but we cannot remain together—or even married.'

Lisa gasped. 'You want to go ahead with the divorce?'

'It is for the best, but I will expect to be involved in my child's life, to see him or her often. In the meantime, we have tonight to get through and, in two days' time, a New Year's Eve party.'

'We?' She glared at him. 'You expect me to accept that you want a divorce yet continue to act the part of loving wife?'

'I will of course make it financially worth your while by way of a substantial settlement, but I have no wish to give the press or society's gossips any further ammunition to create headline news with. Therefore, I expect you to act, as you so nicely put it, the loving wife for the remainder of this evening and on New Year's Eve.'

'You are...' She struggled to find the right words and he added them for her.

'Cold-hearted? Despicable? Mercenary?' The smile he bestowed on her was on the surface real, but in reality it was formed in his hardened heart.

'Oh, yes, all of those and I can add some too.' She at him, anger making her lips press into a firm line.

'Not right now, you won't,' he said softly as he leant toward her, touching her gently on the shoulder. 'You have a role to play and what wife would say such things to the man she loves?'

'I don't see why we have to keep up such a façade.' A smile became firmly fixed on her face. How stupid had he been to almost fall for her talk of love, to almost open up a heart he'd thought had died long ago? He'd been on the brink of letting her into his heart, of allowing emotions back into his life. But not any more. It was over. All she wanted was to prove to herself she could be better than her mother and he'd foolishly believed her when she'd told him her mother always tried to bring her down.

He stepped back from Lisa, calling a waiter over to them, hardly daring to look at how sexy she was in that dress, how the neckline skimmed her breasts, the crossover straps drawing his eyes there even when he tried to avoid looking.

'I am not about to announce to Raul that things have gone wrong in my marriage once again. He knows too much of what is going on between us and I'm not in the habit of admitting failure.' He took a glass of champagne and a tall, elegant glass of elderflower cocktail and handed it to Lisa.

She took the drink, sipped it as she looked out across the room decorated in gold for the party. 'So it's all about what other people think? To hell with what I think.'

She moved away from him to briefly speak to someone and he watched her. He wouldn't have been able to drag his attention away from her if he'd wanted to. The black dress emphasised every curve, sending a spike of lust through him. He clenched his hands into tight fists. Now was not the time to become sidetracked by her—by sex.

As she returned to his side he looked down at her, liking the way she'd put her hair up, twisting it into a tousled kind of knot that made her look as if she'd not long left his bed. Damn. Why did everything come back to sex with this woman?

'Of course it is. I have no wish for Angelina to think there is discord between us on her birthday.' Even to him the words sounded stilted. Rehearsed.

She turned to glare at him. 'Discord?' The word echoed loudly around them. Too loudly.

'Everyone will know if you are not able to lower your voice.'

'I don't damn well care.' Before he could add anything to that she flounced off and although he wanted to go after her, he didn't. It would create more of a scene if someone saw them arguing.

He swigged back his champagne, put down the glass and went in search of a proper drink. At the bar he ordered a whisky and sent it chasing after the champagne, then turned, leaning against the bar, and surveyed the room, the guests.

'I see impending motherhood is wreaking its usual havoc.' Raul's voice jolted him and he turned to see his brother, cutting a handsome figure in his black tuxedo.

There was a smile on his face, but he looked different. Much less tense and not so on edge. More relaxed. Marriage obviously suited him and that fact only made Max even angrier. Why could his younger brother make a success of it and he couldn't?

'I think it's more to do with the stress of the season,' Max offered by way of an explanation. 'We've hardly been in one place for long.'

'So how was Christmas in the English country cottage?' Humour bubbled in each word, only adding to Max's disgruntled mood. What the hell did Raul have to be so happy about? As soon as the thought made its presence felt, he pushed it back. He didn't wish unhappiness on anyone, least of all his brother, who'd also suffered in his childhood due to their so-called father. 'Was it as romantic as you wanted it to be?

It was on the tip of Max's tongue to tell him it was excellent, but something stopped him. Maybe it was some kind of brothers' code he wasn't yet aware of, but he didn't want to elaborate on the truth.

'It all went very well at first.'

'But?' Raul asked, a grave look sliding over his face.

'We want different things. Things I can't give her.'

Raul nodded. 'You have to find the solution to that

yourself, Max. Only you can and only when you are ready.'

Max knew they were talking of the same thing. Hadn't he witnessed it between him and Lydia that day in the restaurant when he'd arrived to meet him? Raul had found his way through the mire of his past and had found love. Just seeing him and Lydia together proved that.

'Any more news on Carlos?' Max changed the subject. This was not the time or the place to have such a talk with his brother, not after he'd told his wife he wanted a divorce.

'He's resigned from the board. He's been in my father's pocket for so long he seriously thought the company would come to him, that he could buy it for a rock-bottom price. I nearly fell for his insistence that I marry Lydia instead of finding you.'

Max remembered well the evening they'd met and talked through everything that had brought them together. How they'd both been convinced that their father had wanted them to find one another, to run the business together. That was why he'd put the marriage clause in the contract Lydia's father had signed, knowing full well marriage was the last thing Raul had wanted.

'But you married her anyway,' Max said, wondering for the first time if it was a marriage that was as real as it looked.

'Only because I realised what a fool I was to let the one woman I loved walk out of my life.' Raul looked at him then took a glass of champagne. 'You'll know what I mean one day, brother.'

'I'm not so sure about that.' Max inhaled deeply and

looked away from his brother. He didn't want to see that smug smile of satisfaction on his face.

'You can't shut it out for ever,' Raul said as he clapped a hand on his back. 'Now if you will excuse me, my new wife is in need of a dance partner.'

Max watched Raul go, watched as he took Lydia's hand and led her onto the already crowded dance floor. He knew exactly what his brother was referring to but he was wrong. Very wrong. Love wasn't shut out of his life, it was completely obliterated—for ever. Wiped out by the actions of his father, a man who hadn't even known the meaning of the word.

Lisa's attention was captured as Raul, leading Lydia by the hand, made his way to the dance floor. A pang of envy rushed through her and she clutched her elder-flower cocktail a little tighter. He was as commanding as Max and she didn't miss the guarded glances from men and the longing looks sent his way by women. Most of the guests here might not have known of him until the story in the newspapers, but they would certainly remember him now.

She turned her attention elsewhere, not wanting to intrude on the lovers, and there was no doubt they were in love. Slowly she ambled through the throng of guests, the laughter and excitement of the evening contagious even though it had been the last place she'd wanted to be this evening, especially after Max told her he wanted a divorce. It just made her feel physically sick, but the prospect of going back to her flat and being alone with her mother's words ringing in her head was far worse.

Across the other side of the room, she saw Max talking to some of his team players and their partners. They all looked very glamorous. The women looked sassy and exciting in their cocktail dresses and the men handsome in their tuxedos, but Max stood out. Like the lion who led the pride, there was no doubt he was the ultimate alpha male. Maybe that was her problem. He could never allow her into his heart because he kept it so well hidden in his pursuit of complete dominance and superiority.

'Penny for them?' A cheeky female voice at her side stopped that train of thought dead.

'Angelina.' Max's sister had changed since she'd last seen her, over six months ago. She looked at the tall, willowy young woman, whose hair was even darker than Max's, she realised how much she'd missed her. From the greeting she'd been treated to, it was a mutual feeling. 'It's so good to see you. Happy birthday.'

Angelina held her champagne glass in one hand, and tilted her head to the side, a big smile on her face. 'So is it true?'

'What?' Lisa smiled with a frown, wondering what was coming next, because if there was one thing you could guarantee with Angelina it was complete honesty.

'You and Max are back together.' Before Lisa could say another word, Angelina hugged her with one arm, holding the flute of champagne at a precarious angle. 'I knew it.'

'We spent Christmas together.' Lisa sketched around the truth, avoiding the reason that had brought her and Angelina's brother back together. While Angelina would have to know her brother was going to make her an aunt, it was up to him to tell her. Just as it was up to him to say he was the one who now wanted to go through with the divorce.

'And I hear congratulations are in order. That you are expecting.' Angelina raised her brows at the elderflower cocktail and stood back, smiling at Lisa, then her expression turned more serious. 'How's Max taking it?'

'Max? Taking it?' Lisa couldn't work out what Angelina meant, but she was going to find out. 'What do you mean precisely?'

'You don't know, do you?' Shock filled Angelina's face, the light and fun mood of moments ago slipped away as if they'd walked out of the party, and if Lisa wasn't mistaken there was pity in her eyes too.

'No, but you are going to tell me right now,' Lisa demanded. She'd get the truth from Angelina, but would she really want to hear it?

Angelina finished her champagne, deposited the flute on a nearby table and took Lisa's arm and guided her away from the fun and laughter of the party. She stopped when they reached a long and very grand corridor. The noise of the party was subdued as the doors closed behind them and Lisa wondered what it was that was coming next that needed such drastic action. She looked at Angelina as nerves took flight in her stomach, bringing back the nausea she'd been struggling to keep at bay since she'd got up this morning.

'My mother, Max's mother, died when I was two years old,' Angelina began, but Lisa's patience was wearing thin.

'I'm aware of that.'

'Has he also told you that she was diagnosed with cancer while she was carrying me and that she delayed treatment, for me?' Angelina swallowed and Lisa knew this was affecting her far more than she was letting on. That she too hid behind a mask of being the bubbly life and soul of the party to hide her pain and that she was telling her this most guarded secret because it affected Max, affected her.

'I'm so sorry.' She reached out and touched the young woman's arm and for a moment the two of them were lost in their own world. 'That must be hard on you.'

'It is, yes. Mostly because it made Max into a dominating brother, always insistent that I do things his way. The arguments he and my father had over everything from what school I should attend to what I should eat or wear were impossible.'

'I have an older stepbrother who doesn't care one jot for me.' Lisa couldn't help confiding in her.

'I'd much rather that.' Angelina laughed, lightening the mood. 'Please don't let on that I told you. I just thought you would already know.'

'I won't.' Already the cloud of doubt was hanging over Lisa. Why hadn't he told her? Was it that he didn't trust her or didn't care enough to tell her? Either way, it rocked the foundations of all the good the last few days had created. Now she knew the only option for them was to go their separate ways. They couldn't hope to remain married, just for the baby. He didn't trust her and certainly wouldn't ever love her. It was over.

'I've been looking for you everywhere.' Max's voice was raised over the noise of the party as he pushed open the doors and stood glaring first at his sister, then at her. 'Are you feeling unwell?'

'She's fine,' Angelina injected as she stood a little closer to her. 'We were just having a catch up.'

'You are required by your guests,' Max said curtly, and a spark of mutiny slipped over Lisa. What would he do if she just walked out now, dropped the act of togetherness? She was on the verge of doing just than when she thought of Angelina. This was her party. She didn't want to give Max the satisfaction of making her spoil it, especially after such a heartfelt admission.

Angelina looked from her to her brother. 'I shall leave you two to it, then.'

'What is that supposed to mean?' Max watched his sister as she slipped back into the party and Lisa bristled with indignation. He didn't trust her and was trying to control her just as he'd done with his sister. From the things Angelina had just said, Lisa guessed that she wasn't the only person Max couldn't open up to. Not that it made any difference. They were finished. She might have felt love for him, but it had only ever been lust in his world and lust would not hold them together any longer.

'She was only congratulating me.' Lisa glared up at him and when he turned and frowned at her, that annoyance increased. Had he dismissed his child from his thoughts already? 'The baby.'

The baby. Those two words dripped through him, heightening his anger, his irritation. He hadn't given any thought to the fact that Angelina might want to be involved in his child's life. Of course she would. As always, she would want to do anything she could to annoy him, anything that he didn't want her to do.

He looked at his little sister and the ever-present guilt rushed forward like a runaway train. He hadn't ever been able to open his heart to her, hadn't been able to love her, just as he hadn't been able to love Lisa. How the hell was he going to be a father, a proper father, one who loved his child unconditionally? Getting a divorce was the right thing to do. Lisa and the baby would be better off with him out of their lives and overhearing her conversation with her mother had been just the spur he'd needed to come to that decision.

'You can talk more later but right now I wish to dance with my wife.' It was the last thing he wanted to do. Just the thought of holding Lisa close, of feeling her body against his as they moved to the slow sultry music now playing, had a bad effect on his senses—his body. One he couldn't listen to, couldn't act on.

Before Lisa could back out he took her hand and began to lead her to the dance floor, but didn't miss the look his sister flung his way. Irritation at having to deal with impending fatherhood in such a public way, brought about by the headlines regarding his brother, Raul, was beginning to take its toll on him. It was as if an unknown force were pushing him backward into his past and everything he'd thought locked safely away, forcing him to drag it all out and own it.

'You could have been a bit kinder.' Lisa's reproach as he took her in his arms and began to move slowly, going through the motions in an obligatory way, only added to his guilt.

'She likes to test me.' The curtness of his words wasn't what he intended and he ignored Lisa's movement as she looked up at him, knowing that if he looked down into her beautiful face he would want to act on the desire building within him. Desire that was totally at odds with the anger and irritation of their situation, with the knowledge that she wouldn't be his wife for much longer.

'I know how she feels,' she said softly, so softly it was hard to hear her above the music that filled the room.

'Because you like to do the same?' He clenched his back teeth together, determined to calm his irrational anger and regain control. This was so unlike him. Only two women had ever done this to him. Angelina and now Lisa.

She stopped dancing and glared up at him. 'Because my older stepbrother hated me too.'

She thought he hated Angelina? 'I do not hate her,' he ground out.

'Well, you didn't sound like a loving big brother,' she said as she pulled away from him, trying to slip from his hold. 'But silly me, that would never happen. You aren't capable of love, are you, Max?'

He tightened his embrace. 'Don't do this, Lisa. Not here. Not on Angelina's birthday.'

'Don't do what, Max? Say the truth?'

'You have no idea what my relationship with Angelina is like.' He looked down at her, aware now they were attracting attention. Every other couple on the dance floor seemed happy and in love and here they were, spitting fire at one another.

'That just proves how little we know about each other and how unsuited we are.'

Before he could respond to her angry tirade she freed herself from his arms and, chin held high, marched through the other couples toward the door. If she wanted to play those games she would be sorely disappointed. He *never* went after a woman.

But it's not just a woman, it's your wife and your child.

Lisa was so angry she could hardly walk in her strappy black heels as she left the party in full swing. There was

no way she was staying there just to make life easier
for Max, not after Angelina's revelations, which had
come hot on the heels of that word she'd never wanted
to form part of her life. Divorce. She'd failed. She was
no better than her mother.

'Lisa, what's the matter?' Lydia grabbed her arm and
Lisa looked at her aghast. She hadn't even noticed her.

She took a deep calming breath. 'Men.'

'In general or one in particular?' Lydia jested, but
there was no mistaking the concern on her new friend's
face.

Lisa sighed wearily. She had to talk to someone. She
couldn't do this alone. 'One in particular, not that I'm
sure you haven't already guessed.'

'And you think running away will help?' The mock
conjecture in Lydia's voice made it impossible for Lisa
not to smile. 'So, come back to the party, tell me what's
upsetting you and give that man something to think
about.'

'I guess you have already tamed one Valdez brother,
not that Max will admit to being such a thing.'

Lydia laughed, then became more serious. 'Anyone
can see he loves you, Lisa, just as it's obvious you love
him. You're made for each other, for goodness' sake.
Just as he has to accept he is a Valdez, he has to accept love.'

Those words hung in her mind as she returned to the
party with Lydia, instantly spotting Max, pleased to see
he looked casually and briefly their way, then looked
again, hardly able to believe she'd had the nerve to return after running out on him so publicly.

'See,' said Lydia as she got them both fresh drinks.
'He can't take his eyes off you.'

'He wants to get a divorce.' The words slipped icily from Lisa as she turned her back on Max, trying to ignore the heat of his glare as it bored into her back.

'No, he doesn't. If he's anything like his brother he knows exactly what he wants, he just doesn't believe he can have it. He doesn't believe he can love anyone.'

Lisa looked at Lydia. 'You and Raul?'

'Yes, me and Raul. That's why I was rushing out of the restaurant that day they first met. As far as I was concerned it was over. He didn't love me, didn't want my love and that was that.'

'What changed?'

'For Raul I guess it was meeting Max. It allowed him to put to rest the ghosts of his past.'

'May I interrupt?' Max's voice sounded from behind her, making her visibly jump. How much of that conversation had he heard?

She whirled round. 'You shouldn't keep sneaking up on people. You might hear things you don't want to hear.'

His brows rose in that sexy way that always melted her heart and buckled her knees and this time was no different, even if he was in a dark mood. 'Perhaps it's the only way to discover what someone really thinks about me. Shall we dance?'

Dance? Was he insane? After all they'd said to one another, all the public humiliation, and he wanted to dance. Raul joined them at that point, whisking his wife away in a gesture that spoke volumes of the love they shared but also left her alone with Max.

'You don't really want to dance.'

'Yes, I do. We need to set a few things straight and

there's less chance of you running off if I have my arms around you, only this time I will be holding you tightly.'

Before she could say anything else, he'd taken her drink from her hand and pulled her into his embrace, dancing their way into the couples already on the floor. He held her so tightly it was dangerously intimate. At least that was how it felt to her, but to him it was all about achieving what he wanted, preventing her from showing him up, from letting the guests see what was really between them. Nothing.

'So, what is it you wanted to set straight?' The haughty tone of her voice made his eyes glitter, but at least it was some sort of reaction.

'I want to ensure you are going to honour your part of the deal.'

'Deal?'

'To attend the New Year's Eve party with me, to act the part of my wife until the clock strikes in a new year.'

'Why should I do that?'

'It was part of our deal.'

'Why when it's obvious we don't work?'

'Raul and Lydia have made honeymoon arrangements around the party. They have put off their plans to be here on New Year's Eve with us and I do not want any questions asked about your absence.'

'Tell them I'm unwell.'

'No,' he snapped and she looked at him as his face darkened, becoming as black as heavy thunderclouds. 'I want you there.'

'So that you don't have to admit your failings to your brother or yourself? Or maybe it's to Angelina.'

'What has Angelina got to do with this?'

'She's part of your past too, Max, and if you trusted

me enough you'd tell me, share everything as I did with you, maybe then we could work.' She fought back the surge of tears, trying to keep the anger in front of the despair.

'And you are part of my present. Those damned headlines have made me the centre of something I have no wish for and until Raul and I have sorted that you will remain my wife and that means being seen with me on New Year's Eve.'

'And if I don't want to?'

'This is not negotiable. You will be there—with me.'

CHAPTER ELEVEN

MAX STOOD IN the grandeur of the hotel's foyer and waited for Lisa as the New Year's Eve party guests started to arrive. He was as mad as hell and couldn't stand still. Pacing the marble floor was the only thing he could do as he watched several sleek black cars arrive. Guests spilled out, full of happiness and laughter. Was he the only damn person here tonight who wasn't happy?

As yet more guests made their way past him he stood tall, trying not to think again of the moment he'd returned to his apartment after Angelina's party to find Lisa had gone. She'd left before him claiming a headache and hadn't even waited to tell him. She'd just left a note on the bed—the bed they'd shared such pleasure in.

> *I can't be what you need me to be, Max, and you can't give me what I want.*

He'd wanted to turn straight round and go after her, drag her from the little flat she'd moved into when their marriage had first fallen apart and bring her back. But he'd stood and looked at his reflection in the windows, black against the night. He'd never chased after a woman and he sure as hell wasn't going to start now.

He swore savagely in Spanish under his breath as yet more party guests arrived and paced to the door. What if something had happened to her? What if she was ill?

No, that is exactly what she wants you to think. Don't give her the satisfaction.

What had happened to his mother wouldn't happen again. He'd finally managed to get that clear in his mind and, by doing so, his emotions had started to unlock, to engage with hers. He'd been on the verge of admitting something he'd never thought possible, but Lisa's cold note proved how foolish that would have been, how weak he had become.

As those dark thoughts roused his anger further, another car pulled up in front of the doors and he watched as Raul got out, then turned and took Lydia's hand as she slid gracefully from the car. She looked stunningly beautiful in her gold dress, but it was the love in her eyes as they met Raul's that really rocked Max to the core, until he felt such violent shaking that he thought an earthquake was happening.

Once inside the hotel, Raul was oblivious to his brother, his attention so fully focused on his wife that Max felt as if he were watching from a distance, that he was seeing something he couldn't have.

'But I love you, Max, why can't you let me in? Let me love you? Maybe then you can love me too.'

Those words that Lisa had said at the cottage, the words that had condemned any chance of them being together, rushed back at him, like an angry dog, snarling and snapping at him. Forcing him to listen. To think and, worst of all, to feel.

'Max?' Lydia's voice saved him from the savage jaws. 'Where's Lisa?'

The lovely smile had slipped from Lydia's face as she and Raul had walked over and, if he wasn't mistaken, there was a cool reserve of suspicion in her eyes. Already the two women had formed a close friendship, so wasn't it only natural that Lisa would confide in her? But had she told Lydia he wanted a divorce?

'She is on her way.' His words were short and he didn't miss Raul's brows flicking upward in question.

'On her way?' The accusation in Lydia's voice was as clear as a mountain stream in the spring. 'From where?'

He sighed, not wanting this inquisition right now. 'She had other plans today and insisted she'd make her own way here this evening.'

When Lisa had finally answered her phone yesterday afternoon she'd been adamant that he was not going to fetch her. The fire of independence in her had raged so strong he hadn't been able to talk her round, but he had sent a car for her, along with the diamonds he'd given her at Christmas as a reminder of their deal. That had been several hours ago, so where the hell was she?

With a sinking sensation deep inside him he realised she wasn't coming. His phone vibrated in his inside pocket and he pulled it out, but the text was from the driver of the car he'd sent for Lisa, informing him that Mrs Martinez had not required it.

'Problems?' Raul asked, his dark eyes watchful and irritatingly knowing.

'Lisa is behind schedule, so I suggest we go on into the party.' He put on his most charming smile and used it to its full advantage on Lydia. It didn't quite have the effect he was hoping for, but when Raul took her arm, urging her to do as Max suggested, the attention was finally off him.

He lingered behind the happy couple as they made their entrance into the magnificent room. He stayed at the top of the wide flight of steps as they descended into the party. He couldn't go down yet, couldn't mingle with such joyous happiness when his heart beat so savagely in his chest.

Not only had Lisa left him, she'd stood him up too.

He absently scanned the room, looking but not seeing the array of colours of the ladies' dresses and the uniform black of tuxedos. The light and melodious sound of a grand piano competed with the cacophony of laughter and voices. He didn't belong here. Not tonight.

'You look like you could do with this.' Raul's voice startled him and he turned to see his brother beside him, a glass of whisky in his hand.

Without a word he took it, swirled the amber liquid round the glass and then looked at Raul. 'Where's Lydia?'

'With friends. Now are you going to tell me what is really going on?'

His first instinct was to tell him nothing was going on, but he didn't want to. There was a connection between him and Raul, a bond made so quickly that he owed it to him, his brother, to be honest. To admit his failings.

He drank the whisky back in one quick gulp and looked at Raul. 'We are getting divorced.'

Raul swore harshly in Spanish, causing guests who were just arriving at the party to turn and look at him as they made their way down the stairs and into the centre of the merriment and celebration.

'She asked for a divorce?' The disbelief in Raul's usually firm tone was all too apparent.

'She did, before she knew about the baby.'

'And you want a divorce?' The disbelief in Raul's voice was clear.

'I do now.'

Raul swore again. 'We can't talk here,' he said, looking around him. 'Let's get another drink.'

He turned and made his way down the stairs and Max knew he had to follow. Not out of any sense of duty or obligation, but because he wanted to. Hell, he had to share this with someone. He needed someone to reassure him he was doing the right thing, because it sure as hell didn't feel like it.

Raul led him through the snooker room and into a bar more reminiscent of a men's club and gestured toward two large leather chairs by the window. Max sat and within seconds two glasses of whisky were on the table between them. Outside the window, Max could see the street and the cars and cabs moving away from the hotel entrance after dropping off their passengers.

Lisa wasn't going to be one of them. His stupidity had made damn sure of that.

'What the hell are you playing at?' Raul looked at him sternly as he launched his tirade, one he deserved every bit of. He'd avoided love, telling Lisa what she wanted to hear, because he thought he could save her from hurt, but he'd only her hurt her even more and now she'd left him. Just as everyone else he'd ever loved had. Hell, even Angelina couldn't bear to be with him for long.

'It's for the best.' He clenched his jaw as his brother looked at him reprovingly.

'The hell it is.' Raul all but growled at him, then launched into a torrent of Spanish. 'What is the matter with you? Can't you see she loves you?'

'Love isn't everything, Raul,' he threw back at his brother in Spanish, finding it liberating to be letting it all out, letting all the emotions he'd been holding behind his dam of hurt burst over the top. 'I certainly didn't get any from my father and I'm damn sure you didn't either.'

Raul leaned forward in a slow and purposeful way. 'I got past that and you sure as hell can too—or regret it for the rest of your life.'

Max gritted his teeth and frowned at him, remembering what Raul's mother had told him at the wedding in Madrid.

'Don't run from the truth, Max, face it. Own it. Make it your friend, not your enemy.'

What was that truth? That he didn't have to be like his father? That he could be exactly who he wanted to be?

Raul stood up, his glass of whisky untouched. 'You told me the day we met I should sort out my love life and now I am offering you that same advice. Sort it, Max, don't allow the past to kill your future.'

Max inhaled deeply, not ready to accept what his brother was saying. 'I will give it some thought.'

'Not thought, action and damn soon.' Raul straightened his jacket as if he'd physically done several rounds with his brother. 'Now, if you will excuse me, I would like to be with my wife.'

Max watched as Raul wound his way back through all the high-backed chairs and out of the room, leaving Max to brood. He was worse than his father, walking out on the woman who'd so honestly declared her love for him, the woman who carried his child.

He looked into the bottom of the whisky glass, but no answers lay there. He put it down roughly, sliding it across the table away from him. He was pushing it away as roughly as he'd pushed away the woman he loved.

The woman he loved.

The icy bucket of truth poured all over him. He'd been trying to fight the one thing he'd always thought would make him like his father, believing that by loving someone it only led to pain and heartache for them and rejection for him. But he'd been wrong.

Very wrong.

Love was the one emotion his father had been incapable of feeling, of receiving, and by allowing love into his heart he was proving he was far more of a man than his father had ever been.

Why the hell had it taken him until now to accept that? He'd pushed so many people away. His stepfather. His sister. Worse than that, he'd forced Lisa to walk out on him.

Lisa took in a deep breath, instilling herself with calm, trying to soothe the heavy thump of her heartbeat. After what Max had said to her, what had made her come here tonight? Was it to see those dark eyes filled with such coldness once more, to feel the weight of his anger, his rejection yet again? Was it one last attempt to suffocate the love she had for him?

The black cab pulled up outside one of London's most prestigious hotels as in the distance Big Ben chimed half past eleven. Just half an hour and all this would be over. The deal. Her marriage. Her love.

She touched her fingers to the diamonds that lay coldly against her skin, annoyed that Max's driver had handed her the package and said he had instructions to take her to the party. With cold anger in her veins she'd taken the package, knowing full well what it contained, and had dismissed the driver, who'd reluctantly left.

At first she'd thought she wouldn't go, that she'd return the diamonds to him by courier, but that plan had slipped from her mind as quickly as it had formed. Only seeing him once more, so cold and heartless that he had insisted on their deal in such a way, would finally kill that foolhardy love she had for him.

She'd take off the jewellery piece by piece, a symbol of her heart, her love, and give it back to him. Then walk away.

'Are you wanting to go somewhere else?' The driver asked as she sat in the sanctuary of his cab, reluctant to get out, reluctant to do what she knew she had to.

Did she want to go somewhere else? *Yes, anywhere but here.* 'No, thanks.'

She passed the fare through to him and opened the door, the cold air of the evening making her shiver, or was it what she intended to do? Walk away from her marriage, the man she loved?

She picked up the emerald-green silk of her dress, holding it just above her ankles, and stepped down from the cab, feeling unsteady on the gold high-heeled sandals she'd bought as she'd wandered aimlessly around London today, proving if nothing else that she wanted—or needed—to be at the party tonight. To see Max one last time. To put an end to it all.

She pulled off the black coat, which hadn't gone with the high-class dress at all, and handed it in, suddenly feeling very exposed. The long dangling diamond earrings felt heavy in her ears, the necklace weighed her down even more, but very soon she would be free of them and all the pain they'd brought her.

She held her head high as she ascended the main staircase of the hotel and followed the sound of music until she came to the double doors of the suite where one of the biggest New Year's Eve parties this season was being held. It was the place to see and be seen. She pushed the doors gently open and stood at the top of a very grand wide staircase and looked down at the most glamorous party she'd ever seen.

It was like being Cinderella arriving late at the ball. She might not have glass slippers, but she did have a dress she'd never be able to afford, not in a million years. And diamonds. As she looked around at couples dancing, groups of people talking and the sheer glitz of the moment her thoughts went back to the fairy-tale films she'd watched endlessly as a child. She might not be about to get her happy ever after, but she was certainly at the ball.

She lifted the hem of her dress slightly again and slowly descended the steps, one hand on the wide balustrade, then all the air sucked out of the room, the voices and the music slowed and became nothing but a steady thump. Or was that her heart?

Max was standing at the bottom of the stairs looking up at her. If this were her fairy tale then he'd be smiling up at her, love shining bright in his eyes. He would rush up the stairs, take her hand and kiss her fingers so gently yet so passionately, then lead her to the dance floor, where they'd whirl around in a mist of love.

But this wasn't her fairy tale. This was reality.

The reality of Max so very handsome in his black tuxedo, his face dark and thunderous as he looked up at her.

Max's breath felt as if it had stopped. No matter how deep he tried to breathe he couldn't. Like a vision of pure loveliness, Lisa stood halfway down the stairs, the green silk of her dress cascading down her body like a waterfall. Her vibrant red hair was piled up in a mass of unruly curls and the diamond earrings sparkled as they moved gently in the light. The necklace seemed to caress her skin, making his fingers want to touch her there, his lips to kiss her.

She'd come. His mouth dried as relief washed over him, but that was short-lived as he felt her gaze fall on him, felt the heat of those alluring green eyes. Around him people chatted and danced, but he couldn't move. Not toward her or away from her. He'd been certain of what he had to do as he'd left the bar, but hadn't expected that moment to come so quickly. He'd anticipated a car journey across London, time to process his thoughts, rehearse his words because he knew he only had one chance and they had to be right.

As if in slow motion she continued down the stairs toward him. This was the woman he loved, the woman he wanted to be with for ever, but could he say it now when that realisation was all still so new and fragile?

She reached the bottom of the stairs and stopped. The diamonds at her neck glittered as she breathed, giving away the strength of her emotions right now, but the look on her face was unreadable. A mask of defiant beauty.

He became aware of people around him staring,

looking from her to him and back again. The strength of the emotion arcing between them was so powerful it was drawing others in and they stepped back, watching, waiting.

Slowly she walked toward him, the emerald silk of the dress shimmering over her body, giving her an ethereal glow. The mutinous spark in her eyes sent a trail of fear sparking down his spine. She looked like a woman with a purpose. The love had gone from her eyes. He'd done that to her.

Then she was standing before him and her heady perfume invaded his senses, making clear and rational thought almost impossible. He knew they were being watched, knew they'd grabbed everyone's attention, but right now he didn't care, not if it meant he could tell Lisa what he had to tell her.

'I'd like to dance.' Her words were lethally sharp. The soft and gentle woman he'd unknowingly loved all this time had been replaced by an ice-cold vision of beauty.

'It will be my pleasure,' he said as he took one of her hands and pulled her gently into his embrace.

It should feel good to hold her against him, to feel the heat of her skin through the fine silk, but it was bittersweet. He looked down at her, but she was resolutely fixing her attention on his chest and he wished this particular scene had been played out anywhere else but the dance floor.

He wanted to ask her why she'd come after he'd been so cruel to her, wanted to know if it meant he had another chance, but the words just wouldn't come. This was worse than a damn game of poker.

'I came here tonight to honour the deal I made with

you,' she said, finally looking up at him, as if hearing his thoughts, but the fierceness in her eyes scared the hell out of him.

'I'm glad you did.' Her delicate brows lifted in surprise, but the hardness remained in her eyes, sparking more brilliantly than the diamonds at her throat.

'Are you?'

'We need to talk, Lisa.' Max pulled her closer as they moved slowly in time to the music. She stiffened in his arms. This wasn't going well. He could feel her more than physically pulling away from him.

'There is nothing more to say, Max.' She stopped dancing and looked up at him as she pulled off one earring, then with purpose she pulled the other off. 'You have said all that needs to be said.'

'Not yet I haven't.' What was happening?

She took his hand, turned it over and placed the earrings in his palm. Puzzled, he looked at them lying there like glittering icicles, but as he looked back at her he saw her reach up and begin to unfasten the necklace.

She was giving them back. Giving back her love— in the most public and final way.

'Stop.' The word came out as a feral growl but it snared her attention. She looked at him, her arms poised ready to unfasten the necklace, the diamonds setting off fireworks of sparks with each breath.

'Why?' The breathy yet fiercely determined word reared up at him like a stallion. Wild and untamed. Hurt.

This was it. This was the moment to put his cards on the table, the moment to tell her everything. Why here? Why like this? But as those thoughts raced in his mind he knew that if he didn't do it now he'd never get another chance.

He took a deep breath, still holding the earrings, which now seemed to burn his palm. 'Because I love you.'

CHAPTER TWELVE

LISA COULDN'T MOVE, couldn't even blink as she looked at Max. She'd waited so long to hear those words that she'd given up hope of ever hearing. In desperation she'd come here tonight to give him back the diamonds and, by doing so, take back her love, her heart, because they were wasted on a cold and emotionless man like him.

A gasp from someone nearby warned her that everyone close to them had stopped dancing and had formed a circle around them. They were the centre of attention, just what he'd wanted to avoid, but she hadn't planned it like this —so public. But somehow that didn't matter, not any more. Her heart thumped hard and she couldn't take her eyes from Max's.

'I should have said it a long time ago.' Regret filled his voice, but she wasn't going to be lured in by such tactics.

She lowered her hands so that he didn't see how much they were shaking. 'Yes, you should have. A long time ago, but you didn't feel it, did you, Max?'

He stood just an arm's length away but it might as well have been across the other side of the room. He was still closed off, still behind that barrier of steel. Those words he'd just said, the words she'd so longed to hear didn't have a ring of truth in them.

'Just as you didn't trust me enough to truly let me in,' she continued. Now that the floodgates of all her pain were open she couldn't stop. 'Even when I'd shared all the darkness from my past. When I'd told you every-thing that had made me so certain that I didn't want you in our child's life unless you could be there all the time, every step of the way. Even then, Max, you didn't open up to me. You couldn't tell me about your mother even though I was pregnant with your child, forcing you to face all that childhood pain and anguish again.'

He stood rigid, tall and proud, seeming to deflect all the emotion pouring from her. She wanted to pummel his chest with her clenched hands, anything to show him her frustration. But she couldn't, not when all around them the party seemed to have stopped, all attention turned on them.

'It was too painful, too raw to share. I guess I've never come to terms with losing my mother so young.' He frowned at her. 'How do you know?'

'Angelina told me.' She lowered her voice, gentled her tone as a wave of sympathy rushed forward like an incoming tide. 'She told me all about your mother, the tough decision she'd had to make.'

'Angelina?' He frowned at her.

'She's hurting too, Max. You're shutting her out. De-nying her your love.' Lisa let the truth flow from her. If nothing else came of this conversation maybe she could make things better between him and his sister, who deep inside was still the little girl who'd grown up with barely a memory of her mother and a cold, distant brother she believed hated her.

'Ten minutes to midnight.'

The excited remark of another party-goer further away roused some of their spectators, eager to get the champagne needed to toast in a new year, but Lisa held Max's gaze, implored him with her eyes to understand her, to forgive her for saying all this here.

'We should talk about this somewhere else. I didn't intend such a public goodbye.' She began to move, to walk away, hoping he would follow her. Instead he grabbed her wrist.

'Lisa, I couldn't tell you. If I did it would have meant opening my heart, letting love in and love has only ever caused me pain—and loss.'

She shook her head slowly. 'It doesn't have to be like that, Max. It can be good, so very good.'

Movement in those around her caught her attention and in the ever-growing crowd she saw Lydia, hands clasped in front of her and pressed firmly against her chest, and the look in the other woman's eyes left her in no doubt that she was doing the right thing, that, no matter who witnessed it, she had to make him see he was worthy of love. Even if it wasn't hers.

'But it can't mend the past.'

'It can ease the pain, but you have to let it into your life. It can't penetrate toughened barriers of steel. It can't reach dark and cold places—unless you want it to.'

'I know that now. When I thought you weren't coming tonight, that you never wanted to see me again, the pain of that was too much—because I love you.' Max gently pulled her closer and she moved unresistingly to him.

'You hurt me so much, Max, when you told me the marriage was over, that you couldn't give me what I wanted, yet I still loved you. That's why that night a few months ago happened. I couldn't stop loving you.'

'But you don't now?'

Max inhaled deeply as Lisa looked up at him, her eyes searching his, her perfume pulling at his senses, flashing all they'd shared together in front of his mind like that of a dying man. Maybe he was. If he didn't have Lisa, didn't have her love, then life would mean nothing.

'Say something, Lisa.' He couldn't do this, couldn't bear to hear her say she didn't love him any more. 'I'm sorry. I've been a fool.'

'It's not your fault. All that happened, all that made you scared of showing your emotions, that's all to blame. But I want more than you can give me, Max— for me and our baby. I want unconditional and honest love.'

Now she'd touched that raw nerve he'd always kept guarded. That he wasn't fit to be a father; that, just like his own, he wouldn't be capable of love. Raul moved into his line of vision and for a moment his gaze met that of his brother. It empowered him. Raul had let go of the past and he was going to damn well do the same. His present and his future were with Lisa.

He opened the hand that had been holding the earrings and offered them to her. 'These are yours. They were a token of the depth of my feelings for you, as was the Christmas cottage. I was just such a damn fool I didn't recognise it as love.'

Lisa looked down at the earrings, then up at him. Did the tears glistening in her eyes mean there was hope? That it wasn't too late? If she took them she would be taking his love and he'd never let her go again.

She shook her head and stepped back as much as she could while he still held her wrist. She didn't want them. Didn't want his love. Pain seared through him as if he'd been physically branded. Branded by her love. Her rejection.

'Oh, no!' someone exclaimed in the crowd around them and a whisper of panic rushed around them, around him, pushing the tension in the air ever higher.

'Please, Lisa.' He tried one last time. If she refused once more, he'd turn and walk away. Accept defeat. Accept he'd messed it all up, thrown away the one good thing in his life.

Lisa looked down again at the diamond earrings that had unwittingly come to represent so much. The tension around her, buzzing in the crowd still gathered, made her head thump and her heart beat so hard. But it was what he'd just said that sent a fierce surge of hope through her.

He'd said he loved her. He'd said the words she'd always wanted to hear and in front of everyone.

So why wasn't that enough?

Because he's hurt you too much. Because he doesn't trust you.

She lifted her hand to his, then stopped. She raised her gaze to his, meeting the darkness that was full of despair. He meant every word of what he'd said. He'd finally opened his heart to her, but if she took them she could be exposing herself to more pain.

'Ten!' someone shouted as, beyond the circle gathered around them, the countdown to a new year had begun amidst raucous delight.

'I can't,' she whispered as her eyes searched his face,

his eyes. 'You don't trust me. You couldn't open up to me even after I'd told you my darkest secrets and it knocked me so far down I don't know if I can come back from that.'

'Nine!'

Max let her wrist go and raised his hand to brush the backs of his fingers over her cheeks. 'That was my insecurity, Lisa, and for that I'm sorry.'

Her eyelashes fluttered closed as he moved his hand, his fingers, trailing down her neck and then to the back of her head. When she opened them he was so close to her she could kiss him if she moved forward just a fraction.

'Eight!'

'It's never been about that.' Her whisper was soft, her breathing fast and deep. She couldn't hold out against this for long. Not when she loved him so much.

'Seven!'

'I was a damn fool, Lisa. You've loved me all along and I abused that love in the worst way possible, but I want to spend the rest of my life making it up to you—loving you.'

'Six!'

'And the baby?' She drew in a ragged breath as he lowered his gaze. 'Max?'

'Five!'

'Our baby will have all the love it can ever want from its father because I'm not my father. I'm not the cold, hard, mercenary man he was, not when I love my wife with all my heart.'

'Four!'

It was just seconds until the new year, until a fresh start, and Lisa knew she couldn't ignore that omen, couldn't turn Max away when her heart ached so badly for him and he'd finally destroyed the barrier of steel he'd spent so long behind.

'Oh, Max,' she whispered as she moved closer, her lips almost touching his. Almost.

The look on his face, the purity of the love she could see in his eyes made any further words so hard, but she managed what needed to be said. What he needed to hear.

'I love you, Max. So much.'

'Three!'

His lips claimed hers in a hard kiss as the hand at the nape of her neck pulled her toward him. Her arms wound around his neck and she kissed him as if her life depended on it.

'Two!'

He pulled back from her, still so close. 'It's time for a fresh start. You and I and our baby.'

'One!'

'The perfect time,' she said softly as the old year slipped away, taking with it all the pain and heartache.

'Happy New Year!'

A riotous cheer went up from those around them and she looked at him, smiling. 'Happy New Year, Max.'

He brushed his lips over hers. 'Happy New Year, and I'm going to tell you I love you every day from now on.'

'Just *tell* me?' she teased wickedly, not caring who was still watching, though from the sound of chinking glasses and popping corks it wasn't many people. Fireworks sounded outside and more cheers went up.

'I will tell you as much as you like here, but when I get you on your own I'm going to *show* just how much.'

She laughed in delight as he lifted her from her

feet and began turning round and round as in a dance of elation.

'That was better than any fireworks,' someone said as Max finally stopped turning.

Slowly her feet touched the floor again and she looked up into his handsome face as he lowered his head to kiss her. She reached up and pressed a finger against his lips. 'I'm going to hold you to that, Maximiliano Martinez. I want to hear that every single day from now on.'

'Then I'd better start now. I love you, Lisa. You are everything to me, always have been and always will be and just to prove it I want you to take these back—and put them on.'

He opened his hand and she looked at him then took the diamond earrings, warm from his touch, just as his heart now was. Without taking her eyes from his, she put them back on then smiled. Diamonds would be a symbol of their love for evermore.

'I love you, Max.'

A round of applause erupted again as he kissed her, deeply and passionately, and she knew that finally her happy ever after had arrived.

EPILOGUE

LISA LOOKED AROUND the crowded party room at the top London hotel Max and Raul had chosen for their New Year's Eve party. It was hard to believe that this time two years ago she'd been ready to walk out on Max, on her dreams of love and happiness, believing them to be futile.

'This is spectacular,' Lydia said as she sat across the elegantly set table, looking as glamorous as ever despite being heavily pregnant with her first child. The deep blue of the gown suited her well. Or was it the glow of pregnancy?

'I'm so pleased Raul and Max have decided to make this our annual family tradition, a new one to clear away all the heartache they have both known and build good memories for our children. When they are older, of course.' Lisa laughed softly at the expression on Lydia's face and wondered if she'd given her secret away.

'Children?'

'Our little Lilly and soon your son or daughter,' Lisa said as she sipped at her cooling lemonade.

'Oh, I have to tell you. I just can't help myself,' Lydia suddenly said, leaning as far forward as her advanced pregnancy would allow. 'It's a boy.'

She took her sister-in-law's hand and squeezed it tightly. 'I'm so pleased for you both.'

Further talk of babies was halted as Max returned to their table, soon followed by Raul. The two men were immaculate in their tuxedos and had commanded equal attention as they'd moved around the room, mingling with their guests.

'Have you seen Angelina?' Max asked as he sat back and surveyed the guests.

Lisa had seen her. She'd been in the arms of the Greek that Max and Raul had been in recent business negotiations with. Although she wasn't sure Max would welcome such news. He was fiercely protective of his sister despite the way she continued to keep him at arm's length. He had tried to mend things with her, but the pain and heartache she'd known was so deep. Lisa briefly thought of saying nothing, of leaving him in ignorance of the obvious attraction between the two, but that night two years ago they'd made a promise to never keep anything from each other again.

'She was dancing with Vasilios Christakis a while ago,' she said lightly, trying to play the situation down.

'I had no idea she knew Vasilios?' Max frowned.

'They've had a few dances, that's all.' Lisa had seen the connection between them, that same spark of instant attraction she'd felt when she'd met Max.

'Where is she now?'

'Max,' Lisa said softly as she placed her hand on his arm. The usual frisson of awareness rushed through her. 'She's twenty-three now. She has to make her own choices.'

'Vasilios Christakis will never be good enough for

my little sister,' he said in a low and menacing voice. 'He may be wealthy and have a good reputation as a businessman, but he certainly doesn't where women are concerned.'

'Will anyone ever be good enough for Angelina in your eyes? I doubt it.'

'You're right,' he conceded with a sigh.

'You'll be the same with Lilly,' Raul added for good measure. 'In about twenty years' time.'

Max glared at Raul, but both Lydia and Lisa laughed, knowing they were fooling around as they often did. Nobody could ever guess they'd only met two years ago.

'And what about you, Raul? If you have a little girl you will be her most fierce protector.' Max goaded his brother just a little more and Lydia caught Lisa's attention with a knowing smile.

'Then I will be the same,' Raul replied firmly, a hint of a smile on his lips.

'I've had enough of this for now. I'm going to dance with my wife while I have her to myself.' Max stood up and took Lisa's hand, pulling her to her feet gently then looking again at his brother. 'That, little brother, is something you are soon going to have to get used to because once that baby arrives it will take up all your wife's attention.'

'Stop teasing, Max,' Lisa chided and began to walk to the dance floor, pulling on Max's hand, forcing him away from the expectant parents.

The music was slow and Max took her in his arms, holding her tight against his body so that she could feel every step he made. 'I hope Lilly is all right.'

'Max, stop fretting, she's fine. She has the best nanny ever. You made sure of that.'

'You're right.' He pressed his lips against hers and she sighed softly. The last two years had been so good, so happy. It was hard to remember the pain and heartache of that Christmas when she'd told him he was going to be a father.

'Do you remember we promised not to keep any secrets?' There was a light teasing in his voice, but her mind flew instantly to what she and Lydia had just been discussing. Had he heard them?

'Of course I do.'

'So is there anything you want to tell me?'

She put her head to one side and looked at him coyly. 'Like what?'

'Like why you are not indulging in the champagne this evening?'

She smiled. 'I was saving it until midnight and now you've spoilt the surprise.'

His eyes narrowed in suspicion briefly then a smile spread across his lips and lit up his eyes, like the night sky full of stars. 'Are you…?' He stumbled over the words.

'Yes, Max. I'm pregnant. You are going to be a father again.'

'When?'

'It's still early days yet, but by the end of July.'

'Another summer baby. Have I told you how much I love you, Lisa Martinez?'

'Often!' She laughed as he dropped a light kiss on her lips. 'But I don't mind hearing it some more.'

'I love you, Lisa, with all my heart. You, Lilly and our new baby are my world.'

The kiss he gave her was so powerful, so full of love she knew without a doubt how happy he was. She kissed him back, not caring they were now standing in the middle of the dance floor kissing passionately. In fact it was becoming a bit of a habit.

* * * * *

If you enjoyed
MARTINEZ'S PREGNANT WIFE
why not explore the first part of Rachael Thomas's
CONVENIENT CHRISTMAS BRIDES *duet?*

VALDEZ'S BARTERED BRIDE

And also these other Rachael Thomas stories
DI MARCELLO'S SECRET SON
A CHILD CLAIMED BY GOLD

All available now!

MILLS & BOON®

MODERN™

POWER, PASSION AND IRRESISTIBLE TEMPTATION

MILLS & BOON®

Coming next month

CLAIMING HIS NINE-MONTH
CONSEQUENCE
Jennie Lucas

Ruby.

Pregnant.

Impossible. She couldn't be. They'd used protection.

He could still remember how he'd felt when he'd kissed her. When he'd heard her soft sigh of surrender. How she'd shuddered, crying out with pleasure in his arms. How he'd done the same.

And she'd been a virgin. He'd never been anyone's first lover. Ares had lost his virginity at eighteen, a relatively late age compared to his friends, but growing up as he had, he'd idealistically wanted to wait for love. And he had, until he'd fallen for a sexy French girl the summer after boarding school. It wasn't until summer ended that his father had gleefully revealed that Melice had actually been a prostitute, bought and paid for all the time. *I did it for your own good, boy. All that weak-minded yearning over love was getting on my nerves. Now you know what all women are after—money. You're welcome.*

Ares's bodyguard closed the car door behind him with a bang, causing him to jump.

"Sir? Are you there?"

Turning his attention back to his assistant on the phone, Ares said grimly, "Give me her phone number."

Two minutes later, as his driver pulled the sedan smoothly down the street, merging into Paris's evening traffic, Ares listened to the phone ring and ring. Why didn't Ruby answer?

When he'd left Star Valley, he'd thought he could forget her.

Instead, he'd endured four and a half months of painful celibacy, since his traitorous body didn't want any other woman. He couldn't forget the soft curves of Ruby's body, her sweet mouth like sin. She hadn't wanted his money. She'd been insulted by his offer. She'd told him never to call her again.

And now…

She was pregnant. With his baby.

He sat up straight as the phone was finally answered. "Hello?"

Continue reading
CLAIMING HIS NINE-MONTH
CONSEQUENCE
Jennie Lucas

Available next month
www.millsandboon.co.uk

LET'S TALK
Romance

For exclusive extracts, competitions
and special offers, find us online:

For all the latest titles coming soon, visit
millsandboon.co.uk/nextmonth

*Calls cost 7p per minute plus your phone company's price per minute access charge